Phishing

A Tiger Lily's Café™ Mystery

By Kathleen Thompson

Phishing

A Tiger Lily's Café™ Mystery

By Kathleen Thompson

© 2015

ISBN-13: 978-1517313876

ISBN-10: 1517313872

Cast of Characters 4

Chapter 1: Classic Rich Boy 10

Chapter 2: Great Neck Lake 20

Chapter 3: A Bundle Of ADHD 30

Chapter 4: Ma'am, You Ain't Winterized 50

Chapter 5: We've Been Hacked! 63

Chapter 6: The Cats Surrounded Their Guests 71

Chapter 7: Best In Show 81

Chapter 8: What's This About Hacking? 91

Chapter 9: Seafood Pasta Salad With A Twist 106

Chapter 10: He Was The Rhinoceros 123

Chapter 11: Syrah And Cheese Curls 131

Chapter 12: What's For Breakfast? 139

Chapter 13: A Good Friend 145

Chapter 14: The Person To Whom So Much Was Given 159

Chapter 15: No! Don't Put Me In The Trash! 175

Chapter 16: Annie Wanted To Sleep In 190

Chapter 17: The Cats Could Not Be Found 210

Chapter 18: Annie Needed Some Alone Time 223

Chapter 19: Just Pray 230

Chapter 20: We're Havin' A Heat Wave 237

Chapter 21: Don't Forget To Pick Me Up 245

Chapter 22: That's On My List! 249

Chapter 23: Go Do Your Cat Burglar Thing 268

Chapter 24: The Brilliant Colors Burst Over The Lake 274

Chapter 25: Annie Barely Slept 284

Chapter 26: We'll See What We Will See 292

Chapter 27: Humor Me 296

Chapter 28: Traditional Christmas Eve Oyster Stew 304

Chapter 29: Santa Claus Found Us! 317

Chapter 30: The Rest Of The Story 326

Chapter 31: New Year's Eve Block Party 342

Cast of Characters

Annie Mack, with the help of her "kids" and a talented staff, owns and manages a B&B, a cafe and other businesses on the south side of The Avenue.

Ben is a college student. He works part-time at the Café. This holiday, he is working at the Inn with his sister JoJo.

Boone has been doing Annie's mowing and snow removal; he just started to do preventive maintenance for her. He grew up in rural Appalachia at the far western tip of Virginia and is married to Harriet.

Candice is the head waitress at Mo's Tap. She and George can't decide if they are dating or not.

Carlos is the manager and baker at Mr. Bean's Confectionary. He supports his mother and younger sisters in Mexico.

Cheryl inherited The Marina from her parents. It's a small deep water marina with basic amenities. Cheryl is married to Ray.

Chris is the Officer in Charge of the Coast Guard Station. His sketches – in charcoal, pencil and pastel – are sold for charity.

Christal is a gorgeous redhead who seems to keep cropping up in George's life, much to the chagrin of Candice.

Clara owns the flower and gift shop, Bloomin' Crazy. She grew up in a tropical climate and is influenced in that fashion.

Cookie probably has another name, but this is what he goes by. He cooks at Mo's Tap and learns what he can from Felicity at every opportunity. He's reticent at best.

Daryl and Donny are the young adult children of Boone and Harriet. Daryl has been working with Boone for a few years; Donny just graduated from high school and will be working with him starting this winter.

Diana is the chief instructor at L'Socks' Virasana (veer AHS ana). She is Mem's daughter; they have a tenuous relationship.

Felicity is the chef at Tiger Lily's Café. She is young, perky and extremely talented in the kitchen.

Frank recently moved to Chelsea to open an antique shop, Antiques On Main. He and Mem are in a relationship.

George is the bartender and manager of Mo's Tap. His only ambitions are to live simply and enjoy life.

Geraldine Foxglove was the leader of the "it" crowd in high school. Somehow, life didn't turn out quite as she expected.

Ginger is the daughter of Pete and Janet. She is a senior in high school and works at L'Socks' Virasana to save for college as well as for high school credit.

Greg is a progressive realtor in Chelsea. His goal is to get the right property to the right owner, always moving Chelsea forward.

Gwen is Annie's accountant. A 60-something motherly figure, her financial acumen is hidden from all but those lucky enough to have her in their corner.

Hank is a member of the Town Council. He opposes Annie in every way.

Harriet (Hilly) will be working for Annie, cleaning all of her businesses. She grew up in rural Appalachia at the far western tip of Virginia and is married to Boone.

Henrie manages the KaliKo Inn. He never speaks about his background. He runs the B&B in an elegant manner.

Holly and Jolly, twins, own DoubleGood, an electronics and hardware store. Holly lives in a wheelchair.

Janet, married to Pete, spent 20 years as a Marine officer's wife. She traveled the world and is now living in Chelsea. She is an outsider, not having grown up here like Pete.

Jennifer and Marie, sisters and nurse practitioners, own The Drug Store and The Clinic. Folks call the sisters before calling 911.

Jerry is the candy maker at Mr. Bean's Confectionary. He learned how to make candy in a minimum security federal prison. He was not an employee.

Jesus manages Sassy P's Wine & Cheese and also selects the wines. His family makes wine; he prefers to choose them.

Joan is a member of the Town Council. She opposes Hank in every way. Clara's pet name for her is "Joan of Chelsea."

JoJo is a college student. She works part-time at the Café. This holiday, she is working at the Inn with her brother Ben.

Laila owns Babar Foods. She has three children, the youngest of whom (Carl) has Autism. James is in high school and Ava is in junior high.

Marco is a police officer in Chelsea. He was recently promoted to "second in command" because he was the only officer that didn't go off-kilter during a hostage situation.

Mem owns the health food store and cyber café, CyberHealth. Her wisdom is reassuring to everyone, including her daughter, Diana.

Mindy is Gwen's assistant at Beancounters.

Minnie chooses perfect cheeses to accompany the rotating wine selections at Sassy P's Wine & Cheese.

Nancy and Sam are Annie's mother and step-father. They have been married since Annie was a child.

Pete is a native of Chelsea. He retired from the Marine Corps and is now the Chief of Police. He and his wife Janet have three children, the eldest of whom is Ginger.

Ray owns and operates The Escape, a yacht fashioned into a cruiser for fishing, diving and pleasure. He is married to Cheryl.

Rusty is a young man who is spending a lot of time with Christal.

Teresa pastors a small church, Soul's Harbor. She came to this community to serve.

Trudie is the barista at Tiger Lily's Café. She is from Jamaica and ended up in Chelsea quite by accident.

Guests at the Inn

Daniela is visiting from Mexico. She is Carlos' mother.

Harrison Jones is in his mid-thirties and entirely clueless about ice fishing. But then again, since when do you have to be an expert when you're on vacation?

Isabel is a special friend of Carlos, visiting from Mexico.

Jeff Bennett is a Special Agent with the FBI. Having experience with Chelsea and now a member of the cybercrime division, he is sent to handle the recent phishing incident.

Jessica, Paul, Jerome and Sally are Annie's niece (daughter of Patti), her husband and two children, visiting for Christmas.

Patti, Fritz, Allen, Percy, Gracie, Ella and Ollie are Annie's half-sister, her husband, and five of her children, visiting for Christmas.

Rosa and Valeria are the sisters of Carlos, visiting from Mexico.

And The Companions

Annie has seven "rescue kitties." From Annie's perspective, each of them rescued her.

Tiger Lily is a beautiful tabby cat with soft green eyes. She is the titular manager of Tiger Lily's Café, the main gathering place for Chelsea. She is generally calm and logical.

Little Socks is a bright-eyed black cat with white socks. She has a commanding personality and is small and sneaky enough to serve as a cat burglar. She spends time at the yoga studio, L'Socks' Virasana (veer AHS ana).

Kali, Ko and Mo are litter mates. They shared a secret language as kittens; Kali and Ko now speak "cat," but Mo still speaks "secret." Kali and Ko can be found at the KaliKo Inn, a lakeside B&B. Mo will be at Mo's Tap, an upscale blues bar.

Sassy Pants is aptly named; it's difficult to keep this girl's attention. She is overly sensitive and will react out of emotion instead of reason. She entertains at Sassy P's Wine & Cheese.

Mr. Bean is the baby of the family and is mostly gray with traces of tiger. He has two speeds: fast and love me.

Claire is a blue point Himalayan whose human is Frank. She's beautiful and loves people. She is stand-offish with other cats.

Cyril is an English setter whose human is Pete, the Chief of Police. Cyril is friendly and calm. He is an excellent hunter.

Honey Bear is a large, golden, long-haired mutt of a cat who believes it is his perfect right to be anywhere. Other cats hate him. Honey Bear is in Chelsea whenever Annie's mother is.

Jock is a Portuguese water dog whose human is Ray, the captain of The Escape. Jock is spirited and affectionate; he loves children.

Chapter 1: Classic Rich Boy

An airport taxi pulled into the parking lot of the KaliKo Inn and disgorged its passenger.

Henrie stood at the top of the porch steps. He was wrapped in a warm coat, hat and gloves. The wind was brisk. The snow had stopped coming down for the moment. A brief moment. He walked down the steps and reached his hand out in welcome as he approached the taxi. "Welcome to the KaliKo Inn."

The passenger, now the arriving bed and breakfast guest, took his hand and responded, "You must be Henrie. Blaine Harrison Jones. I'm here to fish!"

Thus started a several minute period in which Henrie and the driver removed bags, boxes, crates and several unpackaged items from the taxi and set them upon the porch on both sides of the front door.

Blaine stood to the side, moving further and further along the porch as more items took the space in which he stood. From time to time he would slap his gloved hands together as if to keep the blood moving.

As the piles mounted, Henrie was thankful he had stored the porch furniture rather than merely covering the pieces for the winter. There would not have been room had he not. And the porch was quite large.

Blaine Harrison Jones had arrived to fish in Chelsea, a small resort town on the sunset side of a Great Lake. A rambling forested state park surrounded the town on two sides. Nestled into the park and the lake, Chelsea could pretend to be separate from the rest of the world. Only one highway dared to encroach upon its borders, and that highway only glanced by it to the east. Anyone coming to town had to exit the highway onto an access road.

The town circle, a mile from the highway, had just one building, a historic brick Italianate two story structure, which housed the town hall and the police department.

Driving around the town circle, one turned onto Sunset Avenue, a broad street with a median wide enough for benches, game tables and a walkway. Known simply as The Avenue by locals, it traveled one long town block, ending at the convergence of several tourist attractions.

The KaliKo Inn held a privileged position at the end of The Avenue. Just past the Inn, right to left, were the main entrance to a state campground, the main entrance to the state park, a town park with a playground and a brilliant white-sand beach, a parking lot free to anyone and used by everyone, a smaller private beach, another tip of the state park, and a small deep water marina.

Sunset Avenue was named for another tourist attraction. At the right time of day, which changed with the seasons, the median, parks and parking lot would fill with locals and tourists taking in the sunsets that were part of the town's allure. Indeed, even during the winter months, the area would be filled. Walkers strode up and down the beach or headed out to the lighthouse with cameras to capture the reds, oranges and yellows that seemed to last forever then fade all too quickly.

While tourist traffic was heavier from spring through fall, many winter sports kept the town busy year-round. Blaine Harrison Jones was here to indulge in one of the town's prominent winter sports, ice fishing, made possible due to the numerous small lakes in the area.

Chelsea maintained its tourist allure by staying just a little off the beaten path. The airport taxi that was becoming lighter by the minute was in fact a small airport bus out of a regional airline hub in Marsh Haven, a town about twenty miles north of Chelsea.

The driver huffed and puffed as he lugged gear and luggage onto the porch. He was happy to finish, take the tip and get on the road.

Henrie, also puffing a little in his own formal way, saw the driver on his way and leaned against the rail to look at his new guest and the profusion of "luggage" in his wake. This was a high-budget expedition.

Henrie, an elegant man, left a budding career as a manager of a five-star hotel in New York for the pace of this small resort community's premier bed and breakfast. Now, as chief cook, bottle washer, toilet bowl cleaner and concierge, his always-just-so attire, perfect diction, and hard-to-place accent could seem out of place. For some reason, they did not.

Blaine Jones appeared to be in his mid-thirties. He wore two layers of cardigans, black over gray, under a white fleece waistcoat. Black paisley socks showed underneath the hem of his black denim slacks with classic, polished leather shoes that appeared to never touch the snow. A blue and white batik scarf fashionably tied around his neck, a black Astrakhan cap and black leather gloves finished the look. Classic rich boy.

"Mr. Jones, you are certainly the best provisioned ice fisherman to stay at the Inn. You must have a great deal of experience. Is this your first time to fish in Chelsea?"

"I've never held a rod, reel, hook or worm in my hands before. Not once."

Henrie smiled briefly, politely held his tongue and looked around. He was surrounded by gear, and quite frankly, he did not know what to do with it. He envisioned the lovely library cluttered with this…debris. Hopefully, he asked Blaine, "Have you availed yourself of a rented vehicle of any type?"

"No. I thought you would have something. This is your area of expertise, is it not?"

"I see. Well. I will certainly make some arrangements this afternoon."

Henrie vowed to call Frank to ask for the loan of a moving trailer. And some skids. And possibly a forklift. Definitely a forklift. He was not going to carry these items any further.

From the sidewalk came a hearty, "Henrie, how ya doin' today? Cold enough fer ya?" A tall, stocky, warmly-clad man with a couple of days of stubble made his way to the porch steps.

Henrie gave a silent sigh of relief. "Boone, it is wonderful to see you. You have no idea."

Boone stepped onto the porch and looked around. "Well, looky here at this pile of stuff. Hi, young feller. I'm Boone!"

"How do you do, Boone. Blaine Harrison Jones. I'm here to do some fishing."

"Fishin' on the ice?"

"Yes. I guess that would be how you say it."

"And how you gonna get all this here stuff out to the lake?"

"Well, Henrie and I were just beginning to discuss that."

Boone, a big man, rough on the exterior but soft as a truffle on the inside, looked at Henrie with understanding.

"Henrie, I don't think I've ever seen you flustered-like afore this."

"I do not believe I have been confronted with this issue before. I had thought to call Frank to borrow a trailer and perhaps some moving equipment."

"That Frank's purty busy gettin' that store of his'n ready fer the open house. I don't think he can part with that stuff any dang soon."

"Well, then, I am sure we will come up with something. I will call the car rental company and see if they have an appropriate vehicle for, um, getting this equipment out to the lake."

Boone looked at Henrie, then looked over the piles of equipment on the porch. He turned to Blaine. "You a'fixin' to take most of that stuff out ter the ice on that there sled?"

"Yes. I understand that's the biggest and the best. Mother would not have purchased it otherwise."

"It sure is a big'un. And some of these other things are purty long. Henrie, you ain't agonna find what you need here in town. You call up there to Dodd's in Marsh Haven. Tell 'em you want one of them big ole four-wheel drive pickups. Tell 'em you needs a long bed, and with this snow an' all, tell 'em you needs a cover over the bed."

Henrie looked as relieved as he would allow himself to look. "Thank you, Boone; that is very helpful."

Henrie picked up two of the bags that he assumed were personal luggage and started for the door. "Come, Mr. Jones. Let us get in out of the cold for now, and I will make some coffee for you before calling for the vehicle."

As Henrie went through the door, Blaine stood a moment on the porch. He looked at Boone. "I didn't expect to meet someone as formal as Henrie in a fishing atmosphere. I would like to fit in as much as possible, and I don't know whether to speak like him or like you. How do folks here normally speak?"

Boone looked at him in confusion. "Well, gosh, we just opens our mouths and lets 'er fly."

"Oh. Well. I shall do my best!"

Boone picked up two more pieces of luggage on his way into the Inn. Blaine, looking around and finding no one else to pick up the last of his personal bags, picked it up himself and followed.

As he entered the foyer, he dropped the bag with the others and looked around. He saw a silver tray with freshly baked cookies and helped himself to one. "White chocolate and macadamia nuts." he said. "One of my favorites."

Boone picked a couple of cookies off the tray and bit into both of them at once. "Fresh baked."

Henrie was quick with the coffee. He walked into the foyer from a side room with a tray, two cups of steaming brew, sugars and creamers. "Mr. Jones, Boone, please help yourselves." He set the tray on a table, turned and said, "I shall make that call now, Mr. Jones, then show you to your room."

Blaine sank into a comfortable chair and looked around. From his vantage point, he could see into both the library on his left and the dining room on his right. "This is quite an attractive place," he said to Boone.

"It shore is. This is the first time I's been inside. It looks right nice."

"My home is so boring compared to this," continued Blaine. "All of my walls are painted the same color. Mother says it's 'eggshell,' but to me it's just boring. Of course, I like blue, and that seems to be the dominant color. But no room is the same."

"I see whatcha mean. That there room is light purple and that one there is pinkish."

"I think that might be called 'rose.' And all of the windows! I'll bet on a sunny day it's really pretty in here."

"We ain't seen much sun fer severl days, an' I 'magine we won't be seein' it fer quite a while. You know, we's known for our sunsets, but we ain't seen one of those fer quite a while."

Blaine then noticed the cats. The big cats. They sat on the middle step leading up to the second floor landing, and they were staring at him.

"Those cats. Are they safe?"

"Oh, yeah. That there one on the left is Kali and the one on ta other side is Ko. They's the ones whose names are on the sign."

"Oh. The KaliKo Inn. Now I get it. Mother made the reservations. She didn't say anything about cats."

"They's cats in all Annie's places. These two 'uns, they don't allays leave this place. They like to stay to home. But I sees 'em on the porch ever' now and then. They's big, that's fer shore."

Henrie entered the foyer. "Mr. Jones, the car rental agency is checking with their various partner agencies. They will call back shortly. For now, allow me to show you around the Inn and get you settled into your room."

Henrie showed Blaine the coffee room, where all types of coffees, teas and hot chocolates were available. He pointed out the cupboard with snacks and told him about the fresh snacks and truffles that would be available every afternoon.

"And please make use of the refrigerator or freezer if you care to bring anything in. Should you bring fish home from the lake, please allow me to help you store them in a more appropriate place."

Henrie gestured to the second floor landing. "There is a notebook available for you at the desk, and," he paused while walking toward the library, "in here you will find books, games, of course this large-screen television with a library of movies. These areas, and the all-season porch, through that doorway, are available to you at any hour of the day or night."

Boone had followed them on the short tour. "Well, dang! This here is a right fine place, Henrie. No wonders folks likes to stay here."

"Thank you, Boone. Now, Mr. Jones, I will take your luggage upstairs. You may join me in the elevator or take the stairs to the second floor."

"I'll take the stairs, Henrie." Blaine walked off, hands in his pockets, leaving Henrie and Boone to deal with the five bags.

Henrie picked up two bags and Boone took three, holding the handles of two in one hand. He followed Henrie to the elevator. Henrie nodded his thanks.

Blaine waited for them as they got off the elevator. "Your guests must watch a lot of television. Is the one on the landing here used often?"

"Yes, depending on the number of guests. On occasion more than one large group gathers to watch a sporting event or movie. Each guest room has a television as well, for your private viewing pleasure."

Henrie led Blaine to the guest room overlooking the lake, Boone trailing behind. Blaine went immediately to the French doors and looked out. "It's probably a bit nippy for using the patio, but the view is outstanding, Henrie."

"I am so glad you like it. Now, please take your time getting settled. I will be downstairs awaiting that call."

"Thank you, Henrie, and you too, Boone. I hope to see you again." Blaine held his hand out to Boone.

"You have a good time a'fishin', Blaine. I hope you enjoy our little town."

Henrie and Boone left the room, closing the door as they went. Blaine went again to the patio door, taking in the snow-covered beach and the white capped lake. As he turned to unpack, he noticed the two cats. Somehow they had gotten into the room and they now sat on the bed, looking at him with unblinking eyes.

"Well, um, hello there, cats. Kitties. One of you is Kali and the other Ko, right?"

The two big girls didn't move or blink.

"Kitties want a treat?" asked Blaine, clearly nervous. He glanced around the room and saw a packet of nuts. Moving slowly, keeping his back to the wall and his eyes on the cats, he got to the packet, opened it and tossed a few nuts on the bed.

The two big girls, whose eyes had followed Blaine to the packet of nuts, remained still, not even looking at the nuts now scattered on the bed.

Unnerved, Blaine said, "Shoo!"

The two girls remained still.

A little louder, he said again, "Shoo!"

And then again, even louder, punctuating the word with hands waving in the air, he nearly shouted, "Shoo!"

Kali and Ko, disgusted, stared for a few seconds more. They slowly rose, jumped off the bed, and tails twitching and hindquarters waving side to side, they walked out of the room through a cat door he had not noticed. He saw a lock on his side of the door, however, and he quickly snapped it shut.

He looked around the room once more, silently approved his surroundings, and took his time unpacking his bags. The room contained a long, low dresser with six drawers, a taller dresser with six more drawers, and a locking armoire with room for hanging clothes and additional drawers. Even with five bags of clothing and personal articles, there was plenty of space for him to unpack everything.

When finished, he put his now empty bags under the bed and out of sight, took a final look around, and left to explore the Inn on his own, checking once again that the cat door was secure.

Chapter 2: Great Neck Lake

Annie was returning from an early morning appointment with her accountant. She carried a large envelope with some "homework" she had to attend to fairly quickly.

She moved as quickly down the sidewalk as she deemed safe. Boone was doing a great job keeping it clear of snow, but the sun had been out. It had ducked behind some clouds, and the bit of water it had created was turning to a slick overcoat of ice.

The snow she craved for Christmas had come early. With a vengeance. If weather reports were to be believed, they were in for a spell of extraordinary cold, with more snow to follow. There were indications a blizzard would arrive before the week was out. Probably on Christmas. Thank goodness for Henrie. He would make sure they had everything they needed, come what may.

Annie had two styles of dress. Spring, summer and fall brought casual capris, flowing, colorful tops and almost flat sandals. Winter brought denims, longer sleeves, and either stylish mules with crazy socks or fleece-lined boots. Today, she wore fleece-lined boots. She also wore a rainbow-colored scarf and matching gloves with a thigh-length black coat, more functional than stylish.

Annie's straight, dark hair peeked around the sides and back of her scarf. Her hair was graying gracefully, but the lack of wrinkles on her face made guessing her age difficult. High cheekbones gave just a hint of some hidden Native American blood in her background.

She slowed when she reached the porch steps, looking around at the – what? It looked like six guests had decided to check out at once, dumping their very weird luggage on the porch while they paid their bills. But that couldn't be. They didn't have any guests. One was expected to arrive today.

Oh. An ice fisherman. Annie remembered this little nugget and looked more closely at the piles. She saw what could be a tent or shelter, possibly a heater, some poles, coolers, and stacks of boxes of what could be brand new fishing gear. Was that an extra-long sled in the corner? This guy was serious!

As Annie entered the Inn, she was met by Kali and Ko, the Inn's "managers" and chief cats-in-residence. Dilute calicos, all grays and peaches without a speck of another color, Kali and Ko were big. Big. With their litter mate, Mo, they could take up an entire sofa at naptime.

"Hi, girls. What's up?"

Kali and Ko began a string of cat sentences, first Kali, then Ko cutting in, then Kali…. Annie had long since learned not to look at first one, then the other. It could give a woman a neck problem. She had a way of backing her head up just enough to take both girls in at the same time in one long gaze.

When they seemed to finish, she said, "Well! You've had an exciting morning. Did you meet our new guest? I hope you liked him."

This started another string of cat sentences, with a bit of an edge.

"Well, you can stay out of his way. Maybe. I'm going to the kitchen. It smells like Henrie has made coffee, but I'll bet he can get me some hot chocolate. It's cold out there!"

Annie put the envelope on the hall table and shed her outerwear. As she went through the dining room, she saw Boone and their guest drinking coffee and "shootin' the breeze," as Boone would say.

She walked to her guest, holding out her hand. "Hello. Mr. Jones, isn't it? I'm Annie. Welcome to Chelsea and the KaliKo Inn."

"Thank you."

"Did Henrie give you the grand tour?"

"Yes, and I'm learning a lot about the area also, from Henrie and also from Boone. I'll take the day to explore a little bit and start fishing tomorrow."

"If there is anything I can help you find, please let me know."

"I will. By the way, not wanting to be rude, but may I ask about the cats?"

"The cats? Kali and Ko?"

"Yes. Are they friendly?"

"They're very friendly. Were Kali and Ko on their good behavior when you arrived?"

"I'm not sure. I have no experience with cats."

"Oh. Well, you will have by the time you leave here. Normally, you would see all seven of them only in the mornings and evenings, but this week, no matter what time of day you're here, you will have the pleasure of everyone's company."

"All of them? Seven of them? All day?"

"All day." Annie thought her guest might be turning green. "Are you allergic, Mr. Jones?"

"Oh, no. Well, at least I don't think I am. I've just never been around cats before. Do they, um, bite?"

"Oh, no. Well, the one that would possibly bite will probably just leave you alone."

Kali and Ko entered the dining room. They jumped to the buffet and stared at Blaine, unmoving.

"Those two. They're friendly?"

Boone interjected, "They's real friendly, Blaine. Looky here." Boone stood to go to Kali. Everyone in town knew Kali was partial to men. Boone cupped her head in his big hand and scratched behind her ears.

Kali succumbed. She normally liked the male guests, but this Blaine character had an aura about him. She had tried her best to be aloof in his presence, but Boone's ministrations wore her down. She turned her head into his scratches, closed her eyes and purred.

Ko hissed, jumped down and went somewhere to hide.

Annie turned a quizzical glance toward Blaine. "How did you find the KaliKo Inn? Did you go online? Find us on the web?"

"Mother took care of it. She handed the reservation slips to me last night."

"Oh, well, it's just that most people who find us see the cats on the web, and our confirmation reminds guests that cats are around. Did you see the cat door in your room?"

"I found that. I saw there was a lock. I trust it is acceptable to use it?"

"That's what I was going to suggest. When you're in the rest of the house, though, you'll see them. And like I said, there will be seven. It's supposed to be deadly cold, and I intend to keep them all home."

Blaine seemed to come to an inner conclusion. "I'm going to do my best to learn to enjoy them. It will be a learning experience. Mother did not allow me to have a pet, so this should be fun, actually."

Annie almost laughed as she watched the expression on Blaine's face as he went through that last speech. It was almost as if he was convincing himself as he talked. She changed the subject.

"You must enjoy ice fishing," said Annie. "You have a lot of equipment."

"Oh, no."

"You don't enjoy it?"

"Sorry, that's not it at all. It just that I've never fished before in my life, ice or otherwise."

Annie almost made a smart remark, stifled it and covered with a question. "Have you talked to anyone about helping you get started? There are guides…."

"Oh, I can handle it, I'm sure. I've read books and web articles. As long as someone points me in the right direction, I'll be just fine."

"Well, then. I'll call someone that can give you a good start. Are you going out first thing tomorrow?"

"I had hoped to go at first light, but apparently I will have to wait for the vehicle."

"Vehicle?"

Boone interjected, "Henrie's a'talkin' to Dodds up to Marsh Haven to see if he can rent a big ole pickup for Mr. Blaine here."

Henrie came around the corner with a mug of hot chocolate on a tray. He handed this to Annie, who said, "Henrie, truly, will you marry me?"

Henrie responded with a small, formal smile. He turned to Blaine. "Dodds has just the thing for you. They will bring it to the Inn by 9:00 tomorrow morning."

"Thank you, Henrie. I apologize for thinking you would have a vehicle on hand."

"That was certainly not a problem, Mr. Jones. However, I must ask if you have appropriate clothing for this excursion. The temperature is going to be dangerously cold this week. We're looking at an extended period of below zero weather with wind chills. It will feel like an arctic wasteland."

"I'm prepared. Mother purchased all the latest gear to keep everything warm. And I mean everything. I understand I have a shelter, a heater, blankets and all kinds of clothing I've never worn before. Even the proverbial long johns. But they're probably silk. I can't imagine Mother purchasing anything of that nature that was not made out of silk."

Annie looked at Henrie and said, "I'll call Chris and ask him if he can go out with Mr. Jones tomorrow, get him started." And in her mind, she thought, and check on him several times during the day….

"That is an excellent idea. It will give Chris a chance to spend time on one of our lovely smaller lakes, albeit on the ice."

Again, Annie turned to Blaine. "Which lake are you fishing, Mr. Jones?"

"Please, it's Blaine. I'm going to Great Neck Lake."

Boone said, "That there's a big'un. It's real skinny and twisty. They's woods all around it. You can't just stand at one end and see the whole lake. They's noplace you kin see it all."

Annie looked at Blaine earnestly. "It sounds isolated, Blaine, and it probably doesn't have the best cell phone service. Are you sure you want to start with that one?"

"I've heard the isolated lakes are the best if you want to fish."

25

"There are several smaller lakes, closer to town, easier for folks to keep an eye on one another."

"I'm here for the total experience. I want to be able to tell Mother I did it all."

"I hope you'll be able to do that, Blaine. I truly do."

Annie sipped on her hot chocolate, looking at Blaine over the rim. She decided she wasn't going to change his mind, so she turned to Boone.

"Boone, why don't you and I go have that talk we were going to have?" Annie and Boone moved to the library where they could talk in private.

Annie owned the KaliKo Inn and the 1880s era building that started at the edge of the Inn's yard and moved up the block, ending at the town circle. That building was home to several small businesses geared to the resort community's personality. She inherited the properties and the businesses from her father, a life-long resident of Chelsea, even though she had only visited summers before her father passed away.

She hired Boone and his crew last spring to keep the lawns mowed and landscaped. As the snows moved in, he took care of snow removal. She didn't know what she would do without him, although she hardly ever saw him. She knew this had to change, and it would. She would see to it.

"Boone, you have no idea how happy I am you can do building maintenance for us. I haven't done a single thing since Dad left these properties to me. We've been lucky. We haven't had any issues, but it's going to get so cold! This is the time for things to start to go wrong."

"I know what you's a'wantin' from me. Me and my crew, we can take a look at ever'thin' inside and out. We'll make sure ever'thin's workin' good and ever'thin's tight. Work on what needs work, and then get you on a, like a calendar, make sure things get tended to regular-like.

"You can call me anytime, day or night, if they's a problem. And we'll jes keep our snow schedule to goin', and the mowin' and stuff, jes like we been doin'. I'm a'thinkin' you still want me to do both sides of The Avenue, right? I mean with the snow and stuff."

"Yes, and I like the way you've been shoveling walkways from one side to the other. It's working out really well for everyone."

"You're right kind to do this for ever'one."

"Oh, I'm not kind. I'm selfish. I can afford to do it where not all of them can, and I need them. My businesses need them, and I like knowing we're all being taken care of."

"Well, it's still right kind. Do you know, now, who they gots to do their buildin'?"

"I don't think they've contracted with anyone, but they're in the same fix as me. They all moved in about the same time, a few years before I moved to Chelsea, and they're beginning to notice little things that need to be fixed. I've given them your number, and they'll probably be calling you. Is your crew big enough to handle this much additional business?"

"Now don't you go to worryin' 'bout that. I have lots of folks, and they's allays other folks lookin' for work. As long as I keep the new'uns with my good workers, they get things done real good."

"I've never heard anything but great comments about your work. Why don't you plan on doing your building reviews right after the first of the year?"

"Well, now, we're a'gonna look at yer pipes and stuff yet t'day. We'll stay out of ever'one's way. All they has to do is point us to the 'quipment. We won't make no noise or nuthin'."

"I supposed that's best, especially with this cold snap. And then you can start after the first of the year, unless you find a serious problem?"

"That would be jes fine. If we find somethin' bad, we'll get on 'er right away. Now, Miss Annie, my Harriet was awful sorry she couldn't be here t'day to talk about the cleanin' and all. Did you want her to do just this place? The Inn?"

"No, I was thinking about all of them. Henrie's got his hands full here, and so does everyone else. I think the problem will be scheduling it. Each place has different open and close hours."

"She's right flexible. She'd be able to work it out with ya. She's got lots of folks on her crew, but she'd a'prob'ly want to take care of your places by 'erself. At least for awhile. Until she's right clear she's a'doin' things the way you want 'em did."

"I'd like to sit down with her right after the first of the year as well, then. Hopefully get her started as soon as possible in January."

"Well that'll work just dandy. We both likes to give our folks time off over the holidays, so's they can spend it with their fam'lies."

"Speaking of people that work for you, that young man that was doing the snow this morning looked an awful lot like you. Is he your son?"

"Yep. That there were my son Daryl. He's been a'workin' fer me a couple years now. He's gettin' ready to go on down to part time. You know kids. They gots other things to do. My other boy, Donny, he's gettin' ready to start up with me. He gradyated from high school this month. He had hisself enough credits to leave in the middle of the year. He's gonna work part time too. You know kids."

Annie nodded and said out loud, "Yeah, I know kids." At the same time, she thought to herself that if kids don't have the guidance they need, they won't get going in the right direction. It seemed, perhaps, that Boone and his wife Harriet, very hard workers from all outward appearances, were going pretty light on these young men.

But that was none of her business. "Boone, I'd like to invite you and your family to dinner in my apartment. I'll even make it myself, if you would be brave enough to try my cooking. Would there be an evening next week, between Christmas and New Year, that you, Harriet and the boys would be available?"

Boone seemed genuinely surprised. "Well, golly, Ma'am, lets me talk to Harriet and I'll lets ya know. Thankee!"

Chapter 3: A Bundle Of ADHD

Annie made quick stops at each business on her way to the Café. At Sassy P's Wine & Cheese, business was very light. Jesus and Minnie, though, moved quickly. Jesus, born in the California wine country to a family of vintners, purchased the wines and managed the shop. Minnie, his partner in life and at work, did many things at Sassy P's, but her focus was on cheeses. She was raised in Wisconsin cheese country and brought those experiences as well as her European training to this resort town.

Sassy P's was bright and modern with wooden touches. Display counters, shelving and the tasting bar had light walnut finishes, and the bar had a delicate hand-carved trim. The wall behind the tasting bar was painted cranberry red; the other walls were lavender. At the end of the bar were a few café tables; the bar featured highly polished wooden stools with seats resembling hollowed out wine barrels.

Annie was met at the door by Sassy P herself. A small bundle of energy – truth be told, probably a bundle of ADHD – Sassy Pants had the coat of a painter's palette gone mad, with smatterings of tabby and white all over. Annie particularly liked the moon-shaped white spots on her flanks and the brown spot at the base of her chin.

Sassy Pants ran to her mommy, dropped to her back on the floor and wiggled herself into a perfect give-me-tummy-rubs position. Annie obliged by kneeling down to tickle the proffered body part, then picked the little girl up for a cuddle as she continued into the store.

"Minnie, is Sassy Pants helping you get ready for the two parties you have later on, or is she just getting in the way?"

"She's always a help, and to tell you the truth, if she isn't here when our groups arrive, they're disappointed."

"I know, and I'm sorry to say that after today, I'll be keeping the kids at the Inn. Just until the cold spell is over."

"I understand. It's supposed to be deadly cold. It's cold enough now! I hope we don't have a lot of cancellations between now and Christmas. We have a lot of food and wine stocked for the week!"

"What are you serving?"

"We're featuring a new wine from a small winery in Indiana with every Christmas party this week. And I have a couple of cheeses to feature as well. We've been pretty lucky. Everyone wants the same general menu, so we're getting small plate appetizers from the Café that will work for us all week."

"I'm not going to make you stop and explain them to me now. I'll try them when we have our own party."

"We're looking forward to it. Jesus and I will work in shifts. He'll stay here to get our parties started, and I'll switch out with him after an hour or so. All of our staff will go in shifts, too. We plan to be as relaxed as possible this week. We're really busy, but we're prepared. And we're serving everything from the buffet, so there won't be a lot of table service."

"Smart thinking."

Annie turned from Minnie to the little bundle of love. "Mommy's leaving, Sassy Pants. You get home early, now. It's cold out there."

At Mr. Bean's Confectionary, Annie stepped inside the door and sat on the windowsill. Mr. Bean jumped into her lap for some special pets and kitty cat kisses. A young, muscular gray cat with white markings, Mr. Bean was the "kitten" of the family. He loved attention, and he always moved in for the full-on, lick-my-mommy-on-the-lips kiss.

Like Sassy P's, Mr. Bean's had a bright, modern interior. Most of the walls were painted lime green with the exception of a bright white accent wall behind the counters. The accent wall was strewn with lime green and sunburst orange shapes. Glass counters were trimmed in bright white, and the natural light from the front windows was augmented with pendant lights, each one colorful and unique. Only a few café tables dotted the area as most guests took their purchases home to enjoy.

Carlos, the manager and baker, and Jerry, the candy maker, came to the front when they heard Annie enter. Jerry was shy, so shy that Carlos required him to initiate a conversation with Annie whenever they were around one another.

Jerry, becoming more confident every month, asked Annie, "Have you had a chance to try my holiday truffles? I made peppermint and eggnog flavors. The eggnog has a bit of a kick to it, and the peppermint has a bit of crunch."

"I have not. On purpose. I intend to try them at our Christmas party. If I try them now, I won't stop eating them."

Jerry blushed and looked at the floor. With a wink toward Annie, Carlos excused him. Jerry continued to look at the floor and blush as he walked away, but Annie could see the smile.

Jerry had remarkable skill as a candy-maker, learned in his years at a federal prison. While he shared little to no information about his past, Annie and her managers were aware Jerry had not been a prison employee.

Carlos was the perfect supervisor for Jerry. With his natural paternal instincts and no wife and children to use them, he turned those talents to grooming this capable young man who, somewhere along the way, had gotten into some problems.

Annie realized that she didn't let Carlos know often enough how much she appreciated him. "Carlos, the world is a much better place with you in it."

Now Carlos blushed.

Annie gave some last hugs to Mr. Bean and said, "Make sure this little guy gets home early tonight. It's freezing cold. After today, they won't leave the Inn until the cold snap is over."

"The guests will be very disappointed."

"I know. The kids will be, too. I'll have to lock the cat doors at the Inn before they realize what's happening."

Annie stopped at Mo's Tap next. George, manager and bartender, had a couple of guests at the bar and Candice, the head server and George's sometimes and now current love interest, had only a few tables with lunch guests.

During the day, the lighting was subdued but not as "moody" as they kept it at night. The bar was upscale, with a classy, clean, light look. Most of the walls were butter yellow; light taupe served as an accent color. The tables were burnished oak with comfortable oak chairs. Booths, also oak with dark taupe cushions, and several areas with overstuffed chairs and accent tables offered more private seating. A few areas had tables that looked like oaken barrels.

Each seating area had unique pendant lights that could be turned up or down as the mood struck. And candles. The candles were lit at night, when the lights went down and Mo went home. Mo had a habit of sticking his beautiful tail – and other body parts in that vicinity – into the flames.

Blues music played at a moderate level in the background.

Mo himself luxuriated at the end of the bar, snuggling into the hands of a woman with long red hair. The woman talked to the man at her left, but her body language poured into Mo's long, soft gray fur. The man appeared younger. His blond hair was spiked in the tradition of those who wanted to make their aversion to authority known. A number of visible tattoos and lots of metal added to the look. He did not look to be the type the redhead would find attractive, but Annie figured it was none of her business.

Mo, on his back, twisted his face to look at Annie with love-satiated eyes. Annie waggled her fingers at him and sat at the other end of the bar.

As Annie waited for George to break free, her mind wandered. She thought about George, a Chelsea native, a great bartender, a Coast Guard volunteer, and a semi-reformed Casanova.

Slowly, a snippet of a conversation from a couple of months ago came to her. One of her staff, Trudie, told her about some pretty redhead wearing a dress with a plunge down to here and a slit up to there. The redhead had come in between George and Candice.

George and Candice had split, coming back together after a Coast Guard emergency landed George in the hospital. As far as Annie knew, they were still together.

Annie now looked with studied indifference toward the end of the bar, and sure enough, the top half of the redhead looked like Trudie's description. There was certainly a plunge to the neckline. The details were covered up by a large, gray long-haired body, now snuggled into the curves with complete content.

Annie looked across the room at Candice, who had an equally elegant head of hair. Hers was long, thick and dark. She had a fine figure, also, but she didn't care to share the details like the redhead apparently did.

George joined Annie shortly. "Hey, Annie. How's your day going?" While they talked, he stood in front of her in a classic bartender stance, always busy. He cleaned the bar in front of and beside her. He picked up some clean glasses and shined them. He filled the nearby snack bowls.

"Great. You're a little slow today. I would have thought offices from town would be filling you up all week."

"I think that will start tomorrow. The bosses want to get one good day of work out of everyone, then the rest of the week will go to heck. And we'll reap the rewards of the heck."

"Who's the couple at the end of the bar?"

"The woman is Christal. She comes and goes as a regular guest. The man, if you can call him that, he's barely legal, is Rusty. He's been coming in with her lately."

"Kind of an odd-looking couple," said Annie, unable to resist. She might hear a bit of gossip.

George made a face, kind of a grimace, and said, "Lucky me. She shows up again, at Christmas, with a guy that, let's face it, is not the most charismatic, and she always heads for that bar stool." He looked around the room and motioned toward Candice with his chin. "The atmosphere has been a bit chilly around here."

Annie laughed. "One of these days, you'll make up your mind."

In recent months, George seemed to have his mind made up, settling on Candice. Annie couldn't deny that George was the perfect bartender. He knew all the locals, made friends of the tourists, had an open face with open ears, kept everyone's secrets, knew his beers and made killer cocktails. All of his past girlfriends remained friends, which assured the bar business would continue to grow. And the ups and downs with Candice had not affected the running of the bar.

George confirmed her first thought. "That's the thing, Annie. I have made up my mind. But I guess my track record makes it easy for her to doubt it."

"Hang in there, big guy. You can do this."

Annie waggled her fingers at Mo again and said to George, "Make sure the big boy gets home early today, and I'll keep him home for the rest of the week with this cold snap."

"That will be a disappointment for the guests. And, frankly, our bottom line."

George sighed as Christal signaled for another round of drinks.

Annie took that as her cue, and she left. As she walked out the door, she thought about her two bar "managers." Mo and George shared many traits. Especially in the way they were drawn to beautiful women and how those women, like magnets, were drawn to them.

At the yoga studio, L'Socks' Virasana, Annie stopped first at Little Socks' special windowsill. As usual, the little girl was curled into a ball, soaking up what little sun came through the window. Black as night, with white socks and some white on her chest, Little Socks preferred to curl up, covering anything white. And it was absolutely best if she was on something black. She could pretend to be invisible, a chameleon of sorts.

Diana, the manager and head instructor, knew Little Socks very well and empathized with the cat's aloof personality. A few weeks before, she had purchased several large black cushions, setting them along the windowsills so Little Socks could chase the sun and pretend to be invisible.

Annie sometimes forgot to play the game. Today was one of those days. She sat next to Little Socks, leaned over and whispered into her ear. "Hello, big girl."

The ear wiggled. One bright green eye opened a slit. Just a slit. The eye stared balefully, then closed.

"Oops. I mean, I wonder where in the world that pretty kitty has gotten to? All I can see are black pillows. I wonder if she's here?" Annie touched the pillow to her left. "Or here?" She got up and touched the next pillow over on the right. "Well, where in the world could she be?"

Little Socks lifted her head, stretched out both sets of legs, arched her back into the stretch, sat up and licked a front paw.

"There she is! How is my pretty girl?"

Little Socks allowed Annie to touch her head with one finger. Then she dropped to the floor in search of another hiding place.

Annie laughed and waited for Diana to get free. She was teaching a regularly-scheduled class, typically a large one, that today boasted two students.

Another bright space, L'Socks' had a wall of knee-to-ceiling windows trimmed in bright orange and lined by backless benches of various primary colors. The opposite wall was completely mirrored with bright orange trim and a ballet bar that ran the length of the wall. The side walls were painted eggshell and in primary colors were silhouettes of yoga poses.

Diana was a native of Chelsea, like George, but she left town for several years. Those years remained a mystery to everyone. She talked to no one about them. She returned to Chelsea only recently to patch up the relationship with her mother. Or, more correctly, to forge a relationship where one had not existed. Mother and daughter had a silent agreement to never discuss those mystery years.

When Diana came over, Annie asked, "Are you going to be this slow all week?"

"Oh, yeah. It's going to be worse than last year. People want to eat and drink over the holiday, not stay healthy, and this year we have snow and freezing temps."

"Why don't you take a look at the schedule and see which of your instructors can be given some paid time off?"

"Oh, wow! Thanks! I'll see if I can't spread it around and give everyone some time, just make sure one person is here for our busy hours. Really, that seems to just be in the morning."

"Why don't you open as usual and close for the day as soon as your morning classes are finished?"

"Maybe into the early afternoon. By then, people have done everything they need to do and they've gone inside to stay warm for the rest of the day."

By now, the lunch rush would be at full speed at the Café, so Annie left the yoga studio to go to the next, and the last, business in the building.

Tiger Lily was at her standard greeting place, the hostess stand. A brown and gray tiger cat with soft green eyes, she greeted all guests as they entered and said 'thank you' to all guests as they left. Now she greeted Annie, grateful that Mommy was finally here. In cat language, she said, *"It's about time you got here! Look at all these people! There's only one empty table and it hasn't been bussed yet!"*

From experience, Annie knew Tiger Lily was telling her something about the Café. She thought she knew what it was, so she responded, speaking in human language, "It looks pretty busy in here. And here come some more folks, right behind me. Do you think I ought to help out, big girl?"

Tiger Lily narrowed her eyes for just a second then turned to greet the newcomers. She gave her guests the full-on open-eyed greeting, then slowly closed her eyes, gave a small nod of the head and accepted some adoration. When they moved into the dining room, Tiger Lily looked down, behind the stand, where her friend Cyril was napping. He was absolutely no help whatsoever today.

The Café had a casual chic ambiance; it was on a corner, allowing for two walls that were mostly knee-to-ceiling windows with minimal coverings. Annie's father had been able to save the original tin ceiling in this location.

The two walls that were mostly windows were painted mint green, and the walls behind the coffee counter and server station were bright purple. The lighting was an eclectic mixture of track, recessed and pendant lights. The pendant lights were colorful and unique in shape and design.

The tables and chairs matched, but not necessarily at the same setting. The chairs were wooden and painted in every color of the rainbow, with comfortable cushions matching the color of the chair. The tables had brightly painted ceramic tops; each table was unique, with animals, landscapes or artistic motifs.

The tables had another element: platforms on every side. To the uninitiated, the platforms looked like strange places to set a drink, but there was a purpose for them. They allowed Tiger Lily to speak to her guests at table, sometimes offering them a recommendation – by way of a paw placed on the menu – for a meal or appetizer.

Annie waved at people she knew and headed for the coffee bar. She spoke first to the barista, Trudie. "Can I help you out?"

"I'm fine, and the kitchen seems to be keeping up with the orders, but it looks like the servers are in the weeds, getting behind on clean-up."

"I'll do some bussing, then check with Felicity."

Trudie was, as far as anyone knew, the only Jamaican in Chelsea. She was here by accident. Abandoned by a boyfriend at the state park's campground, she was taken in by Felicity and given a job at the Café. She fell in love with the ambiance of the town and made it her home.

Annie couldn't imagine the Café without her. She was indispensable as the barista, the second in command, and a standout fill-in for each of Annie's businesses when the need arose.

Annie left the coffee bar and stopped at the server station, told a couple of hard-working servers she would give them a hand, and headed into the dining room. She deftly cleaned the now three empty tables, wiped them down and reset them for new guests. She walked through the room, greeting guests and picking up empty glasses and plates as she went. She gave holiday greetings to Chelsea locals, welcomed tourists to town, and chatted a bit with several friends.

As she finished circling the room, it appeared the servers had a better handle on things, so she stopped to sit with Pete, the Chief of Police, and Chris, the Officer in Charge of the Coast Guard Station. And her friend. Partner. No, friend. Good friend. That sounds best, she thought.

Pete and Chris had a lot in common, really, although they looked quite opposite of one another and had varied backgrounds.

Pete was a tall man, over six feet, with a physique honed by 20 years in the Marine Corps. Chris was not quite as tall, a little under six feet, and had the slim and erect bearing of a Navy officer.

Pete had a military haircut, mostly black on top but graying at the temples, while Chris's hair, prematurely white, had some length to it. He also sported neatly trimmed facial hair, both mustache and beard.

Pete's family arrived in Chelsea four generations ago via the Underground Railroad; his ancestors worked in the timber industry, then later became skilled wood workers and furniture manufacturers. Chris arrived a few years ago on assignment from the Coast Guard and was the child of a privileged, old-money family.

Pete was eating meatloaf; Chris had the tofu-based groundnut stew with a whole wheat bagel.

Annie had a weakness for meatloaf. She nearly reached for Pete's plate but caught herself in time. "The meatloaf looks good. Is that today's special?"

"You've been all over the room, and you don't know what today's special is?"

"Well, I wasn't taking orders, so I didn't really have to know."

Kathleen Thompson

A server stopped at the table to ask Annie if she needed anything. "Could I have a half order of that meatloaf, please, and ask Trudie if she can fix me one of those chocolate peppermint lattes."

As the server walked away, Annie turned to Chris. "Chris, I have a favor to ask."

"When don't you?"

"Uh, I think I went for three days in early December without asking you for a thing."

"I remember it fondly."

Annie chucked him on the shoulder and said, "Really, this could be important. I have a guest…"

Pete cut in, "Another guest problem? Please, tell me he's not a ruthless killer, a thief or someone on the run."

"None of the above. He's rich and completely out of his element. It looks like he's spent hundreds of dollars on brand new ice fishing gear. He's going out to Great Neck Lake, and he's never been fishing in his life. Not even at a summer watering hole."

"You are kidding."

"Nope."

"Did you know this when he booked in?"

"I knew he was going to be ice fishing. Henrie didn't know he was an amateur either. Oh, and the guy didn't know about the cats. He's spooked by the cats."

"Who in the world gets spooked by cats?"

"He appears to be a momma's boy that doesn't do much without her say-so. A rich momma's boy." Annie aimed a meaningful look at Chris.

"You calling me a momma's boy?"

42

"I've never met your mother, so no, but if the shoe fits…."

Pete laughed and then got serious. "Annie, I know you don't know a thing about fishing or the inland lakes here. Chris, you know everything there is to know about the Great Lakes, but do you know anything about the little ones?"

"Not a thing. I always wanted to be on big water. We Coast Guard types don't care much for the smaller stuff."

Pete shook his head. "Great Neck Lake is the most isolated lake in the county. And as for ice fishing, it's shallow on the edges, but it's deep in the middle. There's a river running through it. It could make for some dangerous situations."

Annie closed her eyes tightly and pursed her lips. "Should I encourage him to go to another lake?"

"You should try. But you can't make him do what he won't do. He sounds a little spoiled. He'll probably go ahead, no matter what you say."

Chris dropped his chin to his chest with a sigh. He spoke from that position. "What do you want me to do?"

"Could you just follow him out to the lake and make sure he gets to a safe spot? Knows what to do in an emergency? Check on him every now and then?"

"I suppose I can do that. Pete, do you know if Ray knows anything about ice fishing?"

"He does. He loves that big lake just like you do, but I remember him doing some ice fishing right after he moved here."

Chris gave Annie a smile. "I'll make sure he gets a good start, and with Ray and maybe some other folks, we'll make sure he stays safe."

"Thank you," Annie smiled, looked at Pete and smiled wider. "Isn't he the greatest?"

Pete and Chris made gagging motions.

Annie was saved from their silent snarky remarks when a small plate of meatloaf was delivered by Felicity, the Café's chef and manager.

Felicity was another person Annie couldn't imagine having to live without. She was bright, perky, always upbeat, a great chef, willing to take risks, and always pushing the envelope as she pushed the Café to new levels of success.

"I brought this out myself because I want to know what you think of the flavor."

"What's in it?"

"Not telling. You tell me."

Annie put a forkful into her mouth and tasted. "Yum. Let's see, there are raisins, and some kind of cheese. Provolone?" Felicity nodded. "And pine nuts. But the meat. This isn't regular meatloaf meat. What is it?"

"Combination ground chuck and ground pork."

"And how did you get this crust so perfect?"

"The crust has some of the raisins, nuts and cheese. They're both inside and rolled over the top before baking."

"This is awesome! What are you treating vegetarians to today?"

"The meatloaf sounded so perfect for a cold day like today, so they have a vegetarian – actually a vegan – option with black beans, quinoa, veggies and a mushroom wine sauce."

"May I have a taste?"

Felicity laughed. "What do you think I have behind my back?" She handed Annie another plate.

Annie tried it, sighed, and said, "I don't know which I like the best."

As Felicity left, Annie looked again at Pete. "Cyril is napping behind the hostess stand. I don't think I've ever seen him nap here before, at least, not when it's busy."

"He's unhappy with me. He knows something is up, and he's a little nervous. And, let's be honest, he's sad."

"About the trip you and Janet are taking?"

"Yeah. We've been on the phone a lot during the evenings. The kids have been excited, and there are piles of clothes and things that will be going into suitcases tonight and tomorrow, but no dog things. Last night he started picking up his toys and putting them on the piles of clothes. Janet and I just left them there."

"But you've told him he'll be staying with Chris, right? He likes Chris."

"I like to think he understands everything I say, but he's not buying this. I think he's worried we're going to leave him and never come back."

"You're leaving tomorrow, right?"

"Yes. Tonight, Chris, Ray and Cheryl are coming over. Ray's bringing Jock. Maybe if he sees he still has friends…."

"And Cyril is going home with you tonight, Chris?"

"That's the plan. He's going to be a Coast Guard dog, at least for a week. That's not much different from being a police dog, except he'll be doing part of his work on water."

At this moment, Cyril walked to the table. A beautiful English setter, the bounce seemed to have gone out of his step. He put his muzzle on Annie's lap and looked up at her with big, sad dog eyes.

Annie smiled down and placed her hand on his head. "It will be fine, Cyril. We're all going to have a great Christmas, and then, in a few days, everything will be back to normal."

Cyril sighed.

"He really does know."

"Of course. But let's talk about happier things. Cyril, let's show Annie what we've been working on."

Cyril perked up and looked at Pete expectantly.

Pete held two fists at dog level. He looked at Annie and said, "Right is yes, left is no."

"My right, or your right?"

"My right. Your left."

"And he understands, right? That it's your right and not his right?"

"Of course he understands."

"Well, just sayin'…"

"Shut up and watch the trick."

"Okay, okay."

Pete looked over at Chris. Cyril, this guy I'm looking at, is he a good guy?"

Cyril reached a paw to touch Pete's right hand.

Pete smiled and looked in turn at Chris then Annie. "See?"

"He had a fifty/fifty chance of getting it right," said Chris with a laugh. "Get it? Right?"

"Lame," answered Pete. "Let's try something else. Cyril, do you want a treat?"

Cyril reached a paw to touch Pete's hand for 'yes.'

Pete reached into his pocket. "Oops. I didn't bring any treats with me."

Annie was taken aback. "How can you leave the house without treats?"

"I just forgot. We're packing. Can he have a bite of your meatloaf?"

"Only the vegan is left. But it's good. Here, Cyril. Here's a treat."

Cyril sniffed the plate Annie offered and turned away, giving Pete an unreadable stare as he did so.

"I'm sorry, Cyril. My bad. Let's try one more thing. Are you ready?"

Cyril looked at him, expression still unreadable.

Pete looked around the room, spotted Tiger Lily and asked, "Is Tiger Lily your friend?"

Cyril looked at Pete, took his paw to choose 'no,' and walked back to the hostess stand to plop down behind it.

Pete looked first at Annie then at Chris. "Well what was that all about?"

Annie and Chris both smiled. Chris was the one that said it. "Fifty/fifty. There is always a fifty/fifty chance he'll be wrong."

Tiger Lily turned around and looked down on Cyril. *"Why did you say I'm not your friend?"*

"It was just a game, and I got tired of playing."

"Why are you so sad today?"

"Pete is leaving me. He's going away, and he's leaving me."

"Pete wouldn't leave you. He's your human."

"*He's leaving me with Chris.*"

"*Forever?*"

"*I don't know. I don't care.*"

"*You do too care. I think, if Pete is leaving you with Chris, there must be a good reason. Sometimes Mommy leaves for a couple of days, and we stay with Henrie.*"

"*That's different. You get to sleep in your own bed, and you know Annie's coming home.*"

"*You know Pete's coming home.*"

"*He's sending me to a new home. Now be quiet and let me sleep.*"

Annie went to the hostess stand as Pete and Chris left the Café. She said good-bye to Cyril, then stood at the hostess stand for a few minutes just petting Tiger Lily and greeting guests as they entered or left. But she was thinking.

When they hit a quiet moment, she stood directly in front of Tiger Lily, held out both of her hands, in fists, and motioned with them. "This one is yes, and this one is no, okay?"

Tiger Lily blinked.

"Is it cold outside?"

Tiger Lily blinked.

Annie waggled her fists. "Tiger Lily, is it cold?"

Tiger Lily blinked.

"One more time, now, is it cold outside?" Annie waggled her fists, looked into Tiger Lily's eyes with meaning, nodded her head as if clueing her in. "This one means yes," she said.

Tiger Lily yawned, turned to the side and licked her paw to clean off the back of her ear. Annie shook her head and left the area.

At that moment, Carlos walked in, Mr. Bean behind him. Mr. Bean jumped up to the stand. *"What's going on?"*

"Mommy is trying to teach me tricks."

"What?"

"You know that trick that Cyril does. This hand means yes, and this one means no."

"Why is Mommy teaching you? You already know how to do that."

"Mommy doesn't know that I know. The important thing is that She. Is. Trying. To. Teach. Me. Tricks."

"What's wrong with that?"

"Mr. Bean, sometimes I think you aren't all there. Cats do not do tricks. Not ever. Never."

"Never?"

"Never. And we can never let humans know that we know how to do the tricks they teach to dogs."

"Why do the dogs do the tricks?"

"They think their humans will love them more if they do it."

"Will they love us more if we do it?"

"No. They love us because we're cats. Cats. Do. Not. Do. Tricks. Not. Ever."

"Okay. Thanks for letting me know. I'll have to stop doing the dance Carlos likes me to do."

Tiger Lily looked at Mr. Bean. *"You do a dance for him?"*

"Yeah. And then he gives me treats."

Tiger Lily narrowed her eyes and stared.

"I'll stop! I didn't know!"

Chapter 4: Ma'am, You Ain't Winterized

When the lunch crowd was nearly gone, Boone stepped into the Café, looked around until he saw Annie and caught her eye. She walked toward the front of the room and waved him to the coffee bar. "Boone, Trudie will make you anything you'd like to drink. What will you have?"

"Well, Ma'am, I'd like a cup of black coffee, if that wouldn't be a bother."

Trudie thought it best not to ask if he preferred Columbian or French Roast. She simply said, "No bother at all, Boone. Go ahead and have a seat. I'll bring it out."

Boone and Annie headed for the back room which had emptied out for the day. As they sat, Boone looked at Annie seriously. "Ma'am, you ain't winterized."

"How bad is it?"

"Purty bad. Dudn't look like your paw did much of anythin' to insulate pipes an' such. You been lucky."

"The temperature is going to nose-dive tonight. Can you do anything?"

"Yes'm I can. I'll have to get in as soon as each place closes taday and tanight, and I'll have to do the Inn too. I'll call all my folks in. We'll get 'er did, but I got to get a'goin' on it."

"Well, get a'goin' and I'll let everyone know. Both Mo's and Sassy P's will probably be open late tonight, because it's Christmas week. Will that be a problem?"

"I'll get severl guys a'goin' at wunst. We'll get started in these other places and the Inn, and it'll probly be late afore we can even get to them two ones."

"Thank you, thank you, thank you!"

Annie did not wait for the managers to send the kids home. The thermometer was dropping fast, so she picked them all up on the way home.

She carried Mo, whose tender feet didn't like to touch the ground in a perfect 70 degrees. Everyone else trotted behind or ran on ahead.

Tiger Lily and Mr. Bean trotted behind, where Tiger Lily continued a lecture on 'how cats behave.' *"Honestly, doesn't any of this come naturally to you?"*

"You're the only cat momma I've known. Well, I guess you're all mommas, except for Mo, who would be a papa, except that I can't understand him."

"Trill!"

Mr. Bean looked up at Annie's shoulder, where Mo's head was draped. His paws were wrapped firmly around her neck. When he replied, his tone was a little confused, a little petulant. *"I don't know what you said."*

Mo closed his eyes and appeared to go to sleep.

Sassy Pants, who had stopped to allow Annie to catch up, said, *"He tries to shows you how boy kitties act."*

Mo opened his eyes, said *"Trill,"* sighed and closed his eyes again.

Sassy Pants said, *"You's welcome,"* and ran on ahead.

Tiger Lily and Mr. Bean just looked at one another, then at Mo, then at the retreating tail of Sassy Pants.

Tiger Lily had never understood Mo, although she was trying to learn how to interpret his trills. Typically, she had to wait until Kali and Ko were around, because they used to speak litter mate kitten language with Mo. They had graduated to speaking 'cat,' but Mo still talked in 'kitten' and appeared to be unable to progress further. Kali and Ko were his normal translators.

Their friends, Cyril and Jock, both dogs, appeared to understand Mo. And now, inexplicably, it appeared Sassy Pants could understand him as well.

When they reached the Inn, Annie put Mo on the floor in the foyer, turned around and reached down to lock the cat door from the inside. She then went to the kitchen.

"Henrie, I'm going to lock all the outside cat doors right now. The kids are staying home until it warms up."

Henrie turned to look at Annie, narrowed his eyes and said, "You do know we will have behavior problems."

"Yes, we will."

"So be it. It is for the best. Allow me to get the doors on this half of the house, before they figure out they've been locked in."

Annie heard some banging coming from the basement. "Boone's folks?"

"Yes. They are a'winterizin' away."

Annie stifled a laugh as she turned to go.

Henrie stopped her with the menu for his afternoon snack. "I have everything cookies, orange and apple slices, and a delectable orange ginger mint tea suggested by Mem. Would you care for some?"

Henrie's everything cookies varied with each reincarnation. They had coconut or oats, two flavors of chips, walnuts, pecans or peanuts, raisins or cranberries, and sometimes a surprise. Annie loved them.

"Yum! Yes! Has Blaine been down this afternoon?"

Henrie set a cup of tea in front of Annie as he said, "Yes. He took a walk around The Avenue but came back fairly quickly, He said the air was 'invigorating but a bit nippy.'"

"Oh, boy. Do you think he'll really go fishing in this weather?"

"Unfortunately, I believe he will do just that. It could be a disaster. Or not."

"Let's hope for 'not.' What do you know about ice fishing, Henrie?"

"I did some web searching this afternoon and learned a few disturbing things.

"First of all, you know we have had an unusual amount of snow since Thanksgiving, and starting tomorrow, it will be frigid. But until today, temperatures have been in the teens. Great Neck Lake is frozen solid around the edges, but the current of a river runs through it and it is quite deep in the middle. Even though it is a narrow lake, there is a possibility the ice in the middle is still quite thin.

"The lake is snow-covered. The literature suggests steering clear of dark spots, or places where the snow is discolored. However, since we have had steady snow, I doubt our Blaine Harrison Jones will be able to distinguish the trouble spots.

"And, as you know, he will be fishing alone. He certainly has the requisite emergency gear, but he will be unpacking it for the first time. There are some things books alone cannot teach you. Unless he takes the gear out to work with it first, he will not know what to do in a crisis.

"And a novice has no business going to such a lake. You know nothing about the smaller lakes, yet even you realized the, shall we say, 'spotty' cellphone coverage and the isolation."

Henrie paused to take a breath.

Annie was a little shaken. "Is that all?"

"Just an observation. He lasted barely half an hour in the cold today, and we have not begun to see the temperatures we will see starting tomorrow."

"Oh, my, Henrie. We've certainly had novices here before. Tourists here to try out a new sport. But I don't believe we've ever had anyone intentionally putting themselves in danger before. What should we do?"

"I think we are taking all the appropriate steps. You will ask Chris to go with him and check on him; we have outlined the dangers as we believe them to be. We must be mindful of his comings and goings and send up a flare if he is late in returning."

"I've talked to Chris, and he's not used to ice fishing either, but he's going to ask Ray to help. And besides that, we wait until the end of the day, every day? Hope he makes it back to the Inn?"

"Unfortunately, we will have two times each day to worry. He will return to the Inn to warm up midday, then go out again sometime later in the afternoon. He is hoping to catch the peak fishing times. He insists on having the 'total experience.'"

Annie had some end-of-year tasks to attend. According to Gwen, her accountant, she needed to make decisions about charitable contributions, and she needed to do it before Christmas so Gwen could prepare checks before the end of the year.

Nestled into the crook of one arm was the envelope she brought home this morning. It was filled with brochures of vetted charitable organizations. One brochure was out and open, balanced on her arm with her fingers holding it and the envelope. In her other hand was a cup of Henrie's tea.

Annie headed for the second floor landing, intending to use the notebook set up for guest use. Blaine was the only guest and he was enjoying cookies and tea with Henrie at the moment. She walked slowly, mostly by feel, as her head was buried in the glossy brochure describing a safe water project.

As she got to the stairway, and before she felt the little foot under her shoe, she heard, *"IIIIIIII!"*

"Mr. Bean! Are you alright? Did I hurt you? Little fellow, you have to stop doing this!"

Mr. Bean was long gone, having run from the stairway into the library. Annie didn't follow him, but she called after him, "Baby boy, sometime or another you're going to get hurt doing this. Tiger Lily, where are you? You need to teach him to not do this!"

Mr. Bean had developed the habit of walking directly in front of his humans, close, but not so close that he would touch them to warn them of his presence. He particularly liked to do this, Annie believed, when his humans were engrossed in an activity. He would stay slightly in front of, but close, to his human and would angle his head up often to make sure the human was still following. Then, often, he would stop to take a good, long look. At which point, more often than not, a human foot would land on a kitty foot.

Tiger Lily heard Mommy calling, but she ignored it. She realized all of the cat doors had been locked, effectively making them prisoners at the Inn. A comfortable and nicely outfitted prison, arguably, but a prison none-the-less. Tiger

Lily was going to make Mommy pay for this sin one way or another. Silence was one way.

Usually, when something like this happened, something unpleasant was brewing. Yesterday she heard Mommy talking to Grandmommy on the Skype thing. Maybe that visit they had talked about was getting ready to happen. Maybe that horrid Uncle Honey Bear was about to make an appearance again.

Tiger Lily sat on a table in front of the street-side window in the library, watching the snow sift down. Once again, the snow was coming, but not heavy. Across The Avenue, people hurried into and out of the shops, pulling coat collars or scarves more tightly around their necks as they hit the cold air.

Tiger Lily wondered if she had been too harsh regarding Mommy's actions. Maybe she thought it was getting too cold for their unprotected paws. Mommy did make everyone come home early today.

From behind her came Mr. Bean's soft kitty voice. *"Tiger Lily, Mommy doesn't like me getting close to her."*

"Mommy doesn't want to step on you is all."

"But I wanted to be close to Mommy."

"You have to wait until she sits down, or wait until she's just standing somewhere."

"But what if she doesn't look down?"

"Then you do what you always do. Stand up and pat her with your front paws. Or if she's walking, get behind her and find a way to touch her. Just keep an eye out that she doesn't turn quickly or something."

"Can I cuddle with you?"

Tiger Lily gave Mr. Bean a long, cool stare. Then she rearranged herself to look out of the window from her side and motioned with her head. Mr. Bean gave a sigh and stretched out behind her, spooning around her back. It took only a few seconds for him to fall asleep, the purr machine massaging her back, his front paw softly kneading into her shoulder.

Tiger Lily looked around and down at the boy and thought, I guess he's a keeper.

Annie hoped Mr. Bean wasn't badly hurt, but he had run away. Certainly, if he could run like that he wasn't really hurt. She hoped.

She sat at the desk and turned on the notebook. She first logged onto the financial records of the Café. They were having a good month. Everything looked right. Guest numbers were solid for December, maybe a little higher than last year, and expenses seemed to mirror last year at this time.

The catering business was solid as well, growing each month and remaining profitable. The second floor facility had a cost center of its own and could be easily monitored. Use of the facility was growing steadily, and there was a lot more holiday use this year than last. Outside catering activities were tracked in another cost center, and they, too, were growing. Of course they had one client they could count on during several months of the year. Ray, who owned The Escape, a cruise and fishing yacht, asked the Café to cater all of his excursions.

Annie confirmed the Café could afford the extra expense of a cleaning crew and building maintenance, as long as major repairs were not needed.

Annie's businesses had varying degrees of profitability. Merging the finances of all of them, she could afford to give a decent benefit package to all of her employees. Employees in the hospitality industry were normally underpaid and under-insured. She realized how lucky she was to be able to do this and had recently begun spending more time looking over the shoulder of her accountant, to be sure things continued to go well. And to learn some tricks of the trade.

Being able to pay better than average and add health insurance helped Annie hang on to the best hospitality employees in town. Spending the "extra" money paid dividends to the businesses in many ways, making them more profitable rather than less.

Taking the burden of cleaning away from them would be another benefit. The managers knew this was coming, and they had shared the good news with the rest of the staff earlier in the month. They would get through this holiday rush, and then life would be easier for them. Staff would still do end of shift and beginning of shift cleaning, but the heavier, weekly stuff would be done by the new crew.

She moved on to the yoga studio. There, benefits were not a big expenditure, as Diana was the only full-time employee. However, she paid the part-time instructors a premium to keep them coming back.

Beyond salaries, there was very little overhead at the studio besides utilities, and the income and expenses seemed to be appropriate. Expenses were steady and the number of students appeared to be on the rise, pushing the studio to break-even, even with the cleaning crew figured in.

Annie next opened up Mo's Tap. The income was good, more than a tick above last year. Expenses had spiked in November and appeared to be spiking again this month. This was going to take some digging into, so she moved on to Mr. Bean's Confectionary.

Wow. A surprising jump in income this year over last, but expenses seemed to be consistent with that increase. This business was very profitable, and, she thought, perhaps the baby boy was responsible for some of it. Oh, and the new pet treats they were selling had to help also. Annie would come back to this one also, to dig a little deeper.

Sassy P's Wine & Cheese had a curious mix of income and expenses. There was a marked increase in income. Jesus and Minnie had made a reputation for the winery, and they found a niche in hosting affairs, both casual and formal.

The investment in walls that could enclose the patio during colder months had paid off. The idea had been a collaboration of Jesus and Minnie, and Mo's Tap reaped some benefit from it as well, as the space was shared. Mr. Bean's Confectionary, nestled between the two, had been remodeled so that only the front half of the building was needed. The back half was torn down and the patio, which included an outdoor tasting bar, was constructed.

In warmer months, the patio opened to a garden reaching almost to the wooded area of the State Park. Now winter, the seating area was smaller but still added an expandable space for parties.

While she would expect an increase in expenses to match new income, the increase appeared to be abnormally high. She would come back to this later.

The last business was, of course, the Inn. The third floor was her private residence, so the entire property was not devoted to making money. However, the Inn was also host to her rental property's income. Each building with apartments on the second floor had separate cost centers in this account.

Annie was lucky in her rentals. Every unit was rented to a staff member, so she was assured of payment on time and good care of the interior. Now Boone would help with the rest of it. Spreading the expense over everything should allow her to keep the apartment rental charge the same.

Annie took a quick look at each cost center. The Inn was doing well, and it was going to be doing better. Her mother and step-father were getting ready to rent one large unit for a month at a time, several times a year. This would be their get-away-from-it-all location. They would pay less than a guest would pay, but it would be constant and would have less expense attached. Overall, a good deal for all concerned.

Their guest room rentals were up for the year; expenses were as expected. Henrie did an excellent job managing things, and his manner and style of first-class-everything had gained them a solid reputation in the industry. As expected, it was paying off in returns.

Relieving Henrie of cleaning duties had been hard. He had more responsibilities than the rest of the staff, and he had no one to back him up. However, he was almost offended when she talked to him of hiring a crew.

Once he realized, however, that he would have sole supervisory responsibility of the crew, at least at the Inn and possibly with the apartments, he decided it "might be satisfactory." He did ask, however, if he could "require the use of the King's English when guests are present?" Annie thought his request was tongue-in-cheek. She hoped it was. She assumed Harriet spoke in the same manner as Boone, and Boone's English was decidedly not the King's type.

Annie knew what the other cost centers would show. There had been no movement of tenants in any rental. She wanted to assure herself Gwen was getting it right. As if she would ever get it wrong. But the maintenance of these units was a big concern to Annie. Not that they had been a problem. In fact, there had been no issues – none – since Annie took over the property. She knew it was time for something to go wrong. Probably sooner rather than later.

The first set of apartments was above L'Socks' Virasana. Entrance was gained from a stairwell in the back that led to a full deck on the back side.

The apartments were fairly equal in size; one had windows facing The Avenue and one had windows facing the back. The "back" included a view of the grassy park-like area behind Annie's building and the woods of the State Park.

Felicity had the back apartment and Trudie the front. They were great friends, and they shared the balcony overlooking the park. Annie didn't have to worry about them traveling to the Café early in the morning or late at night for catering events, unless they tripped down the steps.

Two apartments set in similar style were above Mo's Tap. George had the larger unit. It faced the back but had windows overlooking the garden area between Mo's and the Winery as well. Jerry, from Mr. Bean's, rented the smaller unit facing The Avenue. Annie didn't think they shared balcony use, but then Jerry didn't seem to do much but stay in his apartment and read.

Mr. Bean's Confectionary was a shorter building, with the garden behind it. The apartment was larger than most others and had great lighting from both The Avenue and the back, which overlooked the garden area and the State Park. The deck was quite large, covering the enclosed space of the patio dining below. This apartment was rented by Carlos.

Sassy P's had two apartments similar to the ones above Mo's Tap. Jesus rented the back one and Minnie the front, although for all practical purposes, the two were used as one large unit. Annie wasn't sure how they were using them, where the main bedroom was, the main kitchen, the main living area, but that didn't matter. Living in two units like that gave them the opportunity to be together or to grab quiet space.

Financially, all of the rental spaces appeared to be in good order. Annie went back to Mr. Bean's Confectionary to ferret out the good news.

Pet treats were a big seller. It looked like Carlos was doing more out-source baking, with signature breads and desserts for several restaurants, hotels and even B&Bs in the region. Of course, some of his baked goods came to the Inn, many things to the Café, and even Mo's and Sassy P's used his goods, especially for parties. That cost center was certainly up.

And yes, the store's display baked goods were up, also. And Jerry! My goodness! Jerry was so good the candy was fairly jumping out the doors!

It appeared their lunch business had grown also. Everything Carlos and Jerry touched seemed to turn to gold.

Now, Annie thought to herself. Let's take a look at those expenses for Mo's and Sassy P's.

Chapter 5: We've Been Hacked!

Annie, looking into the bar's accounts closely, had called George to ask about some expenses. "Who are these new vendors we're buying from?"

On the other end of the telephone, George, obviously in the middle of a rush – an exuberant crowd, from the sound of it – had replied, "What?"

"The new vendors. It looks like we're getting a lot of artisan beers from new vendors."

"We don't have any new vendors, and I haven't changed the stock out since last fall."

"And you do all the buying, right?"

"Right. Look, if there's a problem, I can pull Candice behind the bar and come over. Right now, I don't know what you're talking about."

"No, George, that's okay. You're busy. Let's get together early tomorrow, though, and look at this. We'll have to go to Gwen's office to look at the invoices. But you don't have a clue, right?"

"Not a clue. Unless we've been hacked."

A similar situation existed at Sassy P's. There were three new vendors. Two were apparently wine vendors and the third looked like a wholesale grocer. She knew the Christmas parties were going on there, however, so she didn't call Jesus. She would call him tomorrow morning.

The more she thought about it, the more she realized George was correct. They had been hacked. Angry and scared, Annie picked up the phone to call Pete. She called him at home, knowing he would have left the office for the day. As she found his contact and hit the dial button, she remembered he had left the office for the next ten days. Drat!

The phone was already ringing as she had this thought, so she didn't hang up. And she rationalized that he would be the best person to ask, even if, technically, he was now on vacation. She breathed deeply and put on her "calm" voice.

Janet answered on the third ring. In the background, Annie could hear two dogs barking and two or three men trying to calm them down.

Even in her state of near-panic, Annie had to laugh. "What kind of party are you having? And I didn't even get an invitation!"

"Trust me, you would not want an invitation for this, well, if you want to call it a party, we can call it that. Cheryl and I opted for the quiet of the kitchen and a bottle of wine. The two-legged boys and the four-legged boys are having the party. I don't want to know what they're doing."

Janet was the long-suffering wife of Pete. They were a wonderful couple, but Janet often took a back seat to the needs of the town. Well, the word "often" didn't even begin to describe it. Janet was almost always a police officer's living widow, making all household decisions on her own. She had raised their children without much help as well, but somehow, Pete and Janet always made their relationship work.

At the moment, she was entertaining Cheryl, a Chelsea native who owned The Marina. Cheryl and Annie had been friends from childhood. When Annie summered with her father, she spent many a summer day on the lake with Cheryl on one type of boat or another. Tonight, Cheryl's husband

Ray would be one of the two-legged boys having a party in the back room.

Knowing she would not detract from Janet's evening, Annie didn't worry about bothering Pete at home. She pressed on. "I hoped to talk to Pete before the two of you left town. Do you think he can be torn away from his party?"

"Not a problem. There is nothing important going on back there anyway." Janet took the phone away from her ear to shout, "Pete! It's Annie!"

Back on the line, Janet continued. "He'll pick up out there, Annie. I'll say good-bye now and hang up when he does."

"Thanks, Janet, and have a great Christmas. Enjoy that family time."

Pete picked up, Janet hung up, and Annie apologized again. Then she said, "Pete, I think my accounts have been hacked for, I don't know, a lot of money. I won't know for sure until we talk to Gwen tomorrow, but what can I do?"

"Oh, man, Annie, you do stretch my mind and my resources. I've never dealt with this kind of thing before."

"Who should I call?"

"Let me think a minute." Pete paused for about thirty seconds, and Annie said nothing. She concentrated on deep breathing, hoping to calm down.

Eventually he said, "First of all, you probably need to know for sure you've been hacked. Gwen's probably the best person to figure that out. If she thinks that's what it is, call Marco. I'll call him now and let him know what might be going on, and I'll tell him that if he hears from you, he's to contact the FBI office. And listen, Annie, if you've been hacked, don't let Marco tell you he can handle it. Insist on the FBI."

After Annie hung up, she thought for another minute, then put in a call to Gwen's office. She knew voice mail would answer, but she couldn't wait. She tried to keep the scare and anger out of her voice when she left the message. "Gwen, this is Annie. Please call me first thing in the morning. I think we've been hacked."

At Mo's Tap, George hung up the phone and got busy behind the bar. He was summoned shortly by the red hot redhead, Christal, who seemed to need a lot of bartender attention tonight.

Candice was just as busy on the floor. She had assigned all of the tables to the other servers to give them a chance at more tip money for Christmas shopping. Even with having no tables of her own, she stayed busy as she helped bus tables and deliver drinks when the others were too busy.

When a moment came that George and Candice were face-to-face, he said quietly, "We have a problem. We're apparently paying some new vendors for artisan beers that we haven't received."

"What? How can that happen?"

"I don't know. Gwen doesn't pay anything except by invoice. And I email all of those to her myself."

"Well, I've done it when you're gone. Does anyone else?"

"I'll have to ask her tomorrow if she accepts invoices from anyone but you and me."

"Maybe Cookie."

"Maybe, but I think he gives all of his invoices to me. And it would be unusual for him to have a beer invoice."

"Gwen might not know that."

"You're right. For now, let's just keep it between the two of us. I'll know more tomorrow."

"Yes, boss."

"Huh?"

"I've just decided we need to get back on a business-only basis."

"Why? What have I done this time?"

"Oh, be all innocent. Little miss redhead hotty totty can't seem to get enough of your big bar."

"That's her! It's not me! What do you want me to do? Throw her out?"

"You can stop ogling the goods."

"I'm not ogling anything."

"Yeah, right. I have guests."

George shook his head and thought, women! I need to learn to live without them.

He turned back to his duties at the bar, which included tending to Christal who motioned him over. Rusty had been sitting with her, but for now the barstool was empty. Christal leaned in to make her order.

George resisted leaning in as well. He could see just fine without getting any closer. Well, okay, he was ogling. But Christal made it so easy. It was too bad he had personal knowledge the goods were fake ones. That typically ruined the experience for him.

He said, from a safe distance, "Another one?"

"Oh, come on, George, come a little closer."

"I'm close enough, thanks. Where'd your boyfriend go?"

"He's not my boyfriend. He's the one buying the drinks tonight. And he went to the little boys' room. By the way, where's my favorite little boy? Mo."

"Mo is safe and sound at home tonight. It's freezing out there. He doesn't have a good pair of boots to put on."

"Boots. Clever. Georgie, why don't you call me anymore?"

George ignored the use of the nickname, which he hated, because a good bartender pretends to not hear half of what is said. "You know why. I made a mistake with you in the first place. I was with Candice then, and I'm with her now."

"Doesn't look like it to me," Christal simpered. She leaned back, uncrossed and re-crossed her legs so that George and half of the guests in the Tap could see what she had to offer.

George smiled and said, "Thanks for that, but I have guests at the other end of the bar. Do you want another drink?"

"No. I'll wait for the nice guy to come back."

As George walked away, he thought, nice but stupid guy.

At Sassy P's, the Christmas parties were in full swing. Minnie, back in the prep area to restock a tray of cheese, crackers and meats, took the time to glance at her email account. There was another email from Gwen, Annie's accountant. She had received a few of them in the last few weeks.

Typically, Jesus dealt with Gwen; Minnie was initially surprised to receive emails from her. Now, however, she was used to the invitations to join one or another online training program. Unfortunately, the links Gwen sent were not good. Minnie signed up for programs that didn't take place. She would log on at the appointed time and stare at a blank page.

Minnie decided to take a quick look. It was another interesting topic. As before, Minnie filled out the form with her name, business name, address, email address and the last four of her Social Security number to confirm.

Felicity and Trudie had enjoyed a take-out supper from the Café and a bottle of wine from Sassy P's. It was late. The Café opened early the next day. But sometimes, Felicity could just not turn off. She needed to do something to wind down.

After Trudie left, Felicity logged onto her personal email account, Facebook, LinkedIn and the dating site she had joined recently. A new online acquaintance waited for her.

They chatted for a while and eventually the conversation turned to his financial issues. He wondered if Felicity might be able to help with his rent for this month. He was behind and he was going to be evicted.

Felicity lied. She said she, too, was behind on her rent and she couldn't possibly help. She found a reason to end the conversation and, to herself, vowed not to engage with this guy again.

Before going to bed, she logged into her work email account. There was another email from Gwen.

Gwen started sending emails a couple of weeks ago. Felicity had resisted opening the emails, as they were clearly invitations to training sessions.

As a rule, she deleted those emails before opening them, but early last week she had opened one. The training session sounded interesting, so Felicity filled out the online form to register. The session was supposed to be presented late last week, but something went wrong and it did not display.

Curious, tonight she opened this email, and once again, her interest was piqued. She signed up.

And then, just as she dropped off to sleep, she thought, I should check with Gwen, ask if she is taking advantage of the training sessions. And I should ask if she ever has problems logging on.

Chapter 6: The Cats Surrounded Their Guests

Laila came to the Inn bringing fragrant dishes from her native Pakistan, her three children – James, Ava and Carl – a ferret in a carrier and the famous turtle. Annie supplied a rubber tub with water and a rock for the turtle, fruit drinks for the children, wine for the adults, and a container of Felicity's meatloaf, half vegan, half carnivore. Fifty/fifty.

Annie had invited Henrie to join them, but he politely declined. Blaine, their guest, had gone to Mo's Tap for beer and a sandwich.

Dinner was over. The children had tired of playing with the animals and were now in front of the television watching the most recent Captain America movie. Shouts could be heard throughout the apartment. "Watch out, Cap!" "Did you see that?" "Whoa!"

The cats surrounded their guests, the ferret and the turtle, and wondered forlornly what it would be like to have to stay in a carrier or a plastic tub all day long. They all sat as if caged themselves, each on their belly, front paws forward, back paws underneath them, seven tails twitching.

Every now and then a low hiss would come from one part of the circle or another. The guests didn't appear to mind. They seemed to know they were safe and that the cats were thinking about something else.

Tiger Lily said, *"I wonder if Mommy locked us in the Inn for these guys. It doesn't seem like it. They can't go anywhere."*

Kali and Ko said together, *"She told Henrie it was cold out." "She doesn't want our feet to freeze."*

Mo looked at them and said, *"Trill?"*

Kali replied in a couple of soft trills.

Little Socks, secretly embarrassed she couldn't understand Mo, looked at Kali and said, *"What did he say?"*

Sassy Pants looked at Little Socks and said, *"Mo just asktid why Mommy was worried about Kali and Ko's feets cuz they never goes outside."*

Little Socks let out a hiss and said, *"You need to speak English!"*

"I duz speak English!"

Tiger Lily, ever the peacekeeper, and smarter than the average cat, said, *"Little Socks, I think we need to be less concerned about grammar and more concerned with just how it is Sassy Pants knows what Mo said."*

That got everyone's attention. Everyone, including, it seemed, the ferret and the turtle, went silent and looked intently at Sassy Pants.

She looked around the circle at everyone. *"I just reads his mind, is all. I don't know the words he sez. I just reads his mind. It's like pitchers. Kind of."*

"Pitchers?" asked Tiger Lily. In her mind, she saw a vision of herself growing thumbs, picking up a pitcher full of water and dumping it on Sassy Pants.

Sassy Pants gasped and said, *"That's mean!"*

Tiger Lily was shocked into silence, but had the presence of mind to wipe her thoughts clear. Then she looked at Kali and Ko. *"Think about something."*

Together, they said, *"What?" "Why?"*

"Just think about something. Anything."

Kali immediately recalled the nut-throwing incident while Ko thought of the peanut butter cookie pulled off the plate when Henrie's back was turned.

Tiger Lily looked at Sassy Pants. *"What do you see?"*

Sassy Pants looked confused, then realized what Tiger Lily was asking of her. She concentrated, first on Kali, then Ko. *"I sees nuts. Nuts was throwed at Kali. And I sees cookies on a plate and then one cookie. Ko stoled a cookie.*

Kali and Ko looked at one another, then at Sassy Pants, in amazement. Together, they said, *"He did. He threw nuts at us!"* *"I didn't steal a cookie! I didn't!"* Ko had the grace to look embarrassed as she told her lie.

Tiger Lily threw a special look Ko's way, giving a silent admonishment for taking a cookie meant for guests. She turned to Kali. *"What about nuts?"*

Kali, who normally liked all of the men that stayed at the Inn, said, *"This guy Blaine is weird. He brought all that stuff that's still on the porch, and he's afraid of us."*

Little Socks sniffed. *"What's there to be afraid of?"*

"Exactly! But he's afraid, and he threw nuts at us for no reason and told us to 'shoo.'"

Tiger Lily was offended. *"We sometimes get guests that don't like cats, but I don't recall anyone throwing things at us. And we're locked in with him. We'll have to stay away from him."*

She then looked at Sassy Pants. *"Talk about tricks. That was amazing."*

Mr. Bean sat up and smiled. *"So it's okay for Sassy Pants to do tricks? Can she teach me?"*

Sassy Pants, confused, said *"I didn't know it wuz a trick. I don't knows how I duz it."*

Little Socks, even more embarrassed that Sassy Pants, of all cats, could do something she could not, successfully covered her feelings with her signature temper. *"Do it! Do it!"*

she snarled. She was attempting to correct a grammatical faux pas.

"Do what?" asked Sassy Pants, puzzled. *"What duz you needs me to do?"*

Little Socks touched her forehead to the floor and pushed, eyes closed tight, wondering how *"Speak English, you idiot!"* would translate into a picture.

Mr. Bean, missing the point, said, *"I guess she wants you to teach me the trick. I'm a good learner. I learn things all the time. Today I learned that we don't do tricks. Oh. That's right. We don't do tricks. Is reading minds a trick, Tiger Lily?"*

Kali and Ko said together, *"Tricks?" "What about tricks?"*

Mr. Bean, proud of his new-found knowledge, explained, *"We don't do the fist bump like Cyril does. We don't tell Mommy yes and no and stuff like that. I don't know why. I think Mommy would understand us better if we did, but Tiger Lily says we don't do tricks, only dogs do tricks, and the fist bump thing is a trick, so we can't do it. And I can't dance for Carlos anymore. That will make me sad. But now that I know I'm not supposed to, I won't do it. He won't understand. Tiger Lily, I can't make him understand if I can't do tricks to talk to him. So how do I talk to him? Kali? Ko? How do you talk to Henrie if you can't do tricks? What do you think, Sassy Pants? How do you talk to Jesus? Isn't reading Mo's mind a trick? Tiger Lily? Isn't that a trick? But it's okay to do that? Why isn't anybody answering me?"*

Six cats had turned in directions that had them looking away from Mr. Bean. They showed various degrees of frustration or resignation on their little cat faces. Most of them concentrated on personal care on one or another parts of their bodies. Mo concentrated on his privates.

Eventually, Mr. Bean lay back down to take a nap, snuffling to himself a little bit that no one in this family was nice to him. Not even Tiger Lily. Not all the time.

Annie put her feet up and sighed in what seemed to Laila to be immense relief. Laila asked, "So, why are you halfway not here?"

Laila owned the grocery store across the street, Babar Foods, and lived with her children in the apartment above the store. She was Annie's best friend.

"I didn't want to ruin dinner. It's so fun to have the kids here. I wanted to just enjoy the moment. But now that they're busy, I'll tell you.

"It looks like a couple of my places have been hacked. Or, well, to be honest, it could be someone who works for me, but I hate to think that's happening.

"At any rate, we're being taken for a few hundred dollars every week. And it looks like, with Christmas inventory ratcheting up, the thefts have gone up as well. I won't know for sure until I can get together with George, Jesus and Gwen tomorrow. And so far, George is the only one I've spoken with. I hope Gwen has time for us tomorrow."

"What if she doesn't?"

"Well, I don't think anything is coming straight out of the bank. It looks like the bank is only responding when Gwen tells them to pay someone.

"It appears we have several new vendors. I've been paying more attention to the accounts this year, because I know I should. I've been taking for granted that things were going well, and in general, they have been. It's just a good idea for me to be more on top of it.

"But I haven't looked at things for a couple of months. It just jumped out at me when I logged onto the accounts this afternoon. I could tell that it just started a couple of months ago, coincidentally with my absent eyes, but I really think that's just a coincidence. No one knows when I log on, I don't think."

Annie thought about her last sentence and added, "Surely no one knows that. Would they?"

Laila thought about it for a while. Laila was conservative in many ways. For example, she always wore a traditional Pakistani trouser outfit, topped off with a dupatta. Tonight, the dupatta was draped over her shoulders, leaving her head and that gorgeous black hair free.

In other ways, Laila was more progressive than Annie. She had a better handle on social media and the ways in which electronic devices can make your life easier. Or more difficult.

"I think there are probably many ways in which skilled individuals figure out when you log into your accounts, either from your accountant's records or from the bank. I don't know how they do that, though.

"It's also possible they could get to your bank one way or another through your accountant. I'm not so sure you should wait until tomorrow."

Annie, already spooked about the possibilities, went to the bedroom to retrieve her notebook. She brought it to the living room and logged into her accounts at the bank.

"I don't even know what to look for, Laila."

"Don't look for anything now. You're tired. You've had some wine. Just change your user name and password for now. Better yet, make sure you tell them they have to call you before they let anyone log on. You can fix that with Gwen tomorrow. But just give yourself a little extra protection tonight."

Annie followed her instructions and set up the protection. Then she and Laila relaxed and enjoyed more wine and girl talk.

Laila asked, "Have you seen the new stock at Mem's and Clara's yet?"

"New stock?"

"Yes. Mem has new kitchen and gourmet grocery items and Clara added jewelry."

"Why haven't they said anything?"

"You've been busy. They've been busy. And I only found out because I had to go to Mem's to physically drag James home for supper a few nights ago."

"What was he doing?"

"He found a new friend, a gamer. Some young man named Rusty has been hanging out at Mem's in the back. He likes the same games that James does."

"Rusty? A skinny blond guy?"

"Yes. Do you know him?"

"No. I've just seen him is all."

"I've tried to find out about him, you know, just being a mother. James is a few years younger than him, and my radar always goes up."

"So, is your radar going to go up when a young man two or three years older than Ava asks her out?"

"Oh, no, that won't bother me, because I'm not going to let Ava date until she's 25."

They laughed, then Annie's natural curiosity got the better of her. "Could Mem tell you anything about Rusty?"

"She said he's only been coming in recently, so she doesn't know much. She noticed him first when he came in with a redheaded woman. She noticed because he looks like he tries hard to not fit in, and she seems, well, the opposite."

Annie told Laila about the chance encounter at Mo's Tap, seeing Rusty and Christal at the end of the bar. "George didn't say much about him. Does it worry you that James plays computer games with older guys?"

"As long as he goes to Mem's, I don't worry. She and her staff keep an eagle eye on the kids."

"So this isn't unusual?"

"No, several of his gaming friends are older. He teams up with Daryl sometimes. You know him, right? Daryl works with his dad, Boone. Sometimes the younger brother, Donny, does some gaming, too."

"What do you know about them?"

"They seem to be nice young adults. They don't talk to older adults much, though. I think they're shy."

"Does James say anything about them? He must have known Donny in school."

"James says Donny is really smart. He always took more credits than the other kids, and he has enough credits to be done with school now. He took early graduation and is going to work."

"Boone told me he will only be working part-time, and that Daryl is going to part-time, too. You'd think Donny would stay in school if he were only going to work part-time."

"It's hard to tell. It's possible Boone doesn't have enough work to keep them both full-time. Maybe they have to get part-time jobs somewhere else as well. Maybe the family needs the money."

"Maybe. It's too easy to be an armchair nosey-posey."

Laila asked, "Well, nosey-posey, where's Chris tonight?"

"Well, not that I know where he is every night, but he's at Pete and Janet's tonight. He'll be keeping Cyril while they're gone, so he's taking him tonight. Pete said they're getting an early start in the morning."

They got quiet for a minute, then Annie said, "You're coming over Christmas Day, right? With the kids?"

"Wouldn't miss it. My kids are looking forward to meeting your nieces and nephews. Do you think we can lock them all in a room somewhere, so we adults can have a quiet day?"

"No, don't think that's going to happen. Bring earplugs."

As Laila's eyes roamed around the room, she noticed the picture in the dining room. "What's that? A new charcoal? With color?"

"Oh, that. Chris did that last month, after the Halloween block party."

"All of your kids with Cyril, Jock, and Honey Bear."

"Yes. A family portrait of sorts."

"That is outstanding."

Annie smiled. "Yes. An outstanding portrait of some outstanding companions."

In the charcoal, entitled "Friends and Heroes," Annie's cats sat in a row, each in a regal pose. Tiger Lily was in the center, flanked on the right by Kali, Ko and Mo and flanked on the left by Little Socks, Sassy Pants and Mr. Bean. Behind them were Cyril and Jock. Honey Bear peered around Jock's hind legs. Each companion wore a glittering red ribbon from which hung a gold badge.

Annie didn't share the back story, not even with her best friend. Only a handful of people knew the story of the heroic efforts on the part of this group of companions, even, yes, the dreaded Uncle Honey Bear. Chris had honored them with this "trophy" portrait.

Chapter 7: Best In Show

In another part of town, Pete, Chris and Ray played some three-handed poker while Cyril and Jock sat in front of the television. The men paid no attention to the show, more intent on winning the pennies and nickels on the table, and being fairly vicious about it. Every now and then, Cheryl or Janet would stick a head around the corner, to make sure no one was being maimed or killed.

The men were the best of friends. When Pete returned to Chelsea after a career in the Marine Corps Military Police, he brought Janet and their three children with him. Janet was a "city girl," and found out fairly quickly how difficult it was to be an outsider in a small town. Pete was popular, however, which made her fit into small town life go more smoothly.

Ray was retired from armed services as well, the US Navy. He moved to Chelsea to marry Cheryl, a native. Cheryl's parents had owned the small deep water marina nestled into the harbor near the state and town parks. Cheryl owned it now, and Ray owned a yacht fashioned into a cruising and fishing boat, The Escape.

Chris related to the military careers of both men. When he wasn't guarding the coast of the Great Lakes, he was an amateur artist specializing in charcoals. The last pieces he had done for charity sold like proverbial hot cakes, and he was just finishing up some special order pieces, proceeds to go to that same charity, in time for Christmas.

Cyril and Jock were intent on the television show. Pete and Ray knew the best thing to keep their attention was a show with dogs, and Pete had recorded the last Westminster Dog Show, one of the reruns that played both nights in one long time slot. This was good for a few hours of dog entertainment.

Both dogs semi-napped through the first "night" of judging. They liked all types of dogs, but really, they didn't need to watch all of the Hounds. This was a large group of 30 breeds, and while some of them were handsome, this was not the main show, as far as Cyril and Jock were concerned. They woke up to notice the 15 inch beagle took the group. Cyril took note of the name: Lookin' For Trouble.

The Toy group didn't hold their interest at all. Cyril, though, roused to watch the Affenpinscher. That type of dog – maybe it was this dog himself – had won Best of Show not too long ago. The Affenpinscher didn't win this year. The shih tzu took the group. Cyril looked at Jock and said, *"What kind of a name is Rocket Power for a yappy little dog?"*

Jock stayed awake for the Non-Sporting group. Some of these dogs seemed attractive to him. Jock particularly liked the Dalmatian, but he didn't place. The winner was a standard poodle, Hearts On Fire. This was a female. Jock turned to Cyril. *"Cute. She could set my heart on fire."*

The last group of the first night was the Herding group. Some of these dogs were handsome as well. The boys napped lightly, waiting to hear who the winner would be. An old English sheepdog, Bugaboo's Picture Perfect, won. *"Pretentious name,"* Cyril and Jock agreed.

As the commercials played before the second night of judging came on the screen, they took the time to go outside to refresh themselves. Last year, Cyril taught Jock this was the most refined way to describe what they were doing. They came back in, took a quick mouthful of food and a drink of water. They settled down to watch in earnest.

The sporting group was up first. This group included Cyril's breed, the English setter. The announcer talked while the group entered the arena. "They're hunting dogs; they have to work together. Hunting dogs are even-tempered, and they live for their humans. This makes them good family dogs as well. If you turn your head, more often than not, suddenly there's a nose in your face followed by a big lick."

Cyril and Jock exchanged looks and barked, happy to hear Cyril belonged to such a friendly group.

When the English setter was shown, Jock paid attention to what the announcer was saying. "As a family dog, the English setter is unsurpassed. His even temperament, devotion, quiet manner, ease in comfort and training and fondness for children makes him an ideal companion. English setters make good companions whether you live in town or in the country."

Cyril, on the other hand, didn't hear a word as he watched in rapt adoration as Wait Wait Don't Tell took his turn in the arena. Cyril saw a sculptured face, a strong chest, and long, beautiful hair flowing from chest, stomach, legs and tail. *"So handsome,"* came the unsolicited whisper.

When the English setter returned to his place and another dog took the arena, Jock turned to Cyril and said, *"Now I know what you're supposed to look like. Too bad you get all clipped up. Pete ought to let your hair grow like it's supposed to."*

Cyril was secretly jealous of the long hair, but he replied, *"I'm a police dog. I can't worry about being stylish."*

"So, it's okay for you if some lady setter doesn't care for your trim?"

"If some lady setter doesn't care for it, then she's not worth my time," said Cyril. *"Pete says it would be dangerous for me to have the long hair. But look. He leaves a little on my tail."* Cyril raised his tail

while they both looked at it. Cyril thought wistfully about long hair everywhere and Jock stifled a laugh.

Cyril continued, *"Some bad guy could grab long hair and keep me from doing my job."*

Jock howled, literally. *"Instead, the bad guy will be too busy laughing at the bald dog!"*

Cyril decided to take care of his hind quarters until the finalists were assembled. This was the even-tempered thing to do.

After another set of commercials they watched together as the group paraded around the arena. Cyril was devastated when Wait Wait Don't Tell didn't even place. He sat in sad silence while Jock, apparently not realizing his rude manner, said, *"Don't worry. We'll have a winner yet. My group is next. Wait until you see Matisse."*

This started a round of hurtful comments between the two, something that had never happened before. They yipped and snarled at one another and didn't notice that the English springer spaniel, White Diamonds, won the group.

They stopped arguing when the Working group took the arena, but Cyril was still hurt. They both listened as the announcer opened the group's showing.

As the announcer spoke, Jock became noticeably prouder while Cyril pressed himself harder into the floor. Eyes pressed tightly closed, he didn't notice the Portuguese water dog enter the ring.

Cyril thought the announcer went on and on. "Here come the big dogs tonight. And I mean big dogs. They're big, and there are a lot of winners in this group, including the number one dog in the country last year, Matisse, the Portuguese water dog. Matisse is the dog to watch tonight. He won over

130 best in shows last year and is a two-time champion in the working group here at Westminster."

Almost as an afterthought, another announcer added there were several winners in this group, and the first announcer just had to say, "The President even weighed in on this one. He said Matisse is the dog to beat." His second announcer said, "He should know. Two beautiful examples live at the White House!"

Jock whined through several dogs, barely able to contain himself as he tried to wait patiently. Even before Matisse took the ring, the crowd was cheering. He was obviously a crowd favorite. As Matisse was announced, Cyril listened with growing hurt and anger.

"Portuguese water dogs have been valued crew members and loyal companions to Portuguese fishermen for generations. This is an intelligent, independent, spirited breed with a bit of creative mischief in its heart. They can be demanding of attention and manipulative. The Portuguese water dog is always ready for a full day's activity in or out of the water and requires an owner of equal stamina and intelligence."

One phrase stood out in Cyril's mind, and he would remember it often in days to come. "They can be demanding of attention and manipulative." Cyril also noted Matisse seemed to be vain, just like Jock. He had to stretch in front of the camera before taking his turn around the arena. Again, the announcer sang his praises, accenting words, unlike his descriptions with other dogs.

"Matisse! The number one male show dog last year and the number one male show dog in history! He's just great; 238 best in shows. He's beautifully presented, a wonderfully moving dog. Matisse is the dog to beat, not only in this group, but if he survives this group, as I'm sure he will, <u>he'll be the one to beat at the end of the night</u>."

What struck Cyril more than the words – those overly demonstrative words – was the dog himself. Cyril's eyes widened and he sat up a bit to get a closer look. The dog's hind quarters were shaved like a poodle and there was a huge black powder puff at the end of his otherwise shaved tail.

Cyril didn't bother to contain the laugh that bubbled up at the sight of that tail. Jock ignored him until the next dog took his place, then he turned on Cyril with a snarl. *"What is your problem?"*

"Your hero has a poodle cut! And a powder puff tail!" Cyril said through his laughter. To the humans it sounded like a coughing fit.

Jock snarled. *"You're just jealous. Wait until the end. Then you'll see. This is the dog to beat."*

Cyril snorted, busied himself again with personal care, and sighed, content that no judge would choose such a laughing stock as a winner.

Eventually, the group was lined up to take a final turn around the arena. As Matisse was pulled as a finalist, another crowd cheer went up, and the announcer said, "Matisse!" and launched into another verbal praise fest.

Cyril gave a silent gag. Jock sat up straighter, if that was possible.

Then disaster struck for Cyril. Matisse was the first dog pulled from the finalists. The crowd went wild. Jock sat up and barked. The judge took one more look at the finalists and pointed to Matisse as the winner. The announcer chortled, "<u>Matisse</u> wins the working group for the <u>third year in a row</u>!"

Jock couldn't speak. His heart filled with pride, he got up, trotted around to each of the men in the room demanding and receiving attention from all three. He returned to Cyril.

"I'm going to win best in show," he said.

"You aren't in the show."

"You know what I mean. Matisse is going to win."

Cyril rolled over to put his back to Jock and pretended to be asleep while the Terriers – another large group – went through their paces. When the winner of the group was announced, Good Time Charlie, the long-haired Skye Terrier, a dog Cyril would normally have thought of as handsome, he merely spit out, *"He's a yappy little thing."*

Then they were at the best part of the show. From this next segment, the overall winner would be chosen.

Usually, Cyril and Jock were both excited to see the final show. This year, it was difficult for Cyril to take both the show and Jock's high good cheer.

Cyril had to suffer through Matisse's walk around the arena, and the yadda yadda yadda of what the President had to say about him, and all the high accolades. Jock's tail didn't stop pounding the floor. He sat upright, leaning into the screen.

Then, the finalists were called to the center of the arena.

Jock barked as each dog was called out until the Judge was done. Matisse wasn't called out. *"No! Something's wrong! Stop the show!"* he barked out. But the judge kept looking at the other dogs that had been pulled to the center of the arena.

Jock's mouth dropped open, his shock beyond bounds. With disbelief, he whispered, *"Matisse didn't make the cut."*

Cyril rolled over on his back, laughing so hard and so loud that Pete turned to take a look, just to make sure he was okay. *"Matisse didn't make the cut! Hey, Jock, Matisse didn't make the cut!"*

Cyril twisted his head around to see who won best of show. From his upside-down vantage point, he watched as the beagle, Lookin' For Trouble, took the top prize. The reserve best of show was that hairy, yappy Skye terrier, Good Time Charlie.

When Cyril got his laughter under control, he sat up. His laughter was under control, but still present. He couldn't stop it entirely. *"That powder puff tail didn't help."*

And now it was Jock's turn to defend his less-than-stylish look. *"That's a standard cut. I don't have it because I have a job. I don't have time for clips and cuts and stylists."*

"Yeah, yeah, save it for the lady water dogs who think you're a country bumpkin."

This was too much for Jock, who had just been shocked to the core. He snarled and leapt at Cyril, nipping him in the hind quarters. Cyril, startled, yelped more in surprise than in pain, but now the fight was on. Snipping, snarling and gouging with their feet, in an instant, they were grabbed by their humans and pulled off one another.

Pete gasped as he held the strong Cyril. "What in the world?"

Ray spoke in a raised voice. "What got into the two of you?" When he got both Jock and his emotions under control, he continued in a normal voice. "Maybe they've had a long day."

Two women appeared in the doorway, worried about the uproar. Cheryl looked at Ray. "Maybe it's time to go."

"You're right." Ray pulled Jock by his collar toward the door. Jock went, but he continued to growl deep in his chest.

Cyril allowed himself a satisfied huff as Jock was pulled away, but the ultimate injustice was yet to come. Pete let go of Cyril long enough to get the leash. He returned and clipped it onto Cyril's collar.

The leash! Pete only used the leash when they had to pretend he was a real dog! Rarely in town! Never on The Avenue! And never, never, never at home!

And then, Pete handed the end to Chris! Pete was giving him away to Chris!

Chris started to walk toward the door, leash in hand, but Cyril sat still, not moving, staring at Pete, a whine building from his belly to his throat.

Chris acknowledged the resistance. "Come on, big guy. You're going to spend a few days with Uncle Chris."

Cyril didn't move. His pained expression pointed in the direction of Pete, following his every move. Plaintively, he whined, *"I'm sorry. I didn't mean to be bad. I'll be good, I promise!"*

Pete got down close to the floor, took Cyril's face in both his hands, and said, "You need to stay with Chris for a few days. We're going out of town, and several of the places we'll be don't allow dogs."

Another whine escaped Cyril's throat. *"They don't allow dogs? Then why are you going?"*

"I'm going to miss you, but you'll have a great time with Chris, and I'm sure you'll spend Christmas with Annie and the kids."

"Christmas? I won't be with you at Christmas?" came the whine, louder and higher pitched. The whine was now interspersed with high-pitched barks.

"It will be alright, boy. I love you. I'll miss you. I'll see you in a few days."

The whine/bark combo turned into a frantic combination of barks, woofs and high-pitched noises that could have been doggy screams. *"I'll be good, I promise! I'll never fight with Jock again! I'll never fight with anyone again! Pete! Pete! Don't make me go!"*

Chris got down beside Cyril and wrapped his arms around the big dog's neck, holding him close and reassuring him that he would be alright.

At first, Cyril fought the attention, but he knew better than to do anything to hurt Chris. Eventually, he got quiet and sat, head hanging down.

When Chris stood again and said, "Come on, big guy," Cyril got to his feet. His head continued to hang down as they walked out the door and to the vehicle. Cyril noticed dully that Janet had put his bed, food, dishes and toys in the back seat.

In just a few short minutes, he had lost his human. He had lost his family. He had lost his best friend. He had nothing to live for.

Chapter 8: What's This About Hacking?

Annie was in the kitchen, poking around in Henrie's pots and pans, when the phone rang.

The voice on the other end belonged to her accountant. "What's this about hacking?"

"Thanks for calling, Gwen. I don't know for sure that we've been hacked, but either that or someone on the inside is stealing from me."

Annie explained what she had found to Gwen and noted that George had suggested hacking as a possible explanation. "I'd like to come in with George and Jesus today."

"Why don't you come in at 1:30? That will give me time to look through your records."

As Annie hung up the phone, Chris came through the back door with Cyril.

"Hey, big guy," said Annie. Chris leaned over to kiss her on the cheek but missed, as she got on her knees to give Cyril a hug. Cyril twisted his head and neck out of her grasp and walked, slowly and head down, through the kitchen and dining room in search of any friends he might have left in this world.

"Not a good day?" asked Annie.

"I think he's upset that Pete wanted him to come with me."

"Maybe it will get better as the day goes on."

"I can only hope. Have you stuck anything outside yet? It is colder than the proverbial witch's you-know-what!"

"I know, I know. I've got my super special coat, scarf and gloves ready to go, and look." She held out a foot and wiggled it. "I have my spiffy insulated boots!"

"Well…I guess, in this weather, functional is better than sexy. Or stylish."

Annie lost a little bit of her morning bounce.

Chris knew better than to try to repair his faux pas. Instead, he changed the subject. "Is my fisherman up?"

"In the dining room. Go introduce yourself and fix yourself a plate."

"What's for breakfast?"

"Henrie has a fisherman's feast out there. He called it a 'Full English Fry Up.' I've been poking around here, and everything smells wonderful."

"Why don't you join us? That way, you'll have an idea what he'll be doing for the rest of the week." And, he thought, perhaps I can make you forget what I just said about your boots.

Annie introduced the two men while she poured coffee. She and Chris then looked at the hearty breakfast items on the buffet: sausage, bacon, corned beef hash, fish cakes, scrambled eggs, bacon egg and cheese casserole, home fries, cornmeal johnnycakes, wheat and rye toast and Boston baked beans.

Chris asked, "Why does Henrie have baked beans for breakfast?"

"I think the beans and johnnycake make it the 'Full English' whatever."

As they decided what to put on their plates – Annie always had a difficult time with this decision – Chris told Blaine what he knew about the weather.

"It's freezing out there. The temperature today is expected to climb out of the basement to hit five degrees at early afternoon, then start to tumble again. The wind will be steady at about seven miles an hour, and the wind chill will put the temperatures in the minus ten degree range."

He stopped filling his plate and looked straight at Blaine Jones. "Are you sure you want to do this?"

"Positive. It should be an invigorating experience."

As Annie and Chris ate, Blaine talked to them. He told them about his equipment and protective clothing, all of it purchased by "Mother" and none of it familiar to him.

"I really wanted to get started earlier this morning, but I have to wait on the vehicle."

Chris, still worried about this novice in the frigid weather, stayed positive. "It will be better for you this first day to be the last one on the ice. You'll be able to see where everyone else goes, and we can find a good place without uprooting any regulars. So, you aren't familiar with the equipment?"

"I've never used anything before, but it's got to be pretty easy, right? I mean, we're just fishing."

"Fishing can be kind of complicated. But I've got all morning. Let's find a spot on the ice, get the stuff out there, and I'll help you set up."

"Do you know if I'll be able to leave the shelter out overnight? So I don't have to take everything down and put it up again?"

"We'll ask some of the regulars we see on the ice. They'll know."

Annie excused herself. "Since I'm no help at all, I'll be moving along. Chris, thank you again for getting Blaine started, and Blaine, enjoy your first day on the lake!"

Kathleen Thompson

Annie walked through the foyer, intending to check on her kids, to make sure they were finding something to do since they were locked in for the day. A pile of fur in the library caught her eye.

She walked in softly. Cyril was on the floor in the middle of the fluffy rug that was used only in the winter. He was on his stomach, head resting on his front paws, tail sitting limply on the floor. As Annie walked in, he opened his eyes, closed them again, and didn't appear to use a single other muscle.

Tiger Lily was snuggled into his side, underneath his right shoulder. Kali and Ko slept in a pile that fit snuggly into his back legs and stomach, also on the right side. On the left, stretching from Cyril's front legs to his back, were Sassy Pants, Mr. Bean and Mo. Even Little Socks was there. She was squarely on his haunches, face down and feet underneath her body, no white parts visible.

Annie's heart went out to Cyril. He was so sad, and apparently her kids knew it and were trying to comfort him. She didn't realize the cats were also upset. They were not happy about being locked in. Even Kali and Ko, who would choose to stay inside, preferred having the choice.

Annie went upstairs to the second floor landing and was on the telephone with Jesus when the front doorbell rang. She watched as Henrie answered it, ushering a man in some sort of work outfit into the Inn. Henrie called Chris and Blaine, who joined them in the foyer. Annie watched their conversation as she continued her own, and soon, Blaine put on his coat and went outside with the man in uniform.

Chris and Henrie got ready also, and headed for the door. Chris stopped and looked up at Annie. With hand signals he indicated he would return for Cyril.

She nodded her understanding and returned her focus to Jesus, who had just said something interesting.

"Say that again, please?"

"Last night Minnie told me she's been getting some strange emails from Gwen. They have links that are supposed to take her to training sessions, but the links never work."

"Why would Gwen be sending those emails to her?"

"I don't know. Maybe she has an agreement with the people doing the training; maybe she gets a fee for referrals."

"Print one of those out, please, and bring it with you when we see her at 1:30."

"I will, along with the list of invoices I've sent from November through last week. Oh, before I forget, Boone found a potential problem last night. The sink in the patio was starting to freeze, but he's working on a solution. I'll tell you more about it when I see you."

She called George next to give him the meeting time and asked him if anyone from Mo's had received emails from Gwen about training sessions.

"Not that I'm aware, but I'll check around before meeting you there."

"Thanks. How did the night go?"

"Were your extrasensory antennae out last night?"

"I guess so. I don't always ask, do I?"

"Nope."

"So?"

"Remember the redhead?"

"The hotty totty with the cleavage?"

"The very one."

"She was there again, huh?"

"Yep."

"And?"

"Candice asked one of the other servers to do her clean-up, and she was out the door as soon as her last guest was gone. And before I knew she was going."

"George, you have to stop flirting with other women if you want this to work."

"It wasn't my fault! And I wasn't flirting!"

"Not a bit?"

"Not a bit! I stood as far back as I could when I wasn't putting a drink in front of her. But you can't help but see what she's offering. I do have testosterone."

"What else can you do?"

"I don't know. I just don't know."

"How about this. How about the next time she comes, you switch places with Candice? You take the floor and put her behind the bar?"

"I can't imagine working that floor again. I put in my time out there."

"Do you have a better idea?"

"No…"

"Okay, then. It's just a suggestion. I'll see you at 1:30."

As Annie got off the phone, she saw Chris coming out of the library, pulling Cyril by the collar. His face showed pure exasperation, and a semi-circle of seven cats glowered at him. As she got to the bottom of the steps he said, "Any problem with Cyril staying here for the morning?"

"No problem at all, tough guy."

Chris let go of the collar and Cyril returned to his spot in the middle of the rug. The cats waited for him to settle down, then they arranged themselves on and around him.

"I don't even know what to say," said Chris. He shook his head and left, not bothering to say goodbye.

Annie called Boone next.

"Well, Ma'am, we got that Inn and the café and the yoga place and the candy shop done afore the tempercher went all the way down. They's all set now. We waited fer the other places to close down, and the good news is that whiles they was open, they was usin' the water, so they kept them pipes from freezin' fer the most part.

"But that sink out there to the closed up garden? It was a'freezin' afore we got to it. They was a little bit of a problem there, but we got a heater a'blowin' on it and got 'er caught afore it busted the pipe."

"When I talked to you yesterday, I didn't even think about that sink, or I would have had you look at it right away. Are we going to have to stop using it?"

"Well, I thought about that, but it 'curred to me that the wine place is a'usin' it all week for parties and such, so we jawed on it a while, and Daryl, you know, my son, Daryl?"

"Yes, I know Daryl."

"Well, he figgered out that we could keep a heater a'goin' there, an' we put lots of insulation on the pipes that lead up to it. And we kept that there sink drippin' just a bit. And I left a note for that Hey-suse to keep on a'doin' it until his parties is done with. And then, well, you probly had better turn it off until we gets over this spell a' cold."

"And how about the apartments? Did you take care of them?"

"Oh heck yes. We did them at the same time we did the downstairs parts, except for those ones over the bar and the wine place. We did them early on. We was real quiet-like."

Annie remembered how "quiet" they had been at the Inn but stifled any comments. "You have no idea how much I appreciate your work, and getting to it so quickly. Thank you, Boone."

A few minutes later Annie found Henrie in the kitchen and said, "I'm going Christmas shopping. Finally. I don't have the first present yet, and good grief, this is Christmas week."

"Are you going out of town to shop?"

"I don't think so. It's awfully cold, and I'd prefer to stick around here. I'll stop by in the shops across The Avenue, and maybe go up to Antiques On Main. I'll see if I can help Frank get ready for his big party."

"Would you mind taking this punch bowl with you? I can place it in a bag for ease of carrying."

"A punch bowl! You trust me with that?"

Henrie picked up a bowl that looked like heavy crystal. In reality, it was a great plastic knock-off of a heavy crystal bowl. "Not that you are clumsy, or anything of the sort, but I would not ask if it were not my finest plastic."

"You, Henrie? You have a plastic punch bowl?"

"Certainly. We used this one, and two others just like it, for that horrid Halloween punch. I could not possibly use crystal for the vile ingredients."

"Wow. I never knew. I'll go there first. That's the farthest I want to walk, anyway, so I'll get that long, cold trek out of the way first thing."

Annie bundled up with her fleece coat, two scarves, and a pair of insulated gloves. She already had WinterSilks brand socks and leggings and a warm camisole underneath everything else. And of course her "functional" boots. Not for the first time she wondered if she should purchase more stylish outwear. No. Of course not. She would rather be warm and dry.

When Annie arrived at Antiques On Main, she was greeted by Claire, the store's blue point Himalayan cat. "I'll bet you're excited. There will be lots of people here this week," she said, stroking Claire on the back.

"*Prrrrrrrrr!*"

Claire loved people. She didn't care much for other cats. Annie knew another cat with similar propensities. Annie wondered if she should introduce Claire to Honey Bear.

Frank called to her from the back of the store. "Come on back, Annie!"

"You can see me?"

"Cameras!"

"Oh. Well, sure. I have some of those myself. I just don't watch the screen like I should."

By this time, she was standing in front of Frank and she held onto the punch bowl as if it were 20 pounds of lead.

Frank was a newcomer to Chelsea. He settled into the town quickly, though, and less than six months after moving here, he was preparing for the grand opening of his store, Antiques On Main.

He lucked into the building. He arrived in Chelsea looking for a bargain, and while still a guest at the KaliKo Inn, this building was put up for sale.

The main floor needed only a few renovations to become an antique shop. The second floor served as his workroom and warehouse, and he lived on the third floor.

"Let me take that for you! I could have come to get it. Henrie shouldn't have asked you to bring it."

"Not a problem," she said, as he took it and realized his mistake.

"Plastic? Henrie?"

"My thoughts exactly. But you see the quality of plastic. Only the finest. I have a couple of hours this morning. Can I help you with anything?"

"Yes, you can. Don't come in here this week asking that question unless you're prepared to stay for a while! Can you help me put prices out?"

"Sure. Just tell me what to do."

Frank had meticulous inventory sheets that not only described his furniture, bric-a-brac and their provenance, but also showed their location on the showroom floor. Each piece was catalogued with pricing as well. The top price would go on the tag, the median price, or the price he could expect to get was highlighted, and the price below which he could not go without losing money was also noted.

Annie started at the front of the store. She decided she would keep at it until the two front display areas were finished.

Frank designed the space using moveable panels as walls. As inventory moved in and out, he could move or shift the remaining or replacement pieces. The walls were high enough to cover the back of high-topped furniture but low enough to accommodate lights that hung from the ceiling. As this building was of the same era as Annie's, the high ceilings were perfect for Frank's needs.

Frank saw to details in several display areas. They chatted on the occasions they were in the same area. In this fashion and as the morning wore on, she learned that Frank and Mem had decided to continue their relationship on a slower pace.

Annie acknowledged that perhaps they had started too quickly in the beginning. The relationship nearly blew up in October. Well, to be honest, the relationship actually did blow up in October, but they had been working on it ever since.

Frank told Annie he was sure the cold weather and potential snow wouldn't keep antique buyers from coming to town for the open house. Annie verbally agreed but mentally wondered.

Annie reminded Frank that her mother and step-father, Nancy and Sam, would arrive tomorrow and would be in town for at least a month. Frank and Sam had become fast friends when they met last fall.

When Annie looked at the clock and realized it was time for her to get to the Café, she put the price tags and inventory on Frank's desk, redressed in her warm outerwear, and then remembered she was supposed to be Christmas shopping!

"Oh, no! Frank! I was going to do some Christmas shopping! I didn't look at anything!"

"Let me help you. Who's on your list?"

"Well, Mom, Sam, my sister and her husband, several kids, one of her older kids and her husband and their kids, everyone on The Avenue…Chris…."

"Short list."

"Right."

"What would you get for any of them in an antique shop?"

"Don't have a clue. Also don't have a clue what I would get for them in a not-antique shop."

"Hate to shop?"

"With a passion!"

"I think I have an idea for Chris."

"Really?"

"Yes. I've got some experience in what-not-to-do-when-you're-early-in-a-relationship. And since I know when the two of you started to see one another, I mean, when you stopped being just friends, I know you're still early-in. You don't want to get anything too 'too,' and you don't want to get anything too 'not too.' Am I right?"

"You're right. What's your idea?"

"Let's go upstairs." Frank took Annie to the second floor warehouse. "I haven't had time to inventory these pieces, but I hope to get most of them out for the open house. Now where is it…" Frank disappeared around a grouping of furniture, and from behind it, Annie heard, "Found it!"

She followed his voice and saw the perfect gift for Chris. She didn't care about the price. It was perfect for an artist.

"What is it?" she asked. "I mean, I know it's an easel, but what kind?"

"This is a vintage French landscape painter's easel. I'd guess it's from the mid-1800s. It's in excellent condition."

"Tell me about it."

"Unfortunately, I don't know the provenance of this particular piece, but I can tell you about the type. This type of easel came into fashion in the mid-19th century. Artists wanting to paint landscapes – or anything outdoors – were interested in painting what they could see and painting in natural light. Some of the most famous artists in the world have used this type of easel, and they are still in use today.

"See here, the legs telescope in and out, this box holds the paints and supplies, and it folds into a case easily carried wherever the painter wants to go. Whoever owned this piece took very good care of it. It's made of hardwood, elm, and there is scarcely a blemish."

"Oh, Frank, this is perfect!"

"I thought you'd like it. You're on your way to the Café, and I need to take a break. I'll wrap it up and take a walk to the Inn, leave it with Henrie."

"Thank you! Imagine that! The hardest gift is the first one out of the way! If you can, let me start a tab. Put this as the number one thing on the list of items I'll purchase at your open house."

"Done."

Annie got to the Café to find things a bit slow. "What's up with the slow crowd, Trudie?"

"I think there is a tiny blip on the tourist scene, with the holiday coming up. Most people go to see family rather than come to a resort town like Chelsea. And the locals are just wimps when it comes to this cold. Truth be told, so am I. I'm glad my walk to work is so short."

Annie laughed. "Well, if you weren't from Jamaica, maybe you wouldn't be such a wimp. So, I guess you don't need me? I'll go back and see if I can help Felicity with prep work for your various parties and such this week."

"Good idea. Tell Tiger Lily we miss her today."

"I will."

In the kitchen, the ever-perky Felicity was hidden behind boxes of fresh produce that had just been delivered. She was in the process of checking the inventory and getting them into the appropriate coolers. She wasn't looking so perky at the moment.

"Hey, Felicity. I wanted to see if I could help with prep work or anything else you might need."

Distracted, Felicity mumbled, "Huh?"

"Do you need me to help you with anything?"

"No. I don't know. Hang on."

Annie stood silent, realizing that Felicity was deep into something.

Felicity moved over to her notebook, and Annie noticed she was logged into the accounting records of the Café and its catering concerns. After studying the records for a while, moving back and forth between what appeared to be invoices and the checking account, she went back to the coolers and appeared to count again. This time she focused on carrots.

Annie began to get a sinking feeling in the pit of her stomach. "Felicity, what's up?"

This time, Felicity looked up at Annie, and Annie could see a mixture of scare and anger. In a trembling voice, she said, "This morning, I received a piece of returned snail mail. It was a check from the bank. Someone forgot to put a stamp on it. The trouble is, it's a check for a vendor we don't use.

"We use our produce every day, so it's hard for me to get a count that would go directly to an invoice. But I finally realized I could focus on the carrots. We haven't used many carrots recently, mostly I'm going to be using them for one of the dishes at the party. But I realized I could count them and see if there is a problem."

"And you don't have nearly as many carrots as you've purchased."

"Right. Annie, I don't know how this happened, and I don't know how long it's been going on. I'm going to have to really look at it." She looked around the kitchen and lowered her voice. "I don't know who's doing it."

Annie moved closer to Felicity and lowered her voice. "I don't think it's anyone from the Café. I just found out yesterday the same kind of thing is happening at Mo's and Sassy P's. Can you join us at 1:30 in Gwen's office? Bring the returned check and print out anything you think might be important."

"Sure thing. Ben's home from college. I'll call him in to cook for me."

"And Felicity, don't stress over it this morning. Take a deep breath, get back to the business at hand, and we'll worry about it at 1:30."

"Thanks, Annie. Thank you so much." Felicity's perkiness was coming back. "And no, I don't need your help at all. Everything's under control. At least the food is under control. I don't know about everything else."

Chapter 9: Seafood Pasta Salad With A Twist

Annie bundled up and left the Café. She saw Chris and Cyril on the sidewalk, coming from the direction of the Inn. They were almost at Mr. Bean's. Cyril walked obediently at Chris's side, but he was still not the Cyril she knew.

She walked toward them. "Hey, how about lunch at the Confectionary? They're slow here. They don't need me."

"Sounds great."

"You can tell me about Blaine, and Cyril can have some of Laila's special treats."

Cyril seemed to perk up.

The Confectionary was slow also.

"It's too cold," said Carlos. And the boy isn't here to draw in the few folks silly enough to be out in this cold weather."

"We're that silly. What's your special today?"

"We have only one special today for lunch. It's a seafood pasta salad with a twist."

"What's the twist?"

"The first twist is that this is usually a warm weather meal. We're dreaming of sunshine, sandy beaches and warm water. So now that we're dreaming, we use shrimp, smoked salmon and crab meat, add some yellow bell pepper and cherry tomatoes. The dressing is olive oil and lemon juice and it's topped with dill and a lemon twist. And you get the bread of your choice on the side."

"That's what I'm having, and I'll have the 'everything' bagel," said Annie.

"Me, too, Carlos, and could you add some treats for my friend Cyril, here? Cyril, can you show Carlos the treats you want?"

For a moment, Cyril forgot he was supposed to be hard to deal with, and he walked to the case that had his favorite treats. He looked up at Carlos with a smile, tongue hanging out. Carlos obliged and pulled out the tray. With his nose, Cyril pointed to the treats in the center row.

"How many do you want, Cyril?"

Chris answered for him. "Give him three."

Once again, Cyril gave that tongue-hanging grin to Carlos as the treats were placed in a dish and set down on the floor beside Chris.

Annie noticed the dish. "Carlos, what a cute dish. When did you get these?"

"I decided, since we are now serving felines and canines, that they should have the same expectations as our human guests. Only the best. So Jerry got on the web and found these rainbow colored cat- and dog-shaped dishes. Perfect for treats."

Chris and Annie smiled at one another. The dishes were a good idea, but better than that, Cyril, like a child, had been hoodwinked into smiling about something during a sulk.

Annie got semi-serious. "So tell me about Blaine and the lake."

"Blaine and the lake. Oh, my. Where to start?"

As they waited for lunch, then ate, Chris told her a story that was at times funny and at times chilling. In more ways than one.

About ten groups were fishing around the edges of the lake when they arrived, and after a couple of conversations, they learned that Blaine could set up almost anywhere he wanted, but to be safe, he should stay away from the middle of the lake.

Yes, he could leave his shelter out, and some of his equipment. For the most part, the lake was safe and had not yet been discovered by local hooligans. But, just in case, he should take the expensive items home with him.

"You know, he just didn't seem to care. To him it was just money, and he could afford to lose it."

"I wish I could live like that."

"Me, too." Chris continued with the story.

"The regulars asked if Blaine was prepared for this frigid weather, and of course, he gave them his stock answer. 'Mother' had provided for everything.

"It took us forever to find a place he wanted to try, and, Annie, I have to tell you, he is in a very isolated spot. I tried to tell Ray how to find him, but I'm not sure he'll be able to.

"We opened everything. Some things I recognized, others I didn't. We figured out how to set up the shelter, and we got the heater out and going. We figured out drilling the hole and decided which rod, bobbers and hooks to use. He had bait. Did you realize you had live bait in that guest room last night?"

"Ick! I'll have to remember to tell Henrie so he can fumigate or terminate or whatever!"

"Good idea. Oh, and by the way, I tried to call Ray from the fishing site, but I didn't have any bars."

"That's not a good sign. Did Blaine try his phone?"

"He did. His was as bad as mine. I called Ray when I got a little closer to town, and he said he and Jock would go out this afternoon."

Cyril huffed.

At 1:30, Annie, George, Jesus and Felicity were at Gwen's office. The office was small, but they fit comfortably, if a little snuggly, around the conference table.

Felicity carried a large carafe. "You weren't counting on all of us, so I brought coffee."

"Oh, thank you! I was going to fill cups and start the pot again," said Gwen, "but this is much better. It probably tastes better than the swill I make, too."

Felicity, politely, did not agree with that last statement. She said only, "I'm here because this check was returned, but it's paying someone I don't use." Felicity handed over the check and the envelope.

"Oh, my," said Gwen. "This is troubling."

Gwen was a matronly-looking 60-something with glasses that looked like they were straight out of the 1980s. She wore a pink twill business suit which seemed to get a little tighter each time Annie saw it. The light pink blouse under the jacket had ruffles at the collar and at the cuff. Another fashion statement from the 1980s, thought Annie.

While fashions may have passed her by, Gwen was a sharp accountant. She was much in demand in town, and Annie was pleased to have Gwen in her corner.

"I can show you everything from the monitor on the wall. Is that okay, Annie, to show each of the businesses to everyone here?"

"Yes. We're all one unit, really. Everyone works together."

"Great, then, let's get started. I looked at the invoices from Mo's and Sassy P's this morning, and I found these new vendors. Of course, I realized they were new the first time I paid them, but I didn't think anything of it."

George and Jesus looked at the list closely. George shook his head slowly. "Don't know a single one."

Jesus nodded agreement.

"After I pulled these out, I did a search of my email to make sure the invoices had actually come from you. It was so confusing, because they all looked like they were coming from you, George, and you, Jesus. But then I looked a little more closely.

"Look at this one, supposedly from you, George. It's from George at Annie's Lifesavers dot com."

"But I didn't send it."

"You didn't. Your email address is Lifesaver, not Lifesavers."

"Oh…."

"Right. And Jesus, your invoices came in the same way. When all the letters run together in lowercase, and you see the familiar Annie's Lifesaver name at the end, you don't realize the one letter difference."

Annie asked, "And what do you have from Felicity that could match this invoice?"

"Let's look." Gwen did a quick search and found it. "The same thing. It looks like I entered three new vendors this month from invoices received on this email account."

"So, what does this mean? First of all, how did someone do this, and second, how do we stop it, and third, how do we make sure it never happens again?" Annie paused mid-sentence, then continued. "Let's not forget four. How do we find this yahoo and get our money back?"

"I've been thinking about this, and I think we have several things we need to check. First of all, we need to change your email addresses, but we have to be smart about it."

"Smart how?"

"Some way or another, someone has found out how to use your business address to set up a separate URL that is similar, and we don't know how that happened, so we need to stay a step ahead."

Annie, a techno-idiot at best, tried to keep up with the conversation. George, Jesus and Felicity seemed to know what Gwen was talking about.

Felicity explained. "We need to keep the Annie's Lifesaver, but for accounting purposes, we need to change the first name and make it unique, so Gwen will always know the invoices are legitimate."

Annie's confusion had not lessened. "But how does that help?"

Gwen looked at her. "If I get an invoice from Tiger Lily's Café, and the first name is, say, Beetlejuice at Annie's Lifesaver dot com, I'll know it's legitimate, because no one but Felicity, you and I will know that's her new email address, just for accounting purposes."

"Well, darn it, Gwen! That was the name I was going to use! Now I'll have to shoot George and Jesus!"

"Do we need to keep it that much of a secret?" asked Annie.

"I would. That way, it would prevent anyone from even joking about the fake names in front of whoever is doing this. The thing is, it has to be someone you all know, or have met, or who knows at least one of you and knows the names of the others. And it has to be someone that would know the logic of your corporate email addresses."

"But why wouldn't we just change the email addresses altogether?"

"Because a) you would have to change everyone's address and then notify everyone that all of your employees deal with, and b) whoever is doing this would probably be one of the persons that is notified."

"So, secret names."

"For now, yes."

"Then what?"

"First of all, we report this to the police."

"Oh, yes. I'm supposed to call Marco and remind him to call the FBI. Pete was going to leave that instruction before he left town. In the event you thought we were being hacked."

Gwen faced everyone, then looked straight at Annie. "I'm going to do a search of my emails to see who else from Annie's Lifesavers – plural – has sent anything to me. And I have to warn you, Annie, this is probably just the tip of the iceberg. There may be more emails from that person, and you could be attacked from one or more additional angles."

Annie made the kind of a face a child makes to get the "you'll freeze like that" caution from a parent.

"Wonderful. I think I'm going to go have a cup of tea and talk to Mem. Before I do that, I'll call Marco and ask him to contact the FBI. I won't suggest he come here. I'd rather not have him anywhere near you, or he'll start thinking he should investigate."

"Good idea. I'll gather records for the FBI."

"George, Jesus, Felicity, think up some great names, and I'll have Carlos, Diana and Henrie do the same. Should I know the names, Gwen?"

"Yes. You and the person who sets up the email accounts on your website."

"That will be Mem. So we'll change the names, and in the meantime, let's hold off on paying vendors until we have a handle on the extent of the problem."

Jesus pulled some pages from his jacket pocket. "Let's talk about those other angles. Gwen, I told Annie about Minnie's concern. She's been getting emails from you about training sessions, but whenever she tries to log on, there's nothing there. Here's the most recent invitation."

"I've been getting those, too. Are you sending them, Gwen?" asked Felicity.

"I don't have a clue what you're talking about," said Gwen as she looked at the printed email. "Look at this. It's from Gwen at Beancounter, not Beancounters."

"Heaven help us. We all need to search our email for that. Guys, please tell everyone at your places with an Annie's email to do that, and I'll let the others know to do the same." Wistfully, she added, "I wonder if Mem can put some tequila in that tea?"

Annie dialed the police station from the Beancounters lobby and talked to Marco.

"Marco, this is Annie Mack. Did Pete get the opportunity to tell you about the potential hacking issue?"

"Yes, he did. What have you discovered?"

Kathleen Thompson

"We definitely have been hacked, multiple times, it appears. Will you be able to call the FBI today?"

"Why don't you give me the information and let me get started on that?"

"I'd prefer to give it to the FBI. Pete said they would know how to handle it."

"Pete doesn't know everything I'm capable of handling. Where are you? I'll come on over."

"Marco, I will appreciate the local help. When the FBI sends someone, I'll be sure to speak with both of you together." Annie was running out of semi-polite ways to say, Marco, you don't know what you're doing.

Luckily, after a heavy sigh and a significant pause, his next response was a terse, "I'll let you know when they can get someone here."

Beancounters was on Main Street, next door to Antiques On Main. Annie stopped there first before going to Mem's. With just that short walk, her face was stinging from the cold and wind.

"Hi, Frank. I was hoping to see Mem this afternoon, but since I was walking past I thought I'd make sure she wasn't here."

"She just left. She was on her way back to the shop."

Annie stepped out the door into the biting air. She rounded the corner and started down The Avenue, holding her scarf to one side of her face while the other she buried into her shoulder.

This side of the street had one long building that mirrored her own. The tenants of this building purchased at about the same time, a few years before Annie moved to town. They had different stories and different goals, but each was looking

114

for an opportunity to own a small business, and they found a golden egg in this little corner of Chelsea.

Greg, a realtor working in concert with Annie's father, advertised this building throughout the region. His marketing was geared to persons who wanted to own a business and live in Chelsea, and even more specifically to people who had a dream. The incentives included a lower purchase price, as long as the buyers renovated the second floor as a living space.

The new owners worked together to renovate the outside of the building, giving their own business a personal flair while working in concert with everyone else.

At the corner, straight across The Avenue from Tiger Lily's Café, was a nondenominational church, Soul's Harbor. It was painted pale lilac and had a modern art rendition of the cross in darker purple.

The next storefront, CyberHealth, was a combination cyber café and health food store. On the outside it was pale peach with a brightly colored Mayan sunburst.

The next held a grocery store, Babar Foods, with a soft butter yellow exterior. As Laila was from Pakistan, she advertised with a graphic of an Indian elephant laden with baskets of fresh produce.

DoubleGood, a combination hardware and electronics store, was owned by two young women, twins. The mint green storefront sported two 3D silhouettes in forest green. On one side, a woman sat in front of a plumbing disaster. On the other side, a man sat in front of a computer monitor with a cell phone in one hand and a notebook in the other.

The flower and gift shop, Bloomin' Crazy, was rose pink in color with paintings of tropical blooms in red tones.

The last business, the one directly across the street from Sassy P's Wine & Cheese, was a double storefront housing The Drug Store and The Clinic. The two-front expanse was painted light slate blue. On the clinic side, in dark slate blue, was a cartoon of an old fashioned ambulance. Two men ran toward it carrying a stretcher holding a woman who obviously wanted off. The other side was more sedate. It was set off with the name and a few pills spilling out of a bottle.

When Annie moved to town following the death of her father, she spent many hours sitting on the porch of the Inn. As she looked at that building, renovated only recently by the new owners, she fell in love with the rainbow of colors from one business to the next.

When she put her personal stamp on her own buildings – the buildings and businesses inherited from her father – she patterned her color scheme on this one. The building across The Avenue was done in pastels. Annie took the primary color route for her own, turning lilac into purple, peach into orange, butter yellow into sunshine yellow, mint green into grass green, rose pink into red, and slate blue into royal blue.

These colors were her lifesaver, her SASHET, her feeling rainbow. Sad (blue), Angry (red), Scared (green), Happy (yellow), Excited (orange) and Tender (purple). The feeling rainbow served her well and she took every opportunity to share it. [Citation for SASHET: Liberation Psychotherapy, Frank & Dix Morris: www.libpsych.com/articles/sashet/sashet.html]

Annie thought the tip of her nose was getting frostbite when she reached CyberHealth. Inside, she was welcomed by a temperate 68 degrees and the fragrant smells of teas and candles.

The combination cyber café and health food store was warm and old fashioned in front (the tea room) and sleek and modern in back (the cyber café).

For the most part, Mem's foods and teas were sold as grocery items, artfully placed on racks and shelving in the front half of the store. But small tables nestled into private nooks throughout the front, where guests could relax with tea and healthy snacks.

From the small kitchen, Mem made easy-to-prepare dishes, like whole wheat vegetarian wraps, fresh vegetable sticks with spicy yogurt dip and fresh fruits with honey-flavored yogurt. The snacks were served on colorful mismatched china plates that matched perfectly with her eclectic collection of china tea pots and cups.

Annie noticed the new display of kitchen gadgets. The good stuff! Colorful, eye-catching items that No. Cook. Can. Live. Without. They held the promise of cooking with flair and producing picture perfect gourmet meals.

The cyber café was limited in scope, as Mem catered to individuals who did not have internet access at home, students whose families didn't have enough terminals for them to complete homework assignments, and people taking a break from work to do some web surfing. An area in the back accommodated guests who liked to game online alone or in groups. She also used that area for training sessions, although most of her training was done at the local high school or in the homes of the individuals needing assistance.

As a teacher – of navigating the internet, safe travels through social media and the use of technology in general – Mem was current in the latest gadgets, techniques and scams.

Mem was older than most of Annie's friends – more mature, Annie corrected herself – and had the wisdom to command the respect of everyone around her. She was currently navigating a relationship with Frank – one that took a heavy hit a couple of months before – and was repairing a formerly rocky relationship with her daughter, Diana. She lived with Diana in the large apartment on the second floor of this business.

Currently, Mem was behind the counter, helping a guest complete a purchase. As Mem finished with her guest, Annie perused the new kitchen displays, looking for more Christmas presents.

She stood, looking at colorful utensils, cutting boards, knives, storage containers, tableware, and unique preparation tools. She would buy everything she saw, in a variety of colors, but how in the world could you choose kitchen items for people whose kitchens were unfamiliar to you?

Another guest walked in, and Annie moved to the food section of the store. Oh, my, thought Annie. Mem had added new gourmet foods as well. There were jams, relishes, salsas, sauces, and mixes to make cheeseballs, dips and mulled drinks.

In the tea section, Mem had added tumblers, infusers, colorful mugs and double wall iced tea glasses. She had dessert teas. Annie was drawn to both the lemon chiffon and red velvet chocolate. All of her standard teas were still present. There was a selection of herbal, oolong, white, green and black teas, and teas made with a variety of spices. She had increased her selection of honey as well, showcasing local producers.

Mem finished with her guests and came around the counter. "The water is boiling, and I've put some lemon chiffon tea on to steep. Would you like a snack?"

"No, thanks, Mem. I just want some of your time, if I can steal it. And the tea sounds great!"

"I saw you looking at it, and almost came over with a napkin to catch the drool. Grab the table of your choice and I'll be right there."

Mem made tea in the "English" manner. She boiled her water in a tea kettle, used a proper tea pot with more than one hole inside the spout, used a tea cosy to keep the tea pot warm, and used only loose tea with a tea strainer or round tea bags with no strings or outer wrappings or staples. No hurry, no modern conveniences like microwave ovens, nothing but china.

Her tea cosies were whimsical. The cosy that came to the table today was knitted into a rainbow with antennae and eyes. Placed correctly and nestled over the snout and handle, the pot looked like a colorful snail.

Annie first asked Mem about the "Frank situation."

"Frankly speaking," started Mem with a smile, "things are going generally well. He is very busy now, of course, getting ready for that open house."

"And whose idea was it to have the grand opening during Christmas week?"

"Well, something goes on all year round, and he wanted to do it before the year was over. He thought this week would be better than next, in between Christmas and the New Year. He knows he is taking a risk that sales will be slow, but, again, this is more a hobby for him than a business."

"And I noticed how you deftly moved from how the two of you were doing to how busy he is."

"I did. He has been very mindful of me and of my feelings. He asks for my opinions, often. He is keeping a respectful balance between privacy and intimacy. In short, he is being extra, special careful."

"Too careful?"

"Possibly. I'm not going to worry about it until after the holiday. Then, if we can't get past terminal politeness, I'll talk to him about it. But that's not why you're here. I can tell something is going on. What is it?"

Annie told Mem about the hacking, the potential additional issues, and what she was doing. She told Mem about the change of emails and asked her to expect a list of fake names tomorrow.

"But I need to do more than that. I don't understand this stuff, and I have everything – all of my businesses – out there on the Internet. And my staff are young and social media savvy, but perhaps not savvy enough. What do you think? Can you help us?"

"I sure can, and the sooner the better. It sounds like you're getting caught up in a couple of different scams. There is definitely some spearphishing going on, and perhaps some catphishing. I'll bet 90% of your staff are out there on Facebook, Twitter, LinkedIn and possibly some other social media sites, and they could be getting scammed there as well."

"I need to introduce you to the guest at the Inn. He's doing some ice fishing and would probably understand what you're saying better than I."

"Annie, you need to catch up with the times! I thought I had you moving in the right direction!"

"I Skype just fine now, thank you very much. And so does Mom. It's the rest of this stuff."

"You need to get out there before the world passes you by."

"Enough with the lecture! Can you help?"

"Yes. I'll put something together for right after the new year. Of course, you know I'll be doing prevention training. I can't help you with the issues going on now."

"I know. Marco has called the FBI."

"You mean Marco hasn't tried to solve it himself?"

"Well…the FBI wasn't his first choice."

"He means well. You know why he was promoted, don't you?"

"I don't think I understand it completely, why he was promoted, I mean. Well, as much as 'second in command' is a promotion. There isn't a real title to go with it."

"No, the Town Council refused to make a new position, but they did come through with a minor salary increase. And training. Serious training for all of the officers and civilian employees."

"But why Marco? Why was he promoted? It all went haywire on his watch."

"He's the only one that didn't make a complete and utter fool of himself, but it wasn't for lack of trying. It's because he was in the back with the Sheriff and the State Police Detective. The rest of them weren't as well supervised."

Annie laughed. The "rescue" of a number of hostages, including her, Mem, Henrie, Pete, Annie's mother and step-father, all of her kids, her mother's cat, two dogs and some other friends, had resulted in three groups of police officers jumping off before they were ordered to do so. In the end, several officers, including all of Chelsea's local force with the exception of Marco, incurred injuries to both their bodies and their reputations.

If the description of Marco's performance was to be believed, the look on his face when the fiasco occurred was priceless. Mouth open, eyes wide, hand slapped to his forehead. Pure shock. Of course, the Sheriff and State Police Detective looked much the same, but their shocked faces were masked with a bit more professionalism.

The situation had resolved itself before chaos ensued through police activity. In the basement of the Inn where they were being held, the heroic actions of eight cats, two dogs, and an injured and shackled police chief saved the day. Now, months later, it was possible to look back and laugh.

Annie thought once more of the charcoal hanging in her dining room. Only six people knew the whole story. Pete and Janet, Ray and Cheryl, and Chris and Annie. The story was told from the perspective of the only two people whose combined observations could tell it. Pete and Annie were there, and they were the only two that noticed the collective behavior.

No matter how incomprehensible it seemed, the coordinated activities of the cats and dogs saved this group of humans from what would have been a deadly ending.

Annie mentally prepared herself for the blast of cold before leaving CyberHealth to go home.

Chapter 10: He Was The Rhinoceros

Annie walked quickly back to the Inn, wishing she had worn a fur mask. Thank goodness Boone and his crew were keeping the sidewalks and porches clean. She didn't want to slow down to navigate slippery spots.

Seven cats ran from various parts of the house to greet her. Mr. Bean stood as tall as he could with his paws on her legs, mewing as loudly as his little vocal cords would allow.

Sassy Pants, instead of trying to expose herself for tummy rubs, ran in and out of cats and ankles with her signature, *"Meh! Meh!"*

Mo wrapped himself around her ankles, trilling away, pushing Mr. Bean and Sassy Pants out of the way with each turn.

Kali and Ko jumped to a table that she would have to pass and mewed loudly.

Tiger Lily and Little Socks, seeing that everyone else had the same idea they did, stopped mid-foyer, sat on the floor and joined the chorus.

To Annie, it sounded like the circus had come to town. To the kids, the ongoing conversation included the following tidbits: *"Why do we have to stay here?" "Make them go to work!" "It's boring here!" "I want to play with Carlos!" "Please let them leave the house!" "Mommy, I duzn't like stayin' with Socks!" "Trill!"*

Annie couldn't move for danger of landing on a foot or a tail. She leaned in to look around the corner to the library, which seemed to have a few things out of place. Books on the floor. Magazines shredded. A glass figurine on the floor, blessedly in one piece.

She turned her attention to the dining room. It looked like Henrie had put most loose items away somewhere. Then she looked straight ahead at the foyer. The beautiful flower arrangement looked a little worse for the wear. A few smaller blossoms and stems were on the floor, and some of the larger blossoms were missing petals. A lot of petals. She wondered what she would find upstairs in the apartment and decided to not think about it.

Henrie appeared with a cup of hot cocoa on a tray. He appeared unruffled. He watched Annie with a small smile as she stood in the midst of cats. "It is your turn to enjoy the, shall we call it a snow day or a cold day?"

"Has it been like this as long as I've been gone?"

"Yes. There were times I could have sworn we had booked in a herd of wild horses. I stopped picking up after the little dears by 11:00 or so this morning. And until about that time, Cyril helped them create utter chaos. He was the rhinoceros that ran with the horse pack. I hope you do not mind that I leave the rest of it to the end of the day."

"I don't mind at all. Should I lock them in upstairs?"

"I do not think you would want to see your apartment after the first few hours if you did so."

"You're probably right. Certainly they'll settle down and get better with it as the week goes on."

"Certainly," said Henrie, as he handed Annie the cup over the clamoring of the cats.

Henrie continued, "Frank delivered the gift for Chris, all wrapped up. I placed it on the table outside your apartment. And how did the rest of the Christmas shopping go?

"It didn't. Not a single thing, not a single idea. Did you take a look at the present for Chris?"

"I did not, but Frank described it to me. I believe you have chosen wisely."

"That's good to know. One down; 573 to go."

"Have you seen anything interesting?"

"Oh, yes! Have you been to CyberHealth lately? She has great colorful kitchen gadgets. The kind that you just can't live without."

"I have heard about this, but I have not been in. I will be sure to go this week."

"If you see anything our kitchen needs, put it on our account."

"I will be sure to do that. I may look for my own benefit as well. You know, on occasion I cook in my own apartment."

"You don't just use the big kitchen when you want to fix something for yourself?"

"Usually that is what I do. However, there are the odd days, when I have a day off, generally, that I want to remain 'at home.'"

"Henrie, would you prefer to have a place to live away from the Inn?"

"Oh, no. Nothing of the sort. The arrangement we have here is quite satisfactory. I have my own space, at no charge, and use of any kind of cleaning or kitchen appliance I might need, laundry facilities, a beach for the rare occasion I allow my feet to touch sand….No, I am quite happy."

"Would you prefer to have someone working here to give you more time off?"

"I have thought of that on occasion. I know I gave you, shall we say, a hard time, when you suggested hiring a cleaning crew. However, if they are adequate to the task, perhaps I may feel more comfortable leaving you on your own more often with a suitably trained substitute."

"Well, then, we have something to look forward to in the new year. Do you have ideas about 'suitable substitutes'"?

"I have been giving that some thought in this past week. There are times, particularly during the summer, that a college student may be appropriate. I thought about Pete's daughter, Ginger. She is such a capable young woman."

"She is, and it would be great to give her some additional work when she's home. Diana can't give her all of the hours she would like. And she could probably continue to teach yoga at the same time. How about other times of the year?"

"I believe we could keep everything 'in the family,' so to speak. We have part-time employees in every business, and any one of them – of course with the cooperation of the other managers – would probably create an excellent presentation for at least a short period of time."

"Great idea. After the first of the year, we can put out some feelers." Annie thought for a moment. "Henrie, why wait until after the first of the year. You are getting ready to have a truly hectic week, and most of your work will be because of my family. How about hiring a couple of people to help you out?"

Henrie sighed deeply. "I have been worried about this week. You are absolutely correct. We may be late getting started, but I will check around. I will start by asking Felicity if she has candidates for such short notice."

Henrie and Annie were interrupted by the arrival of Blaine, trailed by Ray and Jock. Blaine and Jock were in great humor. Ray looked as if he had seen better days.

Blaine said, "How invigorating!"

Jock said, *"Woof!"* and ran to the all-season porch, seven cats following close on his heels.

Ray said, "Do you have anything stiffer than coffee, Henrie?"

"It will be in your hands directly," said Henrie. Before turning to go to the kitchen, he turned to Blaine to say, "Knowing you plan to go out again this evening, I took the liberty of making sandwiches for your afternoon snack. You'll find them in the refrigerator. There is ham with pineapple and sriracha mayonnaise on the side, and turkey with cranberry sauce. There is a tray of fresh fruit and vegetables as well.

"Ray, please help yourself, or take some home with you. Take enough for Cheryl as well."

"Thanks, Henrie. I'll have a sandwich or two myself; Cheryl is off Christmas shopping at Marsh Haven."

Henrie narrowed his eyes at Annie and went to the kitchen.

Annie caught the look and returned it with her own. She turned to follow Blaine to the coffee and snack room. "Mr. Jones, please tell me all about your day." She turned to see if Ray was following and raised questioning eyebrows in his direction. He was following, and in response, he rolled his eyes, shrugged his shoulders, and then hung his head for a good, long shake.

Annie laughed. Once they were settled with sandwiches and drinks, Blaine told Annie about his day.

"It was an excellent bit of luck for Chris to be available this morning. We stopped at the head of the lake and walked around a bit, talked with some of the regulars. He knew most of them, which I'm sure helped. They recommended that I stay where they could see me, but I really wanted to be on my own.

"So I went with Chris. We drove around, going into this area and that, and finally, I found the perfect spot. We went back to get my truck, found the site again, and he helped me set up. Again, I have to say how lucky it was for me he was there. I would still be staring at the boxes wondering where to begin. Instead, the shelter is up, and the equipment is in reasonable order."

"Chris does know his way around equipment and gadgets," said Annie. "He said something about your cellphones not working out there?"

"No bars. I'll really be roughing it."

"So how did you do once he left you?"

"I picked a place to drill, and with a bit of effort I completed that task. But despite my best efforts, I have not hooked a single fish."

Ray had remained quiet to this point. Apparently, though, the resort nature of the town and their mutual businesses seemed to come back to him and he rallied. "His site looked perfect. It did take me a turn or two to figure out which access point they used, but I know where it is now. And Jock had a great time on the ice. It's snow-covered, so he was able to run off some energy. I'm going to have to get him out on the smaller lakes more often in the winter."

"Did you worry about him getting over a thin spot?"

"He seemed to check it out before he started running, and he appeared to stay fairly close to the edge."

"It's still snowing a little bit out there, Blaine. Are you sure your equipment is okay?"

"It's fine. My shelter is a good size, and I just keep the things I'm not using on that sled. It slips in under the shelter, and I put the gear I was using inside before we came back."

"So, is everything going to be okay, Ray?"

"I'm a little concerned about how far out he finally drilled that hole, but Blaine and I already had this conversation. He is exactly where he wants to be. I will say that Jock stayed back a ways from that spot."

From the porch, they could hear Chris and Cyril come in the front door. "Annie? Ray?"

"We're back here, on the porch," called Annie. "Stop at the snack room and get a sandwich and some coffee."

She could tell that he stopped, but Cyril kept coming. He entered the porch at a trot, saw Jock and the cats in a pile on the other end of the porch, and stopped.

A low growl started in his throat and Jock was instantly on his feet, matching growl for growl.

Annie, shocked, didn't move. Ray got to his feet and grabbed Jock's collar. He called out, "Hey, Chris? Can you drop the sandwich and come on out here, please?"

Chris heard the commotion and was already on the way in. He stayed behind Cyril and got a grip on his collar.

"I think we're just going to go home and calm down. Blaine, I'll see you around 10:00 tomorrow."

Chris pulled on Cyril's collar until he finally moved, but by the time they were headed out the door, barks and snarls had been added to the growls, and Ray struggled to keep Jock in check.

By the time they could hear the front door close, Jock had calmed somewhat and Annie, with a start, realized it was time to start breathing again.

Blaine had been rooted to his seat. He took a deep breath. "And just think. I was worried about the cats."

The phone rang. Henrie picked up in another room. He walked to the porch and said, "It is Marco calling from the police department."

Ray's eyebrows went up. Blaine sat forward in his seat. Annie took the handheld phone.

"Marco, hello. Do you have news?"

"Yes, I do. We have confirmation the FBI has a special agent available to look into the situation. He'll be here tomorrow. I've taken the liberty of setting up an initial appointment at the office of your accountant."

"That's great. What time should I be there?"

"1:00. Would it be possible for me to come over there now, to get information to begin the investigation?"

"I'm sorry, Marco, that won't work. I'll make sure we have everything we could possibly need tomorrow afternoon. And Marco? Thank you so much!"

Annie hung up, looked at the men looking at her and said, "Don't ask."

Chapter 11: Syrah And Cheese Curls

Ray led Jock through the porch by his collar. "I'll take this bad boy home and have a conversation with him. Try to figure out what's going on in his thick head."

Jock seemed to know a lecture was coming. He pulled against the hold on his collar and looked back to the cats for help. They wisely stayed out of it.

Annie asked Blaine, "Are you going out again?"

"No. It's too cold and I've had enough excitement today. I'll call Mother, let her know how things are going. Maybe go to Mo's for a beer."

Annie went to the kitchen to say goodnight to Henrie, telling the kids to go on upstairs for their dinner. Most of the cats went upstairs, but Kali decided to try to get to know her guest a little better.

She jumped to the table and sat, looking with her soft face – as opposed to the hard face she had been using – at this fisherman.

He reached out a tentative hand and touched her back, running his hand from her shoulders to her haunches. Kali started to purr and rolled her body into his caress. She moved closer, and he took a second hand to caress her as well.

Kali was in heaven! Humans very rarely used both of their hands!

When she had her fill, she jumped down from the table and went to the apartment on the third floor.

Blaine, once getting into his own room, looked down at the lock on the cat door. He leaned down and flipped it back open.

The first thing Annie did when she got upstairs was to freshen the cats' food and water. She got the water, and as she turned to get the cat food, she heard a familiar cacophony. It was the nightly version of Tiger Lily putting her foot into the water dish as she drank while the rest of them noted their disapproval.

Some things never change. Well, sometimes, things were a little different. Like tonight. Little Socks jumped to the kitchen counter and leveled her narrowed-eye glare and some snappy ick icks in Annie's direction.

"What?" asked Annie.

"You let Tiger Lily get away with everything!"

Annie shook her head and decided it was best not to try to make up with Little Socks. She was right.

Annie and Chris were supposed to spend the evening together. She didn't know what the status of that date was, following the outburst between Cyril and Jock. She decided to send a text.

"RUUP4IT" (Are you up for it?)

"UTM" (You tell me.)

"IMRU" (I am, are you?)

"ICW"(I can't wait.)

"20M" (20 minutes?)

"45" (45 minutes.)

Annie rummaged through cupboards for snacks and a good bottle of wine. She found a Syrah and some cheese curls, in Annie's mind, the ultimate snack food. She arranged things on the coffee table in the living room and relaxed.

When the knock on the door came, it woke her up. She rubbed her eyes and ran her fingers through her hair as she went to the door. "How long have you been knocking? I fell asleep."

For a couple of months, Chris had been using a key to access the elevator. The key opened the apartment as well, but he still chose to knock. "Just the one time. You weren't sound asleep, or I would be napping out here."

As Chris and Annie talked, Cyril came in, still not himself. He was quickly surrounded by cats, and they went as one unit to the living room.

Chris stepped into the door and closed it behind him. He then did something totally out of character. He put his hands on Annie's shoulders, drew her to him, gave her a deep kiss, then stood there, embracing her, rocking gently back and forth, for what seemed to Annie like a full minute.

While in the embrace, she asked, "Is Daddy having a hard day?"

"Yes, he is. I didn't realize how hard parenting would be."

"Sometimes you just need a hug, right?"

"Right." He continued to hold her. "What do we do now?"

"We let go, back away from one another, go into the living room, maybe put in a movie, have some cheese curls, open the bottle of Syrah, and probably fall asleep on the sofa."

"Syrah and cheese curls. The ultimate pairing." He let go, and they did just that.

In the "cushion corner" of the living room, Cyril lounged in the middle with cats either snuggling against or near him. Tiger Lily got right to the point.

"You didn't tell us this morning what was wrong. Now it looks like there's a problem with you and Jock. What's up?"

"He's a pain in the behind."

"Behind what?" asked Mr. Bean.

Little Socks shushed him while Tiger Lily pressed on. *"You have to tell us a little more than that."*

"He's a braggart. He's demanding. He's manipulative."

A chorus ensued. *"What do you mean?" "He's your friend!" "He's not not manip...moped..whatever!" "Trill!"*

Tiger Lily bopped noses. *"Shush! Let him talk!"*

Cyril explained about the dog show, focusing on the group that included Jock's breed. *"And the dog in the show was a vain poodle-cut, powder-puff-tailed water dog. But he won the contest. Well, he won part of the contest. In the end, he lost."*

"So if he lost at the end, what's the big deal?"

"It's hard to explain..."

Mo drew closer to Cyril, wrapped his tail around an ear and trilled.

Cyril leaned his head into Mo's body and sighed a few times.

Mo said, *"Trill."*

Kali and Ko translated together, *"Cyril's sad." "Cyril thinks he's ugly."*

This time even Little Socks said something nice. *"Cyril! You're handsome!"* Then she caught herself. *"For a dog, that is."*

Cyril leveled his gaze at Little Socks, then leaned back into Mo.

"Why is you think you's ugly?" asked Sassy Pants.

Cyril sighed, and Mo trilled.

"Oh!" said Sassy Pants.

Kali and Ko said together, *"What does he mean?"* *"What about hair?"*

All eyes, except Cyril's, turned to Sassy Pants, who looked confused.

"You duzn't get it?"

Tiger Lily reached over to put a paw on the paw of Little Socks, to warn her to stay quiet. Little Socks spit a little bit. Tiger Lily said to Sassy Pants, *"Why don't you explain it to us. It was a little fuzzy."*

"Oh. Well it was really more like furry."

"Huh?" said Mr. Bean. *"Furry? Furry like a kitty cat?"*

Sassy Pants looked at Mr. Bean with confusion, and then she said, *"Oh. You guys duzn't get it at all!"*

Tiger Lily, patiently, said, *"Just tell us. You can do it."*

"Okay. Mo said that…"

Little Socks cut in, *"Mo said?"*

"Mo has pitchers in his brain that said Cyril saw a dog that was like him but prettier than him."

"Prettier how?" encouraged Tiger Lily.

"With long hair. Hair on his belly and chest and stuff that reach to the floor."

The cats marveled at this, never having imagined such a sight on a dog like Cyril.

Tiger Lily said to Little Socks, *"Come help me."*

The two went to one of Annie's tables that had two large books filled with photographs. Cats were on the cover of one and another showed dogs. Together, Tiger Lily and Little

Socks pushed the dog book to the floor and then to the group.

Tiger Lily explained, *"You see these cardboard things? Mommy calls them bookmarks. One of them is marked at Cyril's page and the other at Jock's."*

Together, they got the book open to the first bookmark. It was Jock's breed. Some of the dogs had curly hair, and some had wavy hair, like Jock. Most were black, like Jock, and there was a beautiful full black tail on many of them. But some of the dogs looked quite different.

"Cyril," said Tiger Lily, *"look at these pictures. Did you see something like this?"*

Tiger Lily pointed to a curly haired dog with thick hair from his head to the back third of his back. From there on, the hair was shaved down to a black sheen, back, legs and tail, all the way to the tip of the tail, where the hair once again grew strong and proud.

Cyril stared. *"You mean there are more of them like that?"*

"I guess so. Sometimes humans get silly notions about dogs. They teach them to do tricks and they do strange things to their hair like this. Just like those poodles that have to put up with those silly cuts."

"Why would they do that to a dog like Jock?" asked Cyril. *"He doesn't have time to look silly like that. He has a job. He works with Ray on the boat, and keeps things safe at The Marina. Don't they have jobs like that?"*

"Sometimes," said Tiger Lily, *"there's just no telling what a human will do. I'm sure the dog doesn't ask for it."*

Cyril looked closely at every dog on the two pages displayed. *"They all look just a little different from each other. This one here looks most like Jock, and he is a handsome dog, alright. Turn the book to my page!"*

Cyril was anxious to see how others of his breed looked.

The cats got the pages turned, and they all crowded around. Immediately, they saw the dog that Cyril had seen. Strong-chested like Cyril, and with the same coloring, mostly white with light brown spots. Long hair flowed from the chest, belly, legs and tail. *"That's him,"* said Cyril sadly. *"I have hair in all of those places, but Pete trims it off."*

"Well look at these other dogs," said Tiger Lily. *"Lots of them are all trimmed up."*

Cyril forced his eyes from the one dog and looked at the others. His breed had more colors than Jock's breed, and there were several different cuts. Some had no long hair showing; others had some hair on their legs and tails but not on their chest and belly. Cyril raised his tail and looked at it. It was trimmed short, but there was still some hair there.

"I guess I'm not the only one that gets trimmed," he said, *"but it's confusing."*

"What's confusing?"

"Why is it that Jock is a working dog, so he doesn't get trimmed, and I'm a working dog, and Pete keeps me trimmed? It doesn't make any sense."

"Well, sure it does," said Tiger Lily, but she didn't know how to continue.

Mr. Bean came to the rescue. *"Do you remember when we found that dead girl in the woods?"*

Cyril looked at Mr. Bean, and Mo seemed to preen.

"What about it?" asked Cyril.

"Mommy had to pull stuff out of me and Mo for a real long time, especially out of Mo, because his long hair got tangled into everything. He looked like a ratty old bush when we walked out of there."

137

Cyril looked at Mo, who said *"Trill!"*

"You're right, Mo."

"What?!" spat Little Socks.

Kali and Ko together said, *"Cyril has to keep trimmed to work with Pete." "Pete needs Cyril to go everywhere, and you can't have that hair everywhere."*

Tiger Lily said, *"So you see, Cyril, it's because you're so important to Pete that he keeps you trimmed up."*

Cyril started to perk up, then saddened again. He said, *"Then why did Pete leave me? He left. He took my family away. He gave me and all of my things to Chris."*

The cats didn't have a thing to say about that.

Chapter 12: What's For Breakfast?

Chris went downstairs, met Henrie in the dining room and asked, "What's for breakfast?"

Henrie said good morning to Chris, asked him to help himself, and made no other comments.

Cyril trotted in and sniffed the air, raising up on hind legs to get a better look at the buffet.

"Go on, Henrie, you can say it. You want to ask me to get a room, right?"

Henrie chuckled. "I will check our cupboards for dog food. Cyril looks hungry."

"Annie gave him a little bit but noticed she was running low. She had to put the cat food up on the counters to keep him out of it and she hoped you might have the dog variety down here. So here I am. Before my first cup of coffee."

"You do not need to explain the circumstances to me."

"We fell asleep in front of the TV," Chris added, "on the sofa."

"Really, you do not need to explain anything at all."

At that moment, they heard someone running down the stairs from the second floor. Blaine burst into the room.

"What's for breakfast?"

He grabbed a plate and started piling on the food. Bacon, sausage and egg casserole, a Danish pastry, an onion bagel with lox and cream cheese, and finally, he took a cereal bowl from the rack and loaded it with fresh fruit.

"I overslept! The fish will be gone by the time I get there!"

Henrie calmly poured him a cup of coffee.

As Blaine sat down, he noticed the other person at the table was Chris. "It's not 10:00 yet, is it?"

"No, Blaine. I'll be meeting you out at the lake by then, though. Take the time to enjoy your breakfast. Give the sun a fighting chance to make it out, and it might warm up a degree or two. You need to make sure to take care of yourself before heading to the ice. If you thought the wind was cold yesterday, that was minor compared to what it will be today."

"You're right." Blaine took a calming breath, looked at his very full plate, and said, "You know what? I'm going to enjoy this. I was going to eat fast, but this is part of the experience, too, isn't it? I'm enjoying the full shot. Something else to tell Mother."

Chris noticed, not for the first time, the reference to telling his mother about his experiences.

"Tell me about yourself, Blaine. Where are you from? What do you do?"

"Oh, there's not much to tell, really, I'm just a guy."

"Well, a guy's got to be from somewhere, and I like getting to know about people. Yesterday we spent all of our time talking about the lake and the equipment. We have time now to talk about you."

"Well, why don't you tell me a little about yourself first, Chris?"

Chris opened his mouth, but nothing came out for several seconds. Finally, he said, "I see what you mean. When you're asked, there really isn't that much to tell."

"Give it a shot."

"Okay, I will. Let's see. I grew up on the shore of another one of the Great Lakes, and I was pretty lucky. My family was well off, and I was able to spend my life on boats, both big and small, on that lake. I went to a private school, played a lot of sports, and several of my friends went to the same college I did."

"Which one was that?"

"Yale."

"Ivy League."

"My parents wouldn't have had it any other way."

"How'd you end up in the Coast Guard?"

"Well, I think I may have disappointed my parents on that score. If I had to choose a military career, they probably would have preferred the Navy. They see the Coast Guard as a pretend-Navy, but I wanted to spend my life on a big lake, not on an ocean."

"So, you've been in for a while?"

"Ever since graduation, so yeah, a while."

"How long have you been stationed here?"

"Several years. I hope this is my last placement. They tried to promote me last year, but I turned it down, said I was happy right here. So far, they've let me stay. Now how about you?"

"Oh, it sounds as if you and I are alike in many ways. I didn't grow up on a lake. I grew up in Dayton, and, well, we didn't lack for money either. I went to a private school, a boarding school. Did you board out, Chris?"

"No. My school was right there in my home town. I went home every night."

"That would have been nice. I went to a school in northern Indiana. A pricy one. Lots of famous kids go there. Or, I should say, kids of famous people. La Lumiere."

"Did you like it?"

"I didn't really fit in. Didn't make a lot of friends. But Mother and Father thought I should stick it out, so I did. Then I went to Dartmouth. Like you, I'm an Ivy Leaguer."

"And what do you do now? I assume you're back in Dayton; you mention your mother every now and then."

"Yes. Back in Dayton. Back home. Literally. It's a big place; I have a set of rooms.

"Well, an apartment.

"Well, to be honest, one wing of the house was built for me. Complete with servants."

"Servants?" Chris, while growing up in an old money situation, was not familiar with this concept. His mother had housekeepers that came in once a week and cooks that helped when she entertained.

"Servants. I have what you would probably call a butler, and then there are the ones that clean and the ones that cook and the ones that take care of the yard. They have their own wing, those that live with us. Some of them are day people. They come in from their own homes."

"So, you live the good life, then?"

"I guess you can call it that. Father's gone, so it's just Mother and me. No brothers or sisters."

"What are you doing with that college degree?" asked Chris, not knowing how else to ask the question.

"I manage the family money. Go to board meetings. Pretend I have an interest in the real estate management firm Father owned. Now it belongs to Mother and me."

"You have to pretend? What would you rather be doing?"

"After graduation, I sought and was offered a position with an international bank. Mother didn't want me to take it. She thought I needed to join the family business. So I did."

Blaine got a faraway look in his eye, and his eyes drifted up and right. "That bank had offices in London, Paris and Berlin. If I had followed my plan, I'd be in one of those cities now."

"You could probably still do that, you know. You're still young."

Blaine focused again on Chris. "I probably could, but Mother...well, Mother has told me for years she won't be around forever, and someone has to look out for the folks that work for us."

Blaine looked sadder and sadder as he talked about himself. Chris thought he had better change the subject.

"So now you're ice fishing. Quite an adventure. How did you decide on this kind of a vacation?"

Blaine gave a self-deprecating laugh. "Mother convinced me I needed to get out more, so, being me, I made a list of things I might like to do. Mother got hold of that list, got on the telephone and made reservations. Fishing was the first thing on the list. In my mind, I saw myself on a boat in the tropics or the Mediterranean, but she's a Midwesterner to the core. She thought I should learn how to fish on the ice.

"I'm doing this for her, but I'm going deep sea fishing this summer, I hope. I'll just have to make that reservation myself. But I might make that reservation here, not in the tropics."

"Here? You've been here two nights, and you're ready to come back already?"

"Well, the last couple of evenings I've met a delightful young lady. The first time, it was an accident. But last night we arranged to meet. Delightful."

"Really? Well, I knew we had some delightful women here, but I'm glad you met one of them."

Blaine smiled to himself and offered no more in explanation.

Chris let the silence linger for a moment as he finished his coffee. "Well, I have to go. I have to at least check in at the Station before I head out to meet you on Great Neck. I'll see you soon." As he got up, he said thank you to Henrie and called out to Cyril. Then called Cyril again.

Chris started toward the library just as Cyril walked slowly into the dining room, head hanging down. Chris got down low, put his arms around Cyril's neck and whispered in his ear. "Pete will be home in just a few days. Everything will be back to normal then." Cyril placed a half-hearted lick on Chris's face and followed him out the door, head still down.

Henrie checked on Blaine every few minutes. When he asked if he could serve more juice, Blaine seemed to come to.

Across his shoulder, Blaine said, "Look at the time! Thanks, Henrie. I have to go!" He put on his coat, grabbed his hat and gloves, and walked quickly out the door. He nearly knocked over a man coming up the front porch steps.

Still moving forward, he said, "I'm sorry! I'm so sorry! Are you alright?"

"Not a problem," said the man. He walked through the door, through the foyer and into the dining room, looked at a startled Henrie and said, "What's for breakfast?"

Chapter 13: A Good Friend

Annie walked through the apartment, picking up cat toys and other things lying on the floor. She was confused to see the picture book of dog breeds on the floor.

The book was turned to the English setter page. She thought Chris must have gotten up in the night to do some research. Funny. She didn't remember that. Also funny were the little cat tooth prints in the pages.

A sharp ring brought her out of her reverie. Annie pressed the intercom button. "Good morning, Henrie. What's up?"

"A gentleman is here to see you and would like you to join him for breakfast, if you have not yet eaten."

"I've just had coffee and can be right down. Who is it?"

"A good friend."

Annie realized that was all she was going to get, so she put on her fleece-lined boots and went downstairs.

In the dining room, a man sat with his back to her, sipping a cup of coffee. Annie walked around to the end of the table, smiled in automatic greeting, and then gasped and laughed at the same time.

"Jeff Bennett! What are you doing here?"

"Once again, I am here to save you."

"You? They sent you?"

"I was transferred to the cybercrimes unit. I was available, unlike others, I didn't have family plans for this week, and I happened to have a perfectly clear desk. So here I am. And I understand it will be my pleasure to work with Marco. At least for this week."

"Yes. It will be your pleasure. Pete will be back next week. How long will it take you to figure this out?"

"It depends on how sophisticated the hacker is. I could finish it this week, or not."

As Annie helped herself to breakfast – she was inordinately happy that Henrie always over-prepared for his guests – she asked, "Do you need a room?"

"I do, and Henrie gave me the last one available, so I'm just lucky all the way around."

"I think that's the one facing The Avenue. Isn't that the room you had the last time?"

"Yes. I remember it well!" he laughed.

For a while they chatted about people they knew in common. Jeff wasn't an old friend, but in a short period of time he had become a good friend.

He was involved in the situation that elevated Marco to "second in command." Jeff had actually been acting undercover, investigating other guests at the Inn, and as it happened, he was on hand when the hostage situation came to a head.

"So you have a full house this week," said Jeff. "Please tell me none of them are criminals."

Annie laughed. "I'm sure not. Only one person is here now. He's a rich young man trying his hand at ice fishing for the first time. At the moment, the only crime he's committing is being inexperienced but blundering forward anyway. The rest of the rooms are set up for families visiting over the holidays. Most of them are my family.

"As a matter of fact, Mom and Sam will be here any minute. They'll be taking the honeymoon suite out in the carriage house, and they'll be here for a month.

"And my sister, her husband and younger children will be on the second floor of the carriage house, her daughter, son-in-law and their children will be in the back room here on ground level. The last two rooms will be used by three young women from Mexico coming to visit Carlos. Do you remember Carlos? From Mr. Bean's?"

"I do. He was one of the intelligent and calming influences on that exciting night."

Jeff continued, "So you're having family in for the holidays. That's good. You probably don't get away that much."

"I don't, but the fact is that I'm the one with the space. This will be the first time we've all been together in years, certainly a few children ago, if you count time using my nieces and nephews. I hope we create a new tradition."

"That's all I have now. Nieces and nephews. Parents are gone, brothers are gone. They were both a lot older than me, so their children are fairly close to me in age. But we live scattered to the wind. We keep in touch, but we've never done holidays together."

"Well, even if you finish your work, you'll probably be snowed in here over Christmas. You know we're expecting a blizzard?"

"I heard that."

"So, you'll be stuck here, and we're planning a huge Christmas day. Some of your new friends will be here, Chris, Ray, Henrie, of course, Mom and Sam."

"I don't want to put you out…"

"You won't be putting us out. Actually, if you were planning on spending a quiet day in your room, we'd be putting you out. So you're going to have to put on your happy face and join us."

"I'll plan on it! Now, I should get busy. Tell me how to find this place, Beancounters. I'm going to set my equipment up there."

Annie gave him directions and Henrie walked him out to the car. He took Jeff's personal bags from the trunk and said, "I will place these in your room. I am so happy to see you again and I hope you enjoy your stay."

When Henrie returned to the Inn, bags in hand, he was met by Kali and Ko, sitting in the foyer, looking first at his face, then at the bags. He looked them straight in the eye and said, in a firm voice, "You girls have been shirking your duties today. You did not come in to greet Mr. Jones at breakfast. You did not realize we booked in another guest, your old friend, Mr. Bennett.

"I know your siblings are locked in and are not able to work this week. You girls, however, are locked into your own place of business. You need to show a bit more attention to detail."

The two girls looked chastened. They hung their heads and walked slowly back to the library.

Henry called out to them, "Just for this week, girls, while everyone else is not working, I will allow you to, shall we say, lighten up, as well." He smiled when he knew they could no longer see his face and took Jeff's bags to his room.

Annie was a little worried. She had expected Nancy and Sam by now. It was so cold. If they had trouble on the road, that would put them in a dangerous situation.

Just as she decided to call them on one or another of their cellphones, she heard them come in and ran from the library to greet them.

"Mom! Sam! I was so worried!"

"Oh, honey, it's good to see you, and thank goodness we made it!"

Sam carried a case containing her mother's precious Honey Bear. Or, as Annie wryly thought, the dreaded Uncle Honey Bear. The bane of her cats' existence.

"I really was beginning to get worried! And Honey Bear. So good to have you here again." Annie nearly swallowed her tongue on this lie.

"You can let him out, Mom. The outer cat doors are locked already. All of my kids are home. I don't want them out in this weather."

"Oh, how delightful! I'm sure he'll go find them and play!"

"I'm sure," said Annie, thinking instead there was nothing playful about this dreadful cat. He was a nice cat, when no other cats were around. That never happened in Chelsea, however.

The case was opened, and Honey Bear put one paw out warily. He looked around, came all the way out, heard a howl of protest from the library, and pulled himself into his most vain pose. He walked regally into the library, and the howl became a chorus of howls, hisses, icks and, was that a growl?

Henrie came to the foyer to greet Nancy and Sam while putting on his coat to go to their car. "I will make sure all of your luggage makes it into the Honeymoon suite," he said.

Sam followed. "Way too much work for one man, Henrie. Remember, we have clothes for a month! And Christmas presents!"

Annie groaned.

"What's wrong, dear?"

"I still have a million Christmas presents to get, and no time to shop." And, she thought, there are eight cats in that library and it sounds like 52.

"Don't worry about it. I'll help you this afternoon, unless you have other plans."

"Oh, no. Shopping. Deciding on some end-of-year contributions to make my accountant happy. Meeting with the FBI about my hacking issue." To herself, again, wondering how to keep my cats from killing yours.

"Hacking issue? Really, Annie, you do find yourself in some messes. What's this all about?"

"I'm not sure. I know we've been hacked, at least three of the businesses, maybe more, and it's several hundred dollars-worth. Actually, we're into the thousands. So in addition to not having shopped for Christmas, I don't know if I can even afford Christmas."

Annie stopped short. She had not intended to admit that to anyone. Not her mother, not even Chris. Certainly not any of her staff.

Thank goodness Henrie was outside. Well, he probably wouldn't have heard it anyway, over the noise in the library, which kept moving from the front of the room to the back of the room to the front of the room….And thank goodness Cyril wasn't here. He would have been eating Honey Bear tartare.

"Don't say anything about that last part, Mom. I don't want anyone to worry."

"I won't, dear, but you don't have to worry, either, you know."

"I don't? Tell me how that works." Was that a magazine being shredded? A book?

"Well, you see, it's like this. It's called insurance."

"Oh. Oh! I've been so worried I can't see the forest for the trees! Of course! I have insurance! Oh geez, I probably should have called them first!" She cringed at the sound of a heavy object falling to the floor. She didn't hear glass shatter, however.

"I think you'll be fine, dear. Call them now, let them know an investigation is starting. They'll understand. It's probably a police matter anyway. Why the FBI and not Pete?"

"Pete and Janet are visiting her family this week, and anyway, he would have called the FBI even if he was here. By the way, they sent Jeff Bennett. He arrived this morning, and he's going to stay here, in the same room he had last fall." Furniture was now being moved. It sounded like an end table. She wondered which lamp was about to fall to the floor.

"Wonderful! It will be great to see him! Will he be here Christmas day?"

Annie nodded, a bit distracted.

"I'll pick up a present for him this afternoon. We are going to make time to shop, I don't care how many other things you have on your agenda. But first, let Sam and I treat you to lunch. I can't wait to see what Felicity is serving at the Café today."

Annie could not understand why her mother didn't hear the cats in the next room. No matter what, cat sounds didn't seem to register with her. She looked at Nancy with what she hoped was a nonchalant smile. "Should we let Honey Bear get settled into his new home?"

Annie tiptoed carefully into the library, located Honey Bear underneath a coffee table, and got on her knees to pull him out. He was dead weight, not offering any assistance at all as she put her hands around his stomach and pulled.

"You are one difficult cat, Honey Bear. I don't know what my mother sees in you."

After Honey Bear was settled in the carriage house and Nancy and Sam had refreshed themselves, Annie came back to the Inn. "Henrie, we're going to the Café for lunch."

Tiger Lily came running out of the library and meowed furiously.

"Tiger Lily, it's freezing out there! You can't be out in that weather." That did not stop her protests.

"Oh, all right. I'll get a carrier and I'll cover it with something. You have to behave! If I let you out of the carrier at the Café, you cannot go outside! Do you understand?"

Tiger Lily stopped meowing and tapped Annie's right foot.

Annie looked at Tiger Lily. Tiger Lily looked back. Annie shook her head, went to the apartment for the carrier and came back with that and a colorful lap robe in hand. "Get in," she said.

Tiger Lily went in at once. Annie thought, why won't she do this during an emergency?

She covered the carrier with the lap robe, put on her own winter bundling and went to the porch. Nancy and Sam were just arriving. "Let's go!"

At the Café, Tiger Lily jumped out of the carrier and greeted all of the staff, something she would have done on any regular day. On this day, however, everyone was deep in the weeds when she did so. That didn't stop her from trotting into the kitchen to jump onto a prep table, into the server station to jump onto the glasses bar, and into the barista's domain to jump to the service bar.

She was greeted with laughs and pets, and her leaving was followed by swipes with antiseptic wipes.

Nancy, Sam and Annie found a table next to a window. Brrr, thought Annie. But the warmth of the room made up for the cold pane of glass.

Their server, JoJo, a college student working over her holiday vacation, said, "Felicity asked if she could choose what you get today. Is that okay with you?"

"It sure is," said Sam. I have my favorite dishes here, that's for sure, but we'll be here for a month. Plenty of time to try everything."

Trudie came to the table with a tray filled with several short to-go cups of coffee. "I labeled them, and there are two cups of each kind, so you can test a little bit of everything."

The cups held peppermint white chocolate mocha, eggnog latte, gingerbread cookie latte, pumpkin pie latte, and brown sugar and cinnamon white chocolate mocha.

"Are you coming to our Christmas party this evening?" she asked Nancy and Sam.

"Well, I don't know. Sam, what do you think?"

"Remember, Nancy, when I called Frank, he invited us to dinner. Mem will be there, too."

"Oh, I forgot. That's wonderful. We'll have our own plans, and Annie won't have to worry about us our first evening here. So, Trudie, no, we won't be coming."

"Well, at least you're getting a sample of what we'll be having tonight."

"Would it be possible for me to get a carafe of one of these? To share with Frank and Mem?"

"Sure. Just let me know which one you want."

Chris and Cyril walked in the door. He was surprised to see Tiger Lily at the hostess stand, but he gave her a pet and left Cyril to take a nap. Annie could hear him say, "Trudie, when you have time, could you bring me one of your eggnog lattes, please?" as he walked to the table.

Nancy got up to give him a hug. "Chris, it's so good to see you!"

"Nancy, Sam. I hope the roads weren't too bad for you."

Sam said, "They got a little worse the closer we got. You know, it's too cold for salt to work. They have that awful stuff on the roads now. Makes the roads more safe, but it's ruining the car, that's for sure."

Annie asked, "Did you find Blaine?"

"I did. That poor guy was huddled in his shelter, covered in blankets, heater going full speed. I asked him if it was time to call it a day, but he insisted he was fine. He was just going to 'warm up a bit' and then get out again. He hasn't caught the first fish, and I don't think he'll quit until he does. I almost stayed with him just to catch one and put it on his hook. Ray will check on him in an hour or so."

"How is Cyril today?"

"He's about the same." He turned to Sam to say, "I'm dog sitting while Pete is out of town. He likes me, but I'm not his human. I'm just a friend."

"Did he like being on that lake?"

"Not so much. He came out with me, sniffed at the hole, but he was, oh, I would say, timid on that ice."

"Good for him. At least he won't fall in."

All conversation stopped when Felicity arrived, pushing a cart filled with small plates.

"You are going to sample what I'm making for the party tonight. Are you coming, Nancy?"

"No. Sam and I have other plans. So this will be a real treat. It will be just like we're going!"

Felicity started her presentation of small plates for them to share, placing each dish as she named it. "We're going a little nutty this year, because we have a nutcracker theme. So if you don't like nuts, you'll go hungry.

"We've got cauliflower hazelnut soup; it's very creamy. We'll have apples on the side tonight. And this is groundnut stew. If you have a peanut allergy, don't try it. Peanuts are called groundnuts in Africa. This dish has a tomato base, tofu, several spices, and we get the peanut flavor from peanut butter. Sometimes I serve this as a stew with a variety of vegetables. Tonight, it will be creamy."

Felicity moved from soups to sides and entrees. "I didn't make this into the tea sandwiches we're having tonight, but this is a dish of the chicken cashew salad. Here is an apple, fennel, celery and toasted walnut salad; this dish is pistachio crusted chicken with carrot raita, and this is a spread for breads or crackers, it's honey walnut cream cheese.

Sam stopped her for a moment. "What's a raita?"

"The idea comes from India. It's got a yogurt base, and you can add any number of spices or diced fruits and vegetables. This one has carrots, curry, coriander, cumin, cinnamon and ginger."

"For dessert, we have basil honey and walnut gelato, chocolate mousse that can be topped with chopped sugared almonds, and a walnut galette with bourbon-vanilla custard sauce."

Sam stopped her again. "What's a galette?"

"That's my super fancy way of saying tart. Sometimes I like to pretend I'm a chef in France or Switzerland."

Nancy raised a spoonful of walnut galatte to her mouth. "And you promise that all fats and calories have been removed?"

"Cross my heart!"

Sam forced a frown to his face. "Well, if this is all you're having at the party, I'm glad we're missing it!"

Annie laughed. "You don't know what Mr. Bean's, Mo's, and Sassy P's are adding to the mix. I hope Diana will lead us in some fancy yoga steps to help us work it all off."

Chris asked, "What will Mo's bring?"

"George will bring artisan beers, but Cookie wants to show off some of his dishes. I don't know what they are, but I know he's bringing two or three.

Even though they had not seen one another in person in a couple of months, Annie kept up with Nancy and Sam via Skype, and often Chris was with her. It didn't take long to catch up. By the time they made it through the tasting session, with comments about the color, taste and texture, they were ready to move on to the rest of the day.

Chris gave Annie a kiss on the cheek. "I'll meet you at the party tonight, Annie. I need to get some things done at the Station, and I don't want to make you late."

"That's fine. I need to meet Jeff, Marco and Gwen now."

"Jeff?"

"Oh, that's what I forgot to tell you! The FBI sent Jeff Bennett to investigate the hacking. We had one room left, so he's staying at the Inn, and he'll join us on Christmas day, too."

"Great! I'll let Ray know. Maybe they can hook up for dinner this evening."

"Good idea. Mom, I'll call when we're finished."

"That will work. Sam is going to Antiques On Main to help Frank, but I'm going to the Inn to rest up a bit."

Plans made, everyone went on their separate ways. Annie said to Sam, "Wait for me to get Tiger Lily and I'll walk with you. I'm going the same way you are."

Annie got to the sidewalk and looked down the street, keeping an eye on Nancy as she walked to the Inn. Once she had seen Nancy take the turn to the carriage house, she and Sam turned as one to walk up Main Street.

"She looks tired, Sam. Is she okay?"

"She seems tired every now and then, but I think she's alright. I think she just doesn't want to admit that she's getting a little older and she needs to slow down. It will be good to be here, where she doesn't have to take care of everything for a month."

Annie and Sam clutched at one another as they hit a patch of ice. When Sam had a firm footing, he let go of her arm. "You don't see this on your sidewalks."

"No. I have the best snow remover in the business. You'll rarely see him or his crew at work, but every day, every hour if need be, someone is there taking care of it. On both sides of The Avenue. And you may have noticed there are some walkways on the median. If you want to get out and walk around, it will always be safe wherever you are on The Avenue."

By then they had reached Antiques On Main. Annie said good-bye to Sam and went to the next door down. Gwen, Jeff and Marco were waiting for her.

"Sorry. Am I late?"

"No, right on time. These law enforcement types are always a little early. They want to keep you on your toes."

With that, and cups of Gwen's, um, coffee – Annie silently apologized to Gwen for the word she almost thought, even though it would have been silent, swill – they got to work.

Chapter 14: The Person To Whom So Much Was Given

Jeff and Gwen outlined their initial findings, and the four decided on a plan of action.

They looked through all Annie's files, from the Inn to the Café. Marco looked for emails with the wrong address. Annie looked for invoices that looked out of place. Gwen focused on payroll records, using a current staff list provided by Annie, to see if someone that had never been employed was being paid, or if someone no longer employed was still being paid.

Jeff searched social media sites, using a list of Annie's current and recent employees. He did not share his strategies with the others.

Tiger Lily walked cautiously amid the piles of files and papers, stepping only once on each keyboard. Just to make her presence known. Then she sat at the corner of the table next to Gwen's elbow and watched her human and the others as they worked.

They had been working quietly for about a half hour, heads buried in piles of paper and computer monitors, when Gwen's assistant, Mindy, knocked and opened the door.

"Excuse me, Gwen. Someone is here to see you and she won't take 'no' for an answer."

Gwen rose with some reluctance. "Pardon me. I'll take care of this and be right back."

Before she could make it to the door, however, Mindy swung one way and the door swung another. A woman held it, standing purposefully just inside the room, one hand on the door and one on her hip, moving her coat aside in the process.

159

"And of course, the person to whom so much was given is the person who would keep others from conducting their end of year business."

The woman glared at Annie, who looked straight back into those gorgeous eyes. Annie was actually staring, trying to determine the eye color of the day. With a smile on her face and in her voice, she said, "Geraldine. It's so good to see you."

Geraldine was, of course, everything Annie was not. She was tall, svelte and fashionable. Her 'girls' were bigger now than they used to be, and Annie could swear her waist was smaller and her hips a bit more rounded. Her hair was always coiffed just so; her make-up was perfect. Her wrinkles were receding into a face that was not as recognizable as it used to be. And yes, even today, Annie could tell through the open designer coat that Geraldine wore a tailored dress. And good grief. Boots with three inch stiletto heels.

Gwen continued on her path to the door and ushered Geraldine out. Geraldine, who had continued to look into the room, of course recognized Marco, wearing a suit rather than a uniform, and she thought the other man also had something to do with law enforcement, but she couldn't place him.

She noticed the computers on the table and the files, and she was able to see, before being so rudely turned around, that the monitor on the wall was logged into the Café.

"So," she said to Gwen, "problems with the Café? What? Is someone stealing from them? Who is that man in there? I've seen him before, but I can't place him."

"What can I do for you, Geraldine? I thought our appointment was scheduled for next week."

"I didn't think that was quick enough. You know, I need to get all the tax benefit I can for my foundation."

"We'll have to talk about that, Geraldine. I think some of your personal records got mixed in with the foundation, and we'll have to straighten that out. We have time. Plenty of time."

"But if I need to make charitable contributions before the end of the year, we need to get on it."

"And from what funds will you make the contributions?"

"Can't we do something on paper, and take care of it next year?"

"It doesn't work that way, Geraldine. I'm sorry, but I have this conference to get back to."

"I don't see why you can't give me fifteen minutes of your time right now. Certainly they can carry on with – whatever they're doing – without you.

Gwen continued to usher Geraldine with a firm grip on one arm. "I'm sorry. I just can't."

By now she had one hand on the front door and was pulling it open. "I'll see you next week, and have a wonderful holiday."

The door closed, and Geraldine was outside.

Gwen stopped at Mindy's desk. "Did she hurt you?"

"No, I'm fine. I'm sorry she got through."

"You didn't take this job to be a bouncer. Don't worry about it. Sometimes it happens and we just make the best of it. Wait until you've been here through a tax season."

In the conference room, Jeff looked at Annie and asked, "The famous Geraldine Foxglove?"

161

"The same."

Marco, almost under his breath, muttered, "A real piece of work."

Gwen rejoined the group, and they worked for another hour. By that time, their eyes and minds were swimming, but they had made progress.

Gwen found no instances of payroll fraud. Marco found fraudulent emails from impersonators of George, Jesus and Felicity, of which they were already aware, and Carlos, whose business was just beginning to pick up.

Annie layed out all of the questionable receipts from the Café, the Tap and the Winery. Apparently, bad receipts had not yet been issued for the Confectionary. The email in fake-Carlos' name had just come through.

"That's enough for today," said Jeff. "I'm making lots of notes on social media contacts, but I don't want to share it with you just yet."

Marco puffed up. "I think you'd better share, at least with me."

"Not yet, Marco. As soon as I have something definitive, you and I will go through the data together. But until then, I'm going to focus on these four people, and probably the person next in line to them in the business. Let me make sure I've got it. Felicity and Trudie, George and Candice, Carlos and Jerry, and Jesus and Minnie. Is that it?"

"Yes, of the businesses that have some apparent exposure," said Annie. "And probably, Henrie doesn't mess with social media. At least, he doesn't appear to be the sort."

"I'll add him and Diana as well. Now, Annie, you know I did a criminal background check on all of your people."

Annie's chest tightened, knowing what he was going to say. "Yes. And…."

"You know there's a felon in your employ."

"Yes…"

Marco looked at Annie and glared.

"I just wanted to know if you were aware. His background doesn't suggest anything that would lead to cybercrime."

Annie was visibly relieved, but Marco was not.

"You can't just bring felons into town, Annie."

"What makes you think I brought anyone into town, Marco?"

"You have Mexicans working for you."

"Yes, and a Jamaican."

"I'm more concerned about those two Mexicans."

"Two Mexicans?" Annie could think of three.

"Carlos and Jesus."

"Oh. Huh. I could only think of Carlos, a cook at the Café and an assistant baker at Mr. Bean's. And you come up with Jesus."

"Well?"

"Well, Carlos has been a citizen of the United States for several years, and Jesus is pure Californian. His family has lived there for centuries, and he comes from at least three, maybe four generations of large land-owning vintners in California. His family was living in California before it was taken over by our government, which makes him native."

"What about that friend of yours, that flower lady, and the grocery store person."

"You mean Clara and Laila? Clara, who, like Carlos, has been a citizen for several years? And Laila, who has the appropriate documentation to be here and whose children were born here? What about you, Marco? What kind of a name is that? What's your background?"

"I'm pure one hundred percent Italian American."

"How long have your ancestors been here and who let them in?" Annie was clearly tired, cross and acting a little out of character.

Gwen crossed to the space of table between Annie and Marco. "This is not going anywhere good."

"You're right. I'm sorry, Gwen. Marco, I'm sorry. That was a low blow. Unless we're Native Americans, we are all immigrants, some of us more recent than others."

Marco continued to glare at Annie. "You can bet I'll find out who that felon is."

Jeff stopped the conversation by saying, "Gwen, I'm finished with your files for now, unless I uncover something that needs some background. Could I continue to use your spare room for a while?"

Gwen nodded in the affirmative while Jeff continued. "Annie, you're officially out of this investigation until it's over. And Marco, I'll get with you as soon as I have something. Are we good?"

Annie put the carrier next to Tiger Lily, who had spent the last several minutes at Annie's side. She looked up at Annie, blinked her eyes, and then walked into the carrier.

Annie covered it and said, "Jeff, are you going back to the Inn? If so, I'll walk part-way with you."

As they walked, Annie said, "Chris said he was going to let Ray know you're in town. You might want to give him a call if you'd like company for dinner. Chris and I have my company Christmas party tonight, or I'd invite you to join us."

"Thanks, Annie. I noticed a message come through from Ray. That's probably what it's about."

"I'm sorry I got cross in there. Marco didn't deserve that."

"Marco did deserve that, so no problem with me whatsoever."

The Café had closed early to get ready for the party, and L'Socks' was closed as well. Annie walked with Jeff as far as Mo's Tap. "I'll leave you here, Jeff. See you later."

As soon as she stepped into the door, she let Tiger Lily out, pulled out her cell phone and called her mother.

"I have time for maybe two shops today, and I thought I'd stop at the flower shop and the drug store. Which one do you want to do first?"

"Let's go to The Drug Store first, then we can spend lots of time at Bloomin' Crazy."

"Okay. I'll do a quick walk through the businesses and I'll be at your place in about fifteen minutes."

Annie hung up and walked to the end of the bar. Candice was there, making drinks that had to be going to a table in the corner, because no one else was present. "The guests miss Mo. Little miss hot-to-trot keeps asking about him."

"Is that her in the corner?"

"Yeah. She was sitting at the bar, but when Geraldine came in, they went to a table. Oh, well, it looks like Tiger Lily is trying to make up for Mo. She just jumped to their table."

Annie turned to look. "Oh, my. I wonder if Tiger Lily needs glasses. She hates Geraldine. But Geraldine and Christal are friends?"

"Yeah. Geraldine is her aunt or something. Little hotty is from Marsh Haven, but every now and then she comes here to stay with sweet Aunt Geraldine for a while. At least, that's what I gather."

"Interesting. Where's George?"

"He's back in the kitchen right now. I think he's hiding."

"Hiding?"

"Right after little miss neckline-down-to-there came in today, George asked me to take the bar because he had something to do, and I haven't seen him since."

"Candice, you're going to have to disguise how much you like this woman. People are going to wonder."

Candice narrowed her eyes, turned and walked to the table with the fresh drinks.

Annie considered going into the kitchen but remembered how Cookie liked to keep his distance. And perhaps he wanted those dishes to be a complete surprise. So she called Tiger Lily, put her in the carrier and left.

At Mr. Bean's, she left Tiger Lily in the carrier until frantic meows changed her mind. She let the girl out and asked Carlos how the day had gone.

"We were busy this morning. Lots of pre-orders for holiday parties. We'll have the same thing tomorrow. Other than that, we've had very few walk-ins."

Carlos looked over the counter at Tiger Lily. "Huh. I've never seen her do that before."

Tiger Lily appeared to be dancing in front of the pet treats display. She put her front paws on the glass, sniffed, moved down a bit, using her hind legs to walk while she walked her front paws on the glass, sniffed, walked again, sniffed, then she looked up to see Carlos and Annie looking down. She quickly sat, staring up at them with implacable eyes.

Carlos reached into the case and pulled out a cat treat. "This is our best seller, Tiger Lily. Let me know what you think."

He handed it to Annie, who reached down to place it at Tiger Lily's feet. Tiger Lily picked it up and took it to the carrier, which she entered after one look back at them.

Annie and Carlos exchanged raised eyebrows, and Annie moved on.

At Sassy P's, once again she let Tiger Lily roam free for a few minutes. Jeff had stopped here, and he was drinking a glass of something dark red, nearly purple. "What have you got, Jeff?"

"Rhapsody!"

"Really. That good?"

"That's the name, and it is that good!"

"This is the first time I've heard of it."

Minnie came to their end of the bar, "That's because we've not served it to you. We will tonight, though. This is the wine we're featuring at our parties this week."

"Can I try it?"

"No, ma'am. Not until tonight."

"You see how they treat me, Jeff."

"I see. Such a problem for you."

"Yes indeed. Minnie, I know you're getting things ready for the party. I'm just making sure everyone sees my face this afternoon at least for a minute, but now I need to go shopping with my mother."

"Are you just now getting to your Christmas shopping?"

"No comment."

"Annie, this is worse than last year. And this year, all of your family will be here. You can't make the excuse that the mail held up the gifts."

"I know." Annie sighed. When I was put together, they forgot to add the shopping gene. Minnie, see you later. Jeff, have a great evening."

"Tiger Lily!" she called. Nothing. "Lily?" Nothing. Annie looked around the display room. She wasn't there. Minnie looked around behind her bar; she wasn't there. Annie and Minnie went into other rooms, Annie to the patio and Minnie to the kitchen/storeroom.

Annie finally found her underneath the sink at the tasting bar. She was peering behind the heater into the hole from which the pipe came. Then she jumped up to take a drink from the small stream of water, holding onto the tap with a paw and leaning into the flow of water with her mouth, little tongue working overtime.

"I'm sorry, big girl. Let's get you home to your food and water." Annie picked her up and carried her to the front window, where she had left the case. "Bye!" She was out the door, walking the half block to the front porch of the Inn.

Inside, she opened the carrier, let Tiger Lily out and yelled to Henrie that she was going shopping with her mother.

Henrie was in the library and came right out. "I am glad you have returned. The temperature has dropped even more. Are you sure you want to take your mother out in this?"

"She wants to go. I'm going to hold on to her."

"Good. We will bundle her up, she will still freeze, and when you both fall you can both break your frozen bones. Keep your cellphone on you at all times."

Annie smiled but was worried all the same. It was getting more and more bitter, and the wind had kicked up. She thought to ask, "Have you heard from Blaine this afternoon?"

"Yes. Ray followed him in just a half hour ago. I do not think he will go out this evening. That will be the second evening in a row, and he was so counting on some evening fishing."

"I'm glad he's getting some sense," said Annie. "How were the kids today?"

"Especially quiet. Perhaps they are now used to being at home during a work day."

"Perhaps," she smiled as she walked out the door.

Henrie looked at the pile of cats in the library. Kali and Ko were not there. Unusual. They had been sticking with their siblings while everyone was home. Perhaps they had grown tired of the large group, as they were used to being alone so much of the time.

Annie and Nancy, appropriately bundled for the wind that now seemed to chill their very bones, entered The Drug Store. It was unusual to see both of the sisters, Jennifer and Marie, behind the counter. Both nurse practitioners, they owned and operated The Drug Store and The Clinic.

Natives of Chelsea, they got the education they needed to remain in this resort community. Their services were indispensable, as no doctors had a practice in town. Through The Clinic they provided wellness and emergency care, and the drug store was well-provisioned for a small town.

As they entered, Annie and Nancy shook off the cold air. "Why are both of you here? Is The Clinic closed?"

"We don't have any appointments for the rest of the week, so we closed it. People know to come here, and of course, we're always on call," said Jennifer.

Marie said, "It's good to see you, Nancy. I hear you're going to be with us for a while."

"For a month, at least," said Nancy, and I'm starting to reacquaint myself with The Avenue today!"

"Well, good for you! You've started at the right place. Are you just visiting, or do you need something?"

"My daughter is just now starting her Christmas shopping, and she insists she is going to buy local."

"Interesting. How many people on your list, Annie? And what ages?"

"About a million, from birth to, um, older."

"It's okay, dear. You can say 'elderly.' If the shoe fits, so to speak."

"So, besides the regular items you find in a drug store, like drugs," started Marie, "and vitamins," added Jennifer, "we have diet products," "personal care items and beauty products," "skin care," "an aisle with seasonal items for the home," "but I don't know, Annie," "yeah, I don't know."

Annie loved the way the two sisters worked together to complete their thoughts and sentences.

They started up again. "We have massagers," "candles," "aromatherapy vaporizers and oils," yoga mats and fitness monitors," "let's not forget sexual enhancers and condoms," "no, we might want to forget those," "okay," "cameras," "pet toys…" "I think we've just about covered it." "Yep. You're right. Covered." "Nope. Gift certificates. You could get gift certificates." "Now we've covered it."

Jennifer looked at Annie and said, "Did anything sound like a present for anyone on your list?"

"No…but I might come back after Christmas to do some shopping for myself."

"Oh, Annie," said Nancy, "go ahead and get whatever caught your fancy. I won't tell."

Annie laughed. Then she thought a little more about it. "I might think about gift certificates." The four women chatted some more, and they said their good-byes.

Moving on, they went to Bloomin' Crazy, a flower and gift shop. The shop owner, Clara, was an attractive woman with jet black hair pulled straight back into a braid that wrapped around her head. She always had a bright red tropical flower of some sort behind her ear. This time of year, it was made of silk.

Clara was bloomin' crazy herself. She hailed from Haiti and spoke with a French lilt, the lilt becoming more pronounced the more excited she became. And she was excited. "Nancy! It's so good to see you! A ray of sunshine in this icy wasteland"

Nancy laughed, "Clara, tell me again why you moved to this state?"

"I want to be reminded, every year, what I love about summer. This winter, we've already received far too many reminders. And what are the two of you doing out on this lovely afternoon?"

"My daughter. She is just now starting her Christmas shopping."

"Nu-uh. No. Do you know when Christmas is? It is this week, right? Did I miss something?"

"This week."

"Well, I'm pretty sure you don't want flowers, probably not even balloon bouquets, unless you're taking things around to the hospitals. So let's take a look at some of my new items."

"I heard you had new stuff," said Annie, looking around for a new display. Then she saw it. In front of the window were several display cases of jewelry. "No! You didn't!" she cried.

"I did. Come look."

Annie said, "I'm shopping for other people, not for me!"

"Are women on your list? Girls?"

"Yes…but jewelry is so personal…oh, Mom, look at this ring!" Annie was holding a ring with a large pink stone, smaller, sparkly stones around it. "It fits. And this!" Now she had a choker necklace with various hues of purple, blue and pink, with matching earrings.

"Annie, come look at these. They're interchangeable." Nancy was standing at a display case of jewel stones. Behind the case were hangers of necklaces and bracelets, clearly made to fit the jewel stones. "Here are some with cats."

"I'm not buying for me."

"Other people like cats."

Annie, Nancy and Clara looked through the jewelry for several minutes, each of them finding pieces to intrigue and delight.

Finally, Annie said, "I can't stand it. Look at me. I'm trying to shop for about a million people, and the only things I can find are things I want for me!"

Clara said, "You know, you could get gift certificates."

"Jennifer and Marie suggested the same thing. If I can't come up with any ideas by Friday, I'll do that. Thanks, Clara. Mom, get me out of here."

"Bye, Clara! See you soon!"

"You too, Nancy. Annie, enjoy your party tonight."

"Oh! The party tonight! I knew I wanted to ask you something!"

"What's that?"

"May I borrow your heated wagon tonight? I want to take the kids, but it's so cold. They shouldn't be walking, but I couldn't possibly handle seven carriers."

"Sure, you can. I'm bringing your flowers over tomorrow, so I'll need it back by noon or so."

"Sure thing. Thanks, Clara." Annie went to the storeroom and came out, pulling a large red wagon, as opposed to the little red wagon she had as a child. A resin hood with a hinged top covered the wagon. Clara had invested in the hood because her best customer wanted fresh flowers in each of her businesses every week.

The wagon could be used with or without the hood. When the hood was on, a little heater fitted to the back end of the wagon could be turned on, keeping flowers protected for a trip across The Avenue. Or, as Annie was preparing to use it, keeping cats protected for a trip up the street.

As Annie and Nancy left, Clara called out, "You let me know how that trip goes. I'd like a picture of the seven of them inside that thing."

"One step at a time, Clara. One step at a time. First we solve the problem, then we get the cats to buy in."

She and Nancy left, this time walking straight into the wind as they tucked their heads forward, walking arm in arm to the Inn.

Chapter 15: No! Don't Put Me In The Trash!

Henrie had convinced Sam and Nancy to allow him to cook dinner, keeping them from having to go out in the bitter cold another time. In private, he reasoned that Frank and Mem were younger and a fall would not be so devastating. He would never say it to Nancy or Sam.

To them, he said, "I have pot roast, potatoes, carrots, onions, any spice or seasoning you desire, and a power pressure cooker. Dinner will be ready in one half hour, and what could be better on a cold night?"

As he and Nancy worked together on setting the table and preparing what was going to be a feast, Sam helped Annie get ready to go to the party.

He didn't have to help her get dressed. He had to help her corral the cats.

When they had completed this little task, they collapsed on the sofa in the library. Sam said, "This was worse than getting them to the safe space last fall."

"It was," she responded. "I think I have to go upstairs and change."

"You look fine."

"I feel like I've been run over by a lawnmower."

"You look fine."

"Oh, well. Everyone else will have hat hair. Maybe I'll fit right in. If I don't leave right now, I'll be late."

In the foyer they heard the plaintive cries of seven cats. Annie felt like a monster.

She knew her staff would be disappointed to have a party without them. She knew she'd pay if the cats realized they had missed a fun time. She had done everything in her power to make this go smoothly.

She put a soft blanket in the wagon; she put some favorite toys in the corners. She and Sam found them all in the library, and she closed the door before they had time to be scared about what was coming. Then the real fun began.

Annie would never understand how they communicated with one another, or what they communicated. If she knew this, things would go more easily.

For example, had she known *"Ick! Ick! Ick! Hiss!"* in an upper register meant, *"They're going to put us in that trash can!"* she could have countered with a calming sentence. Something like this. "That's not a trash can, sweetheart. It's a chariot especially sent to take you to the Christmas party."

Instead, she and Sam had to do their best with their limited knowledge of the situation.

First, each cat had to be caught. At least once.

Then they had to be held in such a way that four sets of claws couldn't find purchase on a human body part.

The hardest thing was getting them into the hinged opening, because the four legs held away from human bodies could so easily grab the sides of the opening, thereby preventing an easy insert.

And while one cat was going in, three more could get out. Which accounted for having to catch some of them more than once.

Finally, all seven were inside. You would think they were sitting in a vat of acid.

When Sam and Annie felt well enough to stand up, they went to the dining room. Annie asked Henrie if he had seen Blaine. "I have not. He said he would be going out to eat tonight, and I suggested he go somewhere close again, given the snow coming down once more. He must have taken the suggestion. His truck is still here."

Nancy said, "I'm sure you've told me, but once again, who is Blaine?"

Annie looked at her mother, gave her a hug and said, "He's just a guest, Mom. I'm glad you're here. I'm looking forward to Christmas." And then she tucked her head so no one would see the tear, grabbed the wagonload of prisoners left for the Café.

She hoped they were warm inside the wagon. The frigid wind whipped at her face, arms and legs, making the trip up the sidewalk difficult and uncomfortable. At least three times she turned to the wagon, mostly to get her face out of the wind, but also to say to the cats, "I hope you're comfortable. You have a heater. Do you know how nice I am to you?"

Annie finally reached the Café and entered through the back door. She pulled the wagon into the elevator with her. There was no way she was going to let the cats out on the ground level tonight. She would never catch them.

Felicity had already made a bed for the kids, in case they tired of the festivities. In a corner overlooking The Avenue was a pile of cushions. The windows were low enough they could see out from their bed.

By now, the cats were quiet. They were probably terrified, thought Annie. But then again, maybe they finally realized where they were and why they were there.

Annie took the wagon to the corner with the cushions and opened the hinged lid. No one came out. She looked in. Seven sets of eyes stared out, a combination of outrage (Little

Socks), fear (Kali and Ko), curiosity (Sassy Pants and Mr. Bean), anticipation (Mo) and inscrutability (Tiger Lily).

"Okay. Stay in there. The fun, the food, and all the people will be out here." She smiled at them, took a chance at putting her hand in to pet each little head, leaving Little Socks for last. She was pleased to come away with no scratches or bites. Times like this, it was a fifty/fifty proposition.

"I'm going to help Felicity and Trudie, okay? Make yourselves at home. It's a Christmas party!"

Trudie and Felicity carried a low coffee table to the corner. It was decorated with a nutcracker-themed tablecloth. They left it near the cushions, each of them looking into the wagon to smile and say, "Merry Christmas, kids!"

Annie looked around the room. There were nutcrackers everywhere, of every size and style. She noticed the six-foot tall nutcracker in the corner. "Where did you find this guy, Felicity? And frankly, where did you find all the rest of them?"

"Clara heard about our nutcracker theme and suggested she call a friend of hers with an interior design shop. She got all of these on loan. Free. We just have to get them back tomorrow."

"You guys are doing all of this work. I need to help out more."

Felicity and Trudie together protested. Trudie finally won out. "You do enough, Annie, in so many other ways. And really, do you want to micromanage?"

"Nope! Happy now. Thank you!" Silently, she made a note to herself to thank Clara later.

Trudie and Felicity were nearly finished setting up the food and drinks tables, but Annie helped them with the final touches. She placed wooden bowls of mixed in-shell nuts throughout the room. Each bowl sat next to a variety of functional – rather than decorative – nutcrackers.

She noticed the cheeses and crackers were already here from Sassy P's, and the breads, pastries and candies from Mr. Bean's were nestled in with the other foods.

Then she noticed the iced barrels with artisan beers and white wine. She looked more closely. The white was a chardonnay, one she recalled as being especially buttery.

Next to the iced bins was another table with red wine bottles. Rhapsody, from a winery called Whyte Horse in Indiana. So this was the wine Jeff thought lived up to its name. She asked, "Are we serving yet?"

"NO!" came the chorus from everyone else setting up.

Several large carafes of coffee were on the next table, marked with Trudie's offerings.

When the elevator opened again, it was Cookie. He pushed a cart with three warming bins. Annie kept a respectful distance, recalling his reticence around her. After he chatted with Felicity, set out his foods and left, Annie ambled over. "May I see?"

Felicity said, "More than that, here's a plate with your samples."

"Oh, yum! Tell me what I'm eating."

"Bite sized pieces of salmon. They're baked and they have a crunchy pecan crust. And this is honey walnut shrimp, obviously with an oriental flair.

"And in keeping with small portions tonight, he made tubettini pasta with tomato, walnut and basil sauce. The sauce could go on any pasta, really, and after today, he's going to try it with penne."

Annie took a bite. "There's spinach in here," she said.

"Yes, and the perfect blend of garlic and other spices."

"He's a gem in the rough."

"You're right about that. I hope he's happy in Chelsea. Otherwise, he'll be headed for bigger places in bigger towns."

Trudie came out of the elevator, a covered tray in her hands. "I almost forgot the most important dish," she said. She opened the cover and Annie saw pet treats. There were candy caned-styled red and green bones for dogs, and green mice and red fish for cats. Trudie took the tray to the low table by the cushions, set it down, picked up a couple of pieces and waved them in the air over the wagon.

That got their attention. Seven cats poked curious heads out, looked around, placed the treat table in their point of reference, and one by one, Mr. Bean in the lead, they came out of the wagon.

By now, others started to arrive. Some came in shifts, from Mo's Tap and Sassy P's Wine and Cheese. Others came in full force, from the Café, Lil' Socks' Virasana and Mr. Bean's Confectionary. Henrie, of course, came as soon as Nancy and Sam's dinner was prepared.

Most brought guests, husbands, wives, girlfriends, boyfriends, just-a-friends. Even those coming in shifts, coming from work or having to go back to work, came with a guest in hand. For the most part, when the employee went back to work, the guest stayed.

The cats mingled with everyone, sat to enjoy a treat on occasion and happily feasted on crumbs from human food that fell to the floor.

Annie enjoyed spending the evening with those with whom she had chosen to spend her life. She spent extra time with the staff she didn't always have occasion to interact, the servers, cooks, assistant bakers and candy makers, yoga instructors.

The year before, she had started a Christmas tradition, presenting a Christmas ornament in the theme of the party with a bonus check to each employee.

In a large basket in one corner were more than enough nutcrackers to go around. They were all about ten inches high and made of wood. But there, the similarity stopped.

There were nutcrackers styled as gingerbread men, Santas, elves and snowmen. There were typical nutcrackers with brown fur hats, black bear hats or white fur hats. There were tall skinny nutcrackers in pink, turquoise, purple or multicolored vestments.

There were blue glitter kings, pink glitter queens, nutcrackers dressed in tiger prints and leopard prints. There were butchers, bakers, candlestick makers, football players, baseball players, and soccer players.

Before the night was over, every employee would choose one to suit their particular personality.

She greeted everyone, and to everyone with the exception of those she worked with daily, she gave an envelope. With each envelope handed over, she said, "Happy holidays, and thank you, from the bottom of my heart."

No one missed the party.

Next year, thought Annie, I'll have to add those that work for us on contract. Gwen, Boone and Harriet. Then she wondered if purchasing flowers from Clara on a weekly basis made her a contract employee. Then there were the venders. And Mem. Mem did a lot for them, including the website and social media. Oh my, she thought. Too much to consider right now.

Chris arrived with Cyril only a half hour after others started to arrive. For the most part, Chris stayed away from Annie, knowing she wanted to spend personal time with everyone and that she had gifts to hand out.

Cyril, once he lifted his head from its now perpetual downcast look, made a beeline toward the cushion corner and the table of treats. He took two treats in his mouth and lay on the cushions, taking up most of the space. There he stayed for an hour or more.

The cheeses and breads were familiar to Annie, and throughout the day she had tasted everything else offered to eat and drink with the exception of the candies, the beers and the Rhapsody. Tonight, she tried each of the candies, and then, with enough food calories to satisfy three days' minimum requirement, she enjoyed the Rhapsody.

Jesus presented it with an explanation. "This comes from a small winery in northern Indiana called Whyte Horse. The wine is a complex blend of sangiovese, cabernet sauvignon and zinfandel.

"No wonder I like it," said Annie. "I want to have some on hand for Christmas day."

She turned to George, "The next time I have a pizza, you're my guy. Until then, I'm in the hands of Jesus and his dry reds."

Before the evening was over, a group of at least twenty people tried to get Diana to lead them in a calorie-burning yoga routine. Diana took one look at the group, estimated the amount of alcohol inside each one, and politely declined.

Diana left before the party was over, saying the morning would start too early if she stayed to the end. Annie figured she was escaping the madding crowd.

Cyril was finally coaxed from the cushions and led around the room by Tiger Lily. He accepted human food treats, pets and accolades. Feeling a bit better, when he went to the cushions again, he was able to nap with a lighter heart.

At some point throughout the evening, each cat found his or her special people and received accolades for their services, admissions of how much they had been missed, hugs, kisses and pets.

Carlos picked up Mr. Bean and gave him a special hug. When Carlos put the boy down, he asked him to do the dance. Mr. Bean looked up at Carlos, then down at the floor, sadly. He turned around and left, tail trailing on the floor behind him. Carlos felt an indescribable sadness as he watched Mr. Bean walk away.

Eventually, seven cats and one dog were on the cushions, cuddled up and wide awake. They had much to discuss.

Tiger Lily asked, *"Are you still sad, Cyril?"*

"Pete hasn't come back for me."

Mr. Bean snuggled into Cyril's chest. *"But Chris is being good to you, isn't he?"*

"It's not the same."

Little Socks gave a snort. *"I'll tell you what's not the same. "That hateful Uncle Honey Bear is back."*

"No!" exclaimed Cyril.

Little Socks continued. *"I wish you had been there this morning. He got there a little while after you left. You could have squished him."*

"Kicked him!" "Bit him!" said Kali and Ko together.

"Trill!"

Cyril looked shocked. *"No, I wouldn't eat him. Yuck. All that yellow hair!"*

Tiger Lily looked at Kali and Ko. *"We haven't had a chance to talk. What were the two of you doing this afternoon?"*

They answered, of course, together. *"We went to see that Blaine guy." "That Blaine guy isn't so bad after all."*

"What's up with him? He seems a little strange."

Together, they answered. *"At first he threw nuts at us." "He seemed really weird at first."*

They looked at one another, then continued. *"Now I know he's just sad." "He cries when he's alone."*

Sassy Pants sat up. *"What's wrong wif him?"*

Ko looked at Kali, giving her permission to tell the story. *"That's why we went upstairs. We hoped we would find out. He called his Mommy when he went upstairs, but we didn't understand what he was saying."*

Cyril was still the expert in evidence collection. *"Pete always says to just say exactly what the person said. If you tell it just as you heard it, we can all learn something. So tell us what he said."*

This time Kali looked to Ko, who continued. *"He said he was fishing now, freezing his butt off on the ice and in that wind and was she happy now."*

Kali cut in, *"But we looked, and his butt was still there. He hasn't lost it yet."*

Little Socks put her forehead to the floor and pressed, willing herself to be silent.

Cyril noticed this but ignored it. Instead, he looked back at Kali and Ko. *"Did he say anything else?"*

"Something about maybe he was stupid."

"It was 'I'll show you. I'm not completely stupid.'"

Tiger Lily, confused and concerned at the same time, said, *"What do you think he's going to do? What's he going to show her?"*

Kali and Ko shook their heads, shrugged their shoulders and looked at one another. *"We're going to pay more attention to him." "We'll check on him tonight and at breakfast."*

Tiger Lily decided to coordinate their efforts. *"There are more of us at home now. Who wants to help?"*

Mo said, *"Trill!"*

Little Socks started to laugh so hard she lost her balance and tumbled down the cushions a little. When she caught herself, she looked at Mo and said, *"Even I understood that. You like women, and not only that, usually men don't pay any attention to you."*

"Trill!"

Kali and Ko started to laugh now, so Sassy Pants translated Mo's statement. *"Mo sez anybody would like him better than Socks and if she dudn't shut up he will bites her tail. Off. Maybe he bites her tail. Maybe he bites it off."*

Little Socks gave a low *"Hiss!"*

"That's enough. Let's talk about the important things that are happening."

"What's happening?" asked Mr. Bean.

"We need Cyril's expertise," said Tiger Lily. *"This is what I was able to figure out today. Jeff Bennett is here because there's another bad thing happening. Somebody is stealing from Mommy and George and Jesus and Felicity."*

"*Trill!*" exclaimed Mo.

Kali and Ko together said, "*Not Henrie?*" "*Is Henrie okay?*"

Little Socks just looked at Tiger Lily more intensely.

Cyril, taking on the role of someone-with-expertise, said, "*Tell us everything.*"

Tiger Lily told them everything she learned at Gwen's office. She ended with, "*It's someone that knows all of them or at least one of them and it's someone that is good with that computer stuff.*"

Cyril, who had remained quiet through Tiger Lily's recitation, asked, "*And Marco was there?*"

"*Yes. He was mean. He said bad things about Carlos and Jesus and Clara and Laila.*"

Sassy Pants and Mr. Bean both jumped up. "*Not Carlos!*" "*Not Jesus!*"

"*Mommy said bad things to him. She got him to shut up, but I think he still doesn't like them. And someone named felon. He doesn't like that person.*"

"*Who's that?*" asked Little Socks.

Once again, Cyril had the answer. "*That's not a person, it's a type of person. Someone who committed a crime. A bad crime, usually.*"

"*Who is it?*" asked Mr. Bean, getting excited. He was thinking, *I can be a hero again!*

Tiger Lily said, "*If that's what it means, I think I know who it is. I think it's Jerry.*"

Mr. Bean was outraged. "*You're mean!*"

"*I didn't mean that in a bad way, Mr. Bean, but we all know about Jerry. He was in prison. That doesn't make him a bad man. It means he did something and he had to go away for a while. But he learned how to make all of that candy there, and Mommy likes him a lot. Mommy wouldn't tell Marco who it was.*"

Cyril looked thoughtful. *"Pete needs to know that Marco is involved. He will screw it up, whatever it is."*

"I think that's why Mommy wanted that Jeff Bennett guy to come. I think she thinks Jeff will fix it up right."

Cyril looked at each cat in turn. *"All of us need to keep our eyes and ears open. That was a lot for one day, Tiger Lily. Did you see anything else?"*

Tiger Lily rolled her eyes. *"Geraldine."*

"Trill!"

Little Socks gave another *"Hiss!"*

Kali and Ko said together, and, for once, perfectly in sync, *"What is that witch doing now?"* But unfortunately, they mispronounced the word 'witch.'

Tiger Lily bopped both of them on the nose for their mistake. Then she continued, *"She came into Gwen's office and tried to see what we were doing. Then she went to Mo's and she had a drink with that redhead that goes ga-ga over you."* She cut an accusing look at Mo.

"Trill!"

She looked around at the likely interpreters. Cyril responded. *"It's not his fault that she likes him, but she gives good pets."* Cyril looked at Tiger Lily and asked, *"What did the two of them talk about?"*

"When we got there, they had been talking for a while, probably a long time, but I heard Geraldine say, 'be careful, you don't know what you're getting involved in.'"

None of the cats liked people who pretended to be something they weren't, but Little Socks particularly didn't like Geraldine. *"I hope Geraldine is doing something she can be arrested for. This time."*

Six cats and one dog nodded agreement.

Tiger Lily wasn't finished. *"At the wine shop there was a pipe that looked like it was being fixed. I could smell Boone and a man that works for him; I think it was Daryl. They cut a big hole in the wall. Lots bigger than the pipe. What could that be for, Cyril?"*

"You can hide things in holes. Or the hole could go to another building. Sometimes people can go from one building to another through holes like that."

Tiger Lily looked at Sassy Pants and Mr. Bean. *"The hole goes into Mr. Bean's. The two of you are going to have to keep an eye on things when we get back to work."*

Sassy Pants and Mr. Bean looked at one another, then back to Tiger Lily. Each gave a solemn nod.

Tiger Lily looked around the group. *"There's one more thing we need to keep an eye on."* Because of her solemn tone, she had their complete attention. *"There might be something wrong with Grandmommy."*

Shocked faces stared back at her. There wasn't a sound. Finally, Cyril said, *"Tell us everything."*

"I don't know what it is. She's tired. Grandpoppy said she gets tired a lot. Mommy is worried. I could feel it."

Six cats promised to be good to her.

Cyril said, *"I'll help you keep an eye on her. We'll figure it out."*

By the end of their conversation, Cyril was feeling much like his old self. He was helping. He still had several good friends. Certainly Pete would come back and take care of Marco. And Chris wasn't a bad sort. He was pleasant, actually. He just wasn't Cyril's human.

At the end of the evening, Annie and Chris helped the managers clean up. It was the standard crew by now, minus Diana, as all of the business were closed. Felicity and Trudie, George and Candice, Carlos and Jerry, Jesus and Minnie, and Henrie.

They laughed. They tripped over seven cats and one dog trying to 'help.' They ate a little more. They gave a few more treats to the companions. They drank a little more.

Finally, someone broke out in song and the room was suddenly filled with off-tune voices augmented by cat and dog howls in an attempt to sing several Christmas carols.

And then, it was time to go. Chris said, "Cyril! Let's go home!" Cyril bounced up and down.

The cats went into the wagon quickly and calmly.

Annie pulled the wagon into the elevator, and they went down and out into the cold, cold night. Annie and Chris, Cyril, and seven cats in a wagon.

Cyril bounded out the door and down the sidewalk. By the time he reached the Confectionary, he realized his mistake. Chris meant "home," as in his home. Not the home of his own human.

Once again, he hung his head while waiting for Chris, Annie and the cats to catch up. He followed behind, determined to come up with a plan to find his human or die trying.

Chapter 16: Annie Wanted To Sleep In

Annie wanted to sleep in the next morning, but she knew the day held too many obligations.

By 8:00, she and seven cats joined Nancy, Sam and Blaine Jones in the dining room. Henrie, replenishing the tray of meats – bacon, apple-pork link sausage and thick slices of ham – took a minute to give Annie a message.

"Jeff has already left to go to Gwen's. He said he would call if he had any questions."

Tiger Lily looked suspiciously at Nancy and Sam, wondering if the dreaded Uncle Honey Bear was now in the house. She sent Sassy Pants and Mr. Bean on a scouting mission. They came back to report he was nowhere to be found. The cats relaxed.

Annie looked at Blaine. "You know it's still drop dead cold out there. It still feels like the Arctic. Are you planning to go back out today?"

"Yes I am. I promised Mother I was going to fish, and that's exactly what I will do."

Nancy looked at Sam, then at Annie, then at Blaine. "I don't want to pry, young man, but if you were my child, I would hope you were fishing because that's what you wanted and not something you thought I wanted on your behalf."

Blaine concentrated on a pumpkin Danish.

Annie pushed a little more. "So, do you really want to be out there on a day like today?"

"I heard it would be warmer today."

"Warmer, yes, but still windy, and there is a threat of some snow coming in today."

"It will be invigorating."

Annie believed this was becoming his mantra. She shook her head. "Blaine, this is the kind of weather that invites frostbite or hypothermia."

"I'm being careful. I have layers, blankets, a heater and shelter. The tent can be quite warm when the wind isn't so brisk."

While they talked and ate, Kali, Ko and Mo seemed quite solicitous of their guest. Kali sat on the dining room table, her tail softly curved around the stem of Blaine's water glass. Ko sat under the table; one soft paw rested on Blaine's shoe. Mo, typically a lady's man, took the chair next to Blaine. He lay on his back; his long, fluffy tail swished up and down over Blaine's leg.

When Blaine finished his breakfast, he sipped coffee and again, at first tentatively then with more confidence, stroked Kali's back from shoulders to haunches, over and over.

Kali purred and curled her head back and forth.

Nancy said, "She likes you."

Annie smiled to herself, turning her head so Blaine would not see it.

Blaine continued to stroke Kali and used his other hand to scratch Mo's stomach. "You know, Kali and Ko came to my room yesterday afternoon, and when I woke up this morning, they were in my bed, along with this big guy here. Maybe I'll get a cat or two when I go home."

Annie couldn't help but be concerned about Blaine. If the cats were paying that kind of attention to him, they were concerned as well. "Will Chris be out again this morning to check on you?"

"I don't think so. I told him I was going to be fine and that he should do what he needs to do at the Coast Guard station."

"You know, you could spend today doing other things. You could go to the lighthouse or the Coast Guard station, do some antiquing, check out the local restaurants, or even stay here where it's warm and watch a movie or read a book."

"Mother thinks I should fish, so that's what I'm going to do."

Nancy, realizing that Annie was dangerously close to becoming a mother hen, decided to change the subject. "Annie, your sister should be here early this afternoon. Why don't we go shopping this morning."

"Good idea. I have to take Clara's wagon back to her, then I was thinking we could visit Laila at Babar Foods and the twins at the hardware store."

Sam weighed in on his plans for the day. "You don't need me underfoot when the rest of the family arrives. I'm going to spend the day at Antiques On Main. Tomorrow's the big day!"

As Blaine left the table, Annie went to the kitchen to call Chris. "He's going out again, and he said he told you not to worry about him."

"That's what he said. On the one hand, I want to treat him like an adult. He can't be more than ten years younger than me. But on the other…I think I'll stop out in an hour or so. Most of the regulars have left the lake by now, either because of the weather or the holiday. It might be empty with the exception of him today."

"Chris, I'm sorry to ask you to go out in this cold."

"My work choices are to take a cutter out on the lake for a run or send someone else to take the run. I'm going to exercise some common sense and the seniority of my position and send someone else. I'll have time to check on Blaine."

Annie thanked him and hung up.

Annie was very happy Boone kept the sidewalks clear, because she could walk swiftly and still keep her head down, out of the wind. She delivered the wagon to Clara and came back to the Inn to get her mother.

Arm in arm, they crossed The Avenue to Babar Foods. The grocery store, typically chilly, seemed like a furnace after their short walk.

Annie didn't have time to say hello to Laila, because Laila ran to Nancy, hugged her tight and started talking to her like a long lost daughter.

"I am so happy to see you, Nancy, and you'll be here for a month! We're going to have to spend some time together. We can talk about Annie and come up with plans to fix her life."

"Oh, Laila, if you have any influence on her at all, I would be so thankful! Let's work on that marital status first."

"Yes. Let's. We have to get her out of that I-can-live-by-myself thinking habit."

Annie knew they were joking. Okay, she thought they were joking. Well, it was possible that they were joking on the outside but they really meant it on the inside. No matter what, she decided enough was enough.

"You guys have all month to discuss my future. Laila, Mom is trying to help me out of my Christmas shopping disaster. You can tell it's a disaster, because I have gotten only one gift on a list that's a bazillion long, and I'm standing in a grocery store."

Laila gaped. When a few seconds had passed, she closed her mouth, looked at Annie, looked at Nancy, looked back at Annie, and said, "I knew it was bad. I didn't know it was this bad. What kind of present could you actually buy in my place?"

Nancy tried to help. "She's decided – late, obviously – that she wants to buy local. And local, to her, means on The Avenue first, elsewhere in Chelsea second, and on that computer with extreme special delivery third."

Laila thought for a few seconds more then offered her best suggestion. I could give you gift certificates. For the people that live around here, not your family, you could give certificates for either groceries or party trays, even some of my nutrition training programs."

"The idea of gift certificates has come up before. I'll keep that in mind. Do I have to be specific? I mean, does it have to say groceries, trays, training, or anything else?"

"No. It will only carry the value. I make them up as customers ask. You can't believe how popular an item this is, especially when giving to people who don't have much. Teresa gets them in bulk all year long and gives them to people in need."

Nancy chimed in, "I think it's better than giving a gift card to one of those big box stores. Your gift stays local and gives a second time. It wouldn't be a very good idea for your sister or her family, though. And I suppose they're on your list."

"They are. But local folks are too. I'm beginning to have a thought, but it's too early in the day for it to formulate. If I haven't gotten any further by Friday, I may be back."

While Nancy and Laila went to the deli counter, Annie browsed through the fresh produce. Laila's deli selections changed from time to time as she introduced the community to one Pakistani dish after another. This week she featured a vegetarian dry fruit korma made with seven vegetables, a paste made from nuts and seeds, the korma itself made with yoghurt, cream, curry, chilies, onions and garam masala, and a variety of dried fruits, nuts and spices for garnish.

Eventually, Nancy met Annie at the cash register. "I have something for us to try tonight with whatever we do for dinner. Laila gave me a taste; you'll love it."

"I always love what Laila makes, so whatever it is, it will be great. I'm going to get a handful of blueberries for now. They'll freeze between here and DoubleGood, and they're always good to eat frozen."

As they bundled up again, Annie took Nancy's arm and they walked out into the nearly deserted street yet again, headed for DoubleGood, the combination hardware and electronics store.

They were met just inside the door by twin sisters Holly and Jolly. When they were younger, they hated their parents for naming them in this fashion. As adults, they had learned to enjoy their names and the heads that turned when they were said.

They were identical twins, but easily told apart. Tomboys both, Holly had an accident at an early age that resulted in a spinal injury. Ever since, she lived in a wheelchair. Annie couldn't think of a single thing that Holly couldn't do.

Nancy laughed with the twins and told them about Annie's Christmas shopping plight, and they came up with several ideas. Much like Jennifer and Marie, the sisters from

The Drug Store and The Clinic, Holly and Jolly talked in sync and finished one another's sentences. They were better at it, though, because they shared the same crib at birth.

Together, they listed cell phones to keep in touch, cameras for those who don't use their cell phones to take pictures, televisions for those who liked to stay at home, blu-ray players to go with the televisions, computers or tablets for anyone, video games for teens and pre-teens, a variety of music devices for any age, GPS units for those that didn't have them in their cars already, binoculars for bird watching or man/woman watching, and finally, batteries.

Holly, reaching that last item, said, "You can never have too many batteries or too many kinds. Not on Christmas morning. Something will always call for some type of battery that you can't get your hands on until the next day."

"Still?" asked a bemused Annie. We still need batteries on Christmas morning? We haven't progressed past that yet?"

"Not entirely. Today's toys, for the most part, come with batteries included. But there will always be someone who buys the perfect something for someone but forgot to get the batteries to go with the gift."

Then Jolly said, "Or you can get gift certificates."

Annie was beginning to believe that this was a conspiracy. Before leaving, she purchased the amount and type of batteries suggested by the twins.

As they left, Annie glanced across the street in time to see Daryl and Donny coming from Sassy P's. They were dressed in their warm clothing with "Boone's Services" on the front and back. Curious, she steered Nancy to Sassy P's before going back to the Inn. "I have to go check on something. See you soon."

Jesus was in the front room, stocking his wine bins at the tasting bar. "Hey, Annie, Nancy, it's good to see you. Are you here for a sample?"

"No, just stopping in. Out for a walk in the cool breeze, you might say."

"There are times I miss California."

"I was just wondering what Daryl and Donny were doing. Is the sink okay, or did it freeze?"

"They were just checking. I'm keeping a trickle going in there, and the heater is working well. I heard them banging around in there, so I checked. They were fitting a cover for the hole they made when they had to get to the back of the pipes. I just looked. It looks pretty good, but no one can see it unless they open the cabinet door and get on their knees."

"If no one can see it, did we need it?"

"That was my question. They said it was necessary just to keep rid of some unwanted pests that may find their way into the plumbing. Old building and all."

"That's a good point. I'm going to take a look."

Annie walked to the back room, got down on her knees, opened the door and looked in. A piece of plywood had been cut to fit the hole, and openings had been cut to fit around the pipe. A clever piece was fitted to the plywood, allowing future plumbers to unhook it, slip it back, and pull the piece out. Curious, Annie did so.

She peered into the hole and saw light coming from the other side. She could hear something that sounded like a hammer on nails, and soon she heard male voices.

"Here, Donny, you gots to do it thisaway. Put 'er down flat like this here and fit it up agin tha other. Yep, that's tha way. Now ifin it fits tight, and it do, let's take this here piece first and…"

A tight piece was going in on the other side of the building, at Mr. Bean's.

Clever, thought Annie.

By the time Annie and Nancy got back to the Inn, the cats were in a tizzy. All Tiger Lily could think about was how in the world the Café was getting along without her. She never took vacation or sick days, and now she was missing for the third day in a row! How could they survive? She met Annie at the front door and told her all about it.

Sassy Pants, tired of being home by now, registered her complaints as well. Certainly Jesus and Minnie were just beside themselves without her, and couldn't she please go check on them?

Mr. Bean, sotto voce, danced on his back legs, paws up on Annie's legs as far as he could reach, kneading and pawing, telling her that Carlos was lost, lost, lost without him.

Mo sat on a chair, willing Annie to read his mind. He envisioned all of the cats being zapped with stun guns so the room would quiet down, then he, Mo, would be elevated to the position of primary importance, and he could tell Annie how he desperately needed to get to the Tap where he could seek out female companionship.

For a moment, Sassy Pants stopped her own whine to look at Mo with disgust. He merely gave her a kitty smile and went on with his dream.

Little Socks stayed above the fray. She sat on a table and stared daggers at Annie in an attempt to convey, *"Get me out of here!"*

Annie could see the butts, tails twitching, of Kali and Ko, hiding under two of the stuffed chairs in the foyer.

Henrie came from the kitchen to see what the hubbub was about. "Thank goodness you have arrived safe and sound."

Annie looked at Henrie. "What?"

"You have arrived."

"Can't hear you!" Conversation was impossible. Annie, finally, at the top of her voice, said, "Enough!"

Everyone froze, humans and cats.

Looking at each cat in turn, Annie said, "Enough with the noise. We humans can't have a conversation over the commotion. I'm sure you are tired of being cooped up in this house for a few days, but the last time I checked, there is an apartment upstairs, guest rooms to invade, an entire ground level, and a full basement. Each and every floor has interesting places to sit or nap, and you have toys everywhere. Literally, everywhere. You do not have to stay in one room; you do not have to stay in a room that any of your siblings are in. You have space, time, food, water, beds, toys, playmates, rooms in which to hide. In short, you have everything you need! And it's warm in here!"

Seven cats looked at her, chastened. Correction. Six cats looked at her, chastened. One continued to stare daggers.

Annie took a deep breath, took her mother's coat and asked if she wanted to go to the kitchen for a cup of coffee or cocoa.

Nancy looked at Annie, possibly confused about something. "Coffee or cocoa? Um, okay."

Henry led Nancy into the kitchen while Annie headed to the apartment with her mother's purchase. With a worried look back at Henrie, she said, "I'll be back shortly." She was back shortly, notebook in hand.

Annie first checked on her mother, sitting with a cup of coffee and staring at the window. "Mom, is everything okay?"

"Certainly dear, I'm just tired." Nancy continued to stare at the window.

Annie sat down with the notebook as Henrie placed a cup of cocoa in front of her. She was happy to be gaining in skills at setting up Skype sessions. She could check in with her staff without leaving her mother. She quickly checked in, saw the scattered nature of affairs, let them know she would not be seeing them face-to-face today, but made sure they knew she would be there if they needed her.

Nancy seemed to rally after drinking a cup of coffee. "How are things, dear?"

"It's a combination of holiday partying and freezing weather listlessness out there."

"What does that mean?"

"There are large groups having way too much fun surrounded by empty tables. And Jerry is concerned that he is handling everything alright. He's on his own today. Actually, it's about time for us to be seeing Carlos. He was going to meet his mother and sisters at the airport in Marsh Haven around 10:00."

"Oh, that's right. I didn't realize they were coming today. I'm looking forward to meeting them."

It was like speaking of the devil. They all turned when they heard the front door open and several people walk in, mostly women, laughing and talking in a lively Latin language.

Annie held Nancy back while Henrie went out to greet them. "He has a regular spiel for all of our guests, and since

Carlos has not asked us to take in his family before, this will be their first time here."

"Are they all staying at the Inn?"

"His mother will stay in the apartment with him, but his two sisters and a friend will stay here. Because most of them are here, Henrie will make sure they all feel welcome to use the facilities during the stay. He's going to make sure Carlos and his mother come over for breakfast every day, too, or at least let them know they are welcome."

"What do you know about them?"

"His mother, Daniela, is apparently an accomplished baker. Carlos says he learned how to bake by watching her from an early age.

"He doesn't talk much about his sisters, Rosa and Valeria, but I know he worries about Valeria. He once told me that Mr. Bean reminded him of her. She's the youngest. He says she's spunky and always happy, even in their village."

"What's wrong with their village?"

"There are gangs. They've taken over. His parents used to own a bakery, but when his father passed away, the gang took it over and gave it to one of their members. They give his mother a pittance every month, and they've tried to encourage Valeria to become one of their, um, well, I'm not sure what you would call it."

"I'm sure there are many names. Has she gone over, to the other side, I mean?"

"I think she may have, then she left them to go home, but it's been hard for all of them."

"And Rosa?"

"I think she is a teacher at the local school."

"That's probably a living for her, but does she support her mother and sister as well?"

"Carlos does that. He sends them about half of what he makes. Every month."

"Oh, my. Why doesn't he just bring them here?"

"His mother won't leave. He has tried to convince her to send his sisters, at least Valeria, but so far, that hasn't happened. I wonder if he doesn't want to impress them with this visit. Pity it's so cold this week. He didn't count on this when he made the plans."

"That is a pity. We'll have to play up the town for the other 51 weeks of the year. And what about the friend? Is she a friend of his mother or one of his sisters?"

"I think – now don't quote me on this because I haven't been told for sure – but I think this is a special friend to Carlos."

"Oh, my," smiled Nancy. "The plot thickens."

When Annie could tell that the tour had come to a close, she went to the foyer so she would see Carlos and his family when they came downstairs. She greeted them warmly and added her invitation to the one she knew Henrie had already given. She also went one step further. "I won't take 'no' for an answer. No matter what else you have planned for Christmas day, you are eating here."

Daniela laughed. "Carlos let me know this when he first invited us to come. He offered me the bakery to make traditional Mexican Christmas cookies to bring for the Christmas dinner."

"What are they like?"

"They're called Bunuelos. They are very simple, sugary, and I add my own little twist. I add cinnamon, or sometimes other spices. I'll see what he has in the pantry and decide what to do."

"I can't wait to try them." Annie wondered if she had clothes at least a size larger in her closet to wear starting the day after Christmas.

Isabel made a point to say hello to Annie. "I have been looking forward to meeting you. Carlos speaks of you often. You, Henrie, Jerry, everyone here. I'm happy he included me in this invitation for the holidays."

"Isabel, I would love to tell you that Carlos speaks often of you also, but he holds you close to the vest."

"Close to the vest?"

Thinking quickly, Annie said, "The vest," and showed Isabel with her hands where the article of clothing was worn. "I guess you could say the vest is close to the heart."

Isabel blushed, smiled, and turned away.

As Carlos and his guests bundled up for the cold walk to Tiger Lily's Café, Annie and Nancy decided to have lunch at Sassy P's. Because it was close. Annie invited Henrie to join them.

Sassy P's was busier than they expected it to be, given the Skype session earlier. Only one table remained, the smaller table by the front window. They sat and Annie looked around.

"Oh, hey, George's hot redhead is eating here today instead of at Mo's."

"Where, dear?"

"Don't twist your neck like that, Mom. Be cool. Take a nice, slow nonchalant look around the room, and when you get to your far right, it's the redhead with the plunging neckline."

After a few seconds, Nancy said, "Oh, my. I'll bet that blouse is drafty in this cold weather."

Henrie, who was always proper, slipped a little. "It is obvious from my vantage point that it is a bit nippy over there."

Nancy and Annie looked at Henrie and burst into laughter.

Nancy continued, "Who is that young man with her? He doesn't seem her type."

"His name is Rusty, and I don't know much about him except that he's a gamer."

"A what?"

"A gamer. Listen to me. I talk like I know what I'm talking about. He plays computer games over at Mem's sometimes. Laila said her son has played with him before. And he spends a lot of time with the hot redhead."

"Does the hot redhead have a name?"

"Oh. That would be more polite. I get caught up in Candice-speak when it comes to her. Christal is her name."

Annie noticed that Minnie seemed to say something to them every time she passed the table. Once it was a short sentence that ended with the three of them laughing, another time she responded to a question, and yet another time, when she was not quite so busy, she stopped by to chat for a while. And at times, it appeared Christal and Rusty were covertly watching the table where she sat with Nancy and Henrie.

And then her better side took hold. Why should she think badly of them looking at her when she was looking at them?

Lunch at Sassy P's would consist of cheeses, cold meats and crackers, all chosen by Minnie. Today, she brought a platter to share. It was in the shape of a Christmas tree. Different cheeses alternated with rows of either red or green grapes, anchored with presents at the bottom and topped with a star-shaped dish of cocktail sauce.

It was clear Minnie had gone for cheeses with different textures. The bottom row of the tree was a firm farmhouse cheddar. After a row of red grapes was a row of gouda. Then green grapes, Parmigiano-Reggiano, a last row of red grapes and a small roundish row of Brie.

The presents that overflowed the bottom of the tree were medium-sized shrimp. Minnie gave them a bowl of mixed gourmet crackers, and Jesus brought a bottle of nonalcoholic sparkling wine.

Henrie, after serving himself a portion of shrimp, cheese and grapes, looked at Annie. "We must do this more often."

"Yes, we must!" Annie then segued to, "Tell me about Carlos' family."

"They seem to be a delightful group. You know, of course, that his mother will stay at his apartment."

"Yes, and I think he's going to try to convince her to move here."

"Yes, he hopes to do so. The older sister, Rosa, would like to move. I gather, from talking to Carlos, she believes she must stay in Mexico as long as her mother insists on living there. The younger sister, Valeria, seems to have a bit of an adventurous side to her. She will be happy no matter where she lives, but given her propensity to change jobs, she will probably live wherever her mother decides."

"What about Isabel? Did you find out anything about her?"

"I can tell you that Isabel's room is on the state park side of the Inn. Other than that, all I can say is she is a lovely young woman who is very solicitous of Carlos."

"I haven't asked, Henrie. Were you able to get some help for the weekend, even though it's a holiday?"

"Yes. A brother and sister, college students who work holidays and summers for the Café, will help with breakfast every day starting tomorrow, and they also plan to help all day from Christmas Eve through the day after Christmas. It will be good for them. They had no plans and can use the extra money."

"Great! You must mean JoJo and Ben."

"Yes. They have worked for Felicity since they were in high school. They both cook and wait tables, whatever she needs. They are quite accomplished and willing to do anything we need."

"Have you made potential blizzard plans?"

"Of course. We have extra everything, enough to feed everyone in Chelsea for a week, should it come to that, and of course we always have emergency pillows and blankets for the stray traveler during disastrous weather. I have made up the suite in the basement for JoJo and Ben. They drive in from the country, and I suggested to them, after seeing the weather reports, that they pack bags with enough clothing to stay the entire time, just in case."

"I don't know how you do it, Henrie. You are always three steps ahead of me."

"If I do say so, I believe that is why you hired me."

"I didn't hire you. Dad did. That must be why he hired you, because he knew I would need you."

Nancy added, "Trust me. He needed Henrie and his good head more than you, dear."

And then, the perfectly nice day that Annie was having crashed to the floor. The chime jingled as the door opened, and in walked three of Annie's not-so-favorite people. Geraldine and Hank and Marco. Oh my.

Unfortunately for Annie, one table had emptied, and it was the table closest in proximity to hers. As the three made their way to it, Annie put on her best smile.

"Hello, Geraldine. It's so good to see you. Again. And Hank. It's been a long time. How have you been?"

"I've been fine, Annie." Annie hoped her smile looked more genuine than his. Hank, when he tried to appear friendly, looked like he was wearing one of those rubber faces with the expression molded on. He draped his coat over the chair closest to Annie and came to the table.

"I don't believe we've met. I'm Hank; I'm on the Town Council."

"Hello, Hank. So pleased to meet you. I'm Annie's step-mother, Nancy."

Henrie and Annie looked at one another, but said nothing. A few more pleasantries were exchanged, and they settled at their table. Nancy, whose back was to the other group, looked down at her plate as she whispered, "I had not met him, but I sure have heard a lot about him."

In the past, Geraldine and Hank had worked together to ruin Annie's businesses. They had their individual reasons for wanting her out of the way, and they found willing partners in one another. Annie had done little else than continue to do business as usual, and both Geraldine and Hank had met with failed business dealings, bad public relations and lost friendships.

And now, thought Annie, they were with Marco, who had inside information about Annie's current problems. Marco, who was unhappy with Annie's insistence on involving the FBI. Marco, who apparently was something of a bigot. Marco, who couldn't tell an illegal immigrant from someone with centuries-long family roots. Marco, who apparently didn't accept even those who became citizens and pledged allegiance to the United States of America.

Annie thought about the people in this building. Minnie was from Wisconsin. She was safe. Maybe. Except for her relationship with Jesus.

Jesus had two or three strikes against him. He was Latino, Annie had defended him during the argument at the meeting with Gwen, and he had a relationship with Minnie.

Henrie was an enigma. His chocolate skin and the lilt in his voice that sounded a bit French didn't bode well for Marco's apparent tastes.

And then Annie remembered something else. Geraldine was the hot redhead's aunt. Annie glanced at that table and happened to catch Christal and Geraldine in the middle of a "meaningful stare." All three quickly looked elsewhere.

What in the world could they be up to? "For goodness sakes. It's Christmas. Why don't they just give up?"

Henrie and Nancy looked at Annie, perplexed. No one followed up.

Nancy, facing the window, said, "Oh, look, there's Jeff." She waved, and he waved back, starting for the door.

Apparently, he changed his mind. He had hold of the handle as he looked in the window, seemed to see something or think of something, let go and waved goodbye. He turned around and went back the way he had come.

"He must have left something at the office," said Nancy.

Or, thought Annie, he saw someone he didn't want to be near.

Chapter 17: The Cats Could Not Be Found

They got back to the Inn just in time for the ultimate in crazy. If Annie thought the earlier greeting by the cats was high drama, she was not at all prepared for the rest of the family.

As Annie, Nancy and Henrie reached the porch steps, a modified school bus pulled into the driveway. Annie got her mother safely up to the porch and hurried to the opening door.

Her half-sister Patti was hurtling out the door and down the steps, right into Annie's arms. It had been far too long since they had seen one another. For once, the cold, biting wind didn't seem to be a problem.

Following Patti out the front door were the youngest three children, Gracie, Ella and Ollie, ages 11, 9 and 5. Going out the emergency exit door were the two oldest that still lived at home, Allen and Percy, ages 17 and 14.

Exiting the front door at a more sedate pace were Patti's eldest daughter, Jessica, her husband, Paul, and their children, twins, Jerome and Sally, aged 18 months. The pace was more sedate because the children were being carried. The one in Jessica's arms slept peacefully. The one Paul carried was throwing a just-getting-into-the-two-year-old-stage tantrum.

Patti's husband, Fritz, sat in the driver's seat, forehead resting on the steering wheel. He sensed Annie's presence and said, face still pressed to the wheel, "Do you know how hard it was to drive this bus in that wind?"

There was motion, everyone rushing and running, and several conversations going on at once. The conversations were about ten decibels higher than childless Annie was used to hearing.

The grandchildren ran first to the porch to greet and hug their Nanna. Allen said a polite hello to Henrie. The younger children passed Henrie completely, running into the house and then in and out of every room on the first floor.

When they hit the stairs to go up, Annie thought to caution them to stay out of the guest rooms, then realized they were probably locked. She hoped they were locked.

The cats could not be found. Of course, that's what the kids were doing. They were looking for the famous cats. The cats that were on the web. The cats for which all of these places were named. Each of the kids called the name of the one they just knew would be their favorite, once they met.

As the calling continued, moving from the second floor to the third, Annie figured the cats had retreated to the apartment. Which was blissfully locked. She could imagine seven cats huddled together under the bed.

She heard Percy and Gracie yelling to their mother. "Mom! Ella and Ollie are trying to go through the cat doors!"

Allen looked mortified. He went into the house, probably to find a hiding place.

There were lots of children in Chelsea. The cats loved children. The children in Chelsea were familiar to the cats and with them. The cats were not familiar with children who were not familiar with cats. And "not familiar," in cat-speak, means "scared of."

Henrie tried both to stay out of the way and to be helpful. Being the consummate professional, he soon focused on the young couple and their children.

"You must be Jessica and Paul. Let me show you to your room. It is here on the ground floor, in the back. It is a larger room, and there is a bed for your children."

"Thank you, Henrie. We can put Jerome down and try to get Sally quiet for a nap. By any chance, are the walls soundproofed?"

This conversation took place as they walked down the hall, so Henrie was able to smile at the question without their notice. "The rooms are well insulated, but I believe they are not entirely soundproof. They are what you would call hotel-quality in terms of insulation."

"It's just that the little ones are not used to having several other children around."

Paul, still carrying a screaming child, said, "This will be a learning opportunity for all of us."

Inside the room, Henrie did not offer a tour of either the room or the house. He merely said, "Please show yourself around the house at your leisure. I will be happy to answer any question or show you anything. The short version of the tour is that everything on ground level and on the second floor landing is yours to use as you choose."

"Thanks, Henrie," came a chorus of two tired adult voices while Henrie closed the door. He was absolutely certain the two adults would be sound asleep within minutes, and he could only hope that Sally would follow suit.

By the time Henrie re-entered the foyer, Nancy was telling Patti about the carriage house. While Nancy and Sam had the lower level, Patti, Fritz and the children would be on the upper level. It would be dormitory-style sleeping for them, but this was the only area large enough at the Inn to accommodate seven people.

Henrie introduced himself to Fritz, who had found and made use of the coffee bar.

"Have you had lunch?"

"We stopped about 11:00 for a bite to eat. Have you ever tried to do McDonald's take-out for this many people?"

"Not recently."

"Trust me, it's an experience you don't need."

"I will trust you on that. You relax. You deserve it. I will take a cart out to the bus to load your luggage. It can go straight to the carriage house."

"Thanks, Henrie. Normally I would say, no, no, I can do that, or at least, oh, here, let me help you. But today…today I'm just going to say thanks."

The carriage cart didn't want to stay in one place in the wind. Eventually, Henrie had the idea of ramming one set of wheels into the snow at the edge of the sidewalk. At last he could let go of the cart long enough to enter the bus.

Annie joined him, and together they did a fairly good job of determining whose luggage belonged to whom. They placed a large suitcase, a smaller matching bag, a diaper bag and stroller for two at the emergency exit and loaded the rest onto the cart.

As Henrie took the cart to the carriage house, thankful the wind was at his back, Annie took the luggage for Jessica and Paul, setting it outside their door without knocking. It took two trips to accomplish the task.

As she took the stroller into the house, she wondered if it would ever be used in this weather. She then realized she couldn't have gotten everything. She went to the bus and looked behind the back seats. Sure enough, there it was. A playpen folded up and neatly placed out of the way.

She looked around the bus to see if anything else should come in and realized she would need a bag or box of some sort. The playpen went into the house and outside the bedroom door, and out went Annie once again, with a box she located in the kitchen.

She filled it with three cellphones, a child's purse, two electronic game players, several stuffed animals and dolls, five pairs of gloves, four scarves, a hat, two pairs of shoes, and a book. She looked under the seats and found a small piece of luggage, a box of crayons and a coloring book, a half-eaten hamburger and a cardboard case of French fries loaded with ketchup.

Thinking this had to be everything, she made sure the back door was closed and exited the front, picking up an empty travel mug as she left.

Annie stood outside the bus, balancing in the wind, holding a box filled to the brim and carrying a couple of items from her shoulders. She looked at the door and puzzled about closing it from the outside. Certainly this was possible, but she wasn't sure how to go about it. She finally pulled at one half of the door and both halves shut almost all the way. She decided she would leave it and ask Fritz, who, when last seen, was draped across one of the sofas in the library, arm flung over his eyes.

As Annie got to the porch she heard a call from the median of The Avenue.

"Hey, girl! What in the world is parked in your lot?"

It was Clara, making her weekly fresh flower run, pulling her heated wagon.

"Clara! Get in here out of the cold." When Clara reached the porch, she said, "This is my sister's bus. When they all travel together, this seems to work out the best. They prefer it to having two large vans traveling down the road together."

Clara pulled her wagon up the ramp that ran beside the stairs to the porch. "It's a good idea. Less gas, probably, unless this is a guzzler. And let me say I'm glad you have this ramp. You wouldn't believe the places I have to make several trips, leaving the wagon at the bottom of the steps."

When they entered the Inn, the yelling had subsided, for the most part. Little Ollie was still putting his head into every room he could as he yelled, "Mr. Bean! Mr. Bean! Come play wif me!"

"Where are Kali and Ko? They always greet me. We have a routine."

"They're hiding. I doubt even you can coerce them out of whatever small space they've found."

Clara laughed and went about the business of trading out the flowers. "What happened to these arrangements? It looks like you took them outside during a tornado!"

"Oh. The kids have been home all week because it's so cold out, and, well, let's say that everything in the house has been rearranged a few times. Poor Henrie. He's had to pick most of it up. Over and over and over."

"Well, maybe these will last at least until Christmas."

"We won't worry about it. I know you've got something beautiful in there, but I'm only going to hope it stays nice. I'm not going to try to force the kids to stay out of it. It's been a stressful week for them, and I'm afraid having a full Inn isn't going to be the most fun in the world."

"Well, here is the little bouquet that I always give the girls. You know they have to approve the arrangements I leave."

"I'll make sure they get it."

Clara always brought two arrangements to the Inn, color coordinated to the dominant color of the interior and exterior, blue. One arrangement was over-sized, for the foyer, and the other was tall, for the dining room table. For Kali and Ko, there was a bouquet of each bloom, tied together with a blue ribbon.

The large arrangement took most of the wagon's space. There was only room for the two because of it. As Clara took the large one out, she said to Annie, "I have to get the rest of them from the shop before hitting your other places. This one was a bit large."

It was beautiful. It was a four foot tall white fir tree, firmly fixed in a royal blue ceramic base to keep it watered. Inserted into the tree were blue irises, belladonna blue delphiniums, blue moon phlox and navy blue roses.

Clara showed Annie the individual water tubes on each stem. "This will be a little more difficult for Henrie. He's going to have to replace these every day. And he may need to trim the stems as he does it."

"That's okay. Henrie has some extra help this week. This will be a good job for JoJo and Ben."

"Remind them to keep the tree watered as well."

Clara worked with the arrangement, now sitting on the round table in the middle of the foyer, until she could declare, "Perfect."

The arrangement for the dining room was in the shape of a Christmas tree. The same blossoms were set into a piece of tall, cone-shaped floral foam that soaked water from a low blue ceramic vase. The tree was accented by sprigs of white fir.

Clara made sure her area was cleared of falling blossoms, closed her wagon, now carrying the arrangements from the week before, and bundled up to go. "I'll see you later, Annie.

My impossible-to-keep-happy customer demands I put flowers in all of her places today."

"You need to find better customers."

Clara went back to Bloomin' Crazy, emptied her wagon and filled it again with the rest of the fresh arrangements to go to Annie's businesses. She went next to Sassy P's Wine & Cheese.

"Minnie, I understand my girl Sassy Pants won't be able to approve the bouquet today."

"That's right. She's home. I'm sure she's ready to get back to work. But you're stuck with me. What do you have today?"

Clara brought out a vase of red Christmas roses, geared to the dominant color of Sassy P's, surrounded by six inch high candy canes, all enclosed with a red ribbon. She looked at Minnie. "Simple."

Minnie smiled. "Perfect."

At Mr. Bean's Confectionary, she was greeted by Carlos and Jerry and introduced to the guests from Mexico. Clara immediately understood there was one mother, two sisters, and one mysterious attachment. She zeroed in on Isabel. "Darlin', you need to spend some time with me while you're in town. I'll make sure to show you everything you need to know about Chelsea. You may need to know, some day."

Isabel blushed. Carlos blushed. Jerry blushed. Daniela beamed.

Clara didn't want to intrude on family time, so she quickly pulled out the bouquet for Mr. Bean's Confectionary, always done in shades of green.

This long, low vase had sprigs of white fir and small pine cones interspersed with green calla lilies. Valeria took the arrangement in her hands with mouth open. "You do this every day?"

"All the time. I'm still making deliveries. Do you want to help me finish this run?"

Valeria looked to Carlos who shrugged, and said, "Yes!"

Clara and Valeria left for Mo's Tap, bundled even for that small trip. When they entered, George and Candice were both close to the front door. They said hello to Clara and looked expectantly at Valeria.

Clara made introductions. "Carlos has family visiting this week. This is Valeria, his sister. She's helping me make deliveries."

Candice was called away to a customer table, but George stayed in the vicinity of Clara and Valeria. At the other end of the bar were two familiar faces, Rusty and Christal. They had a notebook sitting on the bar in front of them this time, and they appeared to be reading what was on the screen.

Clara, knowing all about Christal, needled George. "George. Really. Are you still after that?"

"Are you kidding me? I can't get rid of her. I don't want to get a reputation for kicking former girlfriends out, so I can't say anything. I just wish she would, you know, get a life. She doesn't seem to do anything but sit here in the bar, or at the Café, or at Sassy P's. Everywhere I might stick my head in, she's right there."

Clara laughed and explained to Valeria that Candice and George were dating, and that it was probably a little harder on Candice than George. She then got back to business. "Valeria, let's get this bouquet out and finish our deliveries."

She pulled out a miniature crystal punch bowl filled with gold nuggets and yellow roses. Yellow, green and red marbles in the bottom of the vase kept them in place. In the center of the arrangement was one perfect sprig of mistletoe.

Valeria looked at each detail before setting the arrangement on the bar. "This is beautiful. How do you get your ideas?"

"Well, for Annie's places, I always start with the color. Each of her places has a dominant color. Mr. Bean's color is green; Mo's is yellow. Usually I just work with those colors of flowers, but during special times of the year, like this week, Christmas, I try to work it around the holiday as well."

Buttoning their coats, waving to George and walking out the door, they continued their conversation. It was obvious to Clara that a florist was budding inside Valeria.

At L'Socks' Virasana, Clara found Diana waiting inside. "We've been closing early this week, because no one wants to come to a yoga class in this cold weather. But I knew you would be coming, so I waited."

"Should we even leave a bouquet, if you're closed?"

"We're open in the morning, and honestly, everyone notices the bouquets. They stop and look, either going or coming, and just about everyone has picked up your cards at one time or another. I would hate for the early morning crowd to miss your lovely flowers."

For the yoga studio, Clara had a basket shaped like a sleigh that glittered with flecks of golden tinsel. Two tall sticks of orange candy stood on either end with orange amaryllis piled around them. Here and there were bunches of cinnamon sticks that had been soaked in orange juice and tied in little orange ribbons.

As Valeria and Diana looked at it together, Clara, speaking mostly to Valeria, said, "Never be afraid to do something different."

At Tiger Lily's Café, Clara brought out her favorite piece of the week. The Café had a casual, eclectic atmosphere, but the bouquet was always classic. Always in a tall crystal vase.

This week she had selected dark purple calla lilies, purple hydrangea, and purple wedding cremon. Here and there were touches of bright red winterberries. Trudie accepted the arrangement and chatted for a while, until a customer order for coffees came to her.

Clara had one last delivery to make for the day. She looked at Valeria. "Do you have time to come with me for one last delivery? It will be a big one."

"Sure. Carlos knows where to find me if he needs me for any reason."

Clara and Valeria went across The Avenue to Bloomin' Crazy. As Valeria looked around, Clara once again cleared the old out of her wagon and filled it with new arrangements.

They left, this time walking up toward the town square, taking a left on Main Street. A couple of buildings up, Clara hit the buzzer and they were allowed entrance to Antiques On Main.

Sam was finishing a floor arrangement in the middle of the main area. Frank was at the counter, having opened the door to Clara with a button. Claire sat in what would become her signature position, on a bright red cushion to the left of the cash register.

"Frank, this is Valeria. She's visiting her brother, Carlos. Valeria, Frank is getting ready for his grand opening tomorrow. This lovely cat is Claire. She adores humans. Doesn't care much for other cats."

Claire purred.

"And that handsome gentleman," Sam waved, "is Annie's father, Sam. He and Annie's mother are staying at the Inn for a month. I'm sure you'll run into them a few times."

Sam, from his position in the middle of the room, said, "Actually, if you want to be correct, I'm Annie's step-father. But I couldn't be happier to have her in my life. You're staying at the Inn, right? We'll probably at least have breakfast together a time or two while you're in town."

Clara turned back to Frank. "Are you ready, Frank?"

"I am. Just. Cutting it a little close, but by tomorrow morning there will be nothing left to do but plug in the coffee pot!"

"Coffee pot? You aren't having this catered?"

"That was just an expression. Yes, Felicity and Trudie have gone all out, and they've finagled Carlos and Jerry into helping."

"I have to know. Will there be wine?"

"I thought about it, but then I decided I wanted people to come to look at antiques. So I stopped at coffees, finger foods, chocolates and desserts."

"That's plenty. This is going to be fantastic. Where do you want me to put these?"

"Could you walk around and decide where they would look best?"

"Sure! Come on, Valeria. Let's put you to work for once!"

Clara had eight vases of fresh flower arrangements, all with multi-colored blooms, to go throughout the ground floor for the open house. They were in different sizes and in a variety of shapes; each vase was unique.

They started by picking up an arrangement, one each, and walking around the room to find a likely location.

Valeria, standing at an antique dining table, asked, "What if I think the best place is on wood? Do we have something to put under the vase?"

"Great question, and the answer is yes, and no. I had coasters, but I forgot and left them at the shop."

Frank was ready. "Don't bother going back. I have just the thing." Frank ducked into the back of the room and returned with a selection of vintage trivets. "I had forgotten about these until just this minute. I had intended to put them out on tables. They're already priced for sale."

Frank had eight in hand, a hexagonal pottery trivet of multi-colored tile, a dated and signed Rookwood trivet of vintage grapes, a pottery tray trivet, a hand-painted colorful cat trivet, a fleur de lis pottery trivet, a vintage stained glass trivet, and a Danish modern mosaic and wooden trivet.

Valeria took her cue from Clara, chose a trivet to go with the vase in her hand, and went in search of the perfect place.

Chapter 18: Annie Needed Some Alone Time

Annie needed some alone time. Most people couldn't understand why she needed to close the doors on the world.

She was in the people business with each of her establishments. Every day she connected with almost everyone that worked there plus her customers, friends, neighbors and business connections.

She met strangers easily, she juggled several groups of friends and had good relationships with people in every social strata and every race, religion, creed and sexual orientation she could think of.

But lurking deep in her heart was a bitter secret. Something that was known by only her, her mother, and a few close friends. She, Annie Mack, was an introvert.

The Inn was full. Lots of family was there, that was true, but it was full. The apartment was full. Full of cats whose grievances needed to be heard.

Annie put on her coat, scarf and gloves and braved the cold yet again, leaving for, where? She didn't know. She crossed The Avenue and considered taking a left to walk toward the beach and the lighthouse, but a bitter gust of wind changed her mind. By now, sharp pricks of snow were hitting her face. She could tell the snow had been coming down for a while, as swirls skittered around the sidewalk. Nothing was sticking to the ground. It was all blowing.

She turned right and saw a brilliant Mayan sunburst. Mem's. She would have a cup of tea at Mem's.

Mem saw her walk in, noted a look that said, "I need some privacy," and merely waved. She put some water on to boil, placed a selection of tea bags in a china bowl and brought that and a cup to the table.

"I'll bring you a pot when the water boils. Do you want something to eat?"

"No, thanks, Mem. Just some tea and quiet, please," Annie said with a wan smile.

She noticed Diana sitting at a bar stool next to the cash register and gave her a wave.

Annie sat and sipped tea for what must have been a half hour when she was startled from her reverie by Jeff. "Jeff, please sit down."

He did. "I've packed up and won't be taking space from Gwen anymore. I'll either work from my room at the Inn or maybe from here."

"Do you need anything from me?"

"Not yet. I'm still working a few angles."

"Let me get a cup for you; this is really good tea."

Annie was interrupted by the sound of her cellphone. "When did we decide we had to be so connected?" she asked. She glanced at the phone and saw it was Chris.

"I'm sorry, Jeff, I should probably take this. I asked Chris to keep an eye on one of my guests."

She answered the phone and Chris, breathless, asked, "Is Blaine back at the Inn?"

"What?"

"Is he back at the Inn? I was held up and didn't get out to the lake until this afternoon. He's not there. His truck is there, his gear is there, but I can't find him. I thought he may have gotten a ride back, maybe with Ray."

"I don't think so, but Henrie and I were both gone for lunch, and then we got busy. I'll call Henrie right now and have him check. Where are you?"

"I'm halfway back to town. I can't get a signal at the lake. I'm parked. I'll stay right here until I hear from you. If my line is busy, call back. I'm going to call Ray."

Annie hung up and dialed the Inn. When Henrie picked up, she asked, "Is Blaine back? Have you seen him?"

"I have not seen him. Is something wrong?"

"Chris couldn't find him, but his truck is still at the lake. Could you check his room for me, please?"

"Right away." Henrie kept the phone with him as he went to the second floor. Annie could hear him go up the steps, knock on the door, knock again, then call, then use his passkey to let himself in.

"He is not in his room. I will check the porch and then the library."

Annie waited while Henrie did just that, and then she heard him calling Blaine, as if he might be in yet another area of the house. Once again, Henrie was back, saying, "He is not here."

"I'll call Chris."

"What do you want me to do?"

"I don't know. I guess just call me if he shows up."

As Annie hung up, Jeff said, "You know, I met Blaine briefly on my way in the door when I arrived. And Ray told me about him that night at dinner. Is he in trouble?"

"It's possible. Chris can't find him."

"If I can help, you know I want to."

Annie dialed Chris again. He answered with, "Ray hasn't seen or heard from him. He was just getting ready to go check on him."

"He's not at the Inn."

225

"We need to go out there and look for him. I'll call Ray back and get him out there with Jock. Maybe Jock and Cyril can track him down."

"Jeff is here with me. Do you want him to help?"

"Sure. Send him on down."

"I don't know where to send him. Have Ray pick Jeff up."

Jeff spoke up. "Send him to the Inn. I have to put some different clothes on."

Marco, invigorated from his lunch meeting with Hank and Geraldine, left the police department and went to Gwen's office. Mindy told him Jeff had been there earlier in the day, but he had packed up his computer and notes and left, telling her to have a Merry Christmas.

"So when will he be back?"

"He told me to have a Merry Christmas. He's not coming back."

"Not coming back? He's supposed to be working with me!"

"I don't know what to tell you, Marco. I only know that he's not coming back here, to Beancounters. I think he's still in town. He's staying at the KaliKo Inn."

Marco huffed. This fed was in Annie's pocket, alright, just like Geraldine and Hank said.

Marco stormed out and walked toward The Avenue, intending to turn left at the corner to go back to the police station. When he got to the corner, however, he noticed Jeff go into one of the businesses on this side of The Avenue. It looked like he went into CyberHealth.

Marco stood where he was for a while. The snow bit into his face, and the wind bit into his bones, but he couldn't decide where to go.

Maybe Jeff was working on the investigation, using Mem's computers or checking something out with her, since she ran Annie's websites.

Maybe he was meeting Annie, talking about the investigation without including him.

Well, what the heck, whatever he was doing, he wasn't including local law enforcement. Typical fed. Typical game playing.

Marco stamped his feet and clapped his hands together. They were already cold and getting colder.

Should he or shouldn't he? He had every right. He should. Yes, he should.

Marco turned to walk down The Avenue. He walked slowly, head tucked into his shoulder, hand on the side of his face to keep the sting away. He still wondered if he was doing the right thing.

Geraldine and Hank had given him some interesting information. Information that he should share with the fed. Unless he, Marco, decided to take the investigation in his own direction. He might just do that, cut the fed out of the picture.

Marco had met that fed before. He had worked on an investigation right here, and he hadn't included local law enforcement. And what a fiasco that had turned out to be.

In Marco's mind, particularly after his lunch meeting, this fed was totally responsible for the hostage situation. The whole thing was his fault. If he'd worked with the locals, instead of leaving them in the dark, that hostage situation would never have taken place.

Walking more forcefully, Marco pulled the door to CyberHealth, strode in, looked around, and walked with a purposeful stride to the table where Annie and Jeff sat.

"So, are you going to let me in on this 'investigation'?"

"Not now, Marco." Jeff pushed past Marco, literally running out the door.

"What the…"

Annie was standing now, putting on her coat and getting ready to leave. "Marco, we've got a problem."

"You always have a problem. What is it this time?"

"One of my guests is missing. He was ice fishing out on Great Neck Lake. His gear is there, his truck is there, but we can't find him."

"How long has he been missing?"

"I don't know. Chris just called me. He looked for him and couldn't find him, maybe ten or fifteen minutes ago. But he's been out there since 9:00 or so."

"In this cold? How could you let him do that?"

"I didn't let him do anything! He's an adult!"

"You sure as heck don't take care of your guests as you should, and you're always needing the police department or someone to bail you out. Well this time, you're on your own!"

Annie, shocked, looked at Marco and asked, "So I take it you aren't going to take a missing person report?"

"He's an adult. He has to be gone a lot more than a few hours for me to assume he's missing."

"He's ice fishing in the bitter cold and snow; he's a novice fisherman; he could have fallen into the lake; he could be suffering from hypothermia and in the process wandered into the woods."

"Not my problem."

"Is that your final answer?"

"Call me when he's been gone for twenty-four hours."

Annie pushed past Marco, holding her tongue for the lashing she wanted to give him. Where was Pete when the town really needed him?

Chapter 19: Just Pray

Before leaving CyberHealth, Annie stopped to tell Mem and Diana the situation with Blaine. "I don't know where he is, but if we find him, he's sure to need medical help. Could you please put Jennifer and Marie on alert?"

"I will, and I heard that exchange with Marco. I'll call the Sheriff's Department right now. I'll give them Chris's cell number."

"They won't be able to reach him. There isn't any cell coverage out there. I don't know how to tell you where they are!"

Meme took a deep breath, breathing in deeply, letting out slowly. As she did so, Annie followed her lead and did the same.

Having breathed, Annie could now think. "I've got it. I'll call Ray and have him take some of The Marina's handheld radios."

Annie raced from the store, telephoning Ray as she went.

Marco stood by the table she had vacated, alternating watching after Annie and following Mem's movements. Mem kept her eyes on him but didn't bother to say anything to Marco as she dialed her phone.

Diana picked up her phone and made some calls of her own.

Rusty and Laila's son James were in the cyber room, picking up an online game of chess they had going. They didn't always see one another while playing, but on occasion, they played at Mem's and chatted while the game went on. Usually, though, they concentrated on the game.

Today, Rusty concentrated on the conversation of the gamers next to them. Daryl and Donny were on a break and playing one of the newer X-Men games, yippin' and yowlin' in their colorful language of the south.

They also talked about some covers they had made for two of Annie's businesses, the wine place and the bakery. Apparently, some plumbing was shared by the two, and they had just made some fancy coverings for the holes.

Interesting. Interesting also was the fanciful conversation they had regarding potential uses for the new hiding place.

Soon, Rusty's ears picked up on another conversation. Annie and Marco were going at it, something about a missing man. Rusty turned to look at them. James picked up on his distraction and turned to look himself. Soon, Daryl and Donny were looking as well.

They followed the action as Annie talked to Mem, and as Annie left the store.

As Mem and Diana made their calls, they were unaware of the four sets of eyes glued on them from the back of the store.

Marco, wondering if he had made a bad decision, decided not to worry about that and to concentrate on the new information he had regarding the computer thefts and other criminal activity.

There was a lot to think about. One of the things to consider carefully was Hank's insinuation that he could be in line for a promotion. All he had to do was solve some cases. Bring to light some crimes that had been going on under Chief Pete's nose. Everybody knew Pete wouldn't step on anything that might affect Annie and her businesses.

If he, Marco, could make some highly visible arrests, he would be going places.

Geraldine and Hank clued him in to some of the goings on at Annie's businesses. The felon in town was that guy that made the candy, Jerry. Marco had to run his information through the various databases they had at the office. He could be involved in these thefts, or he could have something else going on.

He, Marco, would stay on top of it. Jerry might not be bright enough to do a computer scam, but he could be running drugs. Or worse.

Then there were the illegals. It didn't make any difference what Annie had to say about them. Citizenship classes? Native? Ha! They were Mexicans! He would take a look at Carlos and Jesus.

According to Geraldine, Carlos, Jerry and Jesus had approached her about providing some, what she called "signature" baked goods, candies and wines. Something they tried to sell her when she owned her café. She thought they were probably just trying to get close to her so they could steal from her. She never trusted them.

And Hank told about a time that Carlos refused to allow him to go back into the bakery's kitchen. He was on official business, being the President of the Town Council at the time, and Carlos had rudely – rudely! – refused to allow him into the kitchen, citing some absurd health department ruling about non-authorized personnel in the area. Certainly, Carlos was hiding something back there. A search warrant might be in order.

That girl that made the coffee was Jamaican, but that wasn't really foreign, was it? She was too cute to be foreign.

And those Mexican assistants that he had overlooked before, they wouldn't have access to the computers, probably, and were probably too dumb to figure out how to do anything sophisticated like computer theft. Otherwise, how could he, Marco, have overlooked them as illegals in the first place?

Now Henrie was another person he could think about, but neither Geraldine nor Hank mentioned him. For the time being, he was going to concentrate on Jerry, Carlos and Jesus.

But let's think about Annie herself. She sure had a lot of fingers in a lot of pies. And that FBI guy was a friend of hers. She could probably lead him to water and get him to drink.

Geraldine and Hank both figured she had some sort of a scam going on. Maybe she was scamming the government for taxes. Or more likely, she was behind the computer thefts herself, and she was going to turn in a big claim to the insurance company.

He would have to figure out what company insured her and put a bug in their ear. Stop that little plan from going through.

Maybe Annie was working with one or two of her people. Maybe she was working with George. Geraldine didn't have anything good to say about him either. She said she had known him from high school, and he was just a boy toy. Love 'em and leave 'em. Geraldine was particularly angry about George. Marco had to wonder if maybe Geraldine had been one of the ones he left behind. Or maybe someone she knew had been hurt by George.

Marco didn't care much for George, but that was mainly because George always seemed to have a pretty woman hanging around. Like that server, Candice. Wow. What a looker. But she had eyes only for that screwball.

Maybe George would merit a special look from him as well.

Game plan in mind, Marco left Mem's and headed back to the office.

The same four sets of eyes watched him that had watched Mem as she made her calls. Rusty's mind worked overtime.

Annie reached the Inn just as Jeff came back out, dressed in warm gear and ready to go. "Ray will be here in a couple of minutes. He went back to The Marina to get some handheld radios, since your cellphones will have no coverage."

"Is Marco gathering a search crew as well?"

"Marco? You've got to be kidding me. He told me to wait twenty-four hours to report it."

Jeff was speechless. Annie brought him up to date. "Mem is calling the Sheriff's Department and will tell them you're on radio."

"I hate to say it, but that's probably the better option. I've seen this police department in action. Too bad Pete's out of town."

"I have a feeling when he returns, he may make a few changes."

Ray pulled up, but before Jeff could get off the porch, Henrie was behind them with a thermos of coffee. "This was all I had time to do. I will make more and get it out to you."

Henrie was already on his way back into the Inn to make more coffee for the volunteers that would join the search.

By now, The Avenue was abuzz with activity. The Police Department may have been a no-show for the emergency, but information flew fast on The Avenue, and others were on their way.

George, a Coast Guard volunteer and always prepared for an emergency, ran down the street to get into the truck with Ray and Jeff. As he jumped in, he shouted an explanation to the startled Annie. "Diana called!"

Jennifer came out the door of The Drug Store, also always prepared for an emergency, and raced to her van, shouting for Ray to wait so she could follow him. Marie stood in the doorway with a worried look.

Diana, having called everyone on Annie's side of The Avenue, George first, ran to the Inn. "Annie, I asked everyone to gather what they could, like kerosene heaters, flashlights and other emergency gear. It will be dark soon, and we have no idea how long they'll be out there. Cheryl is on her way with a van from The Marina, and we'll take it to the lake. She knows how to find the fishing site."

By now, Nancy and the five younger children had gathered on the porch in various stages of dress. The kids were mostly without coats, hats and gloves. And to Annie's horror, her mother was barefooted.

Annie watched the last of the informal search and rescue volunteers get underway. The wind bit into her face, stinging her with shards of snow. She turned to gather everyone to go inside. She spoke to the children, but she took her mother's arm. "Come on, children. There's lots of excitement out here, but you'll freeze your little fingers and toes off. Let's get in!"

Patti and Fritz were already in the kitchen. They made coffee, each filling a large thermos. Henrie gathered cups and napkins. Annie sat Nancy at the table, joined them and filled a bag with protein bars.

Nancy, confused, asked, "What in the world is everyone so excited about?"

Patti looked to Annie, who looked back, then looked directly at Nancy. In a calm voice, she said, "Mom, don't worry about it. We're just getting some things together for Chris and some other folks."

Patti drug Annie to the opposite side of the kitchen and said in a strong whisper, "What is this about?"

"Sam doesn't think anything is wrong. He thinks she just gets tired. She does seem to be more confused after periods of activity. If she rests, she gets better."

"How long…."

They were interrupted by Laila, who entered through the kitchen door.

"I have a cooler of sandwiches. Let me take your coffee to Diana. She'll get it out to the lake."

Fritz, not knowing if he should be in the conversation with Patti or in the thick of things with Henrie, asked, "Is there anything else I can do?"

Laila, Patti, Annie and Henrie, together, said, "Just pray."

Chapter 20: We're Havin' A Heat Wave

Annie had planned to make supper in the apartment for the family and Chris. She didn't want to cause any additional work for Henrie, and dinner for fifteen people, including seven children, a dog and seven cats, could create a nightmare for Henrie the following morning.

Henrie would have an early start to the day. Even with the additional help of JoJo and Ben, she was concerned that with all the extra clean-up help, kitchen items would be put "away" in places that weren't really "away," causing Henrie to have to look for everything.

But now, that meant nothing. She couldn't shut herself up in the apartment for the evening with an emergency that involved two of her guests. Blaine was in trouble and Jeff had intentionally placed himself in harm's way.

She worried about everyone out in the cold, but felt a particular degree of responsibility for these two men.

According to the weather station, the temperature was in the low teens.

Gosh, thought Annie. We're havin' a heat wave.

Winds were now at twenty miles an hour, gusting to twenty-five. Snow was coming down at the rate of a half inch to an inch an hour, but it was the blowing and drifting variety. Visibility was low; residents were urged to stay inside.

Henrie, now planning to eat with the family, helped Annie and Patti put supper on the table with the groceries Annie had purchased.

Together, they laid out a simple meal. There was a platter of ham, turkey and roast beef, three different kinds of breads and buns, condiments, deli potato salad and deli broccoli salad, pickles, cherry tomatoes, olives, Nancy's dried fruit korma, iced tea, water, coffee and freshly made cookies.

Annie had just finished setting the table when the kitchen door whooshed open. Two bundled up people with suitcases stomped their feet on the rug, dropped their cases and clapped their hands together. As they unwound their scarves, Annie recognized JoJo and Ben.

"My goodness! You drove to town in this weather?"

Ben answered. "It was a wild ride, alright! We didn't think we could make it into town tomorrow morning, so we came tonight. Just as we got here, we realized that each of us thought the other called you. I hope that's not a problem."

"It's not a problem at all. But your mother would never forgive me if you had driven off into a ditch somewhere. Let me show you the suite; you can get warmed up, then come back upstairs and join us for dinner. But call your mother first. Let her know you're here safe."

Patti had already reached into the cupboards to get two more of everything.

Chris berated the valuable time lost by having to drive halfway to town to call for assistance, but there was nothing else to be done. He left the scene, and as soon as he had bars, he pulled over to make telephone calls.

Once again he thought through the afternoon, wondering if he had missed something important. He had arrived to check on Blaine, but he was nowhere to be found. Chris looked inside the truck, inside the shelter, into the edges of the woods. Fearing the worst, he lay on his stomach looking into the hole in the ice.

There was no indication Blaine had fallen in, but there was no indication he had not, either. There were no marks, no footprints. The wind had already begun blowing the snow around the ice, and once new snow came down, no prints or body marks were visible.

In short, Chris couldn't tell if Blaine had fallen into the hole, had tried to get to his truck but gotten disoriented, or had gone into the woods to relieve himself and gotten turned around.

With the cold, it was possible Blaine was suffering from hypothermia. He could be disoriented or confused. He could be lying in the woods somewhere, groggy or passed out. He could have removed protective layers of clothing, confusing cold for hot.

As soon as Ray arrived, they took the dogs to the edge of the hole in the ice. Neither dog wanted to get close to the edge, but after being prompted by sniffing a hat Chris found, they dutifully checked the edges and didn't find anything.

Cyril and Jock squared off with one another at first but soon got into working mode and took direction from their assigned humans. Jock, of course, was taking direction from his only human. Cyril would work with Chris, because Chris needed him.

Cheryl and Diana backed in, putting hot coffee and sandwiches within reach of the searchers. All they had to do was open the back door. Jennifer's van was close by, loaded and ready with emergency medical equipment.

Chris took charge. On the most sheltered side of the pickup truck, everyone leaned in to hear him over the howling wind. Chris, Ray, Jeff and George each took a radio and a flashlight. Ray and Chris would cover the lake with Jock and Cyril, each taking off in different directions. Jeff and George would take off in different directions through wooded areas, taking the most likely trails. The remaining radio stayed with Cheryl, who, with Diana and Jennifer, would set up a base camp just in case the search drug on.

As the men left, the women got busy moving Blaine's shelter. They first picked up what they could of the equipment scattered around the hole. Most of his equipment was still inside the shelter, and the sled was there. They loaded the sled and made two trips, hauling equipment and loading it into the covered back end of the pickup.

Jennifer took careful note of everything that went into the truck. She didn't know what he had to begin with, but she noted any piece of emergency equipment that he wasn't using. Heater, blankets, flashlights, knife, extra socks and boots, the hat Chris had found. She hoped they were extra and not abandoned.

Jennifer finished stowing equipment into the truck and put the blankets, the hat and socks, the flashlights and the heater into the back end of her van for the moment.

Three cars from the Sheriff's Department arrived just as Diana and Cheryl pulled the shelter to the edge of the lake. The man in charge, Chief Deputy Fred Smiley, was anything but.

He noticed the activity and asked Cheryl, as she was the one who approached them, what in the world they were doing to his crime scene.

Cheryl apologized and explained they were setting up a base camp for the search team. He growled a response at her to apparently make her feel about two inches tall. Cheryl didn't take the bait.

"I have a different reason for being here. I'm here to put together an emergency medical facility, both for Blaine, when we find him, and for the search team, should anyone be injured. I had need of this shelter. You can arrest me when we've done what we came here to do!"

With that, she handed the keys to Blaine's pickup truck to Deputy Smiley and headed for the shelter. Diana followed her. Jennifer, who was well known by the deputies, brought them up to date, told them who they were looking for and who was out there in the frigid weather looking for him. She also gave them the channel upon which the rescue crew could be found.

This being a resort community with a multitude of organizations having to communicate, the Sheriff's department had radios that allowed them access to nearly anyone. Deputy Smiley raised Chris almost immediately.

Chris was already headed back in, as was Ray. They had found nothing and realized their search over the ice and snow would be fruitless. They had called for Blaine, but they could not see and they could not hear anything except for the conversations over the radio.

Visibility grew worse. Luckily, Cyril and Jock were able to lead them back to the site.

Diana, Cheryl and Jennifer outfitted the shelter with chairs and blankets. Kerosene heaters were placed on every side. A folding table sat in the middle with coffee, sandwiches and three kerosene lamps. Altogether, the shelter was a warm oasis in the darkening winter day.

It should be said the deputies were mighty happy to have the shelter, even though it was a piece of tampered-with crime scene. Potentially.

Shortly, Chris and Ray were warming up with hot cups of coffee, talking with the deputies.

Jock and Cyril sat on blankets, breathing heavily behind their humans. Cheryl brought out dog dishes and filled them with water and food. They managed to figure out how to share without communicating. Jock ate first, while Cyril drank, each keeping a wary eye on the other. Then, keeping a wide berth from one another, they switched places. Chris and Ray noticed this but didn't comment on it.

Deputy Smiley was getting ready to send two parties of two men each into the woods. He and his partner would stay with the shelter, now the command post. Chris and Ray were going out again.

Then they heard from George.

"Chris, I need help out here. How do I let you know where in the blinkin' skies I am?"

Marco had a productive day at the computer. He found out about that candy maker, alright. Jerry had done time in a federal prison. It was for murder. Annie had a murderer at the bakery.

Well, the guy had a good attorney and the offense was pled down to manslaughter. But that's murder, just the same.

And to top it off, the guy whacked his mother!

This guy was good for something. Marco just didn't know what, at the moment.

Then there was Carlos. Marco was able to find many times that Carlos had gone back to Mexico. And right now, there were people from Mexico visiting him. They had to be running drugs. Some kind of cooked drug, like meth or glass. They probably had a system for getting it across the border, maybe they packed it up in coffee and sent it through in their checked luggage.

Marco spent a half hour looking at the ceiling, wondering how he could come up with a search warrant to go through the bakery and the Inn, where some of them were staying. He didn't come up with a legal way to do anything.

He couldn't find anything on Jesus and thought he would have to give up on him. For now. And that perfect George was clean as a whistle. As his sainted mother would say, gran' disgraziato!

Marco had found the name of Annie's insurance company, and he Googled the main office. As he sat, discouraged about the lack of anything bust-worthy, he sent an anonymous message to Annie's insurer, telling them he had reason to suspect Annie was running a scam on them, and they should investigate.

Deputy Smiley assumed command from Chris. "This is Chief Deputy Fred Smiley. When you communicate via radio, you need to identify yourself. Please do so now."

First, there was silence. Then a perturbed voice in a dramatic tone with something of a southern accent came over the air. "This is mobile one-seven-niner, out here in the blippin' cold and snow; toes, fingers, nose and you-know-what all frozen to yonder."

Dramatic voice gone, a purely agitated voice yelled, "I need help out here! I've got a coat on the ground, not completely frozen yet, so it hasn't been here long. Is there any way you can locate me using this radio?"

Silence.

Then George again. "Over, dag blast it!"

Chief Deputy Smiley was getting ready to say something negative. He was saved when someone else got on the radio. "George, this is Chris. You went through the woods to the left of the truck, as you face the truck from the lake, correct?"

"Yes."

"Stay right there. Ray and I are coming with the dogs."

A click came on the radio. "Negative, Chris. Send one of those dogs in for me. I'm all turned around. Oh. Forgive me. This is Jeff Bennett. I guess I'm mobile one-seven-tenner."

Despite the situation, Chris and Ray laughed. Ray got on the radio and said, "This is Ray. Mobile one-seven-eighter. I'll be there with Jock directly."

Chief Deputy Smiley wasn't smiling. He did, however, send both units of deputies into the woods with Chris and Cyril.

As they left, he turned to his partner and said, "I was at that Inn a couple of months ago. This town and everyone in it is just one big circus act."

Chapter 21: Don't Forget To Pick Me Up

While the adults were worried about the rescue on the lake, they kept up a good show for the kids. The tables in the dining room rang with laughter and conversation.

Annie and Nancy caught up with Patti and Jessica; Sam, back from Antiques On Main, had a long conversation with Fritz and Paul. He had talked with Annie privately earlier, and was keeping a close eye on Nancy, but from a distance.

The twins sat at high chairs, laughing and throwing as much food at one another as they ate.

After the meal, Henrie, helped by all of the adults, quickly cleaned up the dining room and kitchen. He kept a scanner on, listening for anything that sounded like a lake rescue. Nothing was on the air.

JoJo and Ben quickly made themselves useful by taking Patti's younger children in hand to go through the video game library. They chose a couple of games and settled in front of the large screen television on the south end of the large room.

Eventually, Annie sat in the library in front of a roaring fire on the north end of the library, feet curled under her legs on a reclining chair. She was surrounded by Nancy, Sam and Patti, all conversing quietly with books in their laps. Eventually seven cats quietly came from upstairs, one at a time, looking warily toward the south end of the room, sneaking over to the chair and finding a place to curl on top of Annie.

Peace reigned for a long time when families with children were involved. At least fifteen minutes. Eventually, the children realized cats were in the room and pandemonium ensued once more. Tiger Lily recognized the danger first and was able to get under the chair before she was seen. Six other cats, not as quick on the uptake, dug into Annie as they jumped in every direction. She was sure she was bleeding from at least twelve new holes in her body. Kids and cats ran everywhere, kids laughing and calling cat names, cats running as fast as possible.

This was the scene when Carlos entered the Inn with his family and friend.

Annie invited them into the library, and they all settled in for the evening. Carlos was, of course, aware of the ongoing lake rescue. No one knew anything more than had been known at least three hours ago, so the room soon lapsed into silence.

Ray and Jock located Jeff fairly quickly. As they returned to the campsite, Ray insisted, "Jeff, I've had a break, you haven't. You get in there and warm up. I'll go on with Jock."

Jeff and Deputy Smiley had met before. When Jeff ducked through the opening and stood, he was face-to-face with one of the men with whom he had breached one of the entrances to the Inn during the hostage crisis. They had breached early. Much earlier than they were supposed to have breached.

It wasn't their fault.

Still, their meeting today was a bit awkward

Jeff realized Smiley was now on the defensive, but he was generally a magnanimous guy. He held out his hand. "Deputy Smiley. Jeff Bennett with the FBI. It's good to see you again. I'm glad you can put an official face on this unofficial rescue operation."

"Do you mind telling me why it's unofficial? Why we seem to be here after everything has gotten started? Again?"

"Well, we did inform the local police department, but they declined to take a missing person report until the person was missing for twenty-four hours."

"You don't say. I thought the Police Chief was sharper than that."

"He is. He's on vacation. Out of town. We're dealing with the second string."

"We did this once before."

"Yes, we did. But, the second string isn't even here. The people out there are capable and accomplished in their own right. You may not have recognized them. We've got the Chief of Station of the Coast Guard, the captain of The Escape, a veteran Coast Guard volunteer, and me. And two of the best dogs in the business. And here at the site, we have some extremely capable medical and communications personnel. We might appreciate it if you cut us a little slack while we all work together to bring this man back."

Chief Deputy Smiley was spared a response when the radio lit up again.

"This is Chris. Ray, get out here with Jock as soon as you can."

"I'm already on my way. It's getting a little dark. Moving slower than I did before."

"George is standing at the site where he found the coat. Cyril had a hard time figuring out a trail. Blaine seems to have circled around a bit, took off in one direction, doubled back. We're following one trail. George will point you in the direction I want you to take."

"Where are the deputies?"

"Two with me. Two will go with you."

By this time, Ray was at the site. The next voice on the radio was George. "They've gone off on that trail, Chris. I'm going to stay right here. Don't forget to pick me up after you find this guy."

Chapter 22: That's On My List!

Friday morning dawned bright and clear. Beautiful sunlight streamed through the east windows. This was late December, and the sun heralded a household sleeping in late.

Annie and Chris slept the sleep of the dead, fully clothed and on top of the covers, an afghan pulled over for warmth.

Way too early, Cyril jumped on top of Chris while Mr. Bean jumped onto Annie's chest to give her good morning kisses flavored with cat food crumbs. At least it wasn't litter.

From a distance Annie could hear the sounds of the town's snowplows, clearing off the streets to get traffic moving once again and preparing for the blizzard that was yet to come.

Annie mumbled, "We have to get up."

"I know," came a voice muffled by bed clothes. Cyril had his face pinned with his big chest.

Annie, realizing she had guests, and remembering her long list of things-that-must-be-done-today-without-fail, finally jumped up. "I'm first in the shower."

Most of the cats still hid under the bed, but it was time for breakfast, and they crawled out, trotting expectantly to the cleaned-out cat food dishes. Cyril had wiped them out, leaving only a few crumbs for Mr. Bean. He had taken most of their water as well.

That got Cyril a hiss and a spit from Little Socks. Cyril didn't care. He hopped around at the apartment door until Chris opened it and followed him downstairs at a trot. Front door open, Cyril bounded outside, refreshed himself and bounded back in. He knew where to go. Upstairs was not the place for him. Cyril ran to the kitchen in search of the real master of the food, Henrie.

When Chris got back to the apartment, Annie was out of the shower and dressed. "You have a set of clothes in my top dresser drawer, and I stocked some shaving supplies and other things for you in the bathroom."

Chris looked surprised. "When did you do that?"

"Oh, a while ago," came the response. And she was gone, headed downstairs to begin her day.

The kitchen and dining room were high on the energy of the day. Carlos was at Mr. Bean's, but his mother, taking advantage of Boone's snow clearing, made it to the Inn for breakfast, joining her daughters and Isabel. "Do you know," she said to Annie, "that wonderful crew keeps all of our steps cleaned as well? I came outside, and the deck and stairs were cleaned and salted, and the sidewalk around to the front. I thought I would have to wade through five inches of snow to get to you."

"Boone is a wonder. He and his crew. I have to do something for them today. That's on my list!"

Daniela, Rosa, Valeria and Isabel had a private table for four in the corner of the room. It wasn't so private, as everyone talked with everyone else, but they sat together.

Patti's five younger children sat at another table with Cyril nearby. The twins, from their high chairs, continued to throw as much food as they ate.

Patti and Jessica sat at the head of the table. Patti complained, "Henri gave us a lecture today. We went in to help with breakfast, and he told us to get our behinds out of his kitchen!"

"He said that?"

"Well, not that, really. It was formal Henrie-speak. It was more like, 'I would advise you to leave the cooking to the professionals.' But I interpreted it as getting my behind out of his way."

Annie laughed. "Last night was certainly an exception to all of our rules. It was a unique night. Now we're back to normal, and Henrie's kitchen is Henrie's kitchen. Get used to it!"

"But how are we going to cook our traditional Christmas Eve dinner?"

"We're going to do that in my apartment. I have everything we need. Except the oysters. Laila will have them for me today."

"I'll pick them up for you. I want to go over there today. That dish Mom got was fantastic. She says Laila has all sorts of things like that."

"You'll have to go into all of the shops today, including the shops on Main Street, particularly Antiques On Main. His open house is today."

The family would go their separate ways during the day today, allowing Annie to do the things she needed to do. When Nancy and Sam arrived for breakfast, they all made plans.

Sam would go again to Antiques On Main to help Frank. Nancy, Patti and Jessica would go on a shopping spree that would include interludes of lunch at the Café, dessert at Mr. Bean's and afternoon wine at Sassy P's. Patti was going to be sure her mother had time to sit and rest after one or two shops.

Fritz and Paul would take the older children on another kind of shopping spree, hitting some of the big box stores at the edge of town. At some point in the afternoon, they would drop the kids at the Inn and head to Mo's Tap. Only for a short while, they said.

JoJo and Ben, already ensconced in the suite, would stay through Christmas, and after they helped Henrie with a few things, they planned to take the younger children for a walk on the beach and over to the town park. Between Boone and the town, a path had already been made down to the lake front, wide enough for the double stroller.

Chris and Jeff hit the dining room at the same time, looked at the group of people, took one look at one another and announced, in unison, "We having breakfast at the Café!"

Tiger Lily, hiding under the buffet, ran to Chris and pummeled his right shoe with both front feet. "Lily! What do you want, darlin'?"

Annie looked and saw what Tiger Lily was doing. "It's warm enough for her to go to the Café, but I still don't want all the kids getting out today. Will you carry her to the Café and let her stay there today?"

"Sure." After he put his coat on, Chris leaned down to pick her up. She purred and cuddled into his shoulder, settling in for the ride to her special place, which, today, was anywhere-away-from-the-children.

Little Socks, not wanting to be left behind, ran out from under the buffet to wrap herself around his legs, over and over again.

Chris looked at Annie, who understood the silent question. "Sure. Little Socks, someone will have to carry you. Do you understand?" Little Socks, standing by Chris, tapped his right foot one time. Annie closed her eyes and breathed deeply. Chris looked at the green-eyed monster, wondered about the gesture, then looked back at Annie. "Are you sure it's safe to pick her up?"

Jeff beat him to the punch. As he leaned to pick her up, he said, "You love me, don't you, girl?"

Little Socks didn't purr, but she didn't hiss, spit, bite or claw, either. She allowed herself to be carried on his shoulder, staring at Tiger Lily the entire time with a, "Do not ever remind me of this moment again" kind of a look.

Annie noticed, as Chris and Jeff left, that Jeff's laptop case hung from his shoulder.

As they got to the door, Chris stopped, as if remembering something. "Cyril! Cyril, come on, boy. Let's go to the Café for breakfast!"

Cyril, covered up in small children, shouldered his way to his feet and followed obediently. Gracie, Ella and Ollie wailed in disappointment.

The day was clear and sunny; the temperature had climbed into the twenties, and only a light breeze tickled their noses.

Annie, finally realizing what they had all been missing, said suddenly, "We all have to get together to watch the sunset tonight! There will finally be one!"

Nancy and Sam could hardly contain their excitement as they told the rest of the family about the beautiful sunsets here at the Inn.

Annie continued, "This is going to be the only day we'll be able to see the sun at sunset while you're here. The blizzard is supposed to hit tomorrow, and it's supposed to snow through Christmas day.

"It will be a tight fit, but we can all watch it from my balcony. Daniela, you and the girls will have to come, too. I know Carlos has told you about our sunsets."

Henrie came to the dining room. "I can prepare a light repast, and you do not have to go upstairs. It is lovely from up there, but we can put a buffet on the all-season porch, and those who care to brave the winter cold can go outside. It will be much warmer this evening than it has been."

"You're right, Henrie. Budding photographers can go up to the apartment, and those of us who just want to bask in the color can stay down. The sun will set shortly after 5:00 tonight, so plan to be back here by 5:00 at the latest."

No one mentioned the guest who was not present at table.

Annie had a long list of things to do. First on her list was to deliver gift baskets to her most important suppliers, which included everyone on the other side of The Avenue. Even Pastor Teresa, she reckoned, was an important supplier of faith, hope and peace.

She stopped first at Bloomin' Crazy to pick up Clara's wagon. Her next stop was at Mr. Bean's, then Sassy P's. Carlos and Jesus were ready for her.

Annie reveled in the sunshine on her face as she walked up Main Street to Beancounters. As she walked past Antiques On Main, she noticed a crowd of people inside. The weather had cooperated, thank goodness. Main Street was packed with the cars and trucks of shoppers and buyers. Even the town lot up the street appeared full.

Mindy got up to help with the door as Annie pulled the wagon inside. "You brought flowers?"

"No, just the flower wagon. I do have a present for Gwen. Is she in?"

"She is!" came Gwen's voice from the hallway. As Gwen stepped into the outer office, she came to Annie and hugged her. "Merry Christmas to you, Annie. I'm glad you're here."

Gwen handed Annie a thick envelope. "Thank you, Gwen! May I open it now?"

"Please do."

Annie opened the envelope and found a hilarious Christmas card. Inside the card was a gift certificate to her favorite restaurant outside Chelsea, a romantic place in Marsh Haven. "Oh, Gwen, you shouldn't have!"

"But I did. Now, have you made that decision I've been on you to make?"

"I did. But first, I have something for you." Annie pulled out a basket that contained a bottle of sweet white wine, one of Gwen's favorites, individually wrapped cheeses and baked goods, and a box of Jerry's truffles, topped with a candy cane ribbon.

"Perfect. This will feed my family on Christmas Eve."

Annie reached in and pulled out a similar basket for Mindy. "For all that you do, even when you have to act like a bouncer."

Mindy blushed. "I never expected...thank you!"

Mindy turned and ran to the back of the building before Annie could say, "You're welcome."

She turned back to Gwen. "Now about that decision. The information you gave me was outstanding. But I'm going to go a different way."

"You can do whatever you want to do, Annie."

"I want to give an equal amount to the charities that we on The Avenue chose for the block parties this past year, including the charity we'll have for our New Year's Eve party."

"That will be wonderful. They are all 501(c)(3) organizations, so that will work out just fine. What is the charity for New Year's Eve?"

"It's the local human service organization. They can use the gifts for food, shelter, utilities, whatever the needs are over the winter season."

"Then the gift will be timely."

"For now, let's plan to do that every year. We'll come up with the total amount I should be giving for tax purposes, and then divide it evenly among those places. They'll be different every year."

"It's a great idea. And your gift stays right here at home, most of the time."

Annie left, walking again past Antiques On Main and hoping that some good selections would be available by the time she could get there.

Her next stop was at the first place on The Avenue, Soul's Harbor. Teresa was in the gift shop.

"No volunteer today?"

"No. The campers went home before this weather set in, and all of my local volunteers have something else going on."

"It's just as well. I need to talk to you."

"How can I help?"

"It's a problem of Christmas gifts."

"We have a number of things here in the shop. Do you need help finding something?"

"No, not really. I want to get some charcoals that Chris has done for Mom and Sam, Patti and Fritz and Jessica and

Paul, but I want to do something more meaningful for the kids."

"Meaningful, how?"

"I've been doing my late Christmas shopping, as usual, and since I can't seem to make up my mind, everyone suggests that I get gift certificates. So I've been thinking about that, and I wondered if I could get a kind of gift certificate that was, like, a contribution to a charity of some sort. But I want it to mean something to them. I want to be able to tell them what they are giving to."

"That's a wonderful idea, and even though you're late – you do know when Christmas is, don't you Annie? – I think I can help."

Teresa walked to a display case that had colorful brochures about a variety of charities.

"Here's an example. If you make a gift to this safe water project, you can give this brochure to the person you are making the gift for. And here are several other projects. All you have to do is decide to whom you're giving, and in whose name, and I can print out a certificate and put it with a brochure."

"These look familiar. Does Gwen shop here?"

Teresa laughed. "Gwen has customers that she has to push into making end-of-year contributions, and she gets lots of her ideas from me. I think you might have a bunch of these already."

"I think I do, but I haven't had time to look through them."

"What do you want to do?"

Annie gave Teresa the list of names of all of the children, chose an equal number of charities, decided on a total amount, and left it in Teresa's hands.

"Before I leave, let me choose three charcoals."

Chris was a prolific artist. He showed many of his works to Annie, but many he brought to Teresa before Annie ever saw them. She loved to go into the gift shop to see what he may have done without sharing. She was not disappointed today.

For Nancy and Sam, she chose a landscape that included the lighthouse. This was similar to a landscape she had purchased as an open house gift for Frank the previous fall. Nancy had been with her and admired it. As with the previous charcoal, Chris had put amazing detail into the lighthouse itself. The bricks themselves were visible. The lake stood behind the lighthouse, and the flash of color was the brilliant orange, rose and yellow sunset to the west. This picture was entitled "The Last Sunset."

For Patti and Fritz, she chose a scene at the beach on a summer day. The perspective was one of an artist standing far behind the crowd. The charcoal captured the choppy water of the lake, a lifeguard on the stand, groups of families on blankets and under umbrellas, and children playing at the water's edge. The one area of color was a rainbow colored umbrella protecting a large family. The picture was entitled, "Summer Daze."

For Jessica and Paul, she chose a picture of a couple, backs to the artist, holding infant twins, heads together. Chris made this after hearing about Annie's niece and her twin children. He had said nothing to Annie about it. The adults did not resemble Jessica and Paul, as Chris had never met them. But the thought and the love were there. There were two pieces of color in this charcoal; the tip of one baby blanket was peach and the tip of the other was lilac. The title was simple. "Love."

Annie left the charcoals there. She would pick them up later in the afternoon when she picked up the certificates for the children. Before leaving, however, she gave Teresa a basket of baked goods, truffles and cheeses with a gift certificate to Tiger Lily's Café on top.

Annie made stops at all of the shops on The Avenue, leaving similar baskets for everyone: Mem, Clara, Holly and Jolly, Jennifer and Marie and Laila. At Laila's, she also left a basket of toys for the younger children and a gift certificate for gaming time at Mem's for James.

She spent some extra time visiting with Jennifer and Marie, getting a perspective of the rescue attempt that she had not heard before.

Annie next made special trips to each of her businesses, the Inn included. For Henrie, Minnie, Jesus, Carlos, Jerry, George, Candice, Diana, Trudie and Felicity, she had envelopes with an annual bonus and a generous gift certificate for any place on The Avenue, good all year.

Annie made an arrangement with her friends on the other side. When someone presented them with a certificate, they would write the store name and amount on the back, so everyone could keep track. The store would let Annie know the cost of the purchase; Annie would pay at that time.

Annie thought this gift certificate idea was a great one, and she was happy the Karma of the week kept presenting this idea to her over and over and over.

She made most of the trips quickly, having so many things on her to-do list today, but she spent some extra time with

Diana, allowing her to cry as she recounted the harrowing rescue events. Diana had ridden in the back of Jennifer's ambulance on the way to the hospital once the rescue attempt was concluded.

Annie put the last two gift baskets in the Inn's SUV. She first drove through the town's parking lot, making use of the few lanes that had been plowed earlier in the day. Stopping at The Marina, she saw Cheryl through the large windows.

Annie smiled. She had not spent enough time with her childhood friend in the last couple of months. She took the basket in, and they stood together at the doorway, hugging one another.

Annie had placed the basket on the floor for the hug. Now she picked it up and took it to the seating area. They sat side by side on the sofa as Annie asked how she was doing.

"I'm okay. You know, I'm getting a little tired of rescuing our own. Well, Blaine was a guest, not a resident, but you know what I mean. Ray had gotten to know him pretty well in just a couple of days."

They sat together for a while, then Annie left to complete her to-do list.

The last gift was similar to the others but larger, since she was gifting four people. It contained loaves of fresh bread, a pie, cupcakes, scones, fresh cookies, a large box of Jerry's truffles, three kinds of cheese and some sausage, gift certificates to the Café, and two bottles of wine, one red, one white. Annie didn't know what to choose, so she chose one sweet and one dry.

She started driving, not sure exactly where she would end up. She smiled to herself, thinking again of the conversation with Boone the day before, when she had asked if she could come to his house.

"Why shore. We'd be might proud to have ya. You go on out to that road that goes around the lake, you know, that dippy thing that it makes out past the state park, and you go till you gets to a sign that sez 'Harley's Bait Shop.' Wonst you sees that sign, look fer a road that goes off to the left, off towards the lake. There ain't a sign there. It's real private-like. It's jest a gravel road. You gets on that road and you winds around until you gets to the end of it, and there we'll be a'waitin' on ya."

Annie had traveled this road many times, but she had not looked for this particular sign or the gravel road Boone mentioned. Today she kept her eyes sharp, happy to have bright sunshine instead of blowing snow.

She saw the sign, found the road and turned off, thinking immediately, what in the world have I gotten into? The lane was only wide enough for one vehicle. Trees crowded the edges. Annie prayed she would not meet someone coming toward her. The trees left her nowhere to go and the curves presented blind spot after blind spot.

At least it had been plowed. Annie wondered who took care of this road, the town or the county. But that thought didn't linger long.

The center lane, even in December, still had tall weeds that drug the undercarriage of the car. Her vehicle lurched left and right when she drove over potholes filled with snow and ice.

She began to worry more when she thought about what might be at the end of the lane. This was far too narrow for her to turn around. If she couldn't turn to drive out, she would have to back up all the way.

Suddenly, she rounded a curve and the lane became an asphalt-paved road. The trees that had encroached upon the edges of the lane gave way to a landscaped drive. At least Annie thought it was landscaped. It was hard to tell with the snow. Sitting in the near distance, on top of a hill overlooking the lake, was a two-story mansion. That's what it was. A mansion.

The front looked southern gothic. The center rose, showing off the tall nature of the rooms within. Columns, six of them, rose to surround and support verandas on both the first and second floors. To each side of the house were two-story sections, substantial but shorter than the center expanse. To the right appeared to be kitchen and dining rooms and to the left the parlor and library. She assumed the upstairs rooms were a combination of bedrooms and dens. The master bedroom must be in that tall middle section.

Windows were everywhere. The house was easily large enough for four or five bathrooms. From what she could tell, the house was deep and had a landscaped area overlooking the lake. There was probably something, maybe steps, leading down to the water.

Annie struggled to close her gaping mouth as she parked on the circular driveway in front of the house. She exited the car and went to the passenger side for the gift basket. As she got the basket in hand and turned around, she saw Boone standing in the doorway, waving to her in welcome.

"Boone, this is lovely. I never knew this house existed."

Boone, sounding completely unlike Boone, replied, "Our lane into the driveway does the trick for us. We have never had unsolicited visitors."

"You speak the King's English, Boone."

Boone laughed as he took the basket from her and walked her up the steps and into the foyer. "Sometimes I have difficulty making the transition either from King's or to King's, but essentially, that is the only language spoken in this house."

A twelve foot tall Christmas tree dominated the entryway. It was beautiful. An elegant white fir with large red and gold ornaments, ribbons streaming down from the top. A blazing fireplace in the library caught her attention. The wide mantel held a nativity scene. Porcelain figures, Joseph at least three feet tall, belied the meaning this family gave to the season.

Boone continued to lead Annie to the right. In the kitchen, a tall elegant woman turned from her task of making tea.

Annie was startled. "Hilly, it's good to see you."

Hilly smiled and held out her hand. "Annie, it's time I introduced myself to you. I'm Harriet, Boone's better half."

Annie laughed. She knew Hilly from the Café and everywhere else on The Avenue. She was a common attendant to the block parties held on The Avenue. She dressed in a stylish manner, was friendly and unpretentious, and she was very private. No one knew much about her except her name. And apparently they didn't even know that.

"How it the world have I heard so much about you, about the good work that you do, from the people that hire you, and they don't have a clue that it's you? I may have had conversations about you with you standing right there!"

"That happens a lot. I know small towns, Annie, and I know how people put other people into boxes of expectation. I have guarded my privacy religiously. Either Boone takes care of meeting my business clients or one of my staff does. I make it a point to stay out of the businesses we clean when anyone that works there could be around. On occasion I've had to muss up my hair and throw a scarf over my head to remain anonymous, but there you have it. It's worked for years."

"And yet, here you are, allowing me to meet you at last."

"I sense a kindred spirit with you, Annie. I trust you will keep my secret, actually our secret, and I know you will not treat any of us any differently just because you have some knowledge about who we are."

"Boone said you would be doing our places yourself while you figured out what I wanted. That works with every place that closes, but the Inn doesn't close. How's that supposed to work?"

"I'll have to trust Henrie with my little secret as well. And I suppose that handsome man of yours, Chris."

"We can be trusted."

The door apparently leading to the garage opened and Daryl and Donny entered. They stopped, shocked to see Annie. Donny mumbled, "Hello, Ma'am. It's good ta see ya," while Daryl kept his mouth shut.

Annie smiled. "Hello, Daryl, Donny. It's good to see you as well."

The boys exited the kitchen through the back door and Annie could hear them pounding up some steps in the back of the house.

Boone chuckled and said, "Let's open one of these bottles and sit by the fireplace."

Sitting in front of the fire, Annie said, "I can only stay a short while. I promised Frank I would get to his open house, and he'll be closing in a couple of hours. I just have to say that I would love to stay longer."

"Well, you can come back anytime. But you're here for a few minutes now. Tell us about yourself."

Annie told them what she thought they might like to hear, about spending summers with her father here in Chelsea, coming here to live after he passed away. About her mother and half-sister, her sister's family. About her cats. Then Annie asked them about themselves.

Boone and Hilly looked at one another. Hilly finally started. "Boone and I have been married for nearly thirty years. When we first married, we decided we wanted more for our children than what our families were able to give us. We both wanted to go to college, but we couldn't afford it. So we made do with an informal education."

She waved her hand toward the bookshelves, and Annie looked around, noticing books from almost every section of a public library.

"We decided the best thing we could do for our children was to work hard, instill in them a respect for education, and if possible provide them with a lovely home."

Annie mulled this over a bit. Then she timidly asked, "But what if the manners you teach them are not apparent to others?"

Hilly laughed. "People will see what they want to see. When Boone and I moved here, we looked and talked just as you see us in everyday life. By the time we had learned to become a bit more cultured, the boys were already into late grade school and junior high. They were already pegged as 'white trash.' Intelligent, but still white trash."

Boone took up the story. "Both boys took early graduation. Daryl could have gone straight from high school into college, but he wanted to make sure our business was solid, and he wanted to make sure this house was paid in full. So he worked full-time and put half of his income on the mortgage. Our family Christmas present this year is the final payment."

Hilly continued. "Now he'll go to the community college and so will Donny. They'll both make an income, and both were able to get scholarships to help pay for their education."

Boone cut in with a burst of pride. "They will be the first from either side of the family to get a college degree."

Hilly took the story back. "They kind of like their public personas for the time being, but I think, once they get to college and start meeting girls that don't automatically think of them as white trash, they'll start to shed it and become the boys they are here at the house."

Annie had to know. "And the two of you? Will you come out of the shadows, Hilly, and Boone, will you shed your public persona?"

Hilly and Boone looked at one another. "Maybe yes, maybe no," said Hilly finally. We like our privacy. But eventually, the boys will come home with wives and children, and they will want to know who their grandparents are. So at some point, we will probably have to."

Boone picked it up. "It's so easy to be the Boone that everyone knows and loves, that everyone counts on, but that no one invites to dinner. But then, you invited us to dinner. So maybe, maybe someday we'll drop the act.

"Frankly, it's a great thing that no one knows where we live. When people see our truck turn onto that lane, they think that we're coming to a place of no consequence or, if they know the house is here, they think we're doing a job."

Annie thought about their lifestyle. She decided to let a couple more people in on her secret. "You know, I'm an introvert. It is sometimes painful how much I want to close the world out. I would never want anything more in my life than to be so anonymous that no one knew who I was, where I lived, what I did. I envy you. I wish I could have a do-over and live this life myself."

Annie finished her wine and placed the crystal goblet carefully on the coffee table. "Thank you for a delightful afternoon. Now, can we pick a date when I can host you in my much less elegant apartment?"

Chapter 23: Go Do Your Cat Burglar Thing

Everyone at the Café was excited to see both Tiger Lily and Little Socks. Little Socks got away from the hands as quickly as she could and found a shelf at the back of the hostess stand in which to take a nap.

Tiger Lily took the time to walk around and greet everyone who worked there and all the guests she had neglected – by her absence – to greet.

Once the amenities had been cared for, however, she went to her special seat at the hostess stand, looking down in disgust at Little Socks.

"You can't work from there."

"I'm not working. I'm hiding."

Tiger Lily sighed and got back to the task of greeting guests. Apparently, people were happy to be here on such a sunny day, but they talked a lot about some kind of thing coming. It sounded like they were saying lizard, but she knew that wasn't right. Where was Cyril when you needed him?

Tiger Lily and Little Socks knew they were not to leave the Café. That was understood from Mommy's reluctance to let them come at all. Since she had not specifically forbidden them from leaving, they held that as a loose understanding.

As long as they stayed on this side of The Avenue, certainly, everything would be fine.

Tiger Lily wanted to get Little Sock's opinion of the hole in the back of the sink at Sassy P's. Tiger Lily thought that someone small, like a cat, could get from Sassy P's to Mr. Bean's from that hole. She explained the issue to Little Socks.

"Go do your cat burglar thing and go from one place to the other. Tell me what you see."

"*Right now?*"

"*Yes. Right now. We don't know when Mommy will come take us home again.*"

Little Socks grumbled, but she stretched, sat to lick her right paw, then stood up. "*What if she locked these doors too?*"

"*I don't think she remembered to do them. She just wanted to keep us in the house.*"

"*Okay. If I get locked in somewhere, it will be your fault.*"

Tiger Lily closed her eyes and shook her head. Then she turned to greet her next guest. It was Geraldine.

Tiger Lily was as polite as she could be. That meant she did not hiss, spit, claw or bite. She also did not close her eyes to nod her head, and when Geraldine reached in to touch her head, she moved to one side. Ick. Geraldine wanted to touch her. And that Hank was right behind. Ick again.

Little Socks slipped down and out the door behind them, apparently unnoticed. But then, that's what a cat burglar does.

Little Socks decided to check things from Mr. Bean's side first. She knew if Carlos or Jerry saw her, they would call Mommy to ask about Mr. Bean. That would be the end of it.

To avoid being taken home by Mommy, she waited until a couple of people were at the counter, then she slipped through the cat door and back to the kitchen. Every now and then she had to slip underneath a counter or hold herself tightly against a shelf, but she made it to the back of the kitchen without being seen.

She was able to get the cabinet door open because there was no latch, but when she looked at the plumbing, there wasn't a hole. She jumped inside to investigate, sniffing all of the interesting parts. She smelled two people. Two of the men that went into the basement of the Inn a few days ago, working on the plumbing there. Daryl and Donny.

Once satisfied she had learned all she could, she opened the cabinet door a crack, then slipped out, going out as quickly and quietly as she had come in.

She didn't have to wait at Sassy P's. Minnie's back was to the door and Jesus was nowhere to be seen. Little Socks ran through the main tasting room and peered cautiously into the back area. Seeing no one, she duplicated her efforts to see the hole at the back of this sink.

She found the same thing. No hole but something covering it. This one had different smells, though. She smelled Daryl and Donny and someone else. She didn't know the smell of the third person.

Little Socks turned to leave the cabinet but stopped when she heard Jesus. She stood still. Jesus was talking to someone and he was not happy. It was Marco.

Little Socks listened to the conversation and didn't leave until she was sure she was alone in the back room. She went swiftly out the way she had come.

As she ran up the street to the Café, she saw Marco inside Mr. Bean's. Curious, she slipped one more time into that doorway.

Marco was being mean to Carlos and Jerry. One of the women visiting Carlos was there, that Isabel lady. She sat at one of the tables with her hand over her mouth, eyes wide, while Carlos had an angry conversation. Jerry stayed behind Carlos, but Little Socks kept hearing Marco say his name. Jerry looked scared.

Little Socks slipped out the door just as Marco looked like he was finished. She almost ran into a man coming out of

Mo's Tap. She startled, fell back against the wall and stayed there, looking up at him. He looked down at her and pretended like he was going to kick her, but he didn't. He went on his way, and Little Socks saw him go into Sassy P's.

He was human smell number three.

Before she could rouse herself to go back to the Café, Mo's door opened again and that redhead stepped out. She turned and went to the Café. Little Socks followed, slipped in through the cat door as the big door was closing, and jumped behind the hostess stand.

From her vantage point on the floor, she couldn't see where the redhead went, but she was curious. She followed, looking up and around, but essentially following her scent, until she found her sitting with, ick, Geraldine and Hank.

Little Socks took a careful sniff of the redhead's boots, and sure enough, she detected traces of human scent number three. This woman had been with that man at Mo's.

Little Socks barely made it back to the hostess stand before Marco stepped into the door. He saw Geraldine and bee-lined back to her table. He didn't even stop to allow Tiger Lily to offer a greeting.

Tiger Lily said, *"One of us needs to go listen."*

"Not me. I have to get my thoughts together on what I've just learned. You go. It will be good to have two sets of ears on this, and I'm the first set."

Tiger Lily didn't wait for an explanation. Time was a'wastin'. She jumped to the floor and walked sedately to their table, curling around the ankles of the redhead, then hopping to the table ledge at her side. The redhead liked Mo. Tiger Lily figured if she could get the redhead to pet her, she would ignore her very presence. It was funny how humans did this. The closer the enemy, the more stupid they became.

It worked. Tiger Lily got an earful.

The afternoon was moving on, but Annie had two more stops to make. First, she parked at Soul's Harbor to pick up the charcoals and gift certificates. She then walked up the street to Antiques On Main.

The refreshments were nearly gone. Trudie and a couple of others had kept the food and drink filled on the buffet, but closing time was coming, so they were winding down.

Annie got a much-needed cup of coffee and a small sandwich. "This is lunch," she said, sad face begging for sympathy. Trudie reached into the cooler and made up a plate of crudités and put another tea sandwich in the middle.

"Frank almost cried when I told him today's catering was your Christmas present to him."

Annie smiled. "It was a great gift. I didn't have to shop and you and Felicity did all the work."

She went off in search of a bargain. She found a few things.

By 4:00, Annie had paid for her purchases, including the Christmas present from earlier in the week, and walked out with the promise to send someone to pick up her finds after Christmas.

Annie spoke to Trudie on the way out. "I purchased some things for the catering hall. We'll need to get them before the New Year's Eve party. I'll ask Chris if he can get some folks to help before then."

"What did you get?"

"I found a peacock hand-painted antique buffet in tones of purple, and a French buffet sideboard, painted turquoise. There was also a hostess stand, I think French, antiqued in rose tones. I think they'll go well with the other things we have. They'll add to our eclectic collection."

"There have been lots of people here all day. Did Frank say how he did?"

"He sold well beyond his expectations. Of course, having the open house on the one day all week that people were comfortable getting out didn't hurt."

"And the one day before the next day everyone will be cooped up again."

Annie drove back to the Inn and unloaded her treasures. Henrie took her purchases to the apartment and hid them under the bed. He had to move two cats to do so.

By the time Annie got to the Café, Tiger Lily and Little Socks sat innocently on the hostess stand. Little Socks gave a simpering little bow of welcome. Tiger Lily bopped her on the nose for her rude behavior.

Annie laughed. "Girls. Is this how you've been greeting folks all day? We're going home. It's not so cold that you can't walk, and since I didn't bring a carrier or wagon, that's what you're going to do."

Two girls looked at her. Then Annie said the magic words. "Sunset tonight."

They jumped down to follow Annie out the door.

Chapter 24: The Brilliant Colors Burst Over The Lake

Everyone gathered in the all-season porch, anxious to see the famous Sunset Avenue sunset. Sam was exhausted, but he was still solicitous of Nancy.

Nancy, who had been remarkably normal to this point today, appeared to be a little confused.

"Why are we sitting out here? We should be in by the fire, where it's warm."

"Here, Mom, use my sweater," this from Patti. "We're going to watch the sunset."

Patti made sure Nancy was sitting at a table and put coffee and some appetizers on a plate in front of her.

"Why, Patti, what are you doing here? Do you live here now?"

"No, Mom. I'm visiting. I brought the family."

"How wonderful. I'd love to see the kids."

The kids were outside, running around in the snow with JoJo, Ben, Paul and Fritz, but very visible to everyone on the porch.

Sam whispered, "Just let her drink that coffee and sit for a bit. She'll be fine."

The cats were getting used to the kids. Or it should probably be said that the kids were getting used to the cats. They were no longer chasing them everywhere, so the cats had ventured out to the porch to watch the brilliant colors.

Jeff, Chris and Cyril had seen someone during the day and knew to be there by 5:00 for food and a good time, and Carlos brought his mother over in time to get one of the best seats. Of course, Isabel got up to give her great seat to Daniela.

Annie saw the look that passed between Isabel and Carlos but didn't have time to ask what it was about.

Soon, the sun was setting, the brilliant colors took over the conversation, and all else was forgotten. For a moment.

The cats and Cyril sat in the corner, just as happy as the humans to see the sunset. This was the best reason to live right here.

They watched as the brilliant colors burst over the lake, then started to sink, still glowing bright.

Tiger Lily got down to business. *"We don't know how long we'll have Cyril to help tonight. I heard Chris say he was going home in a little bit because he needs sleep."*

Mr. Bean, always missing the larger point, asked, *"Why does he need to go home to sleep?"*

Tiger Lily shushed him and continued. *"Cyril, you need to listen to what we all have to say and help us figure out this mess."*

They got to it. Little Socks started. *"I went to investigate the holes under the sinks in Sassy P's and Mr. Bean's."*

Tiger Lily was ready and put one paw each on Sassy Pants' and Mr. Bean's noses to keep them quiet.

Little Socks continued. *"There were covers over the holes. They made a hiding place."*

Mo said, *"Trill!"*

Little Socks, angry about the interruption and her inability to translate, hissed in his direction.

Sassy Pants said, *"He hadded a good question. He askted if anything is hidded there."*

275

"I don't know. I couldn't open them."

Mr. Bean added, *"It was a good question. Can we go find out?"*

"No! I can't open them!"

"But you're a burglar."

"I burgled my way into the places without being seen, when they were open and people were there. No one else could have done that!"

"Mighty Mouse could have done that."

"What does Mighty Mouse have to do with anything?"

Tiger Lily sat on Mr. Bean's tail to shut him up and said, *"Let Little Socks finish. She's got some important things to say, and I have more."*

Mo said, *"TRILL!"*

Little Socks closed her eyes and started to put her forehead to the floor, but Sassy Pants explained, *"He wants to know who putted the covers over the holes."*

Little Socks huffed but made a grudging admission. *"That was a good question, Mo. At Mr. Bean's place I smelled Daryl and Donny, you know, the snow guys and the plumber guys. But at Sassy P's I smelled a third guy, and I'll talk about him in a minute."*

Little Socks glared at Sassy Pants, Mr. Bean and Mo, daring them to interrupt her, took a deep breath and started again. *"So I went to Mr. Bean's, then Sassy P's. I realized we couldn't get into either side to take a look, and then I heard Jesus arguing with Marco."*

Sassy Pants sat up and started to speak. Tiger Lily put a paw on her nose.

Little Socks kept going. *"Marco was talking about Jesus being illegal and he'd better get back to Mexico. And Jesus said he wasn't from Mexico. He was from California. But then Marco said he looks like he's from Mexico and was he helping Carlos deal drugs. And Jesus, he got really mad and told Marco he'd better get out. And Marco said you can't talk to a police officer like that. And Jesus, he said, 'I didn't realize you were here in an official capacity,' just like that, and then he asked if he was being charged with a crime and Marco said not yet."*

Little Socks stopped for a breath. Kali and Ko, together, said, *"What happened next?" "Did Jesus get arrested?"*

Little Socks continued again. *"Marco finally left and told Jesus not to leave town, and Jesus called Carlos on the telephone and started to tell him what Marco was saying. He didn't get to finish his sentence, because Carlos cut him off."*

Mr. Bean said, *"Why was Carlos rude to Jesus?"*

Tiger Lily, now putting a paw on Mr. Bean's nose, said, *"Just be quiet. It will all be clear in a minute."*

Little Socks looked around the room to make sure she still had everyone's attention. *"Okay, so now I can sneak out, and I'm running back to the Café, but I see that idiot Marco in Mr. Bean's place."*

Tiger Lily lifted a paw, but Mr. Bean stayed silent.

"I burgled my way in again, and Marco was accusing Carlos of running drugs and using his family to run drugs. Carlos was pretty much not saying anything, but then Marco started going on about Jerry being a murderer, and how could Carlos sleep at night knowing that Jerry could murder his own mother in her own bed."

That shut down all thoughts of conversation. The cats and Cyril were shocked. Tiger Lily let the silence linger, then said gently, *"Tell them the rest of it."*

"Then Carlos told Marco to get his fat — he said a bad word — out of Mr. Bean's Confectionary and to not come back, ever, unless he came in with a search warrant or an arrest warrant."

The cats and Cyril were still shocked.

"*Keep going, Little Socks.*"

"*Okay, and then Marco left, and I left, and I almost ran into this guy coming out of Mo's.*"

Mo perked up.

"*He was funny looking, yellow hair all sticking up, tattoos and jewelry everywhere.*"

Mo said, "*Trill!*"

Kali and Ko said together, "*His name is Rusty.*" "*You're talking about Rusty.*"

"*Okay. Now we have a name, that's good, because he stopped and was going to kick me, but for some reason he didn't. I had a chance to smell him, though, and he was the other human smell on the sink thing.*"

Little Socks looked around, checked with Cyril, who nodded to continue, and she did.

"*Then I started to go to the Café again, and that redhead that Candice hates was leaving Mo's to go there. I followed her in and she went to sit with Geraldine and Hank.*"

A chorus of "*Oh no!*" "*Ick!*" "*Not them!*" "*That's Christal!*" and "*Trill!!!!!!*" followed.

Little Socks sat down and licked both of her front paws, signaling that she was finished with her report.

Tiger Lily started up. "*And then Marco came in. He sat down with them.*"

Looks of pure disgust were on every face.

"*I went to the table to listen to what they had to say, and every bad thing you want to think about these people would be true.*"

Tiger Lily looked at Cyril. "*This is where you have to pay real close attention.*"

Cyril nodded.

Tiger Lily went on. *"That redhead, Christal, told Marco that Carlos offered to sell her some meth and said it was real good stuff, that it had just come up from Mexico."*

"No!"

"Mr. Bean! Let her finish!"

"Marco asked Christal if she could tell him anything else, and she said whenever Carlos sold her drugs, he went into the kitchen and she thought he went to the back of the room, and sometimes there was a little water on the plastic bag, so maybe it was hidden in the plumbing somewhere.

"And that Hank, he asked if there was anything that Jesus could be arrested for. Marco said he didn't think so, he didn't have anything worthy of getting a warrant. Then Geraldine, she said, what if the drugs were hidden where either Carlos or Jesus could get to them, and he said that would work. And then, Marco left and said he had work to do."

Cyril was beside himself. *"He was going to get warrants. He's going to search those places, he's going to find drugs that Rusty planted, and he's going to arrest Carlos and Jesus."*

The cats were dumbfounded. Then the proverbial doo doo hit the proverbial fan.

The sunset had ended, the families on the porch were cleaning up their supper dishes, and Marco walked in with two officers behind him.

Annie, still angry with Marco for any number of reasons, said, "And this is why we need to start locking the front door, Henrie."

Marco said, "I'm here on official business."

"Oh, would that official business have anything to do with the rescue that you didn't involve yourself in last night?"

"He was not a missing person. He hadn't been gone long enough, and you really stepped into it, going over my head to call the Sheriff's Department."

"Well as it turns out, we didn't even need them. Four volunteers and two dogs found him. But they were there, and they did help carry him out, and they did give Jennifer a sirens and lights escort to the hospital. So, no, we didn't need them and we didn't need you, but no thanks to you, a man is still living. A little worse for the wear, but still living."

Kali and Ko breathed a sigh of relief. They had been hiding from the children and did not hear what happened to Blaine, and no one talked about it today. He was alive. He might be sick or injured, but he was alive. Maybe they would be able to see him before he went home to his Mother

Marco, covering for his embarrassment about that particular decision, said, "I'm here for another reason."

"And what would that be, Marco?"

Chris moved behind Annie and put his hands on her shoulders in an effort to keep her calm.

"Well, while your friend," putting emphasis on the word 'friend' and pointing to Jeff, "has been running around in the woods and hanging out at all the finest places Chelsea has to offer, I've been investigating your theft problem.

Annie and Jeff looked at one another. Jeff wisely kept silent and Annie followed his lead. She looked back at Marco.

"I haven't solved that crime. Yet. But I've solved another crime or two."

Annie continued to stare at him.

"I'm here with a warrant for the arrest of your head baker, Carlos."

Annie's face went white. Daniela, Rosa and Valeria screamed. Isabel grabbed Carlos by the arm but remained silent.

"On what charge?" asked Annie.

"Dealing methamphetamine."

Annie almost laughed. "On what evidence?"

"Several packets of meth hidden between those two sinks that are back to back between the bakery and the winery. Meth from Mexico. You're going to need a darn good lawyer, Mexican, because you're going to be convicted, you're going to serve time, and then you're going to be sent right back to your rightful home. I've already got your partner in custody. Jesus is headed to the County jail for booking, and eventually, when he gets his one phone call, I'm sure he'll call you, Annie. His little girlfriend wasn't there when I picked him up, so you might want to get down there and lock the place up."

Annie had so many things running through her head she didn't know what to do or say.

Henrie spoke up. "Annie, you stay here and arrange for attorneys for Carlos and Jesus. I will go to Sassy P's right now to make sure everything is taken care of." Henrie went to Carlos, put his hand on his shoulder and said quietly, "This will be cleared up quickly."

He turned to leave, remembered his favorite television shows and turned back. "Talk to no one until Annie has secured an attorney." Then he left, staying far away from Marco and not looking in his direction.

Annie finally tore her eyes away from Marco and looked at Carlos, who was looking at her with almost desperate eyes. She said, "Don't worry, Carlos. We'll take care of everything."

Carlos only said, "Take care of Jerry. He's going after Jerry next."

Chris looked at Marco. "Who do I talk to about making bail?"

Marco actually smiled. "These boys aren't going to be able to talk to anyone about bail until their arraignment, and that won't happen until Monday. I'll see to that."

Jeff looked squarely at Marco. "I'm calling my superiors right now. If this is a drug arrest, and if you are alleging the drugs came from Mexico, then we're getting involved. We'll want to see the evidence, all of it, and we're going to review the search warrants and the evidence produced to get the warrants."

"I had good evidence. It was an informant. A good one."

"He or she had better be good."

Annie, finding her courage again, said, "And it better not be Geraldine or Hank or any of their cronies."

Marco, covering for any questions he might have about the legality of his bust, said to Jeff, "You're just upset that I'm moving ahead and you aren't. I'm going to solve your case too, and I'll probably do it before Christmas."

Marco threw a nasty look at Annie and jerked at Carlos, now handcuffed, on the way out the door.

Before Jeff called the FBI office, Annie put her hand on his arm.

"I hate to say this. I really do. I saw Boone's sons put those covers up just yesterday. Jesus and Carlos probably didn't even know there was a space there. I hate to think those boys had anything to do with it, but I know Carlos and Jesus didn't."

"Maybe the boys didn't do it, Annie, but maybe they can lead us to who did."

Chapter 25: Annie Barely Slept

Annie woke up early on Christmas Eve. Well, let's be honest. Annie barely slept the night before.

The cats stayed in bed with her, rarely moving except for a rare visit to the litter pan or, in Ko's case, a few trips to the cat food dish.

The night before was a blur. No one in the house went to bed before midnight.

Annie couldn't sit still. She was on the phone. She texted. She comforted family and friends. She thought through issues and problems. She brought food and drinks from the kitchen. She cleaned up. She was the glue.

Annie didn't know a criminal attorney, so she called the only person she could think of. She called Greg, a realtor friend, who immediately called an attorney he trusted from Marsh Haven.

Annie talked to Kelsie after she left the County jail. She was allowed to speak to Jesus and Carlos, separately, of course, but she was unable to secure their release. Kelsie informed Annie that if nothing happened by noon today, they would be incarcerated until their arraignment on Monday morning. Of course, Monday was the day after Christmas.

By this time, Sam had taken Nancy to bed. She had grown more confused as the evening wore on.

Minnie came to the Inn for comfort. She had been shopping and returned to find Henrie locking up Sassy P's.

Jerry came to the Inn for confession. Isabel called him, knowing him to be alone and pacing in his apartment, and insisted he come.

Henrie, talking with JoJo and Ben about helping at Mr. Bean's and Sassy P's, was stopped by Daniela. She was the baker. She would go to Mr. Bean's early in the morning to get the baked goods going while Jerry kept up with the candies. Tomorrow being Christmas Eve, they would be very busy keeping up with pre-orders. Isabel would help as well.

Rosa and Valeria asked Minnie if they could help her at Sassy P's. Minnie thought about it, and decided they could do everything but serve wine. They could sell unopened bottles, however, and she could certainly use the help.

Annie had never known the crime that sent Jerry to prison, but Carlos did. With Jerry's permission, he had shared the story with Isabel after Marco left. Now Isabel sat next to Jerry as he began his story.

Jerry, a most private man, was not ashamed of what he had done. He only wanted to forget about it. That's why he never discussed it.

Jerry's mother had terminal cancer. The cancer was wretched and painful, and it tore at Jerry to see her in this state. She knew she only had months, possibly weeks, to live, but the pain was nearly unbearable.

She begged Jerry to take care of her, to end her pain. He refused, believing in miracles, and trusted that she would somehow get better. But she didn't. And she wouldn't. And she couldn't take the pain any longer.

Jerry did his research, determined which of his mother's pills would do what she wanted, filled the prescriptions, did what had to be done, and sat with her until she was gone.

And then he called the police. Eventually, the case was turned over to federal jurisdiction, and he entered a plea of guilty to active euthanasia, the active participation in a suicide.

Fritz, being a man of even temper barely prone to anger, took great offense at Marco's treatment of Jerry. Fritz was also familiar with small town gossip. Knowing absolutely nothing about baking or making candy, Fritz planned to leave at 5:00 AM to be the counterman for the day and to help deflect gawkers and gossipers.

Annie made sure the rest of her staff knew everything she knew so they, too, could deflect the gossipers and could get the real story out.

But what was the real story?

Annie got to breakfast around 7:00, which was early for her. Patti and Jessica were already there, helping their children to food and drinks. Henrie, with the help of JoJo and Ben, had again produced a masterpiece.

Poached eggs covered with cheddar cheese, swimming in cream and ready to be placed on a bread of choice, wheat or rye toast, or toasted English muffins. Canadian bacon, Polish sausage slices and thickly sliced ham. Fresh fruit salad. Oatmeal with walnuts and apples. Hot cinnamon buns. Lox, bagels and cream cheese. And for the children, a variety of dry breakfast cereals, the individual boxes that children love to fight over. Henry had made sure to have several boxes of every variety so the fights would not be too intense.

The one large box of cereal was Cheerios. That box had been open and used before. Today, as with other days, Jerome and Sally ate one, threw some, ate another one, threw some more. And laughed.

The air was heavy with the promise of a snowstorm. Annie said, over the clamor, "If there is anything you want to do outside or on The Avenue, you need to do it this morning.

It will start snowing early this afternoon, and it's not going to
let up until sometime tomorrow. Maybe."

"Aunt Annie, where's the Christmas tree?"

"Yeah, Aunt Annie, we haven't seen a Christmas tree here.
Where is it?"

Annie turned to look at the children. "Well, guess what.
That's one of the things we need to do today. We need to
help Henrie drag that big ole tree up from the basement and
put it up in the library. And someone has to decorate it!"

"Me!" "Me!" "No, me!!!!!"

"We'll all help. Okay? And we have to decide where to put
the stockings. You know Santa will be looking for stockings."

"By the fireplace!" "He'll come down the fireplace!"

Annie looked at Patti to see if she had remembered to
bring the stockings for the kids. Patti had large stockings with
names embroidered on each one. She even had stockings for
Jessica and Paul, Jerome and Sally. Mothers and
grandmothers do things like that. Aunt Annie was generally
clueless.

Patti, of course, had remembered.

Jeff ducked his head into the dining room, looked at
Annie and pointed to the door. He was headed to the Café.

Annie called Felicity and asked that she make sure Jeff ate
at no charge for as long as he was in town, since this was the
second breakfast he was missing at the Inn.

Annie then said to Patti, "I have to do some things today
in Marsh Haven. Of course, this wasn't in the original plan."

Patti nodded understanding.

"In my apartment there is everything you need to make
Christmas cookies. I don't have video games up there, but if

the kids want them while you're baking, take some from the library. Just make yourself at home."

She turned to go, turned back and said, "Oh, if I'm later than I think I'll be, all the stuff for dinner is up there, too. But to tell you the truth, if I don't beat the snowstorm, it will be really late before I get back."

Annie remembered one more thing. The big thing. The thing she had problem solved the night before, after Patti and her family had left for bed. "Patti, what do you think about having a large slumber party over here tonight, and maybe tomorrow night, too?"

"What?"

"The snow is going to be fierce. I'd just like to have everyone under one roof. The only way I can think to do that is to put mattresses in the library."

"What about Mom?"

"Blaine won't be coming back. He'll leave the hospital and go directly home. Henrie is going to pack his things this morning. We could bring over enough for them to be comfortable several days in that room." Of course, she thought to herself, the dreaded Uncle Honey Bear would now be spending Christmas Eve, Christmas Day, and possibly a few more days right here.

Patti thought about all the faces she'd seen in the last few days. "Should we make sure Daniela gets over here too?"

"Isabel is going to take a break later this morning and bring her things over. They'll share Isabel's room."

Paul spoke up. "I've been wondering how I could get out of Christmas tree duty, and this is it! I'll help Sam move some things in, and I'll bring all of our things over. We'll move into the library and, um, I guess use Jessica's bathroom."

Annie laughed. "There are plenty of bathrooms to go around. I'm just sorry you won't be in the more comfortable space."

"We spend all day over here, anyway. I'll bring some of those mattresses over as well."

"Make sure Henrie gets the luggage cart out for you."

Then she checked in with Henrie, made sure he could help Pattie and the rest of the family with the trees and the luggage, bundled up and left for the Café.

Jeff sat at a large table with Chris, Ray and Cheryl. There was room for at least one more, thought Annie, so she sat down without receiving an invitation to do so. Immediately, she had a doggie face on each leg, but as soon as one saw the other had the same idea, each huffed and went back to their humans.

"What in the world is wrong with these two? Do either of you know?"

"Not a clue," said Ray. Chris shook his head.

"They worked well together at the lake. Well, when they were working, they worked well. When they were resting, they couldn't get close."

Annie looked at Jeff and asked, "What can you tell me?"

"I'm waiting on orders, but I believe, by 8:00, I can go to the police station and then the Sheriff's Department with orders to take over the case. I can take a look at the evidence then, and I'm going to start with the search warrant. I first want to see if I can get them out, on bail if nothing else, before noon today.

"After that, I'll be looking at the evidence to see what holes I can find."

"I hope that Carlos and Jesus are your first priority, and I don't want to move you off that path, but while you're sitting here, what do you think about Marco's statement that he can wrap up the computer theft by today?"

"I don't think he knows what he's talking about. I spent all of yesterday moving around, watching the people that I think are involved, and I think they've thrown up some smoke screens."

"What kind of smoke screens?"

"I can't talk to you about that, Annie. Trust me. I won't be able to finish that today. But it won't be long. And Marco…well I don't know what Marco thinks he knows, but trust me again, he doesn't have a clue about this cybercriminal."

Diana joined them at the table. "Annie, if we're going to go to the hospital, we have to go this morning. Driving will be impossible this afternoon."

Indeed, they didn't need a weather report to tell them how bad this storm was going to be. All they had to do was look over the lake to see the dark clouds approaching.

Annie said, "We have to stop by the Inn before we go. Henrie has packed a bag of things he knows Blaine will need, and the rest he's going to load into the rented pick-up truck."

Chris asked, "How is that equipment going to get to Ohio?"

"Ben is going to drive it after Christmas, after the snowstorm has passed. Dodd's pushed back the rental agreement."

"And Ben is going to drive it on his own?"

"He's taking a friend. Have you seen that truck? It's got all the bells and whistles. This will be a dream road trip for a couple of young men."

"Have you heard how he's doing?"

Diana choked up a bit. "I think he'll be alright. Eventually. We'll know more after we see him today."

"Give him my best."

"Mine, too," said Ray. "For a guy who didn't know what he was doing, he sure went at it with everything he had."

Annie finished her breakfast. She had Felicity's Christmas Eve special, a Monte Cristo open faced sandwich: French toast topped with a mixture of eggs, diced ham and turkey, topped with shredded Swiss cheese and strawberry sauce.

"I have to stop and pick up some identification papers for Jesus and Carlos' attorney. She needs a passport for Jesus and citizenship papers and passport for Carlos. Marco made a stink that they were illegals."

"Okay. I'll pick you up at the Inn in, what, fifteen minutes?"

"I'll be there."

Annie went around the table to give Chris a kiss on the cheek and Cyril a bite of ham she had saved. As she left, she reminded Chris and Jeff that Christmas Eve dinner would not be the same if they were not there.

Chapter 26: We'll See What We Will See

Annie and Diana left at the same time, but Diana went across the street to her apartment while Annie went first to Mr. Bean's, to get Carlos' paperwork from Daniela, then to Sassy P's, to get Jesus' passport from Minnie.

She then walked to the Inn, entered through the kitchen door and picked up the bag Henrie had packed for Blaine. "Tell Mr. Jones how sorry I am not to say good-bye to him in person."

"I will, Henrie. I wish I could take Kali and Ko with me. Turns out they really liked him."

"Some hospitals allow feline and canine visitors."

"You know, some do. I guess the worst that can happen is that they kick me out."

Annie started thinking furiously. "I need a double cat carrier."

"Well, you know," said Henrie slowly, "you do have three mesh carriers. You could take two of those, place them in the double stroller, and take them in that way."

"You know what, Henrie? You're a genius!"

Annie ran to the back room where Jessica was having a "discussion" with Sally. "Jessica, do you need your stroller this morning?"

"No, we aren't going to go anywhere. Why?"

"Could I borrow it to take Kali and Ko to the hospital?"

"Huh? You know, sometimes I think Mom's right. I think you were born without all your parts."

"We'll talk about that later, but could I please borrow it?"

"Sure. Take it."

"Thanks!"

Annie ran upstairs to the apartment where she opened the closet for her carriers and came out with two mesh ones. She checked under the bed to see if Kali and Ko were still hiding there. They weren't.

She then went downstairs to the library and found two tails sticking out from underneath the television table. She had Kali in a carrier before Ko realized anything was happening. That was lucky, because she soon had both of them.

As they wailed, she explained, "I'm going to take you to see Blaine. You wanted to see him, didn't you? He's in the hospital, and we're going to go visit him."

They got quiet, but Annie only half believed it was because they understood her.

Diana waited at the kitchen door, Blaine's bag in hand. She started to laugh when she saw Annie push the double stroller. The mesh carriers allowed two very large cats to sit up, looking very much like children with mosquito netting.

"It works! Henrie, you're a genius!"

In the car, Annie asked Diana, "Do you think we should take him a present?"

"I got balloons from Clara. They're in that sack in the back seat."

"Will that be enough?"

"I don't know what else to take. I don't know what he's allowed to eat, or what he likes to read, or if he reads, or anything."

Diana had started to tear up again.

"Do you want me to drive?"

"No. I'll be fine. This is good for me, to be doing something, I mean."

Annie heard the story the day before. Blaine and Diana met on his first night here, quite by accident. But every evening following the first, they had arranged to meet. They were taking their time, getting to know one another. What they knew to date, they liked very much.

Diana told Annie a bit about Blaine's relationship with his mother. To say she was overbearing would understate the attribute. Blaine didn't use the word, but as he described their relationship, Diana did. She thought of Mrs. Jones as a monster.

Blaine was a sensitive man. On his own, he didn't have the personal fortitude to stand up to his parents, and later his mother alone.

He had dreams that he could not live.

Diana understood some of that. In retrospect, Diana was able to see that her mother had never wanted to keep her from living out her dreams. She had mistaken her father's disappearance as an indication her mother could not be trusted. She now knew nothing could be further from the truth.

But Blaine was truly stuck. He wanted to unstick himself, but he didn't know how to do it. Diana had hoped she would be able to help, but now...now she didn't know.

Annie had been lost in her own thoughts when she realized Diana had pulled into a parking space near the attorney's office.

"I'll just be a minute," said Annie. She hopped out, went into one of the storefronts and was out very quickly.

Annie got into the car and said, "She doesn't know anything yet, but she's hoping to hear from Jeff soon."

Quiet, thinking their own thoughts, Diana continued the drive to the hospital.

Once there, they arranged Kali and Ko into the stroller again. Annie pushed the stroller while Diana carried the balloon bouquet and Blaine's bag.

They checked the directory and headed to the third floor.

Down a long hallway, they came to a door marked "Psychiatric Ward."

They stood back so the camera could see them as they pushed the door buzzer and were granted entrance.

As the door opened, Annie said, "We'll see what we will see, Diana, and then, time will tell."

Chapter 27: Humor Me

On the way back to Chelsea, neither Diana nor Annie said a word. They had not stayed long, so they were ahead of the storm.

Annie asked Diana to drop her at the church. Annie had to ring the bell, because the gift shop was already closed.

When Teresa got to the door, Annie smiled and asked, "Have you cancelled Christmas Eve or Christmas morning services yet?"

"I've been putting it off."

"How many people do you expect to come out?"

"None."

"Good. Then it's time you closed, put a sign on the door, changed your voice mail message, put a shout out on Facebook and planned to come to the Inn for both time periods."

"I feel really bad doing that. Some folks might want to come."

"Then tell them where you'll be, and tell them if they feel the need of spiritual guidance to come on over. You can have services at the Inn."

"But maybe the weather won't be as bad as they say it will be."

"Teresa, have you seen all the weather reports?"

Teresa nodded.

"Have you looked at the sky?"

They both looked over the lake to the forbidding clouds.

"Do you feel that?"

Snow had started to swirl, and as Annie stood in the doorway of the church it picked up.

"I just feel so bad."

"Think about all the people that are supposed to help you with those services. They deserve to know sooner rather than later that they won't have to put themselves in harm's way to get to church."

"You're right about that."

"Come over as soon as you can and pack a bag. You can sleep on my hide-a-bed in the apartment."

"Surely I can walk home from the Inn."

"Humor me. Pack it, and if you go home, you can either take it or get it after Christmas dinner."

Annie turned, wrapped her scarf around her face and started back down The Avenue. For the last time this weekend, she hoped.

It was after noon when Annie hit the Inn. Henrie figured she would come straight home without stopping for lunch, so he brought out a plate of sandwiches and relishes.

The rest of the family had eaten while they decorated the tree in the Library. It was in front of the window, close to the fireplace. Perfect for a blizzardy night.

Paul and Ben found an old dresser in the basement and brought it to the library so they could unpack again. They were leaving the morning after Christmas and would not move back into the carriage house.

Paul also helped Sam and Nancy settle into Blaine's old room.

And Honey Bear was accepting all kinds of attention from Ella and Ollie. Honey Bear was exceptionally good at accepting attention from humans of all ages. Dreadfully awful at getting along with cats.

Annie looked all over but couldn't see a single Mack cat on the first floor.

Annie went to the second floor landing and looked up and down the hallways. Jeff's door was open; she went to the door and knocked on the frame without looking in. He answered with a, "Come on in, Annie."

She did. He sat at the desk, computer open, face inscrutable.

Annie sat on the edge of the bed. "Were you able to get them out of jail?"

"No. Marco stalled every way that he could so that I didn't get a look at that warrant information until almost 11:00. By the time I worked my way through it, the Judge had gone home for the weekend."

"Oh, my. Do the others know?"

"I haven't had a chance to tell anyone, but I'm sure they've been watching their clocks."

"Give me your gut feeling, Jeff."

"The warrant reads like someone who contacted the police department just recently, yesterday probably, and said she could always count on getting drugs from Carlos. She even knew to say the drugs were sometimes damp, so they were probably stashed in or around plumbing."

"She?"

"She. The name was not used, of course, but Marco doesn't know how to write up a warrant request without giving up some information."

"Did he give up anything else?"

"That the informant was not known to him, but a family member and a family friend were known to him and well-known in the community."

Annie thought about seeing Geraldine and Christal at Mo's, seeing Geraldine, Hank and Marco at Sassy P's, and of course seeing Christal and Rusty together. She wondered what Rusty's involvement could be.

"Jeff, I have to tell you some things that may or may not be pertinent to your investigation. Do you want to hear them now, or do you want to put me in some sort of formal interview?"

Jeff thought about it. "Well, let's just say you are a witness. Do you mind if I record our conversation?"

"No. Please do."

"Let me shut the door."

Annie gave him everything she knew about Geraldine and Hank, starting with their attempts to close down the Café and other businesses, working through their failed attempt to ruin her last fundraising event, and then taking him through what she knew and what she surmised about their current activities on The Avenue. She made sure to include her fears about Marco and his involvement with the two and Geraldine's relationship to Christal, who seemed to be spending an inordinate amount of time in Annie's businesses.

"Christal's friend, who doesn't look at all to be her type, if typing people is even possible, spends a lot of time at Mem's. He's a gamer. Laila said he has played at times with her son,

James. I've wondered from time to time if he and Christal might be involved in the phishing matter, but if so, what in the world could they be doing with drugs?"

"Annie, you've left the realm of giving me information and have started to speculate."

"I know. I'm sorry. I'm just beside myself here."

Without Annie's knowledge, Tiger Lily and Little Socks had come in through the cat door. They had listened to almost everything Annie had to say.

Jeff turned off the tape recorder, told Annie that the information was very helpful for a number of reasons and opened the door. As he opened it, Chris's hand nearly hit him on the head.

"Chris. Come on in."

Cyril came in first, jumping on the bed beside the cats, alerting Annie for the first time to their presence.

Chris gave Annie a kiss on the forehead, sat in one of the easy chairs and asked, "Who's going to bring me up to date on what first?"

Jeff filled him in. "I'll tell you what I can tell you about Carlos and Jesus. It appears the warrant was written on bad information, but we couldn't ferret that out until too late in the morning to get them out of jail. So they'll be in custody until the arraignment on Monday.

"I haven't had a chance to look at the actual evidence, but I was able to see that no prints were taken from either the drugs or the sinks, and now, of course, they are contaminated with any number of prints from our ungloved police officers.

"It seems they were more interested in taking selfies with the evidence than preserving it.

"Annie and I just concluded an interview in which she gave me some very interesting information. But I can't tell you which pieces of information may fit into my investigation at this point, Annie.

"Unfortunately, I'm working alone here. The office couldn't send a partner, so I have to do all the legwork. It goes much more slowly this way. That may have contributed to the delay in getting to the Judge.

"Now if you two will excuse me, I'm going to try to conduct a few interviews before the snow makes travel impossible."

Annie was too tired to think, but she knew she should do something. She finally realized what it was. She reached for her cellphone and called Minnie.

"Minnie, you know it's past noon. It will be Monday before we can get Jesus out of jail."

"I know, Annie." Minnie cried softly but still maintained her composure. "I'm getting ready to close up here, and I'm going home to take a hot bath. Then I'm going to bed to sleep until Monday."

"Minnie, come to the Inn. Take your hot bath, then get dressed and come over here. You can't stay by yourself."

"I'll think about it."

"We have plenty of rooms. You can stay with people or get lost and be on your own. Up to you."

"Thanks, Annie. Rosa and Valeria will be there soon. They were very helpful. And you may see me later."

Annie then called Mr. Bean's. Isabel answered.

"Are you ready to close for the day?"

"Yes. Jerry said the last pre-order has been picked up, and we're ready to go. Daniela and I are leaving now, so she doesn't have to walk through snow that's any deeper than it is now. Fritz will be coming in a half hour or so."

"Great. Unless I forget, thank you again for keeping Mr. Bean's open for business today."

"You're welcome. If the circumstances were any different, I would say it was fun."

"I'm glad for that. Look, Isabel, you know the noon hour has come and gone…"

"Yes, Annie, I'm aware. We won't be seeing Carlos until Monday."

"That's right. I'm so sorry."

"Please. It was not your fault. Daniela and I will be there soon, and she took the time today to make her famous cookies."

"I can't wait. Let me talk to Jerry, please, and I'll see you soon."

Jerry came on the line within seconds. "Annie, do you have good news about Carlos?"

"Yes and no, Jerry. The bad news first. He'll be incarcerated until his arraignment. But the good news is that the evidence is flimsy at best."

"I just don't know what to say. I hope you're right and that he will eventually go free, but you know as well as I do, that once someone is tainted, he is always guilty in the eyes of his neighbors. We have to do more than help him go free. We have to figure out how to prove he is innocent."

This was the longest conversation Annie had ever had with Jerry, and he was much more articulate than Annie had assumed.

"You're right, Jerry. But for now, we're taking one step at a time. And our next step is to keep you from being alone during the holiday. Close up, freshen up after your long day, and come over here for Christmas Eve dinner. Bring some candy."

"I have a box of my best Christmas leftovers and today Isabel baked the rolls and cupcakes Carlos was going to take to Christmas dinner. I'll bring it all over this evening."

Cyril was sad again. Tiger Lily tried to cheer him up by kneading his shoulder, but that didn't help.

"What's wrong?"

"I've decided I have to escape."

"Escape? From what? To where?"

"From here. I have to go home to find Pete. If I can't get Pete back, I don't want to live."

Even Little Socks was moved. *"Don't say that! Cyril, you've got us!"*

"I know. But you aren't enough. I need Pete."

Little Socks and Tiger Lily looked at one another and shook their heads.

Chapter 28: Traditional Christmas Eve Oyster Stew

People arrived at the Inn from every part of The Avenue. They came through the front door both snow-covered and wind-blown. Wet coats, gloves, hats and scarves piled up in the entryway.

Teresa came. So did Minnie and Jerry. Chris and Cyril were already in for the weekend. Ray and Cheryl were here with Jock, and they packed a bag. They would not try to get to their home in this weather.

Tiger Lily snuggled up next to Jock and appeared to whisper something in his ear.

Tomorrow, Christmas Day, everyone else that lived on The Avenue, and a few who did not, would be in the house. Most of them could walk – or wade – through the snow. Candice was the only person who didn't live within a block's walking distance, but Annie assumed she was staying nearby tonight.

It was getting dark and Patti, Jessica and Nancy were in the kitchen. Henrie's kitchen. Annie's plan of a smallish family dinner in the apartment had long since gone by the wayside.

Ingredients for the family's traditional Christmas Eve oyster stew were ready to go into a monster-sized kettle. A turkey, two chickens and a ham roasted in the catering style ovens. Salads filled the refrigerator, green beans and corn warmed slowly on the stovetop.

Ray and Chris stepped out to the sheltered side of the porch. They wanted to watch the snow while Cyril and Jock took a refreshing walk. The dogs did not walk together, but Jock seemed to walk just a little bit behind Cyril.

Soon Jock came back. He sat obediently on the porch waiting for his human to give the command to go back into the house. He loved the snow, generally, but this was just too much. Too much snowing, too much blowing, and altogether too much everything. And he worried about Cyril. A whine escaped.

Chris and Ray talked about this and that, watched the snow, talked some more. Jock continued to whine.

At some point Chris realized Cyril had been gone far too long. He started to call. And call. Ray joined in. They walked several feet away from the porch, still calling.

Jock stayed on the porch. He whined, barking occasionally.

Chris began to get a sinking feeling in the pit of his stomach. "I have to go look for him. He's run off."

"Why would he run off?"

"He's been upset ever since that night at Pete's house. I think he believes Pete gave him away for good."

"That's silly."

"Well, you know and I know that most dogs bond with their humans for life. I think Cyril believes he's been given away."

"Then we need to find him."

The two men went inside and dressed as warmly as they could and still walk. Ray got Jock's leash. They talked to Annie and Cheryl and took off.

Jock seemed anxious to go.

The men started walking where they last saw Cyril, but Jock tried to lead them to Ray's truck. Ray pulled on the leash, but Jock pulled back. He still reached for the truck.

The cats gathered in the only place available to them with any degree of privacy, in the apartment on the table looking over The Avenue.

Mr. Bean asked, *"Where did Cyril go?"*

Tiger Lily answered. *"He's going home."*

"In this weather? You can't see the tail in front of you!"

"I know. But that's what he said. He said as soon as he got the chance he was going to try to go home to spend Christmas with Pete."

"But Pete gave him away!"

"Pete didn't give him away. Pete left him with Chris for a few days. I heard Chris tell Mommy Pete would be home Monday."

"Monday? Why can't Cyril wait for that?"

"He didn't believe me."

The cats were silent for a while, hoping against hope that Cyril would be okay in this weather.

Mo finally said, *"Trill."* It was a soft, sad trill.

Kali and Ko looked at him and sighed.

Little Socks looked to Sassy Pants and asked, a little testily, *"What did he say?"*

"He sez sorry 'bout Blaine."

"What about Blaine?" asked Mr. Bean.

Kali and Ko sighed again.

Tiger Lily said, *"Come on, girls. One of you needs to talk to us."*

Ko sighed, but Kali gathered herself for the story. *"We went to the hospital to see him, and really, we expected to find him in a bed with broken stuff, like broken legs or arms or something."*

Ko didn't want to be left out, so she started to chime in with occasional notes, like this one. *"Or maybe with his butt frozen off."*

"Yeah. Maybe that. But he wasn't in a bed. He was in another place in the hospital."

"He had a bedroom, but there was also a big room, and that's where Mommy went to talk to him."

"He was sitting in a chair in that room, in front of a television, and he just stared at it."

"Mommy and Diana tried to talk to him, but he didn't say anything for a long time."

"Then he looked at Mommy and said he was sorry he caused all the trouble."

Ko and Kali grew silent. Mo said, *"Trill."*

Kali continued. *"He meant he was sorry that everybody had to look for him. He wished he could have died out there. He said that would've been better all around."*

Mr. Bean asked, *"What did he mean?"*

"He told Mommy that his mommy didn't care if he came home or not, he was such a failure."

"A failure?"

"Yeah. If he couldn't even fish, then what in the world could he ever do."

"She said that?"

"Mommy asked the same thing. Blaine just said he knew that's what she was thinking."

Tiger Lily joined the conversation. *"Well that's silly. Everybody knows humans can't read minds. Some of us can, but humans can't."*

Little Socks spit a little bit, but Tiger Lily went on. *"Just look at Sassy Pants. She can read minds. But Mommy can't."*

Mr. Bean asked *"What do you think will happen to him?"*

Kali and Ko said together, *"I don't know." "I wish I knew."*

After a few minutes of silence, Tiger Lily and Little Socks shared what they learned from listening to Mommy and Jeff talk. It was good to know Marco didn't have a lot of information to keep Carlos and Jesus locked up for long.

Then they all turned back to the window, hoping against hope that Cyril would come running onto the porch.

Outside, Ray looked at the disobedient Jock and said, "We have to find Cyril."

Jock continued to pull at the leash while he looked up at Ray.

"Find Cyril."

Jock didn't move from his stance.

Ray looked at Chris. "Well, this was a heck of an idea."

Chris knelt close to Jock, in front of him and looking straight into his eyes. He talked softly, and without thinking about it, his hands rested on his knee, in front of his body and within touch of Jock. "I know there's something going on between the two of you. Something happened that night we played poker and you watched television."

Jock picked up a paw and touched Chris's right hand.

Chris was surprised, but he kept going. "Cyril is still your best friend, isn't he?"

Jock picked up a paw and touched Chris's right hand again.

"Did Cyril run away?"

Jock seemed to consider his response, then he touched Chris's left hand.

Chris was bolder now. "I know you don't want anything bad to happen to him. Do you know where he went?"

Jock touched his right hand again.

"Is he trying to go home?"

Again, Jock touched his right hand.

Chris looked up at Ray. "Let's get in your truck. We're going to Pete's."

And they did. While Ray backed out of the drive, he glanced at Chris. Finally, he said, "Were you just talking to my dog?"

"Yes, Ray, I believe I was."

"And how did you do that?"

"Pete taught Cyril the yes-no-fist-bump. I think either Cyril taught it to Jock, or Jock learned by watching Pete."

"Huh."

"Yeah, huh. You know, there's a fifty/fifty chance I misunderstood the entire conversation."

Cyril, going home as the crow flies, had a shorter distance to travel, but the snow blew furiously and he couldn't move quickly.

Ray had trouble navigating in the weather. The roads were not plowed and wouldn't be until sometime the next day, but he had an all-wheel drive vehicle. Slowly and steadily, he was able to maneuver through the drifting mess.

They arrived at Pete's place at just about the same time. Cyril had just gotten to the kitchen door. He scratched and barked to gain entrance as the truck pulled into the drive.

Cyril turned, expecting to see Pete, but he saw Jock jumping out of the back seat and running toward him.

Cyril got himself into a defensive stance, not knowing what to expect, but Jock stopped in front of him, put his front legs on the ground and his hips in the air, tail wagging, inviting Cyril to play.

Cyril looked at him, confused.

Jock hopped this way and that, continuing the invitation to play.

Finally, Cyril tentatively made a playful motion which was countered by Jock. Then, suddenly, the sadness lifted and Cyril was able to run and play with Jock.

They stayed in the front yard, running and jumping, diving into snow drifts and holes where the snow had blown away.

Ray and Chris stayed in the truck, watching through the window. Eventually, the two dogs came back to the truck. Ray got out, opened the back door, and they both jumped in, happy as clams to be together again.

Chris turned around in the seat and looked at Cyril.

"Cyril, I need you to understand something. Pete will be home in just two days. He loves you. He misses you. He wants you to stay with me for just a couple of days more, and then you can come home."

He placed both of his fists over the back of the seat and asked, "Do you understand?"

Cyril looked at the two fists for several seconds and finally lifted his paw and touched the right one.

When they arrived at the Inn, supper was being served. What a Christmas Eve feast it was! The food was served buffet style, because adults and children were everywhere. Tables were filled in the dining room and the all-season porch. A few sat in the kitchen. Some sat in groups with plates on their laps in the library and the foyer.

Through the windows, they watched as the snow danced and rose in height, dipping into hollows in some places and rising into drifts in others.

No one would be traveling tonight. Not even Jeff.

Annie suddenly said out loud, "Where's Jeff?"

She ran up the steps and knocked on his door. No Jeff.

Henrie called his cellphone. No Jeff.

Annie, Chris and Henrie checked their phones for messages. No Jeff.

Chris walked through each room downstairs. No Jeff.

Trying to be calm, he asked in a voice loud enough to be heard over the crowd, "Did anyone here talk to Jeff about where he might have been going?"

The house grew silent. No one knew anything.

Chris took a deep breath, took Annie by the shoulder and pulled her to a quiet corner of the library. Ray followed. So did Cyril and Jock.

"He said that your interview gave him some good information. He may have been going to interview people you named. Let's come up with a list."

Annie reached into a drawer nearby and pulled out a pad of paper and a pen. "Okay. I don't need to list anyone that's here right now. Marco, Geraldine, Hank, Christal, Rusty. Now let me think."

Chris didn't say anything, but one look at Ray confirmed his suspicious. Calling any of these individuals would be fruitless.

Annie sat up and grabbed Chris by the arm. "I told him Rusty was a gamer, and he played sometimes with Laila's son, James."

She reached for her cellphone to call Laila, who answered on the second ring. "Laila, this is important. Did Jeff, the FBI agent, come by this afternoon?"

"Yes, he did. He wanted to talk to James about one of his gaming partners."

"Rusty?"

"Yes. Annie, what's wrong."

Chris took the phone from Annie, who was far too agitated to gain much information.

"Laila, this is Chris. Can you put the phone on speaker and get James?"

"Right away."

Chris put Annie's phone on speaker as well, and after about half a minute, a young voice said, "This is James."

"James, this is Chris, Annie's friend."

"Yes sir. Mom said you wanted to talk to me about the FBI guy."

"Yes. Tell me everything about your conversation."

"Well, he asked me if I played video games with this guy I know, Rusty, and I said yes, and he asked if I had played with him recently. I said yes again and told him we played online chess the day before yesterday at Mem's."

"What else did you tell him about that game?"

"He asked several questions, and I answered them. I have to think for just a minute, sir."

"Take your time."

"Um, he asked if Rusty said or did anything unusual, and I said no. He asked if anyone else was there, and I told him Donny and Daryl were there. I play with them sometimes, too. And then I saw Annie and Marco. They got into it."

"Did Donny and Daryl say anything that you picked up on?"

"He asked me the same question, but I have to give you the same answer. I have to concentrate real hard when I play chess, so I didn't hear anything that anybody said until Annie and Marco got into it. And I left right after that."

"Thanks, James. If I have any other questions, is it okay for me to call you back?"

"Sure."

Chris hung up the phone and said to Ray, "I think his next move would have been to talk to Donny and Daryl. How do we contact them?"

"I have a phone number for Boone. There is no way we could get to their house tonight."

Annie dialed Boone's number and gave the phone to Chris. Again, he put the phone on speaker. When Boone answered, Chris identified himself, told him the phone was on speaker and that Annie was with him.

"For the second time in a week, the Inn is missing a guest. He works for the FBI. We think he might have tried to contact your sons to ask about a case he was working on. By any chance, have you seen him?"

Boone, in his public persona, said, "Well, that young feller was at our town gee-rage this afternoon, and he talked to the boys. Does you need me to do anythin'?"

"Not right now, Boone, but are your boys there? Could they tell me what they talked about?"

"Well, I could tell ya that. That Donny, he's a young'un, and I stayed right there in with 'im. They talked about playin' games at that Mem's place tha other day, and he askted them about the feller playin' next to 'em, that blond boy with all them tattoos and pins and such."

"His name is Rusty. What did they tell him about Rusty?"

"Well, they duzn't know him that well. They only sees him around town. He never goed to school here."

"What about that day? Did he ask questions about that day?"

"Well, now this wuz a little strange, if'n you ask me. He askted about did they – did my boys – talk about anythin' that day that tha other boy coulda heard."

Boone paused for a minute. "Oh, yeah, at first they couldn't member much, but then Donny, my young'un, he sez, Daryl, you member I askted about how you figerred out how to puts those pieces together fer them sinks, and Daryl, he sez, well yeah, we talked about that.

"An den, the guy askted if they wooda said where those pieces wooda been, and the boys, they thought maybe they mighta said somethin' 'bout that, you know, talkin' 'bout the Bean side or the Sassy side.

"An den, the guy askted if that wuz all, and my boys, they got real shy-like. Finely, I had to say to 'em, boys, you gots to tell tha man. Donny, my young'un, he sez, Daddy you and

Momma will be shamed of us, and I sez, no, son, I's a gonna be shamed of you iffen you don't tell the man.

"So he sez, well, we wuz a'talkin' about all the things we could do with that hidey place we made tween those two sinks, like we could rob a bank and put money there, or we could rob a jewlry store, or we could hide drugs we wuz runnin'. We wuz laffin' 'bout it, Daddy. We wuz funnin' is all. And then that man, he said thankee very much, and he left."

"What time was that, Boone?"

"Well, it weren't dark."

Annie, Chris and Ray looked at one another. Annie finally said, "We have to call him."

"No."

"Yes. We have to call him. I think Marco is a bigot and a lout, but he's still the acting police chief. At least for another couple of days. And we can't wait for Pete to get back."

Ray read their minds. "Okay. I'll make the call. I have fewer demerits with him right now than the two of you."

It took nearly half an hour, but eventually Marco responded to the call made to the police station. Ray gave him the short version. Jeff was missing, the storm was raging, he was conducting interviews, and the nearest they could figure he was last seen at Boone's garage in the late afternoon, before dark.

Marco's response was priceless. "He isn't a missing person until twenty-four hours have passed."

"Marco, he was investigating a crime. He's working without a partner. This is a missing police officer, a missing FBI agent."

"Then call the FBI. I'm off duty, and unless you haven't noticed, there is one heck of a snowstorm out there tonight."

Chris and Annie, listening in on speaker, closed their eyes and shook their heads. Then Chris picked up his phone and called information for the regional FBI office.

Chris had connected to a voice on the other end of the telephone when Annie's phone rang. It was Geraldine.

Chapter 29: Santa Claus Found Us!

"Mommy! Daddy! Santa Claus found us! Get up! Get up! It's time to open the presents!"

Groggy heads came out from under covers from every corner of the house. Except the kitchen. Henrie, JoJo and Ben were already making breakfast in the kitchen. The smell of fresh coffee, cinnamon rolls, Christmas morning egg casserole, and any number of side dishes wafted in the air to tempt other adults to get up, get up, get out of bed!

Teresa had stayed on Annie's hide-a-bed. Chris was on the sofa, Cyril beside him on the floor.

Ray and Cheryl were in Annie's bed, Jock on the bed at their feet. Annie slept in the recliner, seven cats keeping her warm.

Patti, Fritz and the kids were in the Library. Patti and Fritz had their heads under the covers. The kids jumped on their floor mattresses.

Jessica and Paul slept soundly in their room. They had a year before the twin's excitement over Christmas morning would wake them early.

Minnie decided she couldn't be alone after all, and she slept on a sofa in the foyer. Jerry was on the other one.

The rooms upstairs were full, of course. Nancy and Sam, with the dreaded Uncle Honey Bear, Valeria and Rosa, Daniela and Isabel.

And Jeff.

Jeff made it home last night with an FBI escort. The two men who escorted him were sleeping on the all-season porch. They courted death by vehicular suicide when they drove through the storm to pull him out of the vacant house where he had been bound and abandoned.

When they arrived at the over-flowing Inn, one asked jokingly if they should be making arrests for any code violations. Annie calmly told them, taking Jeff in hand and walking him up the stairs, that there were no paying guests in the Inn that night. And since this Inn refused service to no one on Christmas Eve, would the two of them kindly get out of their wet coats and let Henrie find them a place to sleep.

It had been another late night at the Inn, and Annie was ready for a vacation. Instead, she went downstairs to witness the wonders that waited under the tree.

The opening of Christmas stockings and presents collided with breakfast. Everything happened at once.

Daniela and her girls, of course she included Isabel in this thought, shared their gifts under the tree with everyone else. They did not mention their disappointment that Carlos was not with them.

Breakfast was a moving feast as people ate one course here, another there, starting at waking and finally ending when Henrie cleared the breakfast foods completely by noon.

Henrie had conceded that breakfast could be "a problem," and he grudgingly used paper plates and plastic cutlery. "Only the best," he had growled, as Annie put them on a shopping list the week before. This morning he appreciated her insistence on the vile things.

Henrie made his way through the house with his eyes always looking up. That way he could only see the clutter in a glancing fashion. He could almost convince himself it was totally proper to leave items on the floor. All kinds of items.

Wrapping paper, batteries, parts of toys and games, underwear, socks, and of course that fetid pile of wet coats.

The cats, dogs and children had made some kind of pact. The children no longer ran them down and screamed their names; the cats no longer hid; the dogs no longer had to put up with children lying on top of them or trying to ride them from one room to another.

For the most part, however, Annie's cats, Honey Bear and the two dogs spent the day in Annie's apartment. Annie left her door open for the dogs to come and go as easily as the cats.

Annie showed Chris the charcoals before giving them to the intended recipients. The accompanying cards noted they were from "Annie and Chris." Nancy loved her lighthouse. Patti and Fritz were captivated by the beach scene. Jessica and Paul told Chris how beautiful the portrait of the twins was, and told them where it would be hung in their home.

Annie found a quiet moment to talk to each of the children – except the twins – about her gifts in their honor. Each seemed to appreciate it. Jessica said she would start a keepsake box of Christmas gifts from Aunt Annie, and said she hoped all future gifts would be as appropriate.

Of course, Annie received gifts as well. She had received gifts throughout the week from friends and co-workers. Today she received them from family. She thanked each giver warmly and placed them on the bureau in her bedroom. She would consider each one later.

Annie was well aware of her the traits she considered to be shortcomings. To name a few, she had a disability, an inability to remember names. She was an introvert. And she was reluctant to accept gifts.

She had discussed this at length with Mem. Mem suggested she could possibly internalize the belief that she wasn't actually taking a gift; she was instead offering someone else the joy of giving. Annie was working on it.

Chris accepted Annie's gift with an expression of pure joy. He thanked her with a hug and a kiss on the cheek.

Chris did not have a gift for Annie, and he didn't say anything about having one. This became an unspoken "thing" that affected Annie more than she thought it should.

It was Christmas Day, after all, and Sunday. No one showed up for church services, even though Teresa left messages everywhere she could think, so she conducted an impromptu service over the noon hour in the library.

Everyone in the house attended.

Teresa declined to take up an offering.

Jeff and the other agents ate a massive breakfast. Annie sat with them while they ate. "You know, the roads are going to be bad all day. It's still snowing and blowing. There is no reason for you to try to make it back today."

One of the agents, Todd, looked at Jeff. "Is breakfast always this good?"

"Always."

He looked at Annie. "Would the accommodations tonight be the same as last night?"

"Probably. No one is planning on leaving, and since I am well over the legal capacity, I won't be charging anyone to stay. Or eat. And you'll still be on sofas in the all-season porch."

"This isn't a gift, right?"

"Not a gift, right."

"It's a matter of caring for travelers during a weather emergency."

"Weather emergency, right."

Todd looked to his partner, Joe, and a silent decision was made. Todd turned back to Annie.

"Then we'll stay. But we have some business to take care of first."

"How are you going to do that during a weather emergency?"

"You saw what we're driving?"

"Yes. A monster truck. Looks like it can seat eight people and go through six feet of snow in the middle of a hurricane."

"That's about right. We're only driving locally, though. We'll finish here in Chelsea this afternoon. Jeff seems to have everything almost wrapped up. Good thing, since he's going to make us miss our Christmas dinner."

"You won't miss it. We're having Christmas dinner around 5:00 here at the Inn. The best cooks, bakers, candy makers, and cheese and wine choosers in the country will be right here."

Todd looked at his companions and said, "Let's go. Time's a'wastin'!"

Christmas dinner would be a smashing success.

Patti and Fritz corralled the children into picking up all of their Christmas gadgetry, clothes, and what-nots. Paul went through the house three times with a garbage bag, picking up wrapping paper, bows, tinsel from the tree, plates, cups, napkins and silverware.

Jessica found a place in the basement to put out drying racks for the still-wet coats, hats and scarves. The basement was dry, and before the day was over, the outerwear would be dry also.

With the ability to see all of the furniture, JoJo and Ben decorated every table and conceivable dining surface, like coffee and end tables, with holiday tablecloths or placemats. They put out candles, unlit of course, nutcrackers, Santa Clauses, angels and other holiday decorations.

Ben found several laser lights that would throw stars across the walls and ceilings. He set them around so that overhead lights and lamps would not be needed during dinner.

Annie missed seeing her collection of nativity sets. She had them in porcelain, wood, resin, china, plastic and bronze. There were classic sets, sets with baby faces, one set of children acting out a nativity scene and one of cats outfitted as the nativity characters.

They were stacked in a closet in her apartment. She planned to get them out on Christmas Eve, but that day was lost to her given unplanned events.

She thought to herself that she would appreciate them all the more next year. Those and her Dickens village. She missed the village, also stored in the closet.

Henrie made three fruit pies and two cream pies. He coordinated the efforts of everyone who wanted to contribute a dish. That was, well, almost everyone. Some worked in Henrie's kitchen, others in Annie's.

Daniela, of course, had her cookies; Jerry had truffles, rolls and cupcakes; the children were excited to add their Christmas cookies to the table.

Isabel made taquitos; Rosa and Valeria collaborated to make bacalao, dried salted codfish with tomato sauce.

Ray and Cheryl already had the ingredients for a seafood paella; Chris made crabmeat appetizers.

Nancy made scalloped oysters; Patti made her secret recipe herbed turkey breast; Jessica made cornbread pecan dressing; Paul made his mother's baked beans.

Teresa raided Annie's personal freezer and refrigerator and found ingredients for her buffet-style Spanish hotdogs, ground beef, sliced hot dogs and sauce with a honey barbecue base; Minnie made a raid as well and came up with curry chicken salad with grapes and pineapple.

Sam and Fritz stayed out of the way on the second floor landing. They could see all of the comings and goings, but they were in no one's way and they were not called upon to do anything special. For the most part.

Annie hid.

Eight cats, yes, even Honey Bear, and two dogs stayed in the dining room of Annie's apartment. The cats sat or lay on the table overlooking The Avenue, where they could watch the snow continue to come down. From their vantage point, it was peaceful and beautiful. The dogs lay together on a large cushion in the corner.

And then the rest of the guests arrived with their dishes. They trudged through the snow. It was still coming down, still blowing and drifting. As the other guests arrived, the cats and dogs, one by one, made their way downstairs to mingle and wait for crumbs.

The town made no pretense of plowing the streets, and Boone had given up on the sidewalks sometime the afternoon before. He couldn't get to town to do them, and they wouldn't stay "done" if he tried.

George and Diana brought two cases of artisan beer. Chris and Ray fixed a bin to keep them cold on the sheltered side of the porch. Diana went with Minnie to Sassy P's to bring a case of wine, half buttery chardonnay and half Rhapsody. Minnie picked up the cheese tray made the day before at the same time.

Trudie, rather than fight her way through the snow with carafes of coffee, brought the coffee and mixes to make using Henrie's equipment; Felicity brought onion and apple crème fraîche and puff pastry.

Jennifer and Marie brought a salad of mixed greens, apples, walnuts, peppers, oranges and sunflower seeds with a light Asian dressing.

Holly and Jolly called when they were ready to come. Chris, Ray and Fritz went across The Avenue to carry Holly and her wheelchair while Jolly carried a crockpot of Wassail.

Clara came with Diana. Clara brought Blanc-Manger, a molded Haitian dessert made with heavy cream, gelatin, almonds and raspberries topped with raspberry sauce. Diana brought her signature dish, salmon with spinach and quinoa.

Laila and her children brought the ferret and the turtle. They also brought Badam Pasanda, a lamb curry with yogurt, cream, ground almonds and spices. She warned Annie it was a little spicy and those with tender palates should be careful.

Mem and Frank were the last to come, bearing a basket with a variety of teabags, gourmet nuts and crackers and a savory cheeseball.

Henrie had to think of a creative way to present the buffet. On one kitchen counter went salads and appetizers. On another went desserts. The kitchen table, which was tall and also served as a preparatory island, held the desserts.

The main courses and vegetables were on the main buffet in the dining room. Coffee and the overflow from the main buffet went on the side table in the dining room.

At 5:00 on the dot, Jeff, Todd and Joe stomped their feet on the hallway rug. Henrie, as he had with all other guests, gathered their coats and told them they "could be found drying in the basement the next time you need to avail yourself of their use."

Finally, Teresa said grace, asking a special blessing for everyone in the house on this Christmas day, so special in so many ways, and the next two hours were given over to the meal under the starlight that Ben had provided.

Chapter 30: The Rest Of The Story

Late Sunday night, after the food was put away, the dishes washed, the gifts put away for traveling the next day, the children put to bed, and all of the guests from The Avenue back in their own homes, the Inn settled into a quiet stupor.

The snow had stopped coming down, but the wind still blew it around. Visibility was poor and town streets remained drifted shut.

Todd and Joe drank beer and watched a re-run football game in their "bedroom," the all-season porch.

On the second floor landing, Daniela and her girls played a game of Malilla, a point-trick card game for four that they normally played every Sunday evening in Mexico.

Nancy and Sam were sound asleep, as were Jessica, Paul and the twins.

Fritz and Annie were comfortable on recliners in front of the fire on the north side of the library. Fritz read a book from Annie's library on the healing power of crystals. Patti read a brochure put out by the Chelsea Chamber of Commerce. She made a list of things to do when they returned. The children slept on the south end.

JoJo and Ben were online on their smartphones in their basement suite. They had a tray of snacks on the coffee table and some of Henrie's homemade lemonade in a cooler.

Henrie had his feet up in a recliner chair in front of the television set in his apartment, a bottle of Rhapsody and a crystal wine glass on the side table. Two dark chocolate truffles waited beside the glass.

Ray and Cheryl were still not able to get home. They were in Annie's dining room with Chris, Annie and Jeff. Annie and

Cheryl shared a bottle of Rhapsody. Chris, Ray and Jeff kept a tub of artisan beer cool on the balcony.

The dogs and cats, yes, even Honey Bear, continued to rest in their favorite places, the cats looking out the window at the swirling snow and the dogs on the cushion.

Ray and Chris looked at the dogs often, assuring themselves they were still getting along.

The friends were anxious to hear Jeff's story. Jeff had been bound, gagged and abandoned in a deserted and unheated house in one of the poorer sections of town.

Geraldine called Annie to tell her about Jeff's situation and to give her the location of the house. Chris was already on the phone to the FBI and he relayed the information.

Chris and Ray were ready to go to the house themselves, but the FBI ordered them to stand down. Then followed a few anxious hours of waiting.

Jeff told them everything, even though arrests had not yet been made. He did not bore his friends with the information they had already. He told them what they didn't know.

Jeff had gone to interview Rusty about the drugs, but Rusty had surprised and overpowered him. Rusty and Christal carried a groggy Jeff to his car and drove to an abandoned house that Rusty had planned to use as a meth lab. His plans now evolved, as he realized he had to leave town. No longer needing the house, they left Jeff duct taped to some plumbing fixtures.

They hid Jeff's car in the garage behind the house and assumed the blowing and drifting snow would erase all traces of their activities. They figured Jeff would be found, dead, several weeks or even months later. They counted on the winter weather to keep the smell down, and they believed they had time to get away after the snow abated.

Jeff and his partners had much of this information because Geraldine, in their interview of her this afternoon, had provided it. Jeff told Geraldine's story.

When Geraldine learned of the kidnapping of a federal agent, she considered her options, realized her own culpability, and decided to cut her losses.

Wisely, instead of calling Marco, she called Annie. Geraldine knew her niece would be arrested, but she could not abide such a heinous crime.

Geraldine was a veritable fount of information. After the trio satisfied their need for information on the assault, kidnapping and attempted murder of a federal agent, they moved on to the other items on Jeff's list.

Jeff asked her to start by telling them of the cybercrimes perpetrated on Annie's businesses and other businesses in the area. Geraldine had raised hands in surrender and declared, "Everything I did was to lead you away from my niece in this disaster, and this is what you start with!"

According to Geraldine, when she saw the group in Gwen's office, she put two and two together and came up with four. Her niece, Christal, had been hanging out with that horrible creature, Rusty, and she was positive they were up to no good.

Geraldine had approached Christal and asked her to just stop doing what she was doing, but Christal said she was getting too much money. And it was fun. Geraldine said she didn't ask, but she was sure other businesses were targeted, and probably not all of them in Chelsea.

Geraldine didn't understand what they could be doing and had asked Christal to explain it to her. Christal spun an incredible story of what she called a combination of spearphishing and catphishing. The point was to get close to people who might unwittingly give information that could be used to steal from either the person or the person's business.

In Chelsea, Annie's businesses were obvious targets, because they worked so closely together.

Rusty and Christal, in their own names, connected to Minnie on Facebook, LinkedIn, Instagram, and there could have been another site or two.

Through these sites, they got her work email, and they figured out the way that all the company emails were set up. In general conversation, they learned that all invoices went to Gwen, and that Gwen took care of paying the vendors. She wouldn't know if a new vendor was a scam or not, so they set up false business information and sent invoices for payment to Gwen.

Working that angle backwards, they tried to rope a few people from Annie's businesses into going online for training sessions, and they collected personal information in the process. They had plans for using this information down the road, but Christal wasn't clear with Geraldine about how that would work.

Through a false persona, while Christal stole George's attention a couple of months ago, Rusty connected with Candice on a dating site. Unfortunately, George and Candice got back together before Rusty was able to make inroads through that avenue.

Rusty created another false persona and connected with Felicity on that same dating site. Christal told Geraldine she thought this was going to go nowhere.

When Rusty was successful, as he had been with other women, he created some kind of situation in which he would ask for money, and the woman, if hooked, would either send money from her personal funds, or, if she was really hooked, she might steal from her place of employment to come up with more cash.

Geraldine did not approve of any of these activities, but she also didn't want to see the family name besmirched.

The group laughed, as if the name was not already besmirched in Chelsea.

Geraldine formed a plan to misdirect the investigation. She drew in her faithful partner in such schemes, Hank. She didn't tell Hank about her niece, and she believed Hank was ignorant of her niece's culpability in the cybercrimes. He was certainly aware of everything that came after.

In an aside, Geraldine suggested to the agents that they not interview Hank until the arrests had been made. She believed Hank to be untrustworthy.

This got another laugh from the group of friends. It was the pot calling the kettle black.

Geraldine and Hank found a kindred spirit in Marco.

Geraldine insisted to the agents that she and Hank had merely planted seeds in Marco's mind. She admitted this was not at all difficult. They found Marco to be a malleable sort of person.

Geraldine and Hank told Marco that Annie possibly had someone from witness protection in her employ, and did the town really need that? A few months before, Geraldine had thought to hire Jerry away from Annie, purely for his candy-making skills, but she hit a wall looking into his background. He was probably hiding from somebody here in Chelsea. Perhaps he was connected to the mob. Perhaps worse.

Geraldine and Hank told Marco their concerns about illegal immigrants, and certainly Annie was aware she employed illegals. Jesus and Carlos were most assuredly getting by on fake papers, and Annie probably knew about it. She or that pretentious father of hers, may he rest in peace, probably helped them get their papers.

Geraldine and Hank took their game even further. They told Marco they were positive Annie was running a scam. How in the world could someone who owned all of those small businesses be so successful? Perhaps Annie was cheating the government for tax purposes.

Geraldine, talking with the agents, said that she had a brilliant plan of misdirection. It would seem but an afterthought to that completely idiotic Marco, and Hank would be none the wiser. Working that plan, she planted her last seed with both Hank and Marco.

Near the end of their lunch meeting, Geraldine appeared to have an idea from left field. She sent the spark, Hank fanned the flame, and in the end, Marco seemed to have a blazing fire in his heart.

Hank and Marco talked themselves into the idea that Annie herself was behind the phishing scheme. She was the culprit, and she would claim the losses on her insurance policy to double her take.

Annie didn't know what to think about that. She kept quiet, though, allowing Jeff to continue to speak.

Geraldine told the agents that she kept in touch with Marco, just to be of help, you know, should he need it. He informed her that he had run Jerry's name through his databases and he discovered the federal offense. He wanted to know if she, Geraldine, was aware that Jerry was in fact a murderer? Of course, she was shocked!

At this point, Geraldine wanted to impress upon the federal agents that hiring a murderer had to be a crime, and couldn't they find some way to arrest Annie for this egregious offense?

Annie had a thought, reached for her cellphone and sent herself a text. A reminder for her to-do list.

Marco also told Geraldine he discovered Carlos traveled regularly to and from Mexico. He was aware family was currently in town from Mexico, but he didn't have anything upon which to base a search warrant. He found nothing upon which to base a search warrant for Jesus.

Luckily, Christal called Geraldine with a fantastic idea. Rusty had found the perfect thing to frame a couple of Annie's key employees, and they just happened to be the Mexicans.

Rusty heard Boone's boys talking about this hiding place that connected the Confectionary and the Winery. This would be a perfect place for a set-up, and did Aunt Geraldine want Rusty to provide something? Say, drugs?

Geraldine set up a meeting with Marco; Christal provided the false information; Rusty planted the meth. All in time for Marco to get search warrants, find the drugs and make the arrests. And for good measure, the holiday weekend provided a period of time for Annie's friends and for Annie herself to have to suffer.

Geraldine didn't even have to suggest that to Marco. He was already primed to provide as much suffering as he could.

At this point, Jeff had to ask her questions that led in more than one direction. For the first point, he asked how they induced Marco to become a player.

Geraldine said that was easy. She convinced Hank to promise him Pete's position once Pete was dismissed for neglect of duty. Hank had tried to have Pete dismissed once before, and he welcomed the idea that Marco might be able to help.

When asked how Pete would be found neglectful, Geraldine was succinct. "For protecting his friend Annie in her illegal activities, including harboring illegal immigrants."

For the second point, Jeff wanted to know what Geraldine hoped to gain by making all of this trouble for Annie and her employees.

Geraldine appeared to answer this point honestly. "My initial intent was to misdirect the investigation away from Christal. But then things got out of hand and I was having so much fun…."

Jeff described Geraldine's expression as she finished this sentence. She looked up and to the right and a perplexed look crossed her face.

Chris laughed. "She must have realized she was acting just like her niece."

Continuing his story, Jeff said he pressed her about the cybercrime angle and asked if she and Marco had communicated further about it.

Geraldine appeared at this point to be somewhat evasive. She informed the agents that Marco had not relayed any particular information about his activities in that regard.

Jeff went into dramatic mode, relaying the entire conversation at this point. "Ms. Foxglove, this was the most important issue for you, was it not?" "Yes, it was." "But you didn't follow up on this area of Marco's investigation?" "Well, yes, I guess you could say I followed up." Silence. "Could you elaborate?" "Oh, well, certainly I asked him, but he only told me he would have to get back to me." "And you were satisfied with that answer?" "Well, yes, you see, I had to be satisfied. What else was I to do?"

Annie said, "Well, certainly! What else was she to do?"

They laughed together, but Jeff had a caution to offer. "Annie, I wouldn't be surprised if they did something that has yet to be revealed."

"What in the world could they have done?"

"I'm not sure, but she wasn't being honest at this point. I wonder if one of them may have said something to your insurance company, told them you were creating a situation so you could submit a fraudulent claim."

Annie shook her head, wondering how that would play out.

Chris and Cheryl spoke at the same time. "If they did, you'll be cleared." "They've made arrests, for goodness sakes. You'll be fine."

Jeff continued his story. He asked Geraldine if she had tried to throw any additional smoke screens, and Geraldine said yes. She had tried to throw George under the bus as well, because Christal was hopelessly attracted to him. And of course, he was not attracted to her. At least not anymore. But unfortunately, Marco could find nothing on that rascal noteworthy of any kind of investigation.

Jeff, Todd and Joe promised Geraldine immunity if she said nothing to any of the other players and if she testified at the appropriate time. Otherwise, they had a list of federal crimes with which she would be charged.

They spent the rest of the afternoon firming up a case against both Christal and Rusty for the cybercrimes. Jeff had developed a good deal of evidence against them throughout the week, and Geraldine's statement provided confirmation.

They found a federal judge to issue arrest warrants for all the crimes that had been committed. The Judge was a bit perturbed to get the call on Christmas afternoon, but he was assured flight was imminent and that the arrest would be made early Monday morning before the roads were clear.

Annie finally spoke. "What time are you going to make the arrests?"

"About 7:00 tomorrow morning, when the city streets are just getting clear. Travel to any federal facility, all of them north of here, can't be made until at least Tuesday. We're looking forward to walking them into the town lock-up so Marco will have to deal with them."

At this, everyone laughed again, and eventually the conversation turned to more pleasant topics.

By Monday night, almost everything was back to normal. Carlos and Jesus were released on bail. Their attorney, Kelsie, was loaded for bear and ready to take on all comers. She knew, of course, about Rusty, Christal and the drugs and could wait for the FBI to complete their investigation.

She looked forward to a total exoneration, a public apology from the police department and a full and complete press release regarding the matter. And reparations. She was going to go for reparations. She had promised her friend Greg to take the case pro bono unless reparations would be involved.

Patti, Fritz and the busload of family, heading south where the roads would be clear, were gone.

Boone cleared the sidewalks and other walkways on The Avenue. Henrie helped Nancy and Sam move back to the carriage house. And, of course, Uncle Honey Bear went with them. All of the cat bade him good-bye. Tiger Lily noted that perhaps they would see one another soon.

Todd and Joe were gone, leaving the transport of Rusty and Christal to other, lesser, agents.

Jeff was still in town. He had to wrap up a few loose ends.

Ray and Cheryl had gone home, taking Jock with them. The parting of Jock and Cyril was sad to watch.

JoJo and Ben had returned to the home of their parents and were back to work at the Café. Ben would leave in two days for Ohio.

Cyril sat in the corner at Mo's Tap. His current human, Chris, was here for supper. Cyril looked out the window into the dark and snow-covered street, hoping against hope to see his true human. Chris said he would be here, but would Pete really come back for him?

Chris and Annie, over a sandwich and beer, laughed as Jeff told them about the arrest.

Jeff, Todd and Joe arrested Christal and Rusty on a variety of charges. They were shocked to see Jeff alive. Christal's eyes showed her horror. Her very own Aunt Geraldine had turned them in.

They were taken to the police department with an official written request for their detainment until Tuesday afternoon, when federal agents would take custody and deliver them to a federal facility.

Marco, having used Christal as a confidential informant, was blindsided. He took several minutes to study the documents presented, reading every word. He noted among the charges all of the activities leading up to the false accusations of Carlos and the planting of drugs that led to the arrest of both Carlos and Jesus.

He also saw the charges related to the cybercrimes, not only of Annie's businesses, but of other businesses in Chelsea and the surrounding area.

Jeff could only imagine the thoughts going through Marco's mind, including potential lawsuits against the department and the town and the wrath of his boss, who would return to work tomorrow.

Jeff had just finished his story when Cyril started to bark. It was a joyful, yapping bark. He jumped up and down, then ran to the door, and Pete came in. Pete! His human! His human had really and truly come back for him!

The humans remained seated as Pete and Cyril said their hellos. This included jumping, hugs around the neck from a dog standing on hind legs, tummy rubs for a dog rolling on the floor, full body pets for a dog standing completely still, leaning against the legs of his human. His human.

Chris finally got up and made a hand gesture. Pete threw him some car keys, and Chris went outside to transfer the dog bed, toys, dishes and other items from his car to Pete's.

By the time Chris returned, Pete had a beer at the table. Annie had just finished telling him that there was much he needed to hear about the activities of the town and of his police department in his absence.

Pete looked at the three of them. "I'm sure tomorrow is going to be one surprise after another. Give me the short list of the things I need to know."

By the time Jeff finished, Pete was on his third beer.

He said nothing. He shook his head. He hung his head. He looked at the ceiling and blew out long sighs.

He finally looked at Cyril and said, "It's time to go home."

Annie wished she could have been at the police department when the two men in suits arrived. The look on Marco's face must have been priceless.

It was Tuesday afternoon, shortly after federal agents picked up Christal and Rusty to transport them to other, less friendly places.

Two men in suits walked into the police department and asked to speak to the Chief of Police. When the nature of their visit was revealed, Pete asked Marco to join them in his office. After some conversation, the two men in suits asked to speak with Annie.

Henrie opened the door to the Inn when the bell rang. Four men entered. Pete was in the lead, two men in suits followed, and Marco brought up the rear.

Pete asked if Annie was available. The two men in suits looked intense and not so happy. Marco looked at the floor. Pete looked amused.

Annie met them in the foyer and led them to the library, where Henrie served coffee and fresh-baked peanut butter cookies. The two men in suits looked intense and not so happy. Marco looked at the floor. Pete looked amused.

Once they were settled, coffee in hand, Pete explained the reason for their visit. According to the two men in suits, Pete's computer was used to submit an anonymous complaint about Annie Mack. The complaint alleged Ms. Mack had perpetrated a phishing scheme on her own businesses and had then submitted an insurance claim against the alleged thefts.

Annie clarified a point. She had in fact reported the investigation to the insurance company, but she had yet to submit a claim.

The two men in suits concurred with her clarification. They still looked intense and not so happy. Marco still looked at the floor. Pete still looked amused.

Pete explained to Annie that in their earlier conversation, he informed the two men in suits that an arrest in the phishing case had been made by the FBI. The FBI concluded that two individuals had perpetrated the crime against Ms. Mack's businesses as well as several other businesses in Chelsea and the surrounding community.

The evidence was solid, confessions were in hand, and there was no indication that anyone else had been involved in the crime, including Ms. Mack.

Pete explained to Annie that in their earlier conversation, he informed the two men in suits that he had been on vacation when the complaint was submitted. Several individuals had access to his computer at the time the anonymous complaint was made.

It was apparent that either a concerned citizen made an honest mistake about Ms. Mack's activities, or someone willfully made a false complaint.

In point of fact, if the two culprits were as skilled as they appeared, they could have made the complaints themselves in an attempt to misdirect investigators, and they could have hijacked the IP address so that it appeared to come from Pete's computer.

Pete explained to Annie that this time, the two men in suits would decline to investigate a potential false complaint.

Pete paused for a moment to take a drink of coffee and a bite of cookie. The two men in suits continued to look intense and not so happy. Marco continued to look at the floor. Pete continued to look amused.

Pete cleared his throat, looked again at Annie, and explained that the two men in suits wanted to interview Annie to assure themselves that she appeared to be innocent of the charges that had been made.

Annie looked at Pete. The two men in suits looked intense and not so happy. Marco looked at the floor. Pete looked amused.

Annie looked at the two men in suits. "What do you need from me?"

One of the men cleared his throat and said, "Ms. Mack, did you commit a phishing crime on your business or on any other business in Chelsea or in the area?"

"No, I did not."

"Do you plan to submit an insurance claim?"

"Yes, I do, once I know the extent of the theft."

"When will you know that?"

"I believe my accountant will have a figure by the end of the day."

"Were you aware these crimes were in process, and did you allow them to continue in order to, um, increase the amount of the insurance claim?"

"No. As soon as I became aware of the crimes, I stopped every outlay of finances that could go to inappropriate parties."

"Are you satisfied that the crimes have been solved?"

"Yes. However, the preventive measures put in place last week will continue and I will probably add additional preventive measures."

"Do you intend to inform the insurance company of the preventive measures you are adding?"

"Certainly. As soon as we firm up our new procedures, I'll contact my agent."

"Thank you, Ms. Mack. Do you have any questions of us?"

"No. Thank you."

"Well then, I believe that concludes our business."

Everyone stood up.

Annie shook the hands of the two men in suits, who still looked intense and not so happy. She nodded to Marco, even though he couldn't see it, as he still looked at the floor. She nodded to Pete, who still looked amused. He nodded back.

They left, Pete in the lead, the two men in suits following, and Marco bringing up the rear.

When they were gone, Annie and Henrie collapsed in laughter.

Chapter 31: New Year's Eve Block Party

By now, the folks on The Avenue could almost put a block party together with their eyes closed, a hand tied to a foot and a chair duct taped to their behinds.

Almost.

They still had to coordinate a few things.

Annie didn't want the "honor" of chairing the event every year, but because she had easy access to everyone, she couldn't seem to get anyone else to take over the role.

She had called "Skype meetings" a couple of times earlier in December so that plans would be well in hand before Christmas week. That turned out to be a great idea, since so many things fell off the track around the holiday.

The New Year's Eve block party was typically held on the second floor of Tiger Lily's Café, their catering venue. The size of the room alone limited the number of activities, although the last two events of the night were always held outside. Unless, of course, a Christmas-sized blizzard roared through.

Clara, Diana and Jolly planned decorations. The theme this year was Pre-Resolution New Year's Eve, and since no one could come up with a better idea for decorations, Clara would provide balloon bouquets. Around the room would be mini-stations with markers to allow party-goers to pick a balloon, write their resolution on it, and take it home.

Jennifer, Mem and Jerry coordinated the activities. Because of the size of the room, there would be only two stations inside.

One station would be a resolutions board. Attendees could choose to participate in one or two ways.

Some would write down attributes they wanted to give up, for example, greed or gluttony. The note would be folded and placed into a decorated shoebox. At 12:05 AM on New Year's Day, Teresa and anyone who cared to join her would take the box to a bonfire in the park behind the building. She would conduct a prayerful ceremony to send those attributes on their way as she threw the box, carefully taped shut, into the fire.

Some would write down their resolutions and put them into envelopes that they would self-address; Teresa would mail the resolutions out in mid-February as a reminder of their good intentions.

At the children's station, a resolution game would be ongoing. Children would be encouraged to write down a resolution that they would be willing to share with others. The resolutions would go into a top hat, and one at a time, each child would pull out a resolution and the group would guess to whom it belonged. This game was run by Cheryl and Laila who would make sure it was held in fun. No child would be embarrassed.

George and Candice would keep a bonfire going outside in the fire pit. The bonfire, which would be used by Teresa at the end of the evening, would be available for those who wanted to warm up as they played war games in the snow. Ray and Pete would help supervise the building of snow forts and snowball fights.

The committee chose the local multi-purpose human service organization as their charitable recipient. This organization helps with utility assistance, food for the needy and shelter for abused women, among other things. Donation stations would be grocery bags placed at the entry, the resolution station, at each end of the food table and at the drinks table.

Felicity, Carlos and Cookie planned a menu of finger foods. The menu had meatball sliders, roasted shrimp cocktail, spinach artichoke dip with a variety of crackers, sausage stuffed mushrooms, bacon wrapped pineapple shrimp, fried olives, roasted garlic bruschetta, salted caramel brownies and chocolate babka.

Holly and Marie would have a heated tent close to the bonfire with hotdogs, marshmallows, buns, condiments and the makings for s'mores.

As they shared the menu with the committee, most of whom could be seen drooling into their computer screens, Felicity said, "And we're going to have cards for memberships to the yoga studio with discounts throughout January for those who try to eat some of everything. Annie's face turned a bright shade of red"

Carlos, at the last minute, decided to add mini-muffins in a variety of flavors. He suggested streusel, snickerdoodle, ginger-lemon, gingerbread, ginger-fig, cherry-chocolate, candy cane, and Mexican hot cocoa.

Trudie, Jesus and Laila planned the drinks. They would have lemonade and orange juice, regular and decaf coffee with flavorings and flavored creamers from Trudie's coffee bar, hot tea, hot chocolate and a self-serve Bellini bar. Fruit purees would on the bar. Attendees could choose a flavor, peach, orange, strawberry, blackberry or raspberry, pour it into the bottom of a champagne glass, and choose a sparkling drink to top it off. Jesus would supply sparkling wine, nonalcoholic sparkling wine, champagne, ginger ale and lemon-lime soda.

Annie made flyers and handed them out to local businesses and organizations in early December, and newspaper and radio advertisements went out about the same time. Mem took care of marketing on social media sites.

George and Jesus were responsible for the grand finale. This would be the first year for their planned finale, and they were positive they could put it together.

This year, with all of the unplanned events the week before, they were unable to get to work on their project until two days before the party.

Annie, on the Friday before the Saturday party, watched them work on it and heard the French they were speaking. She picked up her cell phone.

"Boone, would one or both of your boys be available to help with a project we have to finish by tomorrow?"

"Well shore, Ma'am." Boone, in order to keep his persona intact, did not change the way he spoke to Annie. "When and where duz you need 'em and what kinds of tools will they be a'needin'?"

"It's a construction project. Have them go to Mo's Tap just as soon as they can and George will explain the problem to them."

On Saturday evening, the air was cold and crisp, the sky was clear, bright stars studded the sky over the lake.

The roads had been cleared, parking lots were open and on-street parking was finally available.

This party started a little later than the others because some wanted to stay to see the New Year in. People would start to arrive by 8:00.

The air was still colder than normal. Late that afternoon, Annie picked up Clara's wagon, and by 5:00, she was doing the dance she and Sam did so well a little over a week before.

Working by herself, it took about a half hour to get seven screaming cats inside the heated wagon. But she did it, and by 6:00, she and the cats were in the catering hall to get ready for their guests.

Ray and Cheryl had arrived earlier to help set up. Jock waited for the cats in the corner on the cushions reserved for the most special guests.

Annie, Henrie and Chris would spend the evening greeting guests and helping wherever needed. Mostly, Henrie and Chris went where help was needed and Annie greeted guests.

Their first guests were Nancy and Sam.

"Mom! You did make it. I wondered if you would stay up this late."

"Sam is taking real good care of me, dear. I had to take a nap this afternoon or he wouldn't have let me come."

"But we're going home by 10:00," added Sam. He had a carrier in his hand, and Annie was surprised to see they had Honey Bear.

Nancy noticed Annie's expression. "He just stood by his carrier and wouldn't move. So, I decided, when in Chelsea, do as the Chelseans do. If he wants to get out of his carrier, will you make sure he gets home?"

"Sure, Mom. But you know, this is new for him. He might run off. Have you thought about that?"

"Yes, I have. I have to let him go if this is what he wants to do."

Annie shook her head, took the carrier to the corner where the cats rested and let the dreaded Uncle Honey Bear out. To her surprise, her cats seemed to welcome him to the group.

Annie rejoined the group at the entryway. "So far, so good. No one spit, hissed, clawed or bit anyone else."

Annie took Sam aside and asked how Nancy was doing. "She's just fine, Annie. We had a good report from the doctor. I think by this time next week I won't have to pay such close attention to her."

Earlier in the week, Annie made an appointment for her mother with her own doctor in Marsh Haven. Her doctor seemed to think that Nancy had a vitamin B12 deficiency. He was still waiting on the results from some tests, but he believed he was on the right track. In the meantime, Sam made sure Nancy did not become over-tired.

"You have other guests coming. We'll walk around and leave you to it."

Frank was the next person to enter; he had come up the stairs, and he, too, had a cat carrier with him.

Annie closed her eyes and breathed deeply. "Frank, you brought Claire. How nice."

"Now, Annie, pull in your claws. I thought I would try it. I don't think she'll run off, but we'll see how she gets along."

"The rest of the cats are in the corner. Who knows? Maybe Claire and Honey Bear will begin the next great cat romance."

"Maybe."

When Frank took Claire to the cushions, Annie noticed some movement and noise, but she didn't see any blood, so she turned back to greet guests.

The party was better attended than they expected, so the room was probably filled beyond capacity. Annie was getting used to that.

She had just directed a crying toddler to his mother when she turned to greet the next guest. Marco.

"Happy New Year, Marco. I'm glad you could come."

"Are you?"

"Yes, I am. You can hang your coat up over there, you'll find food and drink along that wall, and if you want to make a resolution, head over to that corner. And enjoy yourself."

"Thanks, Annie. And Annie, I'm sorry. About everything. I really made some stupid mistakes. And I let some people lead me around by the nose. I should have known better."

"Marco, there's nothing that happened that didn't turn out right in the end."

"But I really created a problem for Carlos and Jesus."

"And you have apologized to them."

"Yes, I have, but I feel so bad about it."

"Then let me suggest that you go to that resolution table and write down the things you are sorry for. Put it in the box, and stay for the burning ceremony right after the New Year begins. Give it up. Let the weight be lifted from your shoulders."

Marco nodded, hung up his coat, and headed for the resolution table.

Chris and Annie had not had a lot of time together during the week, at least little time together alone. Frankly, they had not been alone since sometime before Christmas. This evening, they were once again surrounded by the community, not a chance to be alone.

They were tender and caring to one another, but Annie had become more reserved as the week drew on. She had given this a lot of thought, and wasn't sure what her problem was. On the one hand, she had difficulty accepting gifts. On the other hand, Chris had not offered a gift to her on the one day of the year she would have expected him to do so.

She didn't know what to do with the internal dichotomy.

Henrie, in a moment the two of them were alone, finally said, "Annie, it is absolutely none of my business, but this week, and tonight especially, you seem to exhibit a certain level of sadness. Is there anything I can do?"

"No, Henrie. Thank you. Probably just some leftover Christmas depression. I used to get it as a young adult. Never figured out why I did, and sometime or another it just went away. Maybe it came back. Or maybe everything that happened in the last ten days has finally taken its toll."

"I do not believe a word you just said, but you know where to find me if you want to talk."

Annie smiled at Henrie and blissfully was interrupted by another toddler looking for her daddy.

Around 10:00, an unexpected guest arrived. "Blaine! It's so good to see you."

He had a smile on his face and was walking with more confidence than she had expected. He was with a woman that looked to be about Nancy's age. She was tall, slender and elegant.

"Annie, I'd like you to meet my mother."

"Mrs. Jones. What a pleasure."

"Please call me Elizabeth. Blaine has told me so much about you and about so many people here in Chelsea. When he asked me to come up this weekend, I had to say yes."

Annie wasn't sure if she should ask, but she didn't want to be rude. "Blaine, do you have a place to stay while you're in town?"

"Thanks, Annie. We'll be driving back to Marsh Haven. I'm staying there for about a month. Mother will return to Ohio next week."

"Let me know if there is anything I can do while you're in the area, and please come see us when you can."

They moved on, and Annie watched as Blaine moved his mother toward one of the balloon stations and Diana.

When she turned around, Geraldine was getting off the elevator with her ex-husband and Hank. Coming out of the stairwell at the same time was Joan. Joan of Chelsea. Annie hadn't seen Joan in at least a month.

Joan was elected President of the Town Council when Hank was dethroned from that position. When Hank broke any number of laws in an attempt to close Annie's businesses the previous summer, he didn't lose his elected seat. However, the Town Council passed a resolution to remove him as President.

As they still had to work together, Hank and Joan were on speaking terms, but only barely. Which endeared Joan even more to Annie.

Joan and Annie were both gracious individuals, and they both said a polite hello to everyone coming off the elevator.

Hank and Joan were not gracious individuals. They nodded curtly and went immediately to the coatroom. Ex-Mr. Geraldine was a bit warmer, asking after Annie's cats as he passed by.

When the awkward moment passed, Annie and Joan laughed and hugged in greeting.

Pete and Janet were running a little late. They arrived with two of their three children and Cyril. Their oldest daughter, Ginger, was already helping Diana with balloon resolutions.

Cyril nearly knocked Annie over in his effort to get to Jock and the cats. As Annie watched, it seemed he said hello to everyone, even Honey Bear and Claire. Perhaps this was an omen for a wonderful New Year.

The next person to enter the party was Juanita, the reporter for the local newspaper. The paper was so small the reporter took care of public service announcements as well. Annie worked with her often.

"Annie, I want to make sure we get together as soon after the New Year as possible. I'd like to interview Jerry and get a perspective from you and from anyone else you think might add a different angle."

"I'm looking forward to it. It's a timely story, and Jerry's pleased he can provide some public education about this particular issue."

"You know, my aunt committed suicide. She still had the ability to do it on her own. If she didn't, she probably would have asked me to help her. I don't know what I would have done. I'm anxious to talk to him."

"I'm just glad we'll be able to get the story out, the way it needs to be told."

Juanita moved on as others arrived. The next people off the elevator were Boone and Hilly. A clean-shaven Boone and Hilly.

Annie smiled and said quietly, "You're together in public. What's going on?"

Hilly laughed. "We had such a wonderful time the other night at dinner. Seeing you and Chris together, enjoying yourselves with other people, made us think. Boone and I talked about it, and today we made a decision. We're going to be the people we are, in public, and let the cards fall where they may."

Boone smiled. "It's going to be hard to remember how I'm supposed to talk in public now."

Henrie approached from behind just as Boone started to speak. He came around to the front, looked Boone squarely in the eyes and said, "You have a doppelganger. Yes. Someone in this town looks just like you. He does not speak your language, however, but I am sure he would like to meet you."

Boone and Hilly laughed. Then Boone, looking around the room, asked, "Do you know where the boys are?"

"I think they're outside with George, making sure that grand finale will actually be grand. And not just a finale."

Annie smiled as they moved on, but it was a sad smile. Not for the first time, she thought about Mem's description of her relationship with Frank, that it suffered from "terminal politeness."

Henrie said nothing. He had, of course, heard the mention of Chris, and he had his own ideas about Annie's little nugget of sadness.

In the corner, cats and dogs snacked on treats left by Carlos, slept, talked, snacked, talked, slept some more. The night sky from the window was pretty. Not as interesting as the blowing snow. But pretty.

Throughout the evening, they talked of many things.

When Nancy and Sam arrived, Tiger Lily told Cyril, *"Grandmommy is going to be fine. She doesn't have enough B vitamins, and they're going to give her some more."*

A little later, when Marco came in, Cyril said, *"Pete put him on probation. He has to do a better job for the next three months or he'll be out of a job. And he has to go to training. Something about learning to be more sensitive."*

When Geraldine and Hank entered, anyone standing in the vicinity of the corner would have heard a collection of hisses, spits and one loud trill.

Before the evening was over, Tiger Lily asked Cyril, *"Is everything okay now? Is Pete home for good?"*

"Everything's fine. Pete told me not to worry, but I couldn't help it, and when he left, I just couldn't stand it. But it's good now. Even better. He missed me."

"I missed you," said Jock.

Cyril reached over and licked Jock's left haunch.

A little later, Jock said, *"Ray's been taking me to one of the small lakes to run around. You should tell Pete to bring you."*

"You know Pete doesn't understand me."

"Well, we both figured out how to communicate with Chris."

"But he talked to us. He had to ask us yes/no questions. It's not really communicating."

Mr. Bean said, *"You could dance for them."*

"What?"

"Dance for them. Sometimes they understand what you want when you dance for them."

With a look at Tiger Lily, as if daring her to stop him, Mr. Bean located Carlos, ran over to him, got up on his hind legs and danced. Carlos picked him up and held him tight for several seconds, until Mr. Bean squirmed to get down and run back to the group. Carlos watched after him with a smile.

Tiger Lily didn't say anything to Uncle Honey Bear. She was just happy that on occasion they could get along. She noticed, however, that Honey Bear and Claire sat in close proximity to one another, fluffy tails entwined. She smiled to herself.

Midnight approached. Annie went to the deck to watch the finale, hopefully grand. Only a few people were on the deck as most had gone downstairs and out. Chris came up behind her and wrapped his arms around her shoulders, pulling her close. He rested his chin on the top of her head.

"So, how long is it going to be before we can be alone again?"

"I'm not sure. What's your schedule like?"

"It's not usually my schedule that gets in the way."

"I know."

"Let me ask another question."

"Okay."

"How long is it going to be before you forgive me for not giving you a Christmas gift?"

"I didn't know you needed forgiveness."

"Well, I don't, really, but I do have an explanation."

"You don't need to explain anything, Chris."

"I do."

"Well, if you think you have to, go ahead. But you know I don't expect anything from you."

"Yes, I know that. But I want you to expect everything from me."

Annie remained silent.

"I know more about you than you think I do. For example, I know it's very difficult for you to accept gifts. I've seen that pile grow, and I've even taken the liberty of looking through some of them.

"By the way, I made reservations for dinner at that restaurant you like so much. I'm kind of hoping you'll use that gift certificate and pay for the meal. It's for next Saturday night. Do we have a date?"

Annie laughed, continuing to lean into him. "Sure."

"And I'm going to push forward, especially since you didn't get angry when I told you about looking through your pile of gifts." Chris paused for just a second to make sure it really was okay for him to go forward. "So, what I really want to do is give you a special gift, but I'm afraid that no matter what I give you, it will end up on that pile."

Annie remained silent. After several seconds, Chris continued.

"What do you think I should do? Do you think I should wait for you to go through the pile, decide what to do with all of your nice new things and clean it up, or do you think I should go ahead and give you that special gift? Which is, by the way, burning a hole on my bureau at home."

Annie laughed again, softly, feeling the sadness leave her body. "We can't have anything burning up furniture at your house."

"That's what I was hoping you would say. But I'm going to make it easy on you and strike a happy medium. About that date, how about I plan to give it to you then? You have almost a week to decide what to do with those other things, or leave them where they are."

Annie turned her head up so he could kiss her on the cheek. She felt something at her feet and looked down. Tiger Lily sat next to her right leg, leaning in and curling her tail around her ankle. Tiger Lily purred and looked up, giving Annie the full-on I-love-you-Mommy stare.

Suddenly the crowd below started to cheer. Annie and Chris looked out and saw the grand finale beginning. And my goodness, was it grand!

George had a megaphone and announced midnight to be two minutes away. At that moment, Donny flipped a switch and a large modified disco ball lit up. It sat on top of the flag pole, multi-colored stars shooting from the ball into the night sky.

Felicity killed the lights of the Café, both the first and second floors, while George continued to talk. He invited everyone to find someone to hug and kiss when the ball ended its trip to the bottom.

Soon, it was 11:59. Donny flipped another switch and the ball started to rotate, round and round, as it slowly moved down the flagpole. Stars danced in the sky.

George had a digital watch and counted down the time into the megaphone. Eventually, everyone shouted with him. "Ten! Nine! Eight! Seven! Six! Five! Four! Three! Two! One! Happy New Year!"

At that moment, Annie didn't care who was doing what. Chris had turned her around in his arms for a kiss, and she was lost. The kiss was long and tender. Finally, they stood, locked in an embrace, her head nestled into his chest as his heart beat steadily.

She came out of her reverie when she heard a shout from Candice. Mo had run outside with Teresa. He was next to the bonfire, dancing around the flames. His little butt was on fire. Candice, well-practiced in the art, grabbed him by the tail to put it out.

Thank you for reading <u>Phishing</u>, the third installment of the Tiger Lily's Café Mystery Series. It will be followed later in 2015 with the fourth installment, <u>Holiday</u>.

About The Author

Kathleen (Kathi) Thompson was raised on a small livestock and grain farm in northwest Indiana. She has an undergraduate degree in Sociology and an MBA. She served as a probation officer, parole agent and juvenile residential counselor before moving into administrative, marketing and fund raising positions in human service organizations.

Kathi and her mother discovered an injured kitten of indeterminate age at the family farm. The kitten decided to make Kathi her guardian. She wrapped herself around an ankle, started purring, and wouldn't let go. Against the advice of her mother, Kathi took the kitten home, vowing that if the kitten lived through the night, she would take her to the vet. She lived; the vet diagnosed road burn serious enough to take all the fur from the left side of her face, and the kitten – Tiger Lily – eventually healed and took a huge part of Kathi's heart.

Tiger Lily was joined by the rest: Little Socks (thank you, Aunt Mary); Kali, Ko and Mo (thank you, Connie Hall); Sassy Pants (thank you, Ant Sherwy, better known as Sherry Simpson); and finally, Mr. Bean (thank you, Pulaski County Animal Control).

Tiger Lily's Café has been rattling around in Kathi's brain – there isn't much else up there – for all of the years since, sometimes as an actual café and sometimes as a book. It was less expensive to write the book.

A Note From The Kids

This is Tiger Lily. I want to tell you about writing books. I help Mommy write the books. We all do. We work as a team.

Ko is especially good with papers. She rearranges all of the papers on the desk so Mommy has a better idea where to find things. When Ko has finished her work, I lie down on the papers, because Mommy really does a better job if she can't see anything.

Little Socks helps by lying in front of the laptop, head and paws on the keyboard, moving ever so slowly until she is on the keys, helping to type. Sassy Pants and Mr. Bean keep the excitement going in the house, so Mommy has to take a break every now and then to see "what that noise was." Kali sleeps or cries to be held, because Mommy has to take a break every now and then.

Precious Mo is no longer a part of the family in body, but he lives on in spirit and in these books.

I hope you enjoy reading this book as much as we enjoyed writing it.

Find us on the web: www.tigerlilyscafe.com

Find us on Facebook: TigerLilysCafeMysteries

A List of Tiger Lily's Café Mystery Series Books:

- Turtle Soup
- Boo!
- Phishing

Made in the USA
San Bernardino, CA
21 September 2015